Marion Lennox has written over one hundred romance novels, and is published in over one hundred countries and thirty languages. Her international awards include the prestigious RITA® award (twice!) and the *RT Book Reviews* Career Achievement Award for 'a body of work which makes us laugh and teaches us about love'. Marion adores her family, her kayak, her dog, and lying on the beach with a book someone else has written. Heaven!

Sue MacKay lives with her husband in New Zealand's beautiful Marlborough Sounds, with the water on her doorstep and the birds and the trees at her back door. It's the perfect setting to indulge her passions of entertaining friends by cooking them sumptuous meals, drinking fabulous wine, going for hill walks or kayaking around the bay—and, of course, writing stories.

SECOND CHANCE WITH HER ISLAND DOC

MARION LENNOX

TAKING A CHANCE ON THE SINGLE DAD

SUE MacKAY

MILLS & BOON

First Published in Great Britain 2019
by Mills & Boon, an imprint of HarperCollins*Publishers*
1 London Bridge Street, London, SE1 9GF

Second Chance with Her Island Doc © 2019 by Marion Lennox

Taking a Chance on the Single Dad © 2019 by Sue MacKay

ISBN: 978-0-263-26987-1

Printed and bound in Spain
by CPI, Barcelona

SECOND CHANCE WITH HER ISLAND DOC

MARION LENNOX

MILLS & BOON

CHAPTER ONE

'HEAD LACERATIONS ALWAYS look worse than they are. If you'll help me to a washbasin I'll stop wasting your time. I'm not dizzy any more. Really.'

The woman's voice drifting from the treatment room was warm, husky and a little bit shaky. She was speaking the Tovahnan language, with an English accent overlaid.

Dr Leo Aretino knew this voice well. For the last few weeks he'd been expecting her arrival on the island, but hoping he could avoid her.

He hadn't been expecting her here, in his territory.

The language she was speaking was Leo's native tongue. The first time he'd heard her use it had been over ten years ago. She'd been standing over a microscope, trying to focus. The 'scope had been fiddly, but Anna had been patient. She'd started humming, and then softly singing to herself. In Tovahnan.

It was a tune his mother had taught him as a child.

Leo had doubted if anyone at their prestigious English medical school had even heard of his birthplace, the island of Tovahna, much less known how to speak its language. He'd cut across her song, incredulous. 'Where did you learn that?'

'From my mother,' she'd said. She'd had the slide in

focus at that point and had been looking intently at the nasty little pathogen the tutor wanted them to see.

'Your mother's Tovahnan?'

'Yes, she is. Or she was. She left Tovahna before I was born.' Anna had checked the slide again. 'But it's this little guy we're interested in. You want to look?'

There was a queue. He needed to look at the bug.

His attention was solidly diverted.

Tovahna was a Mediterranean island, sparsely populated, fought over for centuries until its big neighbours had decided it wasn't worth the bother. It was now mostly ignored by the outside world. Few foreigners made the effort to visit, much less learn the language. The women of Tovahna were generally olive skinned and dark haired. Anna had red hair and freckles. This didn't make sense.

'Your mother taught you Tovahnan songs?'

'She taught me the language.' She'd moved away from the microscope, allowing the student after Leo access. 'I think she used it to assuage homesickness. But you've missed your turn,' she'd told him, switching effortlessly into speaking Tovahnan. She'd smiled, a wide, happy smile that had made him feel even more astounded. 'Don't tell me you're…'

'Tovahnan.' And suddenly he'd been close to tears.

Tovahna was tiny, impoverished, its assets gouged for generations by a single family dynasty. Most of its people were trapped in a ceaseless cycle of poverty, but Leo had been so smart at school that the community had rallied to send him to England.

'Get yourself a medical degree and then come home and help us,' they'd told him, and off he'd gone, aged all of fifteen.

At nineteen he'd been doing brilliantly. His English had been flawless. He'd fitted in with his fellow students.

He'd even been enjoying himself, hardly homesick at all. So there'd been no reason why he should gaze at this red-headed, freckled, fellow student speaking his language and feel like…he'd wanted to take her into his arms.

Of course, he hadn't. Not right then. It had been two whole days before he'd kissed her.

It wasn't just that they'd shared a language. Anna had been special.

But that was past history, he told himself as he listened to her voice carrying from the next room. What was between them had been a long time ago. Right now he needed to focus on medical imperatives. A woman he'd met years before was being carried into his emergency room on a stretcher.

He was a doctor and he had to deal with whoever needed to be treated. He needed to haul himself together and go see what the problem was.

The medical problem.

Wow, her head hurt.

The thump against stone had been stupid and entirely predictable. When she'd insisted she wanted to see everything—she now owned a castle and who wouldn't want to see it all?—her late cousin's agent had given her a torch.

'Watch your head,' he'd told her as he'd led her deep into the depths of Tovahna Castle.

What she'd seen had been a maze of tunnels, some built almost a thousand years ago. Secret passages led in and out from the castle walls, to be used in times of siege. There were hidden living areas, ventilation shafts, storage spaces for weapons, for food and water, all dark and dusty and so fascinating it was no wonder she'd finally forgotten to watch her head.

The thump had been solid and the results immediate. The world had spun and then disappeared. She'd surfaced to find blood oozing down her forehead. Victoir, the agent, had been useless, torn between wanting to help and not wanting to get blood on his suit. Finally she'd ripped off her windcheater and applied pressure herself, then had him help her to the surface.

'I don't want paramedics coming down here,' she'd told him. 'This looks worse than it is. You'll have a team of split heads instead of one.'

But emerging to daylight, Victoir's authority reasserted itself. 'I've called the ambulance,' he told her. 'I said those passages were dangerous. They need to be closed off, filled in, before someone's killed. Kids get in and we can't stop them. You've seen the parts that are crumbling. And now this…'

And then a rattletrap ambulance had come blaring down the cobblestoned street to the castle forecourt, and Anna had been bundled inside before she could object.

She could hardly blame them, she decided. She probably did look like something out of *The Texas Chainsaw Massacre*, and, to be honest, she was still a bit woozy. So she'd lain back and let the paramedics put in a drip to compensate for blood loss. She'd felt every bumpy cobble as they'd made their way who knew where, until finally she'd been carried into what looked a plain, businesslike emergency entrance.

'The doctor's on his way,' a middle-aged nurse told her. She didn't attempt to remove the windcheater-pad Anna was still holding. 'Don't worry. Our Dr Leo's on duty and he's the best we have.'

And her bad day suddenly got worse.

Dr Leo. No! Please…

But then the door swung open and a guy in a white coat was beside her trolley. 'Maria, what do we have here?'

And her worst fears were realised.

Leo Aretino. Her first love.

Her greatest love.

How could you be truly in love at nineteen? You couldn't be, she'd decided. What they'd had had been a teenage fling.

He'd broken her heart, but teenagers' hearts were made to be broken. She'd told herself that over and over in the years between then and now. She'd met other men. She'd even fancied herself in love with them, but the thought of Leo had always stayed with her. Tall, dark, intense, speaking the language of her mother, making her laugh, studying with her, making her body sing...

And then walking away...

She closed her eyes. Her head felt like it was about to explode and it wasn't just the pain from the accident.

She'd guessed she might meet him when she came here, but to meet him now, like this...

'It's Anna Raymond.' The nurse's voice held suppressed excitement. 'Anna Castlavara. Katrina's daughter. Victoir was showing her the tunnels under the castle.'

'Of course.' Leo's voice was smooth, unfussed, as if the name meant nothing to him. Had he known she'd be in the country? He must have, she thought. For Tovahna this must have been big news.

It had been big news to her. Her cousin's death. An inheritance so huge she could hardly take it in.

Leo.

'Anna and I have met before.' Leo still sounded calm. Professional. Like she was one of the scores of patients he saw each day. She was a fellow student he'd had a casual fling with ten years ago. No more.

A fellow student who'd inherited most of his country?

'Anna.' His voice gentled and he spoke in English. 'Are you with us?'

'I'm with you.' She couldn't keep ten years of resentment from her voice. 'Unfortunately.'

'Can you open your eyes?'

'I can but I don't want to.'

'Because the light hurts?'

'Because I don't want to see you.'

And the man had the temerity to chuckle.

'Still the firebrand I remember, then, Anna? Okay, keep those eyes closed and I'll check out the rest.'

His hand was on her wrist and the touch made her... what? She should want to pull away.

She didn't do that either.

He didn't touch the pad on her head. He was doing an overall assessment, she thought, checking the IV line, blood pressure, the paramedic notes. Taking in the whole picture.

He was a fine doctor. She remembered that comment at their graduation ceremony. Leo hadn't been there. As soon as his last exam was behind him he'd left to do a fast track course in surgery before heading home. To Tovahna. But at the graduation his name had been read out with pride by the head of the medical faculty. 'Dr Leo Aretino has topped almost every class during his time here and he intends returning to serve his country. He's a doctor we can be proud of, now and into the future.'

So she was in good hands. Leo's hands.

She hurt.

'Is it just your head?' The laughter was gone now—he was all doctor—and that gentle voice she remembered so well was almost enough to bring tears to her eyes. 'Anna, have you hurt anything else?'

'Just m-my head,' she managed, and was ashamed it came out as a stammered whisper.

'Do you remember what happened?'

'There was a cavern with ancient pottery urns. I bent to see and then stood up.' She managed to dredge up a bit of indignation but it was directed at herself. 'Victoir said it was dangerous and I didn't listen.'

'The notes said you lost consciousness.'

'Victoir said I was out of it for a few seconds, but all I can remember is *bang* and then feeling dizzy.'

Leo would be thinking of internal bleeding, she thought. Did they have the facilities to treat that here?

She'd read about Tovahna over the years—of course she had.

Still almost a feudal economy, with one family controlling much of the wealth. Most of the population pay rent to the Castlavaran family, and little is put back into infrastructure. Schools, hospitals, public services are minimal, to say the least.

Tourist sites reported on the medical facilities, too.

Travellers are advised to carry extra health insurance to cover transport to a neighbouring country. Medical services are basic. Complex medical situations often mean either evacuation or a less than satisfactory outcome.

A less than satisfactory outcome. Death?

'If I did lose consciousness it was only for seconds,' she said, more surely now. Wanting to reassure herself as well as him. 'You know split heads bleed enough to make people think you're at death's door.'

'Blood running down faces does seem to frighten onlookers,' he agreed, and she heard the hint of humour return. It was the laughter she'd fallen for. *Oh, Leo...* 'We'll take X-rays to be sure, though.'

'You have facilities?'

'Amazingly, we have.' The laughter was still there, but underneath...the trace of bitterness she'd heard only once but would remember for ever. Old accusations flooded back. *'Your family has sucked our country dry...'*

'I'm sorry. I didn't mean...'

'Let's take a look,' he said, gentle again, and he moved the padded windcheater aside.

The paramedics had moved it to do a fast check but they'd replaced it and bound it fast, thinking it was best not to disturb things until they had a doctor's back-up. Now the bleeding had stopped, and it had become sticky. She felt the windcheater tug on the dried blood in her hair.

She had no choice. Finally she opened her eyes.

Leo was right there, leaning over her. His face was maybe two hand widths from hers. This was a Leo who was older, his face creased a little, with age, with weather, his eyes seemingly deeper set.

But he was the same Leo. Those gorgeous brown eyes. The deep black, crinkly hair, a bit unkempt. The laughter lines. His mouth...

It was as if he was about to kiss...

Um...not. He was looking at her head, not into her eyes.

Oh, but those eyes...

She needed to get over herself.

She'd never intended seeing him. Once she'd got over the shock of her inheritance, her intention had been to come here fast, put the organisation of the estate firmly back into the hands of her cousin's agent and then retreat. She knew the country was impoverished and she had no intention of making it more so. Her uncle and then her cousin had squirrelled away rents and profits.

She needed to figure a way to channel them into charities, and then go home.

Home was in England, where she worked as a family doctor in a village a couple of hours south of London. The community was lovely and she loved her job. She had two beloved springer spaniels, dopy but fun. She'd recently broken up with a rather nice lawyer but they were still friends. She had lots of friends. Life was good.

This inheritance had been like a bombshell. Now, looking up into Leo's face, it seemed even more so.

For the reason things had never progressed with her 'rather nice lawyer' was right here. After all this time, to have this memory messing with her life…

This memory? Leo.

But Leo wasn't looking at her. His fingers—oh, she remembered those fingers—were carefully untangling the matted hair so he could see what he was dealing with.

'This was some thump,' he told her. 'You'll need stitches and a thorough check. Sorry, Anna, but we need to shave some of your hair.'

'Nothing a scarf won't hide,' she said, trying for lightness. 'It was my own fault.'

'But you *were* down in the underground labyrinth.'

'Just checking.'

'Checking your inheritance.'

'That's right.' How hard was that to say lightly?

'I'm sorry about your cousin.'

'Really?' She was trying not to wince at the feel of his fingers. Not from pain, though. He was being gentle.

He always had been gentle.

'Yanni's death was unexpected,' he told her, still carefully probing. 'Although with the lifestyle he led…'

'Eating and hoarding money,' she said. 'I've been

told. My mother said his father—Mum's brother—was the same.'

'And he died of a heart attack as well,' Leo said. 'Twenty years apart, both their deaths almost instant. Your cousin was only thirty-eight, but with the lifestyle he led and his family history… There was nothing we could do.'

'Hey, I'm not blaming you.' She sighed. Her head really did hurt. 'Leo, could you find someone else to stitch my head? To be honest, having you treating me is making me feel a whole lot worse. You don't like anything about me and my family, right?'

'I treated your cousin,' he said, without answering her question. 'Or I tried to. He refused to listen to concerns about cholesterol or weight. But I did my best. I'll do my best with you.'

'You can't imagine how grateful that makes me feel,' she muttered. 'Is there no one else?'

'Not right now. Our only other doctor is in the midst of a birth.'

'You only have two doctors?'

'This island's small.'

'I've read about it. Twenty thousand people. Two doctors?'

'You tell me how to get the money to train them and I'll do something about it. We have a couple of islanders we've trained as nurse-practitioners. They're good, but for a head wound you need either Carla or me.'

She'd known the island was impoverished. Two doctors, though, for such a population… Now, though, wasn't the time for thinking about it. 'I'll wait for Carla,' she said, and she knew she sounded belligerent but she couldn't help it. This man had hurt her in the past and hurt her badly. She didn't want him anywhere near her.

'I doubt if you can wait that long.' He stood back a little, studying her. Like an interesting bug? Like he didn't even know her. 'So what were you doing climbing under the castle without a hard hat?'

'A hard hat…' she said cautiously, and thought about it. Or tried to think about it. The knock had made her feel ill, and Leo's presence was now removing almost all the rest of her ability to think logically. 'Maybe that would have been sensible,' she conceded at last. 'It wasn't offered as an option, though, and I really wanted to see.'

'So Victoir took you underground?'

'He was my cousin's agent. He knows the place.'

'He also knows the rule about hard hats. He didn't warn you?'

'Of course he did. He said it's dangerous. He said the entire underground needs to be closed off, and I guess now I agree. My inheritance states that capital must be used to improve or maintain the castle itself. That's pretty limiting. Victoir's idea is that I close off the underground area and divide the castle into apartments. He says with the view over the sea they'll command exorbitant rent and provide an economic boost for the whole island.'

'I imagine they will,' Leo said dryly. 'And an economic boost for Victoir as well. So he told you that going underground was dangerous.'

'I told you.' She sighed. 'Leo, can we just get on with this? Fix my head, charge me what you like and let me go.'

'You know I won't keep you longer than I must,' he said, formally now. 'But losing consciousness… You know as well as I do that overnight obs are essential. Like it or not, you're stuck here for the night.'

He turned back to the nurse, switching back into Tovahnan. 'Maria, let's get this X-rayed before we do a proper clean-up,' he told her. 'Can you take her through? I'll get some pain relief in first, though.' He turned back to Anna. 'Pain… One to ten?'

She thought about it and decided to be honest. Her head was thumping.

'Maybe…six?'

'Ouch,' he said, sympathetically. 'You do need that X-ray. But a nice shot of something first. Any allergies?'

'None.' What he said made sense. 'Thank you,' she said, and was annoyed at how feeble she sounded.

And astonishingly he touched her hand, lightly. It was the kind of touch he might give any patient he wanted to reassure. It was entirely professional, so why it seemed to burn…

It didn't. She was being dumb. This kind of thump on her head would make anyone dumb, she told herself. He was being purely professional. 'Right, let's get you sorted. Maria can take X-rays. I'll come back with the results as soon as I can.'

'Thank you,' she managed. 'There's no hurry.'

'There's always a hurry,' he said, and suddenly it was a snap. 'That's what my life is, thanks to your family.'

Your family… The words resonated, an echo of what he'd said all those years ago.

'Your family robs my country blind, leeching every asset we ever had. How can I associate myself with any-one even remotely connected to the Castlavarans? I'm sorry, it's over, Anna.'

'So the judgement's still there,' she managed, and stu-pidly she was starting to feel her eyes well with unshed tears. It was the shock, she told herself. A decent thump on the head always messed with the tear ducts.

It wasn't anything to do with this arrogant, judge-mental guy she'd once loved with all her heart.

'It's not judgement, it's knowledge,' he told her. 'Maria will take care of you. I'll be back to sew things up. By the way, I will be charging.'

'Charge what you like,' she muttered. 'And get me out of here as soon as possible. All I want to do is go home.'

He wanted her out of here as much as she wanted to be gone. Maybe more. The thought of a Castlavaran in his treatment room should be enough to make his skin crawl.

Only this was Anna, and what he felt for her...

She was two parts, he conceded. She was Anna Raymond, the redheaded, gorgeous, fun-loving fellow student he'd fallen in love with. But she was still Anna Castlavara, daughter of Katrina Castlavara, who was in turn the daughter of a family who'd held the wealth of this small country in its grasping hands for generations.

'They're nothing to do with me.'

He remembered Anna's response when he'd first discovered the connection. His reaction had been guttural, instinctive, incredulous. For six months he'd been dating her. He'd been nineteen, a student madly in love, thinking life was as good as it could get. And then he'd met her mother.

Katrina had been in America when he'd first met Anna, with a guy Anna had said was one of a string of men.

'We hardly see each other,' she'd told him, but she'd told him little else.

It seemed she'd known little.

'As far as I know, she left Tovahna in her teens and she hasn't been back. She said her mother died young and her father's horrible, but that's pretty much all she'll tell me. I imagine Mum would have been a wild child, so maybe that had something to do with it. Sometimes,

*though...when I was little she'd sing to me, songs like
the one you heard, and in between men, when she was
bored, she taught me Tovahnan. It's always seemed fun,
our own secret language. I suspect she was a bit homesick, though she'd never admit it. She refuses to talk
of her family—she says they've rejected her and she's
rejected them. She's said there's no way she'd ever go
back—that most of the young people from Tovahna end
up emigrating.'*

They still did, Leo thought grimly. The extent of economic activity on the island was to grow olives and tomatoes, fish and pay exorbitant rents to the Castlavaran
landlords.

There'd never been a king, a president, even an official ruler. The island was simply owned by the Castlavarans. For generation after generation they had ruled
with a grasping hand and nothing had disturbed that rule.
There was little on this rocky island to invite invasion. Its
inhabitants were peaceful, ultra-conservative, accepting
the status quo because that's what their parents had, and
their parents before them.

Right now, though, the status quo had changed. The
last male heir, Yanni, had left no descendants. The inheritance had thus fallen to a woman the country didn't
know, a woman who'd been born abroad, a woman who—
as far as Leo could tell—knew little about her ancestors'
homeland.

Was it time for the population to rise up and say,
'Enough'? The land should be owned by the people who'd
worked it for generations.

It wasn't happening. Any kid with any ambition had
one thought and that was to emigrate, and the remaining
islanders accepted apathy as the norm. That meant that
Anna's inheritance was being met with stoic acceptance.

Maybe he should lead a revolution himself, but he was far too busy to think of political insurrection. Work was always waiting.

Like Anna's split head.

'Please let it not be fractured,' he muttered as he left her. Not only for her sake either. He needed to get her out of his hospital and then get on with his life.

His next patient was a child brought in by his grandparents 'because he won't eat', which probably meant he'd been given so many sweets he didn't need anything else. But they'd been waiting for over three hours. The toddler's parents were off the island, visiting the little boy's ill maternal grandmother, and he didn't want them worried, so he took the time to reassure the grandparents. He gave them a chart where every single thing that went into the small boy's mouth had to be recorded, no matter what, and sent them away dubious. But if they stuck to the chart they'd have forty fits when they saw how much they were sneaking—behind each other's backs—into one small mouth.

At any other time that might have made him smile, but he wasn't smiling when he returned to check Anna's X-rays.

All okay. Excellent.

He still had to keep her in overnight. There remained a risk of internal bleeding.

But first stitching.

Carla was still caught up with a tricky birth. He checked in, hopeful, but there was no joy there.

'She may need a Caesarean,' Carla told him. Carla was in her sixties, tough and practical and kind. 'We're doing the best we can. First sign of foetal distress, though, and I'll need you. Don't go anywhere, Leo.'

'I was wondering if you could do a stitching,' he

told her, glancing behind her to the woman in labour. 'Swap places?'

'I've been with Greta all the way,' Carla said. 'It's not kind to swap now.' And then she grinned. 'Besides, Maria tells me she's the Castlavara. I understand why you want to swap. Just treat her like anyone else and then multiply the costs by a hundred. Hey, if you're nice to her maybe we could persuade her to fund us a new ambulance. Put on your charm, Dr Aretino, and go charm yourself our future.'

To say she was miserable was an understatement. She was tucked into a cubicle with curtains around her, cut off from the outside world. The painkiller Leo had prescribed had taken effect but was causing even more fuzziness, and there was still a dull ache. She was in a foreign country, in the hands of a man who'd made it clear ten years ago that he was rejecting her.

She wanted to go home so badly she could taste it, to her lovely little cottage in her English village, to people who treated her as a friend as well as a doctor, to her two happy, bouncy dogs.

It was mid-afternoon. Rhonda, her next-door neighbour, would be walking her dogs, letting them roam in the woods behind her cottage. The dogs would be going nuts, exploring the springtime smells, chasing rabbits, chasing each other, free...

Oh, for heaven's sake, she was close to tears again and she never cried. She was an independent, strong career woman and tears were dumb. How she was feeling was dumb.

She should have asked someone to come with her. Her ex-boyfriend? Martin was a lawyer. They'd had what could only be called a tepid relationship before he'd fallen madly, deeply for her best friend, Jennifer. But they'd stayed friends and when the news of her inheritance had come through both he and Jennifer had been fascinated.

'Summary,' Martin had announced after considerable research. 'The estate's tied up in such a way you can't offload it and the country's in a mess. That mess is not of your making, though, and the Trust doesn't give you much option to do anything about it. My advice? Leave it in the hands of this Victoir guy, who knows the layout. It's pulling in an incredible income. Yes, the settlement decrees most of the income stays with the castle, but as overall owner you're entitled to living expenses and those living expenses can be more than generous. You'll be set for life. Sign the papers and forget about the rest.'

But it seemed too big, too huge, to simply sign and forget. Her colleagues were intrigued and helpful. Rhonda was happy to take care of the dogs.

There was the long-ago memory of a boy called Leo, but Tovahna was surely not so small she'd bump into him in the street.

So she'd bumped into a twelfth-century stone ceiling and she'd found Leo all by herself.

Oh, her head hurt.

And then Leo was back, brisk, formal, hurried. 'Okay, Anna, let's get these stitches sorted. Your X-rays are clear. No fractures. We'll need to keep you in overnight for obs—you know that—but there should be no problem. Maria's bringing what we need now.'

She hadn't heard footsteps. She hadn't heard the curtain draw back. Leo was just…here.

Her head felt like it might explode.

If she'd had a few seconds' warning, if she'd heard him approach, then maybe she could have kept control, but she hadn't and she didn't. She made a desperate grab for the tissue box on the side table and buried her face in a sea of white.

Heroines in movies cried beautifully, glistening droplets slipping silently down beautifully made-up faces, lips quivering as brave heroines fought back overwhelming sadness. Then they'd blink back remaining tears and gaze adoringly at their hero with eyes still misty, and… *most infuriating of all*…not a hint of puffiness in sight. Then there'd be a kiss, with the heroine not even needing to sniff.

But that was in movie land, not on an examination trolley in a sterile, strange emergency room. Anna had to sniff. More, she had to blow her nose and even when she blew it, it kept running. And blinking was useless with this flood. Her shoulders were shaking with silent sobs and she couldn't stop them.

This was crazy.

But maybe she should cut herself some slack.

She'd hardly slept since she'd received the news last week. The journey here had been arduous—where were decent connections when you needed them? Victoir had bombarded her with information she'd had no hope of getting her head around but she knew she had to. And then the dark, the bang, the shock and the loss of blood. She was overtired, overwrought, drugged and still in pain. And finally here was Leo, looking at her like she was something the cat had dragged in.

Leo, whom she'd once loved with all her heart.

She was buried under a wad of tissues but she needed more. She made a desperate swipe for the box but she didn't connect.

And then a wad of dry tissues was tucked into her hand. The sodden ones were removed.

She could hardly thank him. She blew her nose again and struggled to stop the stupid tears.

Everything was shaking.

Stupid drugs. Stupid head. Stupid, stupid, stupid...

And then there was a heavy sigh and she felt a weight on the side of her bed. And arms came around her and gathered her into a warm, strong hug.

It needed only this.

The sensible part of Anna should react with horror. Sensible Anna should shove him away, tell him to take his prejudiced, judgemental self anywhere but here. The sensible part of Anna would...what? Walk out of here, bloodstained and woozy. Call Victoir to come get her?

But right now the sensible part of Anna wasn't big enough to mount a coherent argument. The rest of her was mush, and that mush was being held fast by arms she knew.

She was being held against a chest she loved.

She didn't love. She didn't! But right now she needed. She let herself fold against him, feeling the strength of his arms, the warmth, the solidness.

He was wearing a clinical coat, a bit stiff. It felt okay. More, it felt good. Medicine and Leo, they were a solid combination of safety, surety. Home...

Where had that word come from? Home was England, the dogs, her village, her people.

She could feel his heart beating. Strong. Steady. Leo.

The shaking was easing. Whatever was happening, this helped. She had no strength to draw away and she didn't want to. Drug-free medicine... A hug...

She let her mind stop its useless spinning and focus on just being held.

By Leo.

There was no pressure. He didn't push her away, even

as her sobs subsided. He simply sat and held her, letting her take as much time as she needed to get herself back together.

Letting her take as much comfort as she needed.

And she did need it. She didn't want to draw back.

This was an illusion, a memory of times past, a comfort that shouldn't be any kind of comfort at all.

Oh, but he felt…

'Dressing tray.' The female voice…Maria's?…came from the doorway. And then there was an apologetic reaction as the nurse saw what was happening. 'Whoops, sorry, back in a moment.'

'It's okay.' Finally—to her regret—Leo pulled back. 'Bring it in, Maria. Anna, are we all right to get these stitches in?'

'I… Of course.' The tears were gone. She was blood-stained, puffy-eyed and mortified, but somehow she hauled together what was left of her rag-tailed dignity. 'Stitches and then twelve hours of obs and I'm out of here.'

'That's what we both want,' Leo said, and, comfort or not, the old resentments surged back.

This man was her treating doctor. She needed him to help her. He'd comforted her with a hug.

She still wanted to slap him.

CHAPTER TWO

IT WAS A long night, and it wasn't just medical need that made it so.

The sweet-eating toddler and Anna's laceration were the last simple cases Leo saw. The birth Carla was attending did turn into a Caesarean and a dicey one at that. Greta was diabetic. She'd been desperate to have a natural delivery, had persuaded Carla to let her try, but by the time they'd bailed out her sugar levels had been all over the place. Carla took over the baby's care and Leo was left trying to stabilise mum.

Then there were three injured teens from a street brawl. It wasn't unusual. The kids here were bored. There were few jobs and little to aspire to.

And the woman responsible was in his hospital.

That wasn't fair, he conceded as the night wore on. He snatched a couple of hours' sleep but it was a disturbed rest, interspersed with thoughts of Anna. She hadn't personally been responsible for her family's greed.

But she was now. That one person could inherit such wealth, controlling the misery of so many lives… It made something inside him cold with fury, an anger he'd carried all his life.

Dawn saw him back on the wards. The teens were safe, their injuries relatively minor. Knife wounds, bruising, a couple of fractures, but he could cope with those. Ideally one of the boys should be sent to an orthopaedic surgeon, but where were the funds for that? He'd have to balance cost to the family against using the skills he had.

Breakfast was a fast cruise past the hospital kitchen. Carla found him there. She'd been home and slept. She was sixty but she usually chirped like she was about twenty years younger than Leo felt. This morning she was rubbing her temple, though, and looking tired.

'Headache?'

'I need aspirin,' she conceded. 'Though why I should have a headache when it's you who was up most of the night... Rough?'

He nodded, swigging lukewarm coffee. If there was one thing he wanted more than anything it was to replace the coffee machine.

A new steriliser for Theatre came first. There were always things that came first.

'No deaths?' Carla queried, and he wondered if that was how he looked. Maybe. Anna's arrival had jolted his world.

'No one's dead,' he told her. 'Though there are three kids who tried. Knives, alcohol...' He shook his head. 'Seventeen years old and not a job or a prospect between them. It's a disaster, Carla.'

'So talk to the heiress.'

'You know the rules. The money's tied up in the castle. Even if I could persuade her...'

'You could try.'

'She's a Castlavaran. What's likely to change?' He swigged more coffee and put his mug aside. 'Ugh.'

'But she's an outsider.' Carla suddenly sounded chirpy again. 'And Maria says you've met her before.'

Of course. Nothing in this hospital went unnoticed.

'At medical school,' he said, brusquely. 'I didn't know who she was.'

'She's a doctor?'

'I imagine she finished her training, yes.'

'Wow. That's wonderful. You might even be able to persuade her to help us. Leo, what's needed here is charm.'

'Charm?' He eyed her with suspicion. He and Carla went back a long way. In fact, it had been a much younger Carla who'd persuaded Leo's mother—and the town—to send him to medical school in London. Carla herself had gone there, funded by an aunt who'd emigrated. She was full of energy and ideas and she wasn't afraid to speak her mind. He looked at her now and thought, Uh oh. He knew that look.

'Why not charm her?' she went on. 'Maybe even take it further. She's the same age as you are, and she owns practically this entire country. And now she's a doctor.'

'A doctor who's a Castlavaran.'

'That's prejudice,' she said sternly. 'I've a good mind to march in there and charm for myself.'

'You're welcome. She needs to be checked and discharged.'

'Your patient,' she said, and chuckled. 'And your project.'

'I have work to do. My plan is to get her out of here as soon as possible.'

'The country's stuck with her, though,' Carla said. 'You could put in a bit of effort.'

'Leave it,' he snapped, and then caught himself. Any minute now Carla would be sussing out past history. 'From all I gather, she's here to accept her inheritance and go.'

'So keep her in hospital a little longer.'

'Leave it, Carla,' he said again, and he heard his weariness reflected in his voice. 'We have work to do. Your headache…'

'Nothing aspirin can't fix,' Carla said, and she was watching him now with worry. She'd heard something in his voice. Seen something on his face? 'Leo, what's wrong with *you*?'

'Nothing that getting Anna out of our hospital won't fix. Let's move.'

Leo had written her up for painkillers, so Anna had slept. She'd had some breakfast. A very young nurse had helped her shower, washing away the worst of the bloodstains. She'd be wearing a scarf for a while but she was feeling a lot more in control.

She needed to get out of Leo's hospital.

Her tiny room was clean but shabby, with faded linoleum, a stark iron bedstead, a small wheeled table and nothing else. Its one high window looked out onto a brick wall and the light was from a single bulb, hanging high. It was hardly a room for feeling better in, she thought. It felt more like a cell.

Had Leo put her in here purposely? Was it the worst room he could find?

She wanted to leave, now.

Victoir turned up soon after breakfast with her suitcase. He was appalled—*appalled!*—by what had happened and his volubility made her tired. She persuaded him to disappear while she rid herself of the hospital gown, but the effort of tugging on jeans and T-shirt made her feel woozy. She settled back on the bed, and almost immediately Victoir reappeared, this time carrying a sheaf of documents so thick the ache in her head surged back.

'I can't read them here,' she told him. 'And I need legal advice if they're to do with the estate. Victoir, I'll take them back to England with me and get them checked.'

'I've only brought you the urgent ones,' he told her. 'These are things that can't wait. Like blocking those tunnels. I warned you. The sooner they're blocked—'

'The sooner you can start turning the castle into your dream apartments?'

The voice from the doorway made them both start. Leo. Of course it was. Victoir swivelled and scowled, and Anna flinched—which was stupid. She wasn't afraid of Leo.

She was afraid of how he made her feel.

'Good morning,' he said, edging into the tiny room. 'Victoir, can I ask you to leave while I check Ms Castlavara's condition?'

'I'm Anna Raymond,' she threw at him.

'You own the castle. This entire country knows you as the Castlavaran and I'm not about to argue with my country. Victoir…'

'Ms Raymond's about to sign some papers,' Victoir snapped. 'They're urgent.'

'More important than Anna's health?'

'What gives you the right to call her Anna?'

'I believe she gave me the right some years ago,' he said, meeting Victoir's challenge head on. 'When we met at medical school.'

What the…? Was Leo about to discuss their past history in front of Victoir? She felt herself go cold at the thought.

'We did meet while studying medicine,' she said, hurriedly and grudgingly. 'And he might as well use my first name if the alternative's Castlavara. Victoir, I'm sorry but I'm signing nothing now. Dr…Leo will tell you that

I've been taking strong painkillers, so nothing I sign now will be legally binding anyway.'

'You're fine,' Victoir snapped. 'No one will argue.'

'I'll argue,' Leo said smoothly. 'Victoir, leave.'

'Please, Victoir,' Anna added. 'And take the papers with you. Honestly, I'm fuzzy.'

He knew when he was beaten. He cast her a look of frustration, but then softened.

'I'm sorry. You're right, you're in no condition to consider. But we'll get you home as soon as possible. You'll need a couple of days' recuperation—your castle accommodation will be a far cry from this.' And he cast the room a disgusted glance, Leo an angry one, and stalked out.

Leaving her with Leo, which left her feeling weird. Alone, vulnerable...scared?

'Don't you have a nurse accompany you on your rounds?' she asked, and for the life of her she couldn't stop herself sounding like some sort of sulky adolescent.

'If I was in England maybe I would,' he told her. 'But nurses cost money and this hospital has no money. We run on a skeleton staff. This whole country runs on a skeleton staff.'

It was an accusation.

She didn't know how to answer. He was watching her like she was some sort of unknown entity, certainly not like a woman who'd slept in his arms, who'd shared his life...

Don't go there, she told herself fiercely. Move on.

'My head's fine,' she told him. 'I'm fine.' Being dressed should make her feel better, more in control. It didn't. Somehow it made her feel defenceless.

The hurt she'd felt ten years ago was all around her.

It was ridiculous, she told herself. You didn't mourn a lost love for ten years.

But the hurt had gone bone deep, and it was surfacing again now. This guy was too tall, his eyes were too dark. His hair was too black. He was too much the same as he'd been all those years ago.

'If you're running on a skeleton staff then I'm taking up a bed,' she managed. 'Discharge me now, Leo. The sooner I get out of this cell the happier I'll be.'

'Cell?'

'This room's awful. Why on earth don't you paint it?'

He didn't answer. The look on his face, though…

Uh-oh. She watched his fingers clench into fists at his sides, and then slowly unclench, as if he was counting to ten, and then to twenty, and then maybe to whatever it took to hold his temper.

'We have two private rooms in this entire hospital,' he said at last. 'We reserve them for those who desperately need privacy, usually those in the last days of their lives. We had a death just before you were admitted, which left this room free. Because of your…because of who you are…we believed a single room was imperative. Believe it or not, if we'd put you in a shared ward you would have had half the country visiting the patient in the next bed, just to get a look at you. So we did you a kindness. We put you in what's one of our best rooms.'

'Best rooms…'

'I told you, skeleton staff, minuscule budget, that's what we have. But certainly I'm happy for you to go. We started you on antibiotics last night. You can go as soon as the script's filled. Continue them for the full course— there are bats in those underground vaults and they carry infection. I can't imagine what Victoir was about, taking you down there without protective gear.'

'He was proving the place was unsafe.' There were a hundred other things she could have said but she couldn't get her tongue around any of them.

'It is unsafe. Obviously. But not if you know what you're doing.'

'You've been down there?'

'I'd imagine every adventurous child living within a couple of miles of the castle has been down there.'

'Bats or not?'

'They add to the challenge.'

'Surely my cousin didn't let kids into the castle.'

'There are entrances from outside the castle walls. No one's ever blocked them off. Your cousin and your uncle and your grandfather before him didn't give a toss what went on under the castle, as long as no one bothered their secluded, indolent lives. Let's get your head checked and get you out of here.'

'So I can start my secluded, indolent life?'

He sighed. 'Anna, I have no idea what you intend. I've heard Victoir plans to turn the castle into luxury apartments, with its own internal helipad. An oasis for the super-rich from other countries. With its location, with the Mediterranean right under the battlements, with the right design and your money behind it, such a place could be a celebrity magnet. He hired architects years ago, trying to persuade your cousin that it wouldn't intrude on his privacy. One of those architects left his plans in a local cab and the driver had them broadcast all over the country in minutes. It came to nothing, though. Your cousin wouldn't have seen anything in it for him, and that was all that interested him. Now, your head...'

'So he urgently wants the underground closed off because...'

'It wouldn't do to let it get out that the proposed idyllic retreat can be broached by twelve-year-olds.' He was right by her bed now, too close for comfort, but then anywhere in this tiny room was too close for comfort. 'Your head, Anna. I'm here to examine you, not talk about plans that have nothing to do with me.'

That shut her up.

He checked her head, not disturbing the dressing over the gash but simply noting the extent of bruising. He checked her eyes, her vision, and then retreated to the end of the bed to read the obs chart. Time for discussion was over.

'Headache?' he asked as he finished reading.

'Only when I laugh, and when you're here I find it difficult to even smile.'

He didn't respond.

'Any dizziness?'

'When I stand up fast but that's to be expected.'

He nodded. 'Take it easy for a few days, then. Do what Victoir suggests. Go lie in your castle and enjoy your view.'

Oh, enough. She pushed herself to her feet and glared. 'That's mean. What have I ever done to you, Leo Aretino, to make you act like I'm something the cat dragged in?'

'That's an exaggeration.'

'It's not. What have I done?'

'You haven't done anything.'

'Once upon a time you asked me to marry you.'

'That was a long time ago.' He closed his eyes—remembering?—and when he opened them there was a hint of softness there. Regret? 'We all do stupid things when we're young. Proposing to someone you barely know might count as one of them.'

'You did know me, though. You slept with me for—'

'I don't want to go there. It's history.'

'Which is affecting how you're treating me right now.'

'I'd be treating you the same if we hadn't slept together.'

'That's a lie and you know it. I watched you train as a doctor. I've seen you with patients. You're caring and kind, and last night you couldn't stop yourself moving in for a hug. Now I'm not going to be a patient any more, you're back to cold and sarcastic and all the things you suddenly became the moment you learned who my mother was.'

'Anna...'

'You owe it to me, Leo,' she said, calmly now. 'It's a question that's hung over me for years. I know I should have put it aside, but I've never understood. I suspect I'll be spending a bit of time here now, not only in your country but in this town. We may well meet again.' She took a deep breath, because what she was about to say was a concept so big she was having trouble getting her head around it. 'I may even be the one who decides on funding for this hospital.'

'Are you blackmailing me?' He was suddenly incredulous. 'What are you saying? Tell me why I didn't marry you or you'll cut off our funding?'

Whoa. It was her turn to be angry now.

She'd been confused about Leo for years. They'd had a glorious six months and then nothing. She'd felt hurt, betrayed, sick at heart, but he wouldn't talk of it. For what had remained of their training, he'd avoided any tutorial she was in. They'd been scrupulously polite when they'd been forced together.

She'd hurt every time she'd looked at him.

She'd been a kid, though, and those feelings should have long gone. She was now an experienced doctor in charge of her world—mostly—and there was no way she was letting this man insult her. Her anger was holding sway but she had herself in hand.

'Do you think I'd do that? Blackmail?' Her voice was so quiet that maybe only her dogs would have understood. It was the voice she used when she'd found them with a cornered, injured hedgehog.

Just before they'd decided never to annoy a hedge-hog again.

'It's nothing to do with me, what you do,' Leo snapped.

'If I cut off your hospital funding, of course it's some-thing to do with you.' She was having trouble getting the words out. 'You really think I would?'

'It's your right. Heaven knows, we've had to fight for what we have. You know you own this building? As landlord—'

'You think I'd close you down?'

'You're a Castlavaran.'

'So you think ruthlessness is genetic. It's like the name comes with a money-sucking piggy bank welded to my head.'

'I know the terms of your inheritance,' he said wearily. 'Of your Trust. You have no choice. Money goes into cas-tle maintenance or your comfort. Our funding's limited to providing provisional medical care for Castlavarans and castle staff. We stretch that as far as we can, to provide for the rest of the island. The Trust's been in place for hundreds of years, written into the fabric of our consti-tution. You think we don't know that you can't break it?'

'I know I can't break it but I'm not about to change things. Your hospital is safe.'

'That's great. Thanks very much.'

'Stop the sarcasm.' She was getting very close to yell-ing. 'So I'm not threatening your hospital but there's still so much I don't understand. Ten years ago… Isn't it about time you told me why you wouldn't marry me?'

The junior nurse who'd helped her shower appeared at the door. Her eyebrows hit her hairline.

She disappeared, really, really fast.

Uh-oh.

Anna had spent enough time in hospitals to know what she'd just said would be all over the hospital—all over the country!—in minutes. Hospital grapevines were the same the world over.

Maybe she shouldn't have said it.

But, then, this guy had hurt her. Badly. For ten years she'd needed an explanation and right now she felt strong enough—and angry enough—to demand it.

'I told you why I couldn't marry you.' He raked his fingers through his dark hair, a gesture she remembered. A gesture she could almost feel. She knew what it was like to have those fingers…

Don't go there.

'You said there were family problems,' she threw at him. 'You said you could never marry a Castlavaran. You said if you did then you couldn't come home.'

'Which was the truth.'

'And I said if the feud's that bad then we could leave, go to Australia or Canada. I was ready to go anywhere with you, Leo. But you walked away.'

'I walked back here. To a country that needed me.'

'So you couldn't face family hostility. You chose your family over me.'

'I chose my country over you. I still do.'

'What, like I'm still available?'

'I never said that. I never meant—'

'I don't have a clue what you meant. You never explained. You just closed down.' She sighed. 'Enough. I'm over it or at least I should be. Falling in love with a toe-rag when I was a kid hasn't defined my life and it won't define me now. Neither will this inheritance. I have a lovely life back in England. I'll do what I need to do and go home and let you get on with it.'

'And let Victoir have his way.'

'He's head of the entire castle administration. You think I have any way of figuring out any better plan?'

'You could try.'

'And walk away from my life in England?' She shook her head and the dressing felt suddenly very heavy. 'Why would I do that? You were asked to change your life when you were nineteen and you made it clear that was impossible. Why should I even contemplate doing the same?'

So that went well.

Or not.

Leo left Anna's ward and stood in the corridor, staring at the plain, whitewashed wall in front of him.

Memories of ten years ago were all around him. Of Anna's white, shocked face as he'd told her he couldn't marry her. Of her reaction of total betrayal.

But how could he have done better? How could he have explained the contempt and hatred that was felt to-ward her family? As soon as he'd found out who she was, he'd felt his own dumb adolescent heart break. How to explain that his studies, his time in England, his hopes for his future and the trust his people had put in him, they'd all be destroyed if their relationship went further.

Ten years ago he'd faced a bleak choice. Marry Anna and take her back to Tovahna? Impossible. If her uncle accepted her as part of the family she—and he—would have been incorporated into a family he hated. The community who'd scraped to give him an education would have been betrayed.

And being honest, he had to accept there'd been another problem that had been bone deep. He and his mother had been dependent on charity since his father had died. To marry a Castlavaran and take her home, for her to be accepted as part of the Castlavaran family, and for him to be married to her... It'd be the story of Cinderella turned on its head, and at nineteen, sexist as it was, the idea had made him feel ill.

He'd tried to think of other options. Moving overseas, anywhere where two doctors could make a living without baggage? Cutting all ties to her family and to his island?

He couldn't do it. As soon as he'd heard her name he'd known he had to turn away.

So now... She was still angry? Maybe she had the right to be.

As he'd grown older he'd realised he should have explained better, but at nineteen, bewildered by the complexity of a love he'd been subsumed by, he'd hardly been able to get words out. To explain to his carefree, joyous Anna the abject poverty of his country, the hurt her family had inflicted on his... Explanations would have achieve nothing, he'd decided. It was better to walk away fast.

'Leo, I said you should charm the Castlavaran. I didn't say propose!' Carla's voice from the end of the corridor made him start. It was incredulous.

'What?'

'Luisa said she heard you talking about marriage!'

What the...? 'She was mistaken.' He turned to face her, willing his expression to be bland.

'She was sure.'

'We spoke in English. How's Luisa's English?'

'Poor,' she admitted. 'But she was adamant marriage was in the mix somewhere. She said you sounded intense. If not marriage… You weren't being accusatory, were you?'

'I wasn't.' He sighed and decided to be honest. 'We do have…baggage. Anna and I met at med school when I didn't know who she was. We were in the same class for six months. I haven't heard of her for years.'

'And you didn't tell us because…'

'Because, as I said, we have baggage,' he said, exasperated. 'We dated. Not for long, but what teenager spreads the word about his love life?'

'You had a love life with a Castlavaran?' Carla eyed him with incredulity. But then she winced.

Her wince had him distracted. He wanted to be distracted—he wanted *Carla* to be distracted—but not like this. 'Carla, your headache…'

'It's nothing.' She sounded annoyed with herself. 'It's almost gone.'

'Is there anything else wrong?'

'Apart from too many patients to see? So what's new?'

There was nothing new. The hospital normally had two fully trained doctors and two nurse-practitioners, nurses trained by Carla and Leo to take over many of their responsibilities. It was all they could manage when the cost of sending people abroad for medical training was prohibitive. But Bruno was on leave because his small son had fallen from a tree and fractured his leg. The little boy was currently undergoing corrective surgery in Italy. Freya was recovering from a filthy bout of the flu that had swept through the town, doubling their workload.

Carla had coped brilliantly during their absence, but for the first time ever Leo thought she looked…fragile?

'Carla, you look strained. Are you sure it's just a headache?'

'Truly, I'm better, but thanks for asking.' Their friendship went back a long way, and now she reached up and gave him a swift kiss on the cheek. 'There. A kiss better and I'm done. But a love affair with a Castlavaran? See me astonished. I demand that you take time later to tell me all about it. By the way, you're scratchy and I still think you should charm her. Teenage romances can be resurrected and if you want to charm our heiress you'd better go and shave.'

'I know where I'm going,' he growled. 'Off to check the morning list.'

'I didn't even look,' she told him. 'It's enough to terrify a woman stronger than me. But our heiress—your ex-girlfriend!—is a doctor? Maybe we could ask her to see a few coughs and colds before she goes back to her castle.'

'A Castlavaran? Treating peasants? In your dreams.'

'Don't be so cynical,' she told him. 'It isn't like you, and dreaming doesn't cost anything. I might just pop in and introduce myself.'

'You know there's no time.'

'There's no time for anything but medicine in this place,' Carla said, and suddenly she was deadly serious. 'But this woman holds our fate in her hands and she needs to be onside. I know what triage is, Dr Aretino, and triage says being nice to the Castlavaran is top of the list, for all our sakes. And you… I'm thinking a shave is the least of it.'

'Carla…'

'I know. I need to shut up and see the next patient, like I do all the time.'

The snap was so unlike her that he took her shoulders and forced her to meet his gaze. 'Carla? What is it? You're not coming down with the flu, are you?'

'Of course not,' she said defensively. 'It's just a head-ache.'

'How bad?'

'Nothing a good night's sleep won't fix. Or another doctor. This country…this health service… I try to be cheerful but sometimes it gets me down.'

'It gets us all down but we need to cope with what we have.'

'Or try and charm a Castlavaran,' she said grimly. 'I can but try, even if you won't. Off you go and start our list, Leo. I'll talk to the heiress and join you when I'm done.'

CHAPTER THREE

VICTOIR WAS BRINGING a car back from the castle. It'd be here in ten minutes, the nurse had told her. Anna was ready to go.

She practised sitting and standing a few times. No dizziness. Breakfast seemed to have settled her. Facing Leo should have settled her even more, and in a way it had.

For ten years she'd wondered what she'd say to him, and somehow she'd said it. It felt empty, desolate even, but it was done. It was time to head back to the castle and cope with the enormity of what lay before her. That was enough to make anyone dizzy.

She wasn't dizzy now, though. She was being realistic. What had been landed on her shoulders was far too much for one woman to take in.

Her life waited for her back in England—her dogs, her friends, her lovely little cottage. Her friends had been coaxing her to try a dating site. Maybe she could.

But relationships never seemed to work out for her. Her solitary childhood, her mother's constant abandonment and then Leo's bombshell rejection seemed to have left scars in the trust department. She dated men who were safe and steady, but then there was always that element of…boredom? Whatever it was, it seemed to stop things moving to the next level. She needed to get over it. It was time she dated someone who thought the world was fun.

And this? She didn't need to tell a prospective date about the enormity of her inheritance, she decided. There was nothing she could do about it for another twenty years. She'd hand it back to Victoir and set out to enjoy her uncomplicated life.

She'd have fun without the baggage her mother and then Leo had left her with.

'Can I come in?'

A woman peered around the door, short, rounded, her glasses perched low on her nose. She was wearing sturdy shoes and a white doctor's coat. A stethoscope dangled from her pocket, her white hair was bundled into a tousled bun and her face made Anna feel instinctively that here was someone she should welcome.

'Of course,' Anna told her. She was perched on the bed but stood up. Anna wasn't overly tall but the newcomer barely reached her shoulders.

'I'm Dr Rossini,' the woman said. 'Carla. I'm Leo's colleague.'

'It's good to meet you,' Anna said, and found her hand gripped in a hold that was strong and warm and strangely welcoming. It seemed a warmer welcome than she'd had from anyone in the three days she'd been in the country.

'I've brought you your antibiotics,' Carla said, handing over a box. 'I picked them up from the pharmacy. It'll save you fetching them as you go out. You understand you need to take the whole course?'

'I do. Thank you.'

'And I wanted to meet you,' Carla said. 'You should meet at least one member of the medical staff who doesn't think your name makes you poison.'

'Is that what everyone thinks?'

'Yes,' she said bluntly. 'With reason. If you want me to say nice things about your family you should ask me to go away. But I'm not judging you.'

'That's good of you,' she said wryly, and Carla gave her a rueful smile.

'Sorry. But I thought I should lay our cards on the table. Something I suspect Victoir won't do on our behalf. Maybe not even Leo.'

'Your cards?'

'The country's cards.'

'Right,' Anna said, and the ache in her head suddenly returned. Or maybe it was a different ache. It was the dull throb that had been there ever since she'd realised the enormity of her inheritance.

Strangely, Carla was putting her own hand to her head. Matching headaches? The last thing Anna wanted to do now was talk about the complexities she'd inherited, but she could see strain in the older woman's eyes. She suspected that what was about to be said would be hard to say.

'What's Leo told you about our country?' Carla asked.

'You know I know Leo?'

'He said you dated briefly, at med school. Did he explain the set-up here?'

Briefly? The word hung. It hurt. But she wouldn't talk about Leo. He didn't fit into this conversation—in any conversation she intended having.

Briefly...

'You know the Castlavarans own everything on this island,' Carla was saying. 'Everything. We're a tiny country. We should be centrally governed by a larger state but we've always been independent. Our own language. Our own resources. And, sadly, our own official family, a family that's scourged the land for its own ends and paid to subdue any unrest.'

'I understand that,' Anna said stiffly. 'I also understand there's little I can do about it for now. You know about the Trust? The terms of inheritance are that money from the estate is tightly held, used only for the upkeep of the castle or for my personal welfare. There's a twenty-year holding period before I can change that. Victoir says the Trust was put in place to prevent wild spending by past Castlavarans.

'I have trouble understanding the complexities, but legal opinion says I can't break it. It seems it's best if I go home, forget about it for twenty years and then put a team of lawyers in place to try and sort the mess out.' The ache in her head seemed to tighten. 'Even that boggles me.'

'I can imagine. But meanwhile you could try and help.'

'Like how?'

'Well, a steriliser for a start,' Carla said, suddenly sounding hopeful. And a little bit cheeky? She lifted a spoon from the cup and saucer, left from Anna's morning's coffee. 'This spoon, for instance. This is for your personal use and you're fussy. You could order a steriliser right now, to be delivered as soon as possible. We can't help it if you're discharged before you get to use it, and you could graciously allow us to use it until you need it again.'

Anna's lips twitched, and for the first time in what seemed weeks she found room to smile. In the enormity of what she'd been landed with, this seemed tiny, but the lovely thing about it was that it was something she could do right now.

Carla was looking hopeful, her head cocked to one side. Wondering if she was up to the challenge?

Maybe she was. *Fun.* The word was suddenly right before her. This was a baby step in how her life could continue from now on, but...could she have fun with this? Could she be of use?

'You know,' she said thoughtfully. 'These sheets are scratchy. My welfare decrees I should order non-scratchy sheets, just in case I'm ever admitted again. Could you put in a requisition? Linen can't be kept apart in the hospital laundry so maybe enough for the whole hospital?'

'Yes!' Carla said, chuckling with delight. 'I knew you couldn't be as bad as your cousin. And what about coffee? You surely can't be expected to drink...' But then she paused. She put a hand to her head in a gesture Anna understood. Her own head hurt.

But this was suddenly more than that. Carla's pain seemed to intensify. Her eyes widened and she grabbed for the foot of the bed, as if to steady herself.

And swayed.

And Anna moved as she'd never moved before. She reached her and hugged her under her arms, taking her weight as she sagged against her.

As Carla's eyes became sightless. As her knees buckled.

As she crumpled to the floor.

Leo was in the nursery, checking the tiny baby who'd been born the night before. It was a good moment in what promised to be a frantic day. He gazed down at the newborn bundle and thought, This is what it's all about. Forget Anna. Forget the Castlavarans. Focus on what's important.

And then his buzzer...

Code blue.

He was out the nursery before he realised.

Room Twelve. *Anna's room.*

Code blue meant cardiac or respiratory arrest, or similar medical emergency.

Anna?

What had he missed? Internal bleed? What?

He didn't run—he didn't need to. He'd pretty much perfected his hospital stride, so running would make him no faster.

He turned the corner to Room Twelve and Maria was in front of him, pushing the crash cart.

'Anna…' he said, and he couldn't keep the fear from his voice.

'Worse,' Maria managed. 'It's Carla.'

She'd hit the call button and then she'd yelled. The junior nurse who'd helped shower her had arrived in seconds, taken one look and bolted for help.

Carla vomited as she reached the floor. The first couple of moments were frantic, clearing Carla's airway, getting her into the recovery position, trying to assess her breathing. Anna was crouched on the floor, willing help to arrive. Trying to see what she was coping with. Cardiac arrest? No? Headache, pain, collapse…

And then blessedly Leo was kneeling beside her. The crash cart was being wheeled in behind him.

'Carla…' Leo said, and she heard his voice break.

Carla's eyes were open but she wasn't seeing.

'I don't think it's her heart.' Anna said it intentionally loudly, making her voice clipped and professional. Leo and this woman must be friends. She'd heard Leo's instinctive distress, but she needed a doctor here, not someone emotionally involved.

And he got it. She felt the moment he hauled himself together. The moment he became one of a medical team.

'Fall?'

'Collapse,' she told him. She glanced up at Maria, and Maria anticipated her needs by handing down a towel. Two. She used one to sweep the mess away from Carla's head, the other to help clear her face. 'She looked like her head hurt. She put her hand to her head like there was intense pain and then she passed out.'

'The headache... Hell...' He had his hand on her wrist.

'It's still strong,' Anna told him.

They were squashed together. Maria started working around them, shoving the bed back, heaving the bedside table onto the bed to give them more room.

'Defibrillator?' Maria asked.

'No.' Leo was moving to the next stage. He checked her eyes, and Anna saw the slight sag of his shoulders, relief that he'd seen a corneal reflex. He'd seen her clear Carla's mouth. He'd seen the gag reflex as well.

She wasn't comatose, then, but the speed of the drop from alert to where she was now implied she soon would be.

'It's okay, Carla, we've got you,' Leo said, loudly and firmly. 'Relax, love, don't fight it.'

That made Anna blink. He was assuming Carla could hear. It was good medicine, the assumption, unlikely as it was, that Carla would comprehend what was going on. But not all doctors did it, especially under the stress of an emergency like this one.

'We need to stabilise your airway and get a scan,' Leo said. 'Carla, have you had a head injury? Banged your head?' She didn't respond—how could she?—but once again Anna knew the words had been said to reassure Carla that she was included in this conversation. 'Carla didn't say anything about an injury, Anna? Maria?'

'Nothing,' Maria said, and Anna heard her distress, too.

'Just a headache,' Anna said. 'Leo, this looks like an internal bleed.'

'You must have had a bump.' Leo was back to speaking to Carla. 'You told me you took aspirin last night.'

'She has been taking aspirin,' Maria ventured. 'She's been getting it from the hospital pharmacy. I saw her take a couple of boxes last week. She said she has a bit of arthritis. We were busy and I didn't follow it up.'

'Aspirin won't have done this, though it might have made it worse,' Leo said. 'But if there's a bleed it won't help now. Carla, we're going to have to have a look-see. Get a trolley, Maria. We'll take her through for scans. Now.'

'What can I do?' Anna asked.

'You're a patient,' Leo said roughly. 'Thanks for your help, Anna. You should be right to go.'

The scan showed a bleed.

A big one.

The hairline skull fracture was bad enough. What was worse was the dark shadow underneath the fracture. A subdural haemorrhage. Blood vessels near the surface of the brain had obviously ruptured.

How the hell...?

But the cause of the injury was the least of his concerns. What was crucial was time. Blood had collected immediately beneath the three-layer protective covering of the brain. The brain was being compressed.

In young people a bleed like this was usually triggered by a significant impact. Older people could bleed after only a minor trauma.

Carla was hardly elderly but she'd been taking aspirin. The aspirin would have been thinning the blood.

The greater the pressure on the brain, the worse the

bleeding would become. For her to lose consciousness so quickly…

'I'm going in.' He was talking to Carla, and to the nurse beside him. Maria was looking as terrified as he felt. 'Carla, there's a bleed under the surface. We need to get the pressure off.' He needed to say no more. If Carla was aware enough to take it in then she'd know, and Maria had been a nurse long enough to realise the ramifications of a cranial bleed. Pressure on the brain caused brain damage, and it caused it fast. They had to get the pressure off now.

'Leo, I'm asking again. What can I do?'

The voice came from the doorway. Anna still looked very much the patient. She was dressed in jeans and a T-shirt, but the white dressing showed starkly against her burnt-red hair.

'You need to leave, Anna.' It was an instinctive response.

'I'm a doctor, Leo,' she snapped. 'Get over yourself. Let me help.'

'You're injured.'

'I have stitches from a bump on my head. I imagine Carla's haemorrhaging. Am I right?'

'You're not well. I can't—'

'Do you have another doctor on staff? An anaesthetist?'

He needed headspace and she was messing with it. He opened his mouth to snap back but sense prevailed.

His instinctive reaction to Anna had been that of a doctor to a patient. The internal war, how he was feeling about Carla's illness, physician versus friend, could allow no other distractions.

Anna's question, though, had cut through.

There was no other doctor within hours of travel. Carla

collapsing so dramatically meant that the bleed was sudden and severe. The pool of blood under the dura must be causing damage.

Carla usually assumed the role of anaesthetist if he needed to operate. What now?

'There's no other doctor,' he admitted.

'Evacuation?'

'It'll take hours.'

'Then she needs emergency craniotomy and drainage,' Anna said. Her curt, professional tone helped. 'If there's no one else... Leo, can you operate if I do the anaesthetic? I've done additional anaesthetic training. The village where I work isn't big enough to support medical specialists and there's occasional urgent need.'

She had anaesthetic training? It was like a gift from the heavens. A colleague with anaesthetic skills...

'You have a head injury yourself.'

'I have stitches and bruising. I may also still suffer a bit of dizziness if I stand up fast, but I think I'm over it and I can cover it. I know it's not ideal but given the circumstances... Give me a stool in Theatre and let's move.'

He gazed down at Carla and saw no response. No glimmer of recognition. He looked again at Anna and she met his gaze with a determination that was almost steely. Treat me as a doctor, her gaze said. Get over your prejudices.

She was still a patient. He could hardly ask.

There was no choice.

'Thank you,' he said simply. 'If you're sure.'

'I'm sure. Let's move.'

The surgery sounded simple. Anyone with a decent handyman's drill should be able to do it—in fact, Leo had heard of doctors in emergency situations using just such an implement.

Luckily he didn't have to resort to such measures. Most of their of equipment was second-hand but it was functional. Leo had kept up with a lot of doctors he'd met during training, and when they had been purchasing shiny new medical toys they often remembered him and sent on usable older things. The X-ray department had been set up almost completely via donations from a friend he'd met in final year med school. For the rest they'd scraped and saved and cajoled the community, which meant the theatre he was working in was fully equipped.

And he had excellent staff. Maria, his chief nurse, was rigid about standards and ongoing training, and she ruled her nursing staff with a softly gloved fist of iron.

The only hole in the team was his lack of a trained anaesthetist and that hole had been plugged. In Anna he had an anaesthetist he could trust. From the moment he'd nodded his acceptance of her offer she'd turned almost instantly from patient, from heir to the powers of Castlavara, from his past lover—into a crisp, competent professional.

'Do you have access to Carla's medical history? I need to know what she's taken, allergies… Family? Is someone on their way?'

'Her husband died ten years back,' he told her. 'Her son's in Italy. But we have her history. Maria…'

'Onto it,' Maria said, and so was Anna. Ten minutes later they were in Theatre.

'Glasgow scale deteriorating,' Anna told him. 'I'm losing any eye response.'

He didn't need telling. He knew the pressure would be building.

He needed to focus.

A handyman might be able to operate a drill but what was needed here was precision, care, knowledge. And confidence.

Confidence that Anna could keep Carla alive while he worked.

And strangely the trust was there.

If another doctor had walked in right now, someone he didn't know... If they'd offered to help... Yes, he'd have had to accept their help but there'd be caution. He'd be checking all the time. He'd be torn, though, because the procedure he was performing was out of his comfort zone. He needed to work fast with skills he hardly knew he had.

Anna helped. Somehow just knowing she was here helped.

Carla was in the supine position, facing up. As soon as Anna had the IV line in, as soon as she was sure Carla was under, Maria did a quick shave.

Then it was over to Leo. Two small holes to expose the dura, then careful, painstakingly draining. Hell! The scan had showed a build-up but it shook him to see just how much fluid was in there.

He inserted a temporary drain to prevent more build-up. He'd rather not have—it increased the chance of infection—but with this amount of fluid and with the speed of onset of symptoms, he had little choice.

Then closing.

It sounded straightforward. It seemed the hardest surgery he'd ever undertaken. Why? Because the huge unknown was how much damage had already been done. Had they been fast enough? Had the pressure already caused irreparable harm?

He fixed the drainage tube, dressed the wound and finally stood back from the table.

He'd done all he could do.

Carla was his friend and he felt ill.

What would have happened if Anna hadn't been here? Would he have had to administer the anaesthetic himself? Have Maria do it?

Or wait for evacuation?

He was under no illusion as to what waiting would have meant. Even now, as Anna reversed the anaesthetic, he was aware that they might have been too late. Cerebral haemorrhage was the most frightening of medical emergencies.

'We've done everything we can,' he said wearily. 'A neurosurgeon will need to take over. We've put in a call for evacuation but that's still hours away. Meanwhile, we just have to hope.'

Anna had finished reversing the anaesthetic. She'd removed the intubation tube. Carla was breathing for herself again, but would she wake up? And if she did, what damage had been done?

'You went in as fast as you could,' she said, maybe sensing just how close to the edge he was. 'She has the best chance you could possibly have given her.'

'Partly thanks to you.' Then, almost huskily, 'Thank you.'

'Don't thank me.'

He nodded, dumbly, as the imperatives of surgery faded and the fear for his friend flooded back. What if the damage from pressure was irreversible? What if Carla didn't open her eyes again, or, if she did, what life would she be facing?

Surely they'd moved fast enough.

With this level of bleeding, with the speed with which things had overtaken Carla, there was no way of knowing.

There was nothing more he could do but wait. The pain he was feeling was fathoms deep.

'The Italian neurosurgeons will take over,' he said roughly. 'We don't have the facilities to do more.' While there'd been medical need, he'd been able to put distress aside, but now there was little to do for Carla but wait, that distress was impossible to hide. 'I need to speak to her son. Our receptionist will have contacted him already and he may well be on his way. But enough. Anna, you need to go home.'

'Leaving you alone.'

'Bruno will be back later today. He's one of our nurse-practitioners but his six-year-old fell out of a tree last week. Comminuted fracture of his femur. He needed specialist orthopaedic care.'

'So he was evacuated, too?'

'Yes, but Bruno should be back.'

'But he's not a doctor.'

'He's good. Anna, you need to leave. I'll take over here.'

'And leave you to worry about Glasgow scores on your own.'

'You're a patient, Anna,' he said, reminding himself as well as her. 'Your place isn't here.'

He saw her wince, but there was nothing he could do about it. He had room for nothing but distress for his friend.

And she seemed to accept it. She looked at him for a long moment and then nodded.

'Okay. But you will call me if Carla needs me. If *you* need me.'

'I will.' He hesitated. 'But the castle won't necessarily put my calls through.'

'What the…? Of course they will.'

'Try and see,' he said wearily. 'The outside world isn't permitted to intrude on the castle and its occupants.'

'That might have been then,' she said briskly. 'This is now. If there's any problem, I have my own phone and it's on international roaming. I'll leave my number at the desk. Call me. Promise?'

And he looked at her, a long look where questions were being asked that he didn't understand and maybe she couldn't respond to.

'I promise,' he said at last. 'Not that I think it'll happen, but I promise. Thank you, Anna, but you need to remember you've been injured yourself. It's time for you to leave.'

CHAPTER FOUR

To say Victoir was annoyed was an understatement. He'd come to collect her in one of the castle's limousines. He'd been left kicking his heels for hours.

When she finally joined him he was leaning on the beautiful auto, glowering, looking almost startlingly out of place. The entrance to the hospital was serviceable but that was all that could be said about it. It was a narrow driveway, crammed with people coming and going, mothers and babies, the elderly in wheelchairs or Zimmer frames, people visiting with bunches of flowers or bags of washing.

The ambulance that had transported Anna to hospital the day before had backed into the entrance parking bay, in front of the limo. The limo was practically taking up the entire bay. Paramedics were trying to manoeuvre an elderly lady on a stretcher around Victoir. Victoir, in his immaculate dark suit and crisp white linen, with his hair sleeked back, a man in his forties in charge of his world, wasn't about to move for anyone, not even a patient on a stretcher.

The sight made Anna wince. Not for the first time she thought helplessly about the terms of the castle Trust. Yes, she'd inherited but she had no power. Once upon a time one of her ancestors had mistrusted his heir and made the entailment bulletproof. It would be twenty years before she had any control over funds. She owned it all and yet she didn't own it.

Her cousin hadn't survived his inheritance for the twenty years needed to break the Trust. Her uncle and her grandfather...clearly by the time their twenty years had been up they hadn't bothered. After all, why should they? All their needs were being met.

Men like Victoir had no doubt been lining their own pockets, but to find out how, to explore the complexities of things she probably could do nothing about...

'Leave it and come home,' Martin had suggested. 'A decent legal team can look after your interests from over here. If in twenty years you wish to do something more, you can think about options then.'

It made sense. She knew little about this place except that she now—sort of—owned it. And it was poverty-stricken. And Leo was here and he was struggling.

Victoir was opening the car door for her. 'You should have asked the nurses to carry your gear. That's what they're here for.'

Really? It was a small holdall. To ask one of the overworked medical staff to abandon their work to carry it...

'I can't believe they let you just walk out with it,' he continued. 'If they think they can treat a Castlavaran like—'

'They treated me well.'

'They asked you to work! When you're ill yourself?'

'I'm not ill and I asked to work.'

'They've even demanded to come to the castle. A final check, the nurse said. As if we can't take care of you.'

An offer of a follow-up visit by a district nurse was entirely reasonable, Anna thought. She'd have organised the same for a patient of hers. She didn't need it, though. She was okay.

Except that she was angry.

Usually she was unflappable. She prided herself on her calm in the face of crises.

She didn't feel calm now.

Get a grip, she told herself. Think of the whole situation.

Until now she'd floundered, bowing to Victoir's assumed authority. What choice had she had? But his authority was starting to grate and grate badly. Surely she paid this man's wages?

She didn't know how much. By the look of his clothing and the gold rings on his flaccid fingers, a lot. She'd spent her short time here trying to come to terms with the vastness of her inheritance. Should she stay a few more days and check staff ledgers? She could do that as she lay on her day bed while the staff in question catered to her every whim, she thought, and then she grimaced. The only appealing part of that right now was the day bed.

'You need to remember you've been injured yourself.'

That was what Leo had said and there had been gentleness in his tone.

Of course there had. She was his patient. His gentleness meant nothing.

She'd been judged ten years ago and he'd walked away. How much deeper would that judgement be now that she'd inherited?

'Can you get that ambulance out of the way?' Victoir called, power loading every word. And to Anna's disgust, the paramedic left the old lady's trolley where it was, and went to move the ambulance.

'You'll look after your patient first,' she called, and Victoir's authority was nothing compared to the power she put behind her words. Wow. Where had that come from? Was it the doctor in Anna, or was it the first stirrings of the long line of autocratic Castlavarans in her genetics? Regardless, her words held the weight of ancestry, plus a huge loading of a doctor accustomed to sorting chaos in the midst of medical emergency. It forced all those around her to go still.

The paramedic, the woman about to climb back into the driver's seat, looked at her with doubt. Anna might sound authoritative but she surely couldn't look it. Jeans, T-shirt, bandaged head. What remained of her copper curls tumbling every which way. No make-up. Compared to Victoir she looked a nothing.

But this was a test she needed to pass. Victoir was looking at her as if she'd passed the boundaries of what was permitted. Up until now he'd set the guidelines. He'd made it easy for her to follow his lead, impossible for her to do anything else.

Impossible had to start somewhere. Victoir was invoking the family name? So could she.

'I'm Anna Castlavara and we wait until the needs of patients have been met,' she said. 'Your patient's care takes precedence over my needs.'

'We've waited long enough,' Victoir snapped. 'These people—'

'These people are Tovahnans, just like me,' she said. 'What's best for them is best for me. And what I say goes.'

And she seated herself—firmly—in the rear of the limousine and prepared to wait.

But what she hoped Victoir didn't see was that she sat not because she needed to but because her knees were shaking.

What was she letting herself in for?

And then she glanced out of the window of the car and there was Leo. He was striding out to check on the new patient being admitted.

He'd paused like everyone else.

He'd heard.

So what? She turned away, putting her hands to her cheeks to try and subdue the slow burn spreading across her cheeks. Her knees were still trembling.

She needed that day bed.

She needed space.

She needed to get home to England.

The evacuation team was delayed and delayed again. It happened. Neighbouring countries assisted as they could, but their own emergencies took precedence over Tovahna's. Finally, though, and before evacuation took place, Carla regained consciousness.

It was six at night. She'd been unconscious for almost ten hours. She was confused, her speech was a little blurred and she wasn't sure what was happening or why, but she recognised Leo. She recognised Maria. Her vision seemed only slightly impaired. Her fingers and toes worked, albeit with a struggle.

'What…what…? Tell me what's happened.'

The spectre of unimaginable brain damage faded. It was so much more than Leo had dared hope that it was all he could do to hold back tears.

Maria couldn't. She sobbed, openly. 'Oh, Carla, we've been so frightened. You nearly died. And the Castlavaran, Anna, had to help save you.'

'The Castlavaran…' Carla managed. 'What…? Tell me…'

So Leo sat beside her and held her hand and told her. He wasn't sure if she took it all in. You didn't suffer a bleed on the brain without some repercussions, he thought, but her state of awareness now was a huge promise of a short rehabilitation and total recovery.

'Do you remember banging your head?' he asked, and she looked blank.

'The Castlavaran, Anna, banged her head.'

She was remembering. Better and better.

'She did.'

'And you're dating her.'

Hell. 'I'm not.'

'I remember—'

'Carla…'

'That would be so wonderful.'

And there was no response to that. Carla's eyes were closing. With the amount of drugs on board, the battering her brain had taken, her body was demanding sleep.

But it was sleep, not lack of consciousness. What a gift.

'Thanks to Anna,' Maria whispered. 'We need to let her know.'

'I'll see to it,' he said, and he left Maria watching Carla like a mother hen with her favourite chick.

We need to let her know…

He had Anna's number. He should simply ask the receptionist to ring a message through.

But before he could do anything he was hailed from down the corridor by two young men. One was Ben, Carla's son, who he guessed had hitched a ride in with the evacuation team from Italy. The other was Bruno, the nurse-practitioner. The evacuation team was behind them, signing in at Reception.

He hadn't realised how tired he was until he saw them. An almost-doctor to share his load. A son to take over his love for Carla and to accompany her on evacuation.

Trained paramedics to take Carla to a world-class neurologist.

'You look like a car crash.' Bruno's voice was filled with concern. 'I came as soon as I could. And here's Ben to be with his mother. Tell us the worst, Leo.'

But it wasn't the worst. He felt himself growing even lighter.

'There's every reason to think she'll make a full recovery,' he told them. 'She'll need full neurological assessment but now...the real concern is how she came to have the bleed in the first place.'

'I can tell you that,' Ben said grimly. 'When I rang her last night she said she'd had a headache, then hit her head on the open bathroom cabinet and made it worse. She was making light of it but I could tell she was rattled.'

'But she still came to work this morning.' Hell. They were so short-staffed. Carla would have come to work with more than a sore head.

He might have done the same.

'I'll be having words with her,' Ben growled. 'I know she's popping aspirin for her arthritis. Once she's evacuated to Italy I'll insist on some enforced R&R, and have her visit an arthritis specialist while she's there.' He coloured. 'I have the money to afford it.'

'There's no need to sound apologetic,' Bruno said. 'I just took my son to Italy to have a complex fracture seen to. We each look after our own as best we can.' He glanced up at Leo. 'I hear we even treat Castlavarans.'

'She's not that bad,' Leo said grudgingly. 'You know she's a doctor? She gave the anaesthetic while I operated on Carla.'

'She did what?' To say they were both astounded was an understatement.

'She did all she could.' He told them briefly what had happened. 'She's a talented doctor.'

'Well, pigs might fly,' Bruno said, and whistled. 'All this while she had her own sore head.'

'I need to thank her,' Ben said. 'She's still here?'

'She's back in the castle.'

'Well, that's that, then,' Bruno concluded. 'The castle walls have been broached and sealed again.'

'We don't know that,' Leo told him.

'Really? Does she intend to help anyone else in this country? Like repair the roof on this dump?'

'You know the Trust stops her.'

'Then I'm not interested,' Bruno said. 'It was good of her to help Carla but it's over to us again. Tell Ben where his mother is. Give me a handover, sign off with the evac team and then go home for a sleep.'

Sleep. The word was like a siren song, infinitely enticing.

But he did need to ring Anna. She deserved to know how Carla was.

'Go on,' Bruno growled. 'Out of my hospital. Now.'

'Your hospital?'

'Okay, it's the Castlavarans',' Bruno admitted. 'But there's nothing we can do about that. We just have to make do with the scraps they leave us.'

He wasn't wanted.

Well, he was. There was work for him to do, but Bruno was having none of it. 'You're no use to us dead on your feet. You know if there's a need I'll call you back.'

Bruno was right. He did need to sleep, but how could he head home and sleep after a day like today? He felt wired. Disoriented.

Seeing Anna had done that to him.

He'd promised to let her know.

He went to collect her phone number from Reception but then hesitated.

Anna was less than half a mile away, within the walls of the great castle that dominated the whole island.

She was with Victoir and his precious, urgent documents. Heaven knew what he'd have her sign. Would she even think about what consequences her signature could have over so much of the island?

He glanced out toward the castle walls, vast and imposing. Victoir wanted to turn the castle into apartments for the wealthy, but everyone knew the terms of Anna's inheritance. Funds could only be used for her welfare or the upkeep of the castle. Luxury apartments... How could Victoir get away with that under the terms of the Trust? But if he could... Would Anna realise how much it would hurt the islanders?

Despite its generations of miserly owners, the castle still seemed the beating heart of Tovahna. For hundreds of years Tovahnans had lived within the shadow of its walls. Their forebears—Leo's forebears—had fought for it.

He'd seen Victoir's plans. What they proposed was tearing down sections of the wall to insert massive plate-glass windows, so those lucky enough to afford to stay here could see the islanders going about their business. Victoir knew his market. He wanted the world's rich and famous to use this as a retreat, and quaint island life—at a distance—was a marketing tool.

Did Anna know that poverty was one thing, rubbing the islanders' noses in the riches of others was another?

He thought of Victoir's face as Leo had agreed with Anna's assertion that she was unfit to sign. He'd have the documents out again already, he thought. She might have already signed.

She was his patient. More, she was his colleague and she'd helped save his friend. He needed to see her.

'It's the least I can do,' he muttered to himself.

And then he turned toward the castle.

He took the sea walk to the castle entrance. The walk itself did him good. It was early evening and the harbour was alive with fishing boats unloading, families coming down to help sort the catch, kids playing between lobster pots, cheerful banter between rival fishermen.

It was an idyllic setting. It disguised the grinding poverty underneath.

The idyll paled as he reached the castle walls. The massive stone fortress cast long shadows, and by the time he reached the vast oak and iron gates he felt cold.

Apartments. According to the Trust they'd have to be for Anna's private pleasure. She was a doctor and a good one. He'd seen her immediate concern for Carla. How could Victoir's grandiose plan ever give her pleasure?

And with that came another thought, maybe just as crazy. If medicine itself gave her pleasure then…then…

Don't, he told himself. You're here to protect her, make sure she's healing. Don't think past that.

First, face Victoir.

Islanders worked here—of course they did. They used the tradesmen's entrance, though, but tonight Leo was damned if he'd use the tradesmen's entrance.

He rang the bell and heard its sonorous tone echo behind the great stone walls. Few people rang this bell, he thought. Few people were welcome.

As he'd suspected, it was Victoir who answered the intercom. Victoir who controlled all intercourse between the castle and the world beyond. He'd been Yanni's private secretary, but under Yanni's indolent, indifferent rule his role had gone well past that.

'Dr Aretino...' Leo glanced up and saw cameras above his head. Of course. The castle's massive moat was no longer used for defence, but defences were still there.

'Victoir,' he said, struggling to keep irritation from his voice. 'I'm here to see Dr Raymond.'

'She's resting.' His tone was curt, dismissive.

'That's why I'm here. She suffered concussion. She needs to be checked. I gather you refused the offer of our district nurse when you left the hospital. She needs at least one more check within the forty-eight-hour period after injury.

'I can do that.'

The thought of Victoir checking made his skin crawl. It was all he could do to keep his voice even.

'You'll tell Dr Raymond I'm here to assess her medically and to give her an update on Dr Carla's condition,' he managed. 'I need to hear from her personally.'

'You're not welcome.'

He should turn around and leave.

He didn't.

'You have my patient in there,' he said, each word ringing loudly in the warm dusk. 'I'm concerned about her head injury. I need to be assured that she's well.'

'You can take my word for it.'

'That's not enough. Unless you can produce a medical power of authority, I need to either speak to Dr Raymond myself or I'll ask the local justice to demand access. You know I can do that, Victoir.'

The island justice would like nothing better than an excuse to demand entry to the castle and Victoir knew it. Leo heard the hesitation, the doubt, the weighing up of options.

Having the local authorities demanding entry would not suit Victoir's sense of control.

'She's asleep,' he said, and he sounded almost sulky.

'Do you know how to differentiate between deep sleep and unconsciousness?'

Another pause. And then a heavy click and the vast gates started opening.

'A quick check and you're out of here,' Victoir growled, but Leo didn't bother to answer.

She wasn't asleep. She'd tried hard enough. Home from the hospital, she'd felt weariness envelop her like a dead weight. It was reaction, she'd thought. She'd headed for bed in her over-the-top bedroom but she hadn't slept.

Victoir had opened the door and checked on her—twice—and that had freaked her out. The man gave her the creeps. She wanted to shove a chair against the door to make her secure but that'd show him he made her nervous. For some reason she didn't want him to see that.

She was wearing her yoga gear rather than her pyjamas because that made her feel safer—but not much. She'd feigned sleep and he'd gone away.

This whole place was weird, this over-the-top castle, its living quarters a monument to excess, the rest a derelict shambles. Given other circumstances the gothic setting could have entranced her, but now, alone, her head aching, what was on the other side of her bedroom door made her shudder.

She'd thought fleetingly of ringing Martin or Jennifer. If she said she was in trouble she knew they'd be on the next plane. They were good friends and they were sensible. They'd pick her up and bundle her home.

That was what she wanted right now, her friends, her dog, her own bed in her own small cottage. And yet...

Somehow the events of the last twenty-four hours had made her feel that leaving was cowardly.

But right now cowardly seemed a good way to describe her. This room seemed almost designed to make her feel insignificant, with its massive size, its vast crimson and gold wall hangings, its casement windows looking almost all the way to Italy.

There was a knock at the door and she clenched her teeth so hard she thought she might break them. At least this time he'd had the decency to knock.

'Yes?'

'Anna.'

It wasn't Victoir. *Leo.*

Surely she shouldn't feel relief, but she did. The tension evaporated in such a rush that she couldn't respond. She lay absolutely still.

'Anna?' She must be lying too still, too rigid. There was deep concern in his voice.

Leo…concerned for her…

It made her feel like her world was settling.

She was being dumb, she thought. It was this castle that was unnerving her, this creepy gothic setting, these vast, opulent living areas, this huge bedchamber.

But Leo was here. 'Come in,' she called, and finally she allowed herself to open her eyes and look.

Leo.

Not professional Leo either. He'd ditched the white coat. He was wearing faded jeans and a cotton shirt with the sleeves rolled to the elbows and the top buttons undone. His hair was tousled, as if he'd been walking in the wind.

Once upon a time she'd thought…she'd dreamed…

No.

'Hey,' she said, and summoned a smile—and saw relief wash his face.

He'd been worried. Despite her confusion the thought was comforting.

'You're okay?' he asked, the crease deepening between his eyes. Oh, those eyes…

'Nothing a good sleep won't fix.' She gazed up at him and saw her own weariness reflected. 'Same for you, I bet. What are you doing here?'

'Checking up on you. Victoir knocked back the offer of a district nurse.'

'I don't need the district nurse.' She sat up and wrapped her arms around her knees. 'How can I need anything in this room?'

'I guess you don't,' he admitted. He gazed around the bedroom. 'Great setting.'

'It's ridiculous,' she muttered, and decided she needed to be a bit assertive. She needed to sound as if she was in charge of her world again.

'Really ridiculous,' she emphasised. 'Not just one but two—*two!*—chandeliers. For a bedroom. Ten guest chairs. Two settees and a window seat big enough to seat me, my dogs and a small army of minions—if I wanted minions, which, believe me, I don't. And this carpet… Who chooses crimson and purple carpet with dragons woven into it? And it's not even the main bedroom—I gather this was one of Yanni's guest rooms. *Urk.*'

'I guess you could learn to like it,' he said neutrally, but there was a faint smile behind his eyes. He agreed with her, then. 'Anna, now I'm here… Headache? Pain level? One to ten, you know the score.'

'Two,' she admitted. 'Nothing an aspirin won't fix.'

'Let's try paracetamol instead,' he told her. 'I gather aspirin is what was behind Carla's bleed. She's been taking it for arthritis and then bumped her head. On the medicine cabinet, her son says.'

'Ouch.' They both knew aspirin could make a small bleed worse. 'But now...' She couldn't keep anxiety from her voice.

'She's awake and alert. She's a bit confused but she knows people, events, and there's no noticeable physical damage. Her son's with her. She's on her way to a full neurological assessment in Italy but she may well be in the clear.'

'Oh, Leo, that's wonderful.'

'It is, isn't it?' he said, and smiled and pulled up one of her overstuffed visitor chairs to sit beside her.

Which was discombobulating all on its own.

Leo. Beside her.

Get over it.

'Where's Victoir?' she managed.

'Do you care?'

'He's my...' She hesitated. 'Actually, I don't know what he is. The boss of me? That's what he'd like to think. I'm a bit over Victoir.'

'Good for you. Are you going to sign the release so he can build his apartments?'

She stilled.

She hadn't gone completely to bed. She'd put her head on the mound of glorious pillows and tucked the great crimson coverlet over her. Her yoga gear was pink and purple and covered her nicely.

She wanted more.

She wanted to be in crisp, professional work clothes. She didn't want to be in a room lit by chandeliers and carpeted with dragons. Most of all, she wanted some sort of protection against this crazy situation, where on one hand she'd inherited power and on the other hand she had no power at all.

'What's that got to do with you?' she asked, and then

thought, I sound petty. He must have thought so, too, as his face hardened.

'Everything. You turn this castle into apartments, you rip the heart out of my people.'

'Why does that sound like the overstatement of the year?'

'I'm not exaggerating. The castle takes up almost a quarter of the island. Your grandfather, your uncle and your cousin were appalling rulers but the islanders have accustomed themselves to this life for generations. The people should have risen up long ago but they haven't. They won't. And now… Turn the castle into a glorified gated community where the super-rich can fly in and fly out… Maybe there will be an uprising. I almost hope so, but it'll take years, and meanwhile there's nothing here. There's no hope for the kids. This island needs help, Anna, and right now the only help available is from you.'

'So how could I possibly help?'

'By not being a Castlavaran.'

'Don't you get that I'm not?' Enough. She shoved the coverlet back, folded her arms across her chest and glared.

His reaction wasn't quite what she'd hoped. He looked totally distracted. 'Great outfit,' he said faintly, and the smile returned to his eyes.

'I like pink.' She folded her arms across her chest and glowered. 'And purple.'

'Why wouldn't you? It's amazing.'

'Leo, the last thing I want is compliments,' she snapped, and stood up.

Or tried to. The effects of the last twenty-four hours were still with her. She swayed.

Leo rose and caught her as she staggered. He lowered her gently so she was sitting on the side of the bed.

She should be thankful.

She wasn't.

'I just stood up too fast,' she muttered.

'I know. Anger makes us do all sorts of unwise things.'

'What's that supposed to mean?' She had herself together again—a bit. Oh, she wished she wasn't wearing pink and purple. More than that, she wished she was somewhere neutral, not in this ridiculous bedroom, and not feeling so defenceless. And, yes, angry.

'Don't mouth platitudes at me, Leo Aretino,' she managed, anger growing. 'For ten years you assumed I knew what you were talking about. That I was part of this system. You assumed my cousin's, my uncle's, my grandfather's greed was not only known to me but that their actions were somehow partly my fault. It's not my fault, Leo. So now… I'm not a Castlavaran but I'm stuck.

'The terms of this inheritance are unequivocal. The money's to be used for the castle's upkeep. For my upkeep. Victoir's plan is that he build the apartments, and nominally I holiday in one. The rest are for my so-called friends to join me. We can defend it by saying it's "for my pleasure". It's a way we can close off the unsafe sections and keep the rest of the place functional, even economically viable, while I get on with my life. How else can I stop the whole place from falling down? The way Victoir presents it, I don't see that I have much choice.'

'You can look at options.'

'As if I'd know what they are. So if you have any, tell me, Leo, and stop treating me as the enemy.'

'I never—'

'You did,' she managed. She was so mad she was trembling. Was that still the residue from the bump on the head? Or residue from being dumped ten years ago. Who knew? Not her. 'From the moment my mother told you her maiden name, you've treated me like some form of alien, more, one capable of contaminating anyone who came near. So now... I accept this is your country and your concern. You don't like Victoir's option? Give me another.'

Her anger was almost a tangible thing. There was so much past history here, betrayal, hurt—and a love that had once consumed her.

Get over it, she told herself. Listen.

Without prejudice.

'There is a way,' Leo said, his calm voice trying to break through her obvious fury. 'Anna, can you listen? I'm not sure, but there might be.'

What was he about to say? Break the Trust? Martin had said it was inviolable.

'Like what?' Her anger was still obvious but she couldn't help it.

'Using Victoir's idea,' he said, and she blinked.

'The apartments.'

'No.' He closed his eyes for a moment, and took a couple of breaths. Calm or not, he sounded as if was holding himself in rigid control. Maybe the tension she was feeling between them wasn't one-sided?

If so, good, she thought, and then had the grace to feel ashamed. Yes, he'd dumped her but she'd gone on to have a pretty good life. Maybe her anger was out of proportion. But still, he'd hurt her. She wanted him to acknowledge that.

But he was now intent on his plan. Focussed. For him the past was obviously well behind him.

'Anna, maybe it's a pipe dream,' he told her. 'It came to me on the way here, from something Carla said and from Victoir's plans. But it'd take someone with a massive social conscience.'

'And how can a Castlavaran have a social conscience?' It was an angry mutter.

'You've said you're not a Castlavaran.'

'You don't believe that—or is your memory still selective?' She glowered and then decided to be honest. To lay it all out there.

'Leo, from the moment you told me you couldn't marry me, you acted like you could hardly remember that my name is Raymond. I remember, though, and it still hurts. I know it's stupid, but there it is. I even talked to our clinic's psychologist about it. How needful was that? She says it's tied up with my father walking away, my mother rejecting me over and over—and then you doing the same thing. She says I need to focus forward, not backward. So now… You judging me on my mother's name looks backward to me. Leo, you've checked I'm not dying. I assume you've routed Victoir because he's not here with his horrid documents. So what's left? You can trust me with your pipe dream or you can leave. Take your pick.'

'Anna—'

'Just do it, Leo.'

He closed his eyes and she could see him almost visibly brace himself.

When he opened them again he'd changed. His look was one of pure challenge.

'As you like,' he said formally, as if what he was about to say was business and nothing more. What had been between them in the past was—of course—once again to be forgotten. He sat again so he could talk to her at eye level.

Doctor to patient? Not so much.

'So here it is,' he said. 'I believe it's possible. Within

the terms of the Trust you have a chance to do something spectacular.'

'What?' She wasn't bemused. She was still just plain angry.

'You could turn part of this castle into a hospital. You could provide a base for us to expand and the facilities for us to give first-class treatment. You could be the first Castlavaran who cares. You could prove me—and all of this island—wrong.'

CHAPTER FIVE

To SAY SHE was hornswoggled was an understatement.

'A hospital.' She managed to say it but it was a word, not a concept.

'I know,' he said, gently now, as if he still thought she was ill. 'It's a crazy idea. I guess you're either a Cast-lavaran, in which case you've had greed and indolence bred into you, or you're an English doctor who wants nothing to do with your inheritance because it's twenty years until you can claim it. Either way, Tovahna is the loser. I'm sorry, Anna. I didn't mean to throw this at you tonight. But I just said…'

'Yeah,' she said, dazed. 'You just said…'

'It's something you could think about when you go back to England,' he said. Could she hear a sliver of hope?

'But…' She shook her head and winced. 'First of all you're still being insulting. I'm either greedy or I don't care. And if I'm neither of those then I'll fall on what has to be a preposterous plan. Turn a castle into a hospital?' Oh, her head hurt.

These weeks since she'd heard of this incredible inher-itance hadn't been wasted. She'd learned more of Tovahna than she'd believed possible. She knew the poverty that had kept the people in their places for a thousand years. But Martin and his colleagues had also checked the terms of her inheritance. They'd found it rigidly structured so the heir couldn't make changes.

Money was to be spent for the maintenance of the castle or the welfare of the incumbent. For nothing else.

Incumbent. That was her.

In twenty years maybe she could hand the vast wealth over to some central agency, gift people their own land, do some good. But not before that. Martin had spelled it out.

'The Trust's in the hands of a firm of conservative lawyers in Milan. It'll provide you with a sweet income but there's nothing more to be done for years. Stay home and wait.'

'How…?' she said now, in a small voice because speaking of such a thing seemed so immense, so impossible that even saying it aloud was ludicrous. 'How could I turn the castle into a hospital? How could I possibly fit that around the terms of the Trust?'

And it seemed Leo had an answer.

'The same way Victoir's proposing converting the place into apartments,' he told her. 'The way he's proposing getting around the Trust is that you'd nominally have one set aside for your personal use, and the others would be deemed as being built for your guests. Your guests would pay a hefty price for the privilege but that wouldn't matter. They'd be here for your pleasure. So a hospital…'

'You're saying I could use a hospital? Have the hospital for my own personal use? I'd need to bump my head once a day. More.'

He didn't smile. The intent look didn't fade.

'That wouldn't work. There's no way that'd fit the terms of the Trust. What could work…' Once again, a deep breath, as if what he was about to say was so huge he could scarcely believe he was saying it. And when he finally said it, she could understand why.

'The only way it could work was if this hospital itself was your life,' he said. 'You'd need to live here—really live here—and the hospital would need to be as important to you as the over-the-top sports cars your cousin used to collect. They're gathering dust in the massive garages he had built for them. He could hardly use them because the roads here are so bad. With a little gumption he could have had the roads repaired so he could use them—that would have helped the islanders and been within the terms of the Trust—but that would have taken sense he didn't have. But, Anna, if your passion, your life was a medical centre, to serve not only you but this whole island, then the lawyers in Milan must surely agree. But you would need to live here. Make Tovahna your home. Be the first Castlavaran in generations to make a difference to your people.'

'My people.'

'They are your people.'

'I'm *not* a Castlavaran.' How many times did she have to say it?

'Don't quibble, Anna,' he said roughly, and she thought she detected emotion underlying the tone. How? Because she knew this man. She knew him so well…

Yet she didn't know him at all. He was a stranger, and he was suggesting the preposterous.

What was he asking? He wanted her to stay here, by herself, with the beastly Victoir. He wanted her to forget everything that had happened between the pair of them. He wanted…the impossible.

'I want to go home.' It was a childish thing to say but it was what came out when she opened her mouth. And Leo looked at her as if it was what he'd expected all along.

'Of course you do. Run back to England with your inheritance and forget about us. Well, at least I've tried.'

'You call that trying?' The words were out before she could stop them as anger surged, a swift and unexpected response to his look of disgust.

'What do you mean?' His voice was cold and that made her angrier.

Her legs were dangling over the edge of the stupid over-the-top bed. Her feet were bare. Despite her pink and purple, she felt exposed. Vulnerable.

And still angry.

'I mean I've just been hit on the head,' she managed. 'I'm still tired and headachy. I'm also coming to terms with an inheritance that's made me feel like I've been hit by a sledgehammer. A golden sledgehammer, agreed, but a sledgehammer regardless. Add to that I'm confronted by an ex-fiancé who hurt me. I'm stuck in a thousand-year-old castle that feels like the set of a gothic movie. Plus I have a creepy administrator who comes in here with his indecipherable documents and who takes me underground without a hard hat and almost kills me, just to prove it's dangerous so I'll sign his documents fast. Yeah, I get that, I'm not stupid. And he doesn't even knock when he comes into my bedroom. So now you say I should turn the castle into a hospital and I say I want to go home and you act like what else could be expected of a rich, indolent, money-grubbing Castlavaran? Well, I'm not even a Castlavaran and, Leo Aretino, you can take your castle and your hospital and you can stick it!'

And she picked up one of her massive down-filled pillows and hurled it at him.

It hit him on the chest and slid harmlessly to his knees.

He placed it aside as if it was nothing and she glared and wanted the floor to open and swallow her.

Or Leo.

He was in her bedroom. In her chair.

He was far, far too close.

'Get out,' she said.

'I may just have put my case badly.'

'I don't care. Get out.'

The door opened.

Victoir.

'Get out,' she said again, only this time it was said in unison—with Leo—and it was the break they needed. Or she needed.

Nothing like a common enemy.

'I just…' Victoir started, and she decided it was about time she stopped being Victoir's doormat. Wasn't he her employee? Whatever, at least she could direct some of her pent-up frustration at him.

'You didn't knock. Basic rules, Victoir. Please leave.'

'If the doctor's finished…'

'He hasn't finished. He's explaining something to me that I wish to have explained. He'll see himself out when he's done. Please close the door behind you, and if you walk into my bedroom again without knocking I'll ask the lawyers in Milan to have you removed by yesterday.'

He stared at her and she faced him down.

He left. Fast.

'Wow,' Leo said, as Victoir disappeared and the heavy door was tugged closed. 'Well done. Hey, you really are a Castlavaran.'

'Don't. You'll get me started again.'

'I'm sorry.' He sighed. 'But you're right. You have far too much on your plate for me to be loading you with more.'

'Is that all you're sorry for?'

'You must know it's not,' he said gently. 'Anna, I've been sorry for a very long time.'

And that pretty much silenced her.

The silence stretched on. She was looking at him, seeing strain. She was waiting, but she didn't know what she was waiting for. What she was hoping?

'I'm sorry for not explaining,' he said at last.

'Explaining your hospital scheme? There's still time.'

'No,' he said softly. 'For not explaining ten years ago. For being nineteen and being hopelessly in love and then being dumbstruck by learning who your mother was. For not being able to explain it to you then. For being young and stupid and even cruel. For not being able to control my own hurt to ease yours. I still believe that I had no choice, but most of all, Anna, I'm deeply, deeply sorry that I had to walk away.'

The words left her winded.

After all these years…to have him finally say it.

She felt like a long-faded scar had suddenly split, to reveal there was still infection deep within.

Her psychologist had given her strategies for not looking back. Where was her psychologist now, when she was most needed? Strategies… She couldn't think of a single one.

'You didn't want…' she started, but he shook his head.

'Anna, you have no idea how much I wanted.'

'How can I know that? One minute we were planning marriage and then nothing.'

'I should have asked before. About your mother.'

'My mother was nothing to do with our relationship. She had very little to do with me. I told you she was a wild child. I told you there was man after man after man. What else was there to say?'

'That she was a Castlavaran?'

'As far as I was concerned, she was Katrina Raymond. She'd married my father, even if the marriage ended before I was born. I told you she'd been unhappy at home and her mother had died. I told you everything I knew.'

The only time she'd learned more had been the night she'd introduced Katrina to Leo.

She hadn't seen her mother for almost a year. Katrina had been in the States, but had breezed back to London and decided to drop in on her daughter.

'My head-in-her-books daughter has a man? Well, well, let's meet him.'

She'd been reluctant. To say she and her mother were dysfunctional would have been an understatement.

Anna had always been cared for—sort of. Katrina had access to money. 'It's family money, sweetheart—money's the only thing they're good for.' There'd been funds for an apartment with nannies, while Katrina had been off doing what she wanted. There'd been money to support Anna to study. There'd been no mother love.

Neither had there been any sense of history. Katrina wouldn't talk of home. 'There's some sort of Trust set up so my father has to support me,' she'd told her. 'That's all you need to know. He's an appalling man, Anna. Don't ask.'

So she hadn't asked, and the only part of Tovahna she knew was the language, taught to her in the times Katrina returned to the apartment to get over her latest love affair or to escape from whatever disaster she was in.

Anna had tried to warn him. 'She's unstable, Leo. She'll talk too fast. She'll come across as sophisticated and brittle but underneath...'

Underneath there were scars that Anna could only

guess at. And then that night at dinner, the scars were exposed for all to see.

Maybe it was Leo's gentleness. His kindness. His perception? Even at nineteen he knew how to empathise, and Katrina was captivated.

He spoke to Katrina in Tovahnan and maybe that had been the undermining of Katrina's defences.

'So tell me about your father?' he asked Katrina at last, when the pizza had been replaced by coffee. 'My father died early, but my mother still lives on Strada Del Porto on the island's east side. Is that anywhere near where your father lives?'

What followed was a loaded silence, and Anna looked at her mother in astonishment and thought, Is she about to crack? She'd hardly talked of her father, even to her. But then…

'As far as I know, my father still lives in that great gothic castle he loves so much,' she said, in a voice that was almost a whisper. 'It's the only thing he loves. He sits there and pretends to be a king and he's cared for nothing and for no one. Not my mother, and not me. And my brother's just like him. They can rot in their castle for all I care.'

And Leo stared at her in blank astonishment. 'You're a Castlavaran…'

'Don't say that name.'

'But he's your—'

'Enough.' Katrina pushed back her chair and walked out of the restaurant.

And that was that. One ring returned. One love affair over.

'I was so immature,' Leo said now, and it was so much what she thought that she blinked.

'Well. Good of you to admit it.'

'I should have explained.'

'So should my mother. I'm putting her in the same category. Let's keep Anna in ignorance and let her face the consequences without warning, without respect, without any acceptance of the fact that I had a right to know.'

'Anna…'

'My grandfather and my uncle and then my cousin were all self-serving creeps. I know that now. My mother was a brittle, damaged alcoholic. I know that, too. And you added that up and decided I must be more of the same and you'd cut me out of your life before I could contaminate you.'

'It was much, much more than that.'

'How would I know? Neither of you had the courtesy to explain.'

'I thought your mother—'

'I'd already said she'd told me nothing. She died four years ago, still having told me nothing.'

Unbidden, the hurt of so many years was spilling out, fury at her mother mixed with fury at Leo. But it was crazy, dumb, useless. It was adolescent anger, hurt from a time she should have put behind her.

She understood now, or she thought she did. After that night she'd done her own investigation into her mother's family and she even understood why Leo had walked away. Sort of.

'If I'd stayed with you I could never have come home again,' he said. 'I knew that.'

'And coming home was everything.'

'It was.' He hesitated. 'Hell, Anna, I should have spelled it out. I know that. But this country…you're getting a sense now of how impoverished we are. To send me to London to do medicine…it was a huge deal for the islanders. My father was dead and my mother had no means of support. I should have gone fishing when I was twelve, but my teachers told the town how smart I was. To be honest, most smart kids leave the island as soon as they can but I couldn't walk away from my mother for ever, and the islanders knew it. So when I said I wanted to be a doctor, somehow they managed it. I still don't know how. Because of the draconian rule of your family, every cent had to be accounted for.'

'But they never have been my family,' she managed, and he held up his hands, the same way he'd held them up ten years ago. Warding her off.

'Anna, I've said I'm sorry. I'm also sorry for being too immature to explain properly, for walking away so fast. But to be honest, maybe it was for the best, getting it over with fast.' He hesitated. 'I hope you did get over it fast. You have a partner now?'

What was there to say to that? A woman had some pride. 'Don't kid yourself that I've mourned you for ten years,' she told him, attempting to glower. 'I've had a very good time. I have a great job, a lovely home, dogs. I started dating Martin two years ago. He's a lawyer and a friend, and he'd be here in a flash if I asked him. As would any number of my friends.'

'But not now that you're injured?'

'I have a sore head, not a cerebral bleed. And you…' Two could play at his game. 'Wife? Kids? Goldfish?'

'I'm too busy for relationships,' he said brusquely. 'Moving on. Anna, the idea of the hospital…you're saying no.'

She hesitated. She was trying hard to be grown up, she told herself. She needed to shelve her adolescent self. She needed to get over a pain that surely should be well gone.

A hospital. Here.

Martin's advice had been sound. 'Do nothing. You

can spend twenty years planning what to do when you finally inherit. Just go and look and then come home.'

Home sounded infinitely appealing.

But so did doing something. Something splendid?

'I didn't say no,' she said, slowly now, thinking it through. If she could get over the past, if she could see how this could happen... If she could get over how this man made her feel...

'Tell you what,' she said, pushing herself to her feet again. And once again she wobbled and needed to let Leo take her arm to steady her. Regardless. 'I'm rested,' she said. 'Yes, I'm still a bit shaky but I'm okay. Let's put... let's put everything behind us. You know this castle?'

'I have been in it,' he said. 'I was your cousin's treating doctor.'

'So you've been in his bedroom and in the entrance. Anywhere else?'

'I knew a lot of it as a boy,' he admitted. 'Your uncle ran on a skeleton staff so we could sneak around undetected. As kids...we did do our own exploring.'

'Well, there you go,' she said, determinedly cheerful. Determined to let bygones be bygones. Determined not to let the feel of his hand on her arm make her feel... what she needed to be long over feeling. 'You know it, and you've obviously thought this through. So, Dr Aretino. Let's forget the girlfriend-boyfriend thing. Let's also forget the doctor-patient thing. We're medical colleagues and you have a medical-based proposal. Let's take a walk through this castle. My castle,' she amended, because she was still getting her head around it and if she was going to face Victoir down then she needed the authority. And it wouldn't hurt if this man held her at a distance either.

'Victoir's shown me Yanni's over-the-top apartments and he's shown me through sections that are obviously dangerous,' she told him. 'But I know he has his own agenda. *Let's turn what we can into more opulence and knock the rest down*, is the gist of what he's telling me. So, Dr Aretino, let's go for a tour and you can tell me how any other option would be possible.'

CHAPTER SIX

HE'D DREAMED OF this since he was twelve years old. The night his father had died he'd stood sobbing under the shadow of the massive castle. That night of tears had matured into a vow to create a medical service equal to any in the world—or at least a medical service to stop islanders dying needlessly, uselessly, heartbreakingly.

He hadn't succeeded. Sure, he'd done a lot. He'd got through medical school. He and Carla had badgered the Castlavarans to give enough to provide basic services for themselves, and they'd organised islander contributions. He'd used contacts he'd made during training to plead for donations from abroad. They'd achieved a basic needs hospital with basic needs facilities.

But there wasn't enough staff, enough equipment, enough of anything.

'I need to get my head around the present situation,' Anna was saying. She'd put on shoes and socks. They were heading out from her room into the start of the endless corridors leading…well, he knew where. Anna clearly didn't.

He had his hand under her arm. He wasn't sure whether she needed it but she wasn't pulling away, and he wasn't about to let go.

'What do you want to know?' he asked.

'Everything,' she said expansively. 'But for a start... Why don't you have enough doctors?'

'We have no university on the island.' He hesitated. 'More than that. If we scrape to send one of our students to med school they're offered jobs overseas that are far more lucrative than here. Six years away...they learn to like things that the island can't offer.'

'And sometimes they fall in love and stay,' she said, and he winced. Hell, he'd like to turn back time.

He couldn't. 'As you say,' he said formally.

'So the hospital...'

'We had no funds to build from new. We've knocked four houses into one.'

'Which explains why it's a rabbit warren.'

'We had no choice. Every islander is eking out a precarious existence on what land they have. There are no central open spaces and no money to build.'

And then they turned the last passage to the door that opened to the great hall.

Which was...great.

Leo had been in here once when he was eight years old. He and his mates had burrowed through the tunnels and emerged to explore.

Here they'd stopped, so gobsmacked that they'd forgotten caution. One of the Castlavaran retainers had found them and thrown them out.

He'd thought, over the years, that his impression must have been influenced by his size. Everything looked huge to an eight-year-old.

But it was vast. Columns soared three storeys high to a vaulted ceiling. There was a massive stone-tiled floor. The walls were covered by enormous tapestries, frayed and faded.

The focus point was a fireplace, and what a fireplace.

It took up half the end wall. Blackened by fires from the ages, it reeked of history.

'Victoir's plans have this down as a central gymnasium and swimming pool for the apartments,' Anna said, conversationally. As if it was of no import at all. 'So what would you do with it in your plan? I can hardly see it divided into individual wards. Nurses' station perhaps?'

He smiled. It was the first time he'd felt like smiling for days, and the sensation was...okay.

But he was here on a mission. Focus, he told himself.

'A swimming pool would be a great idea,' he said, forcing his voice to sound calm. To not sound eager instead. 'Can you imagine this place as a rehab centre? A pool, walking routes, grab bars around the walls, ball games, nets and loops, whatever... Right now, if islanders are injured we scrounge enough to get them off the island for immediate treatment. But the cost of overseas rehab is out of the question, so they come back and we do the best we can. But here... Anna, can you imagine what this place would look like?'

He hesitated, catching his passion and corralling it. 'Sorry. I'm way ahead of myself. Setting this place up as a hospital will be costly enough without adding swimming pools. I'm not hoping for the world, just a working hospital.'

'Maybe,' she said non-committally. 'Show me more.'

So he did. Victoir didn't show his face. The small number of servants employed for upkeep were nowhere to be seen.

Leo had seen the rooms used by Anna, and before her by members of her family. He'd been here to treat Yanni for his many complaints, real and imagined. Those rooms were so opulent they were enough to make him recoil in distaste. Staff rooms opening onto the courtyard were clinical, neat and serviceable, but they were a tiny percentage of the castle space.

The rest, seen now for the first time since his childhood exploring, was a vast mishmash of different styles, different tastes, different generations. Dust sheets shrouding ancient furniture. Ancient drapes and wallpaper hung in tatters. Plaster split, cracked, falling. He could see rising damp.

He found himself growing more discouraged as they went from floor to floor, from room to room. The corridors were ill lit, with single light bulbs sparsely spaced. Most of the rooms were lit by the same single bulb, many with frayed, dangling cords. He thought of what it would cost to update the electrics and the thought made him feel ill.

Victoir's idea of apartments might get itself past the trustees as there'd be money coming in, but what he was proposing was surely out of the question. Rooms would have to be knocked together, lifts put in, the whole place practically gutted.

They walked from room to room, from level to level, silent. When he started to speak Anna shushed him.

'Victoir gave me a quick tour on my first day here,' she said. 'He talked all the time, about his apartment plans. About them being the only option. He's pushing me to do it urgently, telling me the place is falling down. I cracked my head over his plans. Let me take time to absorb yours.'

But Leo no longer had plans. As they opened each door the plans faded further and further from the realms of the possible.

Finally they emerged to the vast circle of parapets, to the walkway around long-unused battlements. To a moonlit view that enveloped the whole island, outward to the faint outline of Italy beyond.

This view, and the pristine beach below, long protected by castle walls, were the reason Victoir envisaged apartments for the super-rich, Leo thought. They'd flock here, to an untouched, luxury, Mediterranean retreat. It'd be historic, fascinating, available to only the feted few.

Instead of a hospital.

But his enthusiasm had disappeared. By the time they reached the battlements he was accepting its impossibility. The cost… How could he even have thought it?

The last hint of sunset was fading in the west, casting a faint tangerine hue over the ocean. A lone fishing boat was coming into harbour, its wake a translucent wash. While he stood silently by Anna's side, accepting the impossibility of what he'd dreamed, a pod of dolphins started surfing its wake.

'Imagine recuperating here,' Anna said, finally speaking but talking almost to herself. 'The island's elderly in the nursing home part of that dump you call a hospital… Imagine them up here with the sun on their faces.'

'We can't do it,' he said heavily as the hopelessness of his proposal sank home. 'Now that I've seen the place again…I'm sorry I even suggested it.'

She turned away from watching the dolphins and stared at him. 'Why not?'

'Apart from Yanni's apartments I haven't been in the castle since I was a kid,' he conceded. 'Maybe I was looking at it through rose-coloured glasses, or maybe my memory's played me false. I did remember the great hall. I was imagining it as a major cost, digging out a swimming pool, setting it up for rehab. I knew that was a pipe dream but the rest…a basic hospital… I thought that if your Trust could cover the capital costs we might be able to do it. But tonight… Anna, I see what Victoir means. This place is impossible. To do it up would cost a king's ransom.'

'I have a king's ransom,' she said, and for a moment he thought he'd misheard.

'Anna…'

'Just how much do you think I inherited?' She leaned on the parapet. The dolphins were practically turning handstands behind her but she was focussed on him.

'I have no idea,' he said faintly. 'It's none of my business.'

'If most of that money's been accrued via the poverty and misery of the islanders, then it's very much your business.'

'That's been going on for generations.'

'It has,' she agreed. 'As far as I can see, the lords of this castle or whatever they called themselves have had Miser as a middle name for generations. Early on they apparently spent their rent roll paying mercenaries to protect their stronghold from the marauding hordes, but the hordes seem to have given up long since. But the family didn't relax. The Castlavarans seem to have been saving as if the hordes are still about to attack again. Martin insisted we get an accounting of the entire estate and now I have a number. So…take a deep breath, Dr Aretino, and listen.'

So he took a deep breath and listened.

And the figure…

She said it once and then she had to say it again. It was too immense, too breathtaking, to respond to.

Out to sea the dolphins gave up their acrobatic display in disgust. Neither Anna or Leo noticed.

'I can't…' Leo said at last, and Anna nodded.

'Neither can I. It's left me hornswoggled. But I didn't

think I could do much for twenty years. Restore the castle, yes. Turn it into apartments even. Anything else, no.'

'But…'

'But now you've shown me another way. The Trust is clear. I can spend anything I like on my personal use. The lawyers in Milan say if I want to collect diamonds, as long as I keep them in the castle then that's fine by them. So if I want to create the hospital of my dreams for my personal satisfaction, what's the difference?' She took a deep breath. 'The trustees seem staid, conservative but they have no interest in preventing me doing something like this. Their role is to stick to the letter of the Trust. I'll ring Martin and—'

'Martin…'

'I told you. He's a lawyer and a good one.'

Martin. His thoughts seemed to be jerked sideways.

What Anna was proposing was the stuff of dreams and why a guy called Martin should be getting in the way of his thoughts…

He wasn't here with her. Surely if they were serious he'd be here.

Not important. Not! He fought his way back to what she was saying. What she was thinking.

'You'd really do this,' he said slowly.

'I think,' she said, just as slowly, 'that I might have a responsibility to do it. I could set this up as a state-of-the-art hospital. More. If I really can do anything for my personal use—as long as it's within my remit as castle resident—then my head's starting to spin with possibilities.'

'Anna…'

'Don't stop me,' she begged. 'This is full-on fantasy and I'm enjoying myself. What else? I like travelling to neighbouring countries but I don't like flying. So, yes, I need a helicopter based here for when I'm in a hurry—and, incidentally, for patients who need evacuation to medical facilities even we can't provide. But for my normal day-to-day pleasure I'd like a ferry, one big enough for me not to feel seasick. And the trustees should surely not object if I save costs by letting the locals use it as well. And visiting tourists. Day trippers from the mainland.'

She was off and running, her mind obviously tumbling with ideas. 'The hospital staff...' she said. 'You say you can't keep doctors? I like doctors and I like them living around me. They're my friends and I don't like living in this castle by myself. If we set up accommodation, use some of Victoir's ideas, I could surely entice and pay for the best specialists. They could come and teach me—and, of course, anyone else who's on my payroll...'

'You're making me dizzy.'

'I'm making me dizzy,' she conceded.

She paused. They both paused.

'I've gone from thinking I can do nothing to thinking I can do everything,' she said at last. 'I need to talk to Martin but if I can get around the Trust...'

There he was again. Martin. Why did it shake him out of his fantasy, remind him of reality?

'You'll never do it,' he said, and she blinked.

'Why not?'

'Because you'd have to live here.'

She turned to stare out to sea again, and he could almost see cogs whirring. He should stop her, he thought. She'd been hit on the head. She shouldn't make any decisions yet.

She wasn't intending to, he reminded himself. She was going to talk to a lawyer called Martin.

'I'll need my dogs,' she said at last.

'Would you need Martin?'

That hauled her out of her train of thoughts. She turned to him, eyes flashing sudden anger. 'Butt out of that, right now.'

'Anna...'

'What happens here, the plans for this castle, this hospital, this island... I'll need advice and collaboration. But the personal stuff... You lost the right when you walked away ten years ago.'

'I've said—'

'You're sorry. And that's fine. I'm over a teenaged romance and you should be, too.'

But he had to say it. The night... This woman... 'Anna, the way I feel—'

'Don't you dare,' she snapped. 'Finish that train of thought right now. Moving on. Do you want to be in charge of setting up a hospital to tick the boxes of every islander's basic needs?'

'You wouldn't want me in charge.'

'I'm not a fool, Leo.' Her voice was still cold. 'Basic as it is, from what I've seen, you run your current hospital well. You know the islanders' needs so I'll need your help. I imagine we'll need expert assistance, advice from people who know how to set up the kind of state-of-the-art medical facilities we're talking about. Architects. Heritage advisors too, because my head's starting to think beyond medicine. The tunnels Victoir wants me to close... If they were open to the public...made safe, and with guided tours... We could charge entrance fees to mainlanders coming over on my new ferry. The trustees surely would see the sense in that—spending money to make money. We could even set this up as a hub for international visitors...'

'You think you might be getting carried away?'

'I definitely am,' she said, and she smiled, and suddenly the coldness was gone. This was a great, warm, happy smile, a smile he hadn't seen for…ten years?

A smile that was no longer aimed at him but at a project that was obviously entrancing her.

Entrancing. It was a good word. No, it was a great word.

It described her exactly. An injured colleague, a woman in pink and purple yoga gear, what was left of unruly copper curls, the rest of her head covered with an oversized dressing.

She still had freckles. He wanted to touch those freckles.

'We're running away with ourselves,' he managed, struggling to take the personal out of a situation that held the fate of practically the entire island in its grasp. 'The lawyers in Milan…'

'I'll have Martin speak to them. I can't imagine why I haven't thought of this before.'

'It's only weeks since Yanni died,' he said. 'I imagine you've been in shock.'

'I have,' she admitted. 'One minute I was a nice normal family doctor in a nice normal English village—and suddenly I was an heiress responsible for…' She shrugged. 'Okay, I wasn't sure what I was responsible for until I came here, and Victoir's attempt to make me see the place was dangerous led to a split head. Which led to you.' She hesitated. 'So I guess the split head's lucky. Because it led to you, it led to me thinking outside the box.' But then, as if events had suddenly overwhelmed her, she put her hand to her head and her smile faded.

And instantly he turned back into what he should have been all along. Anna's doctor. Nothing else.

'You need to be back in bed.'

'How can I sleep?'

'I guess you can't. I surely won't be able to. But you need to rest. Anna, this is all supposition until you run it past the trustees. And to stay here… It's a big decision. You'll need to run it past…Martin?'

'And the trustees,' she agreed. 'Mostly the trustees. But also my dogs. My dogs are very fussy about where they live.'

'And Martin?'

'Butt out, Leo.'

He held his hands up. 'Consider me butted. Sorry.'

'But you keep butting in again.' She gazed at him for a long moment, appearing to consider. 'Okay, if we're butting…tell me about you.'

'It's…'

'If you tell me it's none of my business I'll call Victoir.'

'What do you want to know?'

'Like, do you live alone? You say you haven't had time for a relationship. None at all? I find that hard to believe.'

'I live with my mother and her canary called Pepe.'

'Your mother…'

'She's ill. She's been ill for a long time.' Why had he told her that?

'I'm sorry.' A furrow appeared on her forehead. He remembered that furrow. *He liked that furrow.* 'Is that another reason you look so strained? Is there anything I can do?'

It took only that. He'd treated her appallingly and here she was, saying maybe she could spend her inheritance giving Tovahna a medical service that made his eyes water just to think about it. And now she was offering to help with his mother's care?

'She has multiple sclerosis,' he said simply. 'My aunt helps me with her care. Anna, it's me who should be sorry. The way I acted—'

'Was too long ago to be dredged up again and again. Moving on, Leo... Yes, I need to rest. Tomorrow I'll think again.' Her hand went back to her head. 'I ache,' she said simply. 'I need to lie down.'

'Of course you do.' She turned toward the stairs down from the parapets. The stone here was crumbling. He couldn't help himself—or more probably it was the sensible thing to do. He caught her arm and held, supporting her.

He half expected her to pull away. That she didn't...

Why did it make him feel light?

They reached the top of the stairs. Beneath them was gloom. His hold on her arm tightened.

But she paused. Once again he thought she'd pull away, but instead she turned and gazed back over the stonework, over the moonlit sea. An old man was fishing on a low stone jetty jutting out from just in front of the castle walls. While they watched, the line bent. He reeled it in, held it up for a moment.

'Squid,' Leo said softly. 'Luigi and Sondra will have calamari for dinner.'

'You know all the islanders?'

'Pretty much. I'm their doctor. My father was a fisherman and I have relatives all over the island. They trust me.'

There was another admission. Personal.

They trust me.

Why had he said it? Because it was important, he thought. Trust was the reason he'd had to come home. It was the reason he couldn't ever have stayed with this woman.

But now she was here...

It was just as impossible, he thought. The heiress to the Castlavaran fortune? No and no and no.

'Leo…'

'Hmm…?' He was still watching Luigi. The fisherman had caught what he needed. He was now packing up his ancient fishing gear, heading home.

He needed to head home, too. Check on his mother. Head back to the hospital.

'It was good between us, wasn't it?'

That was a blindsider. What had she just said? What had been between them was too long ago to be dredged up again, but here she was…dredging?

Or simply putting it out there?

'It was,' he admitted. 'And I'm sorry it had to end like it did.'

'I still don't get it,' she admitted. 'But I'm starting to think…people can change. You've changed.'

'I don't think I have.'

'You care.'

'I always cared.'

'Not for me, you didn't.'

'I did care, Anna.' And suddenly it was too much. She was gazing at him as if she wanted to see inside; as if she wanted to read his mind. Once upon a time he'd thought she could. 'Hell, I cared. I still care.'

'Leo…'

And what happened next he could never afterwards explain. He was tired. Stressed. The sudden appearance of Anna out of his past had jolted him. The crisis with Carla had shaken him even more. And now…the prospect of doing something amazing with this castle, the vista of a future he'd never dreamed might be possible… Yeah, they were all excuses but they weren't reasons. The reason was that Anna was standing on the castle steps and she was looking at him as he remembered her looking up at him ten years ago.

She'd changed. This was a mature version of the Anna he'd known and loved. She still had her glorious hair and her freckles. Her nose was still snub but the changes were subtle. Her eyes had laughter lines etched at the corners. She hadn't grieved for him too much, then, he thought, and then he thought, how arrogant was that?

But there was that something about her that said she didn't always smile. There was a maturity, a softness, a gentle sense of wisdom.

He remembered thinking all those years ago that she'd make a great family doctor and now he was sure of it.

He was also sure that she was just…great.

She was still looking at him. Asking unspoken questions.

Just looking.

She had a…what? Boyfriend? Partner? Where was this phantom Martin now?

Not here when he should be here.

So where was sense?

He should propel her gently down the stairs, send her back to bed. He knew it. He should become her doctor again.

But her eyes were holding his.

The warmth. The soft wash of the waves beneath the castle. The night.

This was madness.

But, madness or not, it was as if the world held its breath, asking a question…

And the question had only one answer.

He kissed her.

One minute she was hesitating on the stairs, looking back at Leo, feeling confused.

More than confused. Disoriented. Discombobulated.

Was there a bigger word? The way this man made her feel…

She'd put thoughts of him away, had made a life for herself, proved without a doubt that there had been a life after Leo.

But he was watching her now, his eyes troubled, his gaze acknowledging there was unfinished business.

If it was unfinished then she had to finish it. She had to turn away and make her way down the stairs to her ridiculous apartment. She had to close the door behind her, raise the drawbridge, pull in every defence at her disposal.

His hand was still on her arm.

She glanced down at it and then back to his face. His dark, questioning eyes. The look of…trouble?

She couldn't help herself. She raised her hand to his face and traced the harsh line of cheekbone. The touch made her feel…

She couldn't think how she felt.

He was so close.

Did she draw his face down to hers? She didn't know. All she knew was that her world seemed to empty of everything except the sight, the feel, the touch of this man.

And then he kissed her, and her world shorted.

Or that's what it felt like. An electric shock seemed to jar her entire system and then simply shut it down. It left room for nothing. Not one of the five senses was operating—or maybe they all were.

Taste… The way his mouth fused with hers. Glorious memories flooding back.

Smell… The faint smell of disinfectant, the smell every doctor knew so well. But more. He smelt of himself, a waft of arrant male testosterone.

Hearing… She could hear his breath. It was almost as if it was as one with hers.

Sight. Her eyes were filled with the vision of Leo, here, now.

Touch.

And there was the biggie, overriding all. The warmth of his hold, his strength, his tenderness… He was taking what he needed but giving back in spades.

Oh, this kiss… She had no defences from this kiss. The feel of him…the way her body moulded to his…

Somewhere, maybe in church, maybe in some long-forgotten romance novel, she'd read or she'd heard the words describing marriage as two becoming one. Ten years ago, aged all of nineteen, she'd fallen into this man's arms and had thought, yes. That's what this was.

Only of course it hadn't been that. They'd never been one. Over the years she'd reminded herself of the naïve kid she'd been. She'd told herself that marriage was for the long haul. It wasn't a romantic slogan. It was something you entered with your head as well as your heart.

She'd vowed never again to let herself be swept away by emotion, but here she was, subsumed by so much emotion she was drowning in it. This kiss was claiming her, and it was as if…she'd come home.

Only of course she hadn't. This was surely just an ex-boyfriend who'd messed with her past. She needed sense. Now!

She wasn't sure whether Leo pulled away or she managed it, but somehow reality surfaced. Somehow they were inches away from each other.

That knock on the head must have been a doozy, she decided. She was staring at him in dawning horror. 'We can't do this.' She clutched at shreds of dignity but they were nowhere to be found.

Back away, her head screamed. Leave.

'Besides,' she managed, 'you're my treating doctor. I'm concussed. Kissing me is unethical.'

'It's good, though,' he said, and he had the temerity to grin. But the grin was short-lived.

She saw it fade and thought, He's almost as disconcerted as I am.

'I'm sorry,' he said.

'We're both sorry.'

'I need to leave.'

'After you've taken me back to my room,' she said, and suddenly she was panicking. He couldn't just take her up to the battlements, kiss her senseless and abandon her. 'I have no idea where I am. Three storeys up, two parapets across…or is that two storeys up, three parapets…' She tried hard to make her voice light, trying to break through panic, which was only partly caused by the fact that she felt lost—in more ways than one. 'I don't want to inadvertently call on creepy Victoir.'

'He really is creepy?'

'He really is creepy.' Somehow she fought to make her voice sound normal. 'God's gift to women, that's his self-assessment. When I arrived he was already talking about the apartment idea, but it took him about two minutes to realise I wasn't married, and I didn't have two heads. I suspect he has the wedding already planned. Bedding me first, marrying my fortune second. *Ugh.*'

'Ugh, indeed. Would you like me to stay?'

That was another breath-taker. 'You're kidding me, right? Reject Victoir and have you instead? I don't think so.'

'I'm not talking bedding,' he said, and propelled her gently into the stairwell. What had happened between them only minutes ago was, apparently, to be forgotten.

Like it had been forgotten ten years ago?

'I have work to do,' he said, brusquely now. 'But my aunt is staying with my mother tonight. I could come back and sleep somewhere close enough for you to call.'

Time to be honest? There seemed no choice. 'Leo, if I called and I was half-asleep and you came, I wouldn't be the least bit surprised at what might happen,' she admitted. 'Face it, Leo, we've got a thing.'

'A thing.'

'A childish attraction we both need to get over. Thanks but, no, thanks. I'll be fine.'

'What if I send one of our nurses over?' he asked. 'Any one of them would be thrilled for a chance to stay inside the castle. I'll tell Victoir I want observations to be continued—maybe I'm worried about your emotional state.'

'My emotional state...'

'Concussion's a dangerous thing.' They'd reached the landing leading to the passage to her wing. He turned and faced her, smiling, slightly ruefully. 'What just happened was totally out of character, I'm sure. Probably a result of your accident.'

'It was dumb,' she snapped. She felt so disoriented.

'I agree,' he said.

And again she thought, He's too close, too male, too... Leo?

'I was just as dumb. But, Anna, can I send a nurse to stay with you?'

And she looked up into his face and saw concern. Real concern.

This was nonsense. Why was she suddenly blinking back tears?

'I would appreciate...company,' she managed, and he nodded.

'Sensible. I'll send Juana over as soon as I get back.'

'You won't be short-staffed without her?'

'She'll be off duty, here to sleep, but she'll love to see this place. I suspect you might need obs for the entire time you stay here, a different nurse each time.'

'And if I stay permanently?'

'That really is an option?'

She took a deep breath and turned to face outward, through the deep, narrow slit that was used to light the stairwell, or, in more dangerous times, to shoot arrows on marauders threatening to storm the castle.

This castle was ages old, a vast, abiding reminder of Tovahna's history. It was also a cache of Tovahna's wealth, kept from the island's residents because of the greed of a family she wanted nothing to do with.

But she was part of that family, the last surviving remnant.

She could walk away, live in luxury for twenty years and then sell to the highest bidder.

Or she could make a difference.

She turned back to Leo, this man she'd once trusted with her heart. She wouldn't do that again. She wasn't stupid.

But she did trust him…with everything else. This place could be a hospital? She could make a difference?

She thought fleetingly of her lovely little cottage back in England, her cosy life. To abandon everything to live in a castle…

To make a difference.

With Leo?

Dammit, just say yes.

'Yes,' she said, almost defiantly, and then she said it again, loudly, so her voice echoed up and down the stairwell. 'Yes, Leo, staying is an option. In fact, from this

angle, with the trustees' consent, it looks like a certainty.'
And then her voice wobbled again. What was she doing,
making a decision like this so fast?

And he got it. 'You can't make a decision like this tonight,' he told her. 'Think about it. Talk to this…Martin.'
And then he hesitated. 'Anna, let me take you out of here
for a day.' His voice cut across her resolution and she
thought… What?

'Out where?'

'To see what you'd be doing.' His voice was strange,
grim even. It was as if he was struggling between fantasy and reality as well. Was he? She didn't know. Did
she know anything?

'What do you mean?'

'I mean you need to go into this with your eyes wide
open.' He said it almost reluctantly. 'You need to see the
bigger picture. But not tomorrow,' he told her hurriedly.
'You need to rest. But maybe Saturday? Bruno and Freya
will both be back at work by then, and there's no clinic.
I could try for a day off. I'd like to show you the real
Tovahna—the people you'll be helping if you decide to
go ahead with…what you're proposing.'

And she thought, He's like me. He does still think it's
fantasy. 'I think I've already decided,' she said, but that
wobble was still there.

'Anna, you've been concussed,' he said, gently now.
'I can't let you make promises now. But in a few days,
when your head's not aching… Anna, will you trust me
to show you my island, to show you my people? To let
you see how much these fantastic dreams could change
lives? Give me a day.'

A whole day with Leo?

Oh, she felt fuzzy. She felt like she was floating in
fantasy but she had enough sense to realise that what

Leo was suggesting was sensible. She should make no promises tonight.

But a whole day…

Her big, warm, lovely Leo.

No. He wasn't hers. He was a colleague, nothing else. And if he was a colleague and nothing else, then why not?

'Saturday,' she said, before she could change her mind. 'It sounds like a plan to me. A nice island tour and nothing else, Leo Aretino. And now thank you very much but I need to go to bed.'

CHAPTER SEVEN

Tovahna's castle had been built and fortified to defend
the island from barbarians. If I'd been leading them I
might have fought harder, Anna thought. This island was
worth fighting for.

She was sitting in the passenger seat of Leo's ancient
Fiat. The roads were appalling, a potholed mess, but de-
crepit roads and old cars couldn't detract from the beauty
around her.

The coast road alone was enough to take her breath
away. The sea was sapphire-blue, the cliffs were low,
white stone or sandy, and there was bay after bay that
screamed, *Stop, paddle or swim, now.*

They'd left the single row of shops that served the
town, and were now on the sparsely populated far side of
the island. Ancient stone cottages were set far apart, but
people were still around, working in the olive groves or
in veggie gardens, mending nets on the beaches, walking along the road from farm to farm. Leo's faded red
Fiat was obviously well known, because every islander
waved or called as he came into view.

He waved back but he was mostly silent. Letting Anna
see the place without a running commentary?

For which she was grateful. She felt ill at ease with
this man but she did want to see the island. It would have

felt petty to knock back his offer, especially since her alternative chauffeur was Victoir.

But she had to find words soon. It was as if he was waiting for her to take it in, waiting for her verdict.

'It's beautiful,' she said at last as they topped a crest and miles of olive groves and the sparkling sea beyond spread out before her. Masses of wild roses—a species apparently endemic to the island—lined the road sides, breathtakingly beautiful. 'I can understand why you wanted to come back.'

'Needed to come back,' he corrected her. 'Don't let the beauty fool you. It disguises desperate need. Anna, would you mind if we stopped for a few moments? Dino Costa's ninety and he's pretty much bedbound. If I could check on him now it might save me a trip next week. There's a cove below the house. You might like to sit on a rock and watch the water, or take a stroll.'

'Of course,' she said, and then said diffidently, 'Unless you need some help.' She thought of the elderly, housebound clients she'd treated in her years of family doctoring. Social contact was the best medicine. Sometimes an interesting visit could do more good than any medicine she could prescribe.

So say it. 'Unless you think Dino might like to meet me,' she added, and Leo flashed her a look of surprise.

There was a moment's silence, and then, 'You mean it?'

'If you think it could help.'

And he got it. She saw his faint smile. 'For Dino… meeting you? Not only would he love it, it'll bring in every neighbour to hear all about it. For Dino that'd be gold.' He hesitated. 'He won't be polite, though. If you can take it…'

She grinned at that. 'Hey, I'm a family doctor. I've

coped with plenty of abusive patients in my time. Besides, I already know what the islanders think of me. Bring it on.'

So they stopped at an ancient stone cottage set back from the cliffs, surrounded by olive trees that looked as if they hadn't been tended for years. A mass of lemon trees crowded the back garden, loaded with unused fruit. The ground was rough and stony. Apart from the pervasive wild roses, any attempt at a garden had been abandoned long since and the little dog that emerged to greet them looked as dejected as the surroundings he obviously lived in.

But Leo obviously knew him. He knelt and fondled his ears, brushing debris from his dust-coloured coat.

'Hey, Zitto, how's your master today?'

The little dog wriggled his pleasure as he realised he knew this visitor. Tail now wagging, he led the way through the open back door into the house.

'Dino? Are you open for visitors?'

'Leo?' It was a quavering old voice, rising in response. 'Is that you?'

'It definitely is,' Leo called back. 'Dino, I've brought a guest to meet you. Anna Castlavara. Is it okay to bring her in?'

'The Castlavara? In my home? You're telling me lies, Leo Aretino.'

'See for yourself,' Leo said, and ushered Anna in before him.

The old man was seated in a rocker by the fire. The woodstove was burning fiercely, on a day when it was already hot, but Anna was accustomed to visiting houses of the very old. Heat was a medicine all on its own. He struggled to rise but she crossed quickly and stooped to take his hand.

'Don't get up on my account,' she told him. 'I'm just here as background while Dr Leo does his checks.'

'I'll make tea,' the old man said, sounding distressed. 'I should have…'

'Dino's accustomed to Victoir checking rent rolls,' Leo told her. 'He's not accustomed to actual visits from…'

'I'm not a Castlavaran,' she said, quickly before he could finish. 'Signor Costa, I may have inherited the castle but I'm Anna Raymond. Dr Anna Raymond.' She gazed around the kitchen, thinking of the fuss involved in making tea, but of this man's obvious need to be hospitable. Her eyes fell on an empty bottle on the table. There were similar bottles, cleaned and empty, stacked on a shelf, each with a handwritten name scrawled on the front, and there were a couple of full ones on the dresser. A home brew? Excellent.

'Hey, it's almost lunchtime. Could I ask…maybe a tiny limoncello? If you have it?'

It was like flicking a switch. The old man's eyes gleamed with delight. He hauled himself to his feet, pushing away Leo's hand as he instinctively went to help.

'I make it myself,' he told them. 'All my own lemons. Our own lemons. My grandfather went to Sorrento, many, many years ago. Took a job on a fishing boat. Off he went and no one heard of him for years and then back he came with nothing but a bag full of lemon root stock. Femminello St Teresa, the best lemon in the world. "It'll make our fortune," he said, and of course it didn't but maybe the best limoncello is enough.'

He was fumbling in the dresser, producing three dusty glasses—crystal. He wiped them off with a frayed dishcloth, then headed to the refrigerator. Out of the freezer came a bottle like the others—filled, though, with a clear, bright yellow liquid, and frosted over with ice.

Three tumblers full. He poured them with infinite care, struggling to keep his hand from shaking—but both Leo and Anna knew better than to offer to help. Finally he handed them over. He straightened and Anna could almost hear his back creaking with the effort.

'To you,' he said, and raised an unsteady arm. 'You can't be worse than those before you, girl.'

'I might even be better,' she suggested, tilting her glass in response and feeling the amazing tang of frozen lemon burst in her mouth. 'Like your limoncello...you mix local with imported and you get a whole new flavour. Signor Costa, this is the best limoncello I've ever tasted. You know, this island has now imported a brand-new Castlavaran. So, like your limoncello, who knows what you'll get from me?'

Afterwards Leo wanted to check an abscess and it was obvious her welcome didn't extend to sharing that. So she did what Leo had suggested. She found a rock and looked out over the bay.

Leo found her there twenty minutes later. He sat down beside her and did a little bay-watching himself.

'Thank you,' he said at last. 'That'll be all over the island by yesterday—that you deigned to approve his limoncello.'

'I've been trained on Mavis Donohue's raspberry cordial,' she told him. 'She calls it cordial but it's about ninety percent proof. A glass full of cordial, about a teaspoon of soda and she beams the whole time I drink it. Luckily for me—and for the rest of her visitors—she has glaucoma. She has the most amazing pot plants, which I'm sure are now about eighty percent proof themselves.'

'So rating of Dino's limoncello...'

'Dino's limoncello is a thousand times better. There was no way a pot plant was getting that.'

'And it made his day,' he said softly. 'Thank you, Anna.'

'I'm not all bad,' she said, disconcerted by the gentleness of his tone.

'I know that. Not even a tiny bit.'

'Except for...'

'Let's not go there,' he told her. 'It's too good a day. Plus there's a bottle of limoncello for you in the car. He said...and I quote... "It'll sweeten her up, boy, and if anything this island needs it's a Castlavaran with a sweetened heart."'

'I'm not a Castlavaran!'

'And yet you need to be. As Anna Raymond you can return to your life in England. As the Castlavaran you can do good here.'

'But still be treated as the Castlavaran.'

'You can't escape it.'

'No.' She stared sightlessly out at the sea and let her thoughts drift. And finally she let herself say it.

'You can't escape it either,' she said.

He frowned. 'I don't know what you mean.'

'I think you do. You say you walked away because your country would have rejected you if you'd stayed with me. What about your pride?'

'Anna...'

'Victoir told me,' she said. 'I know Victoir's a sleazebag, but he's useful for information. He was warning me against you, or thought he was. He said, "His family is dirt poor." He almost sneered it. "As a child he was ragged, living on charity. For him to demand entry to the castle, to try and lord it over us because he has medical qualifications… He's a nothing. Any approach by him… be warned. He's out for what he can get."'

'Did he really say that?'

'Pretty much.' She cheered up a little then, hauling herself back to here and now. After all, this was history they were speaking of. 'Out for what you can get? That's the last thing I'd think of you. But is that yet another reason you walked away—you were afraid of my fabulous wealth? Rags to riches and you chose rags?'

'Anna…'

'I suspect it's true,' she said. 'But more fool you. I didn't have riches. And how did you know Yanni wouldn't have twelve little Yannis before he died.'

'I was stunned,' he told her. 'I didn't know what to think.'

'And you were being noble as well as dumb.' She sighed. 'And, honestly, I concede. If you'd stuck around I might have sobbed and clung and done any number of the dumb things adolescents do when they're crazily in love. So maybe what you did was reasonable. Anyway, Leo, I've been thinking and I've decided…I forgive you.'

'You forgive me,' he said faintly, and she managed to dredge up a grin. And suddenly it was a real one.

It was a gorgeous day. The sun was shining on her face. The setting was fantastic. She'd just had a truly excellent glass of limoncello and a gorgeous guy was showing her around the island.

So get on with it, she told herself. Get on with your life.

'I know, nobility is my middle name,' she told him, and chuckled. 'So, moving on. I have decided to stay here.'

'With Martin?'

Where had that come from? She was trying not to get

personal, or trying to put personal behind her and here he was, heading right back to where she least wanted to be. To her love life.

But why not be honest? If she was to stay here…

She'd have her dogs. She'd have her amazing apartment. She needed to do something about Victoir but surely she could manage that. And moving on…there might be any number of gorgeous guys on this island.

Leo would be a colleague and maybe a friend. He could ask, she decided, but she needed to set boundaries.

'That's none of your business, and you know it isn't,' she told him. 'Okay, putting all our cards on the table, Martin is actually now my ex-boyfriend. He's also my lawyer. But that's the last time you ask such a personal question, Leo Aretino. If I'm to stay here for the next twenty years I need to make a life for myself. I think I've decided that I can even have a very good time if I try hard enough. Right now, Victoir's intensely interested in my love life and so, it seems, are you. Neither of you have the right. I don't think Victoir and I can ever be friends—in fact, I'm sure of it—but you and I need to be colleagues and if we try very hard I suspect we can be friends, too. So for now I'm nobly forgetting that you ever jilted me and I'm moving on. Are you prepared to move on, too?'

'I guess…' He seemed totally disconcerted.

'Then that's noble of both of us.' She rose and smiled down at him. 'Or sensible. Speaking of sensible, Dino's limoncello was surely an aperitif, meant to be served before lunch. And I'm hungry. Do we need to head back to town to eat?'

'There's a small *taverna* around the next headland.'

'Excellent,' she said, and she smiled her very widest smile. Goading him to smile with her. 'Let's move on, then, shall we? Let's start being sensible from this moment on.'

* * *

Everything she'd said was totally, absolutely sensible. She'd pretty much summarised what had happened between them. She knew his reasons. She'd decided not to hold it against him.

They could move ahead as colleagues and as friends, Leo thought, which was surely the very best of outcomes, so why did things still seem out of kilter?

The *taverna* he'd taken her to was one of his favourite places. Sofia made the best pasta on the island and Giuseppe surely caught the best calamari. Four small tables sat under their olive trees, looking out over the rickety jetty where Giuseppe tied his boat, and there were two tables inside if you were ever crazy enough not to want the view. They wanted the view and today they were the only customers. The menu was one dish, pasta with seafood, but the restricted menu was not a problem.

'Oh, my…' Anna was holding a sliver of squid for inspection before dispatching it forthwith. 'I've never eaten anything so good. Tell me I've died and gone to heaven.'

'It's not all hardship in this place,' he agreed. 'Pasta, olives, tomatoes, seafood…what's not to love?'

'The chef back at the castle seems to cook out of tins,' she said, sighing her pleasure. 'I was thinking twenty years in this place could be torture, but there's this! Hey, I'm a Castlavaran. Surely I can command Sofia to come to my castle and cook for me.'

She'd spoken in Tovahnan. Giuseppe and Sofia had been watching them from the doorway. Three of their children, about twelve, ten and eight, had been running races down to the jetty and back.

As they heard what Anna said they stilled as one, turning to stare at her in consternation.

And Anna stared back, from one to the other. Her face lost all its colour as she realised what they were thinking.

'No! Oh, no, I was joking.' She rose and crossed to where Sofia was standing, so shocked she'd started shaking.

This was why things were still out of kilter, Leo thought. A friend and colleague? She was, but she was still the Castlavaran.

Leo had introduced her to the little family as they'd arrived and they'd reacted with awe. Now he saw Sofia try to back away in fear as Anna approached.

But Anna would have none of it. She held out her hands, grasping Sofia's workworn hands in hers and holding them tight.

'Sofia, that was a joke and a stupid one at that. I won't command anything.'

'You can take away our house,' Sofia said, sounding desperate.

'I can't.'

'You can take away anything you please on this island,' Leo told her. 'It is…yours to command.'

'I won't command anything.'

'It'll take time to prove that to the islanders.'

She looked back at him, dismayed. 'How?'

'It'll take time, that's all,' he said.

'Time. Twenty years?'

'I guess that's what you're committing.'

'I guess I am.' She turned back to Sofia. 'Sofia, please believe me when I say I'm threatening nothing. I may be your landlord but I have no intention of interfering with your lives. I'd like…if possible…to help Dr Leo to build a medical clinic to help all the island, and in time…given trust, maybe I could be a friend?'

But Sofia gave a small, scared smile and retreated. She almost scuttled backward.

The children followed and Giuseppe stood blocking the doorway, arms crossed, an islander in defence mode.

'Help,' Anna said to Leo, distressed beyond measure.

'It's okay,' he said, rising and coming to her aid. He put his arm around her waist, as protective a gesture as Giuseppe's. 'Don't take it personally. You are...'

'I know, a Castlavaran.' She sighed. 'Okay, Leo, I know I am. But I will make a difference. But twenty years... Wow, Leo...' And then she grimaced and pulled herself away from him.

'Please, Giuseppe, reassure Sofia that the last thing I want is to take her away from this *taverna*, from you and your children and this magic place. And you know the reason? I intend to come back here once a week for the next twenty years, maybe even more, and sit under your olive trees and eat your pasta and calamari. If that's okay with you.'

'You will come?' Giuseppe said cautiously. 'With Dr Aretino?'

'Mostly without,' Anna said, suddenly brisk. 'I intend to enjoy myself on this island, but it's starting to dawn on me... I may have to enjoy myself alone.'

She headed back to the table and sat and helped herself to another tentacle. Firmly, as if the action was a vow.

Leo was left looking at Giuseppe. The older man stared at Anna and then shrugged. It's in the lap of the gods, his body language said, and Leo could only agree.

He managed a smile and turned back to watch the woman he'd once loved...

Still loved...

Twenty years?

It was, indeed, in the lap of the gods.

CHAPTER EIGHT

Six months later

SHE WAS ON the beach. It was nine at night. She'd spent the day immersed in plans, in building, in the general chaos of transforming an ancient castle into a modern medical facility. The noise of jackhammers, of carpenters, of architects talking at her, had given her a thumping headache.

This would be the architect ringing, she thought, or one of the builders. It seemed the entire island was determined to get this hospital up and running, and if it needed communication at midnight then so be it.

The last six months had passed in a whirlwind of activity. There'd been an intense meeting with the trustees in Milan, who'd turned out to be astonishingly enthusiastic.

'There's been little we could do from the sidelines over the years. But if you really do want to help Tovahna...'

She really did. They explained the legal intricacies and she'd struggled to understand, but she thought she had it sorted now.

She'd pensioned Victoir off. He might be repulsive but he'd kept her cousin and her uncle happy. In his place Martin had helped her appoint a good financial team.

He and Jennifer had come and stayed for a week. Together they'd helped her understand the financial jargon and they'd helped her face down Victoir. There was something comforting about standing beside a competent lawyer. The alternative would have been to use Leo and she'd made a conscious decision to Not Need Leo.

Her dogs had arrived with Martin and Jennifer, and with them had come a sense of home. She'd explored the island with them. She'd met islander after islander. She'd tasted more home-made grappa and limoncello than was good for her. She hadn't quite dived into the dating scene—as if she could when every islander regarded her in awe—but she'd enjoyed herself.

She still felt an outsider but she'd accepted her lot. The islanders remained wary but she was doing things that made her happy.

And Leo? She scarcely saw him. He made time to be at the planning meetings, but those meetings consisted of architects, hospital planners, builders, suppliers. As soon as they left, so did he.

He had pressures of his own, she knew. Carla told her his mother was fading, and the island's medical need was still oppressive. Until the castle hospital was up and running the trustees couldn't justify her employing medical staff, and she could hardly help herself when there was so much to do here. She was working desperately to get essentials sorted. Some of it was in place but not nearly enough.

And now…her phone was ringing. Drat. She was so over building details.

She was walking in the shallows, kicking up a spray of water with her bare toes, watching her dogs romp ahead of her. The night was almost moonless but at some stage the security-conscious Victoir had had floodlights installed, so the beach was an island of light, backdropped by the castle.

The phone rang out—and then started again.

She sighed and tugged her phone from her back pocket, holding it up so she could see the caller ID.

Leo.

Her heart gave a stupid, crazy lurch.

Oh, for heaven's sake, get a grip. It'd be about planning…something. She hit receive and put on her most efficient voice.

'Hold, will you, Leo? I need to call the dogs. Boris, Daisy, here, guys, home time.'

The dogs wheeled back to her, lanky springer spaniels, glorying in their evening run but equally delighted to be heading back to share their mistress's bed.

That bed was far too big.

Don't go there.

'What can I do for you, Leo?' She started up the steps of the sea wall, her dogs at her heels. She had her voice under control, nicely efficient.

'Anna, I need your help. Two fishing trawlers hit in the harbour mouth. Idiots running without lights. I'm guessing bulbs blown and they saved money by not replacing them, both banking on others to have lights. One of the fuel tanks exploded. Reports of multiple burns. I know your theatre's not ready but I know it's close. First report is six injured crew. I'm on board a boat now, heading out to meet them. Anna, our emergency room is tiny. We can't cope with more than two. We need you as a doctor but we also need space. I haven't been in it for weeks but…hell, Anna, how close are you?'

Six months ago, when she'd returned from negotiating with the trustees, Leo had rejected her offer to help at the hospital. 'Anna, a new hospital is central to the well-being of the entire island. If you can bear being away from medicine for a few months...'

He was right, it had been sensible, so she'd spent six months tied up in bureaucracy. She'd seen not one patient.

But tonight Leo was asking for help.

And she could help.

'Everything's ready to go,' she told him, feeling the familiar surge of adrenalin that medical emergencies produced. 'The surroundings look like a bomb site, but our casualty section's pretty much ready to receive. Equipment's been arriving over the last couple of weeks. We can fit eight in our reception area.'

There was a pause as he took that in. She could hear the sounds of emergency through the phone. She could hear the engine of the boat he was on, the sound of the wind in the background, people shouting. This beach was around the headland from the harbour so she could see nothing, but she imagined him on the deck heading toward flames, gearing up for disaster.

She wanted to be with him. She wanted...

What she wanted was immaterial. It was what she could give that mattered. She thought of the cramped emergency room he usually worked in and she thought of multiple burn casualties. She thought of the alternative.

'You saw it two weeks ago when the painting was done,' she said. 'But we've gone further. When the equipment orders came through I decided it was dumb leaving it in storage until the whole project was completed. Everything's unpacked. I've had the place cleaned, sterilised. Two theatres are ready to go. I don't have drugs yet, but I imagine they'd be easy to transport from your hospital. I have eight cubicles ready.'

Burn victims needed to be treated fast. There'd be blistering, heat welding fingers to fingers or, worse, shock, hypothermia, heart failure. After severe burns these would be more than possibilities. Without swift, competent treatment, death was a probability, disfigurement certain. They'd need evacuation—no small hospital had the facilities to care for major burns victims long term—but initial stabilisation was imperative.

'You can bring them to the jetty under the castle wall,' she said while Leo thought through implications. 'Is Carla at the hospital?'

'Bruno's there, organising receiving. Carla and Freya are on their way in.'

'They could come straight here. How many inpatients do you have over there?'

'Seven but none risky.' There was another silence and she could almost hear the cogs working. 'I'll take you at your word, then. Eight reception cubicles. Surgical equipment?'

'Everything but drugs.'

And the decision was made. 'I've already put out a call for all available staff. I'll have Bruno redirect them to you. I'll leave one nurse at the hospital. It's a risk but a smaller one than trying to cram burns victims into a place geared for four at the most. Bruno can bring the drugs now.' She heard a shout in the background and then another, fainter, in response. 'I'll leave reception to you, Anna. We're reaching the scene now.'

'You don't want me to get on a boat and come out?'

'You're better there. We're only ten minutes from the castle. The boats can bring them straight in. I'll do emergency resus, but everything else will be sent to you. Bless you.'

'Bless you back again,' she said, and she couldn't quite keep her voice steady. She was imagining two boats colliding in the dark, fire, spilled fuel, major injuries. As a family doctor she'd had no experience of the kind of accident Leo was facing. She had the training, though, and so did Leo.

They were both going to need it.

The scene facing Leo was appalling.

Debris was scattered on the water, pieces of still-burning timber. The boat was already a charred hull. The other was a wreck.

He knew these boats, and their crews. World Cup football was being screened tonight at the town hall. The skippers would have been trying to get into port before the game started.

Entering harbour without riding lights? What a way to save money.

The local *guardia* boat was already on scene, as were a couple of other boats, local fishermen who'd also have been on their way into harbour. There were two dinghies on the water, being rowed. You didn't start a motor with this amount of spilled and burning fuel. He saw fishermen hauling someone aboard. A body? Any hope that the initial call might have overstated the seriousness of the situation disappeared.

'Doc…' Pietro, head of the island's *guardia*, called to him across the water. 'We have two on board here, in a mess. There are four on board the *Marika*, maybe less injured but I can't say for sure. Another's being pulled in now but it looks like we've lost him. One unaccounted for.'

'Send the *Marika* straight in,' he called. With patients on two boats he couldn't even assess in the time it'd take to them back to the castle. 'Take them to the castle jetty.'

'The castle…'

'Dr Raymond is waiting.'

'The *Castlavaran*?' Despite the urgency of the situation he heard disbelief. Angelo, the dour skipper of the *Marika*, was calling to him in incredulity. 'We need *you* to treat them. Or Carla. Why would we take them to the *castle*?'

There'd been disbelief at the concept of what Anna was doing. Islanders were taking wages for their work, as generations of Tovahnans had been taking wages, but there'd been little trust.

'It'll turn out to be just for the wealthy; just wait and see.'

Leo had heard the mutterings.

And here it was, suspicion loaded into the one word the skipper had called. He'd said *castle* like another might have said poison. 'We'll take them to the hospital, no?'

'No. The castle's set up for triage. You know we've been working to get it ready, and tonight we're using it. Bruno, Freya and Carla and our nurses are all there. Just go, Angelo.' One of the dinghies was alongside now and there was no time for more persuasion. 'Make sure every airway's clear and there's constant water running over burns. Go.'

And Angelo cast him a look of disbelief—but then moved to obey.

Trust, Leo thought. How hard it had been to earn and how important that he have it. The hatred of all things Castlavaran was bone deep in all islanders. They'd seen what Anna was doing. They'd heard of what she'd done to help save Carla, but centuries of mistrust couldn't end in months. They were all waiting for the drawbridge to slam down. For Anna to show her true colours.

But tonight he'd demanded trust and he had it. The *Marika* was heading for the castle, mistrust of Anna or not, and he had to focus on his own work.

The fisherman pulled from the water wasn't dead. Not quite. He'd swallowed water, however, lots of it, and had probably breathed in burning fumes. It took all Leo's skills to resuscitate him. He was sending him on to the castle on one of the fishing boats as he heard a hail from across the water.

'Doc, we've found Giulio. He was trying to swim to shore. He doesn't look good.'

That was an understatement. What came next was thirty minutes' intense, heartbreaking effort and at the end he lost.

What adrenalin charge had enabled a burned, shocked fisherman to try and swim to shore? Giulio was well into his seventies. He had a weakened heart already and he should have had a valve replacement years ago. *But where's a man like me to find money for a stay in a foreign hospital? I won't put my family in debt. No, this old heart will give out when it decides.'*

It decided tonight.

The final boat took Leo to the castle jetty, with Giulio's body. He stood beside the shrouded stretcher and felt the weight of isolation, of poverty, of the responsibility of being a doctor in charge of a nightmare.

There'd been forerunners of nights like this on the island before, disasters with multiple casualties, and each had left him with the same sense of helplessness. His hospital wasn't geared to cope, and people had died because of it.

What was new? He'd felt helpless from the day his father had died, of appendicitis, of all things, an appendix ruptured because there'd been no doctor, no hospital. Twenty-four hours of agony.

He'd vowed that no one would die that way again. But now he was stuck on a boat and who knew what was happening in the castle? Bruno and Freya were young, inexperienced, full of good intentions but they should be supervised. Carla had come back to work after her illness but she lacked the decisiveness of the old Carla. Her hands shook a little. She faltered when there was no room for faltering.

Which left Anna.

The castle loomed above them as they neared the jetty. Its presence was vast, dark and forbidding.

What had he done, suggesting they use it? Would it create more confusion?

He was depending on Anna, depending on her promises, and he, of all people, should know that promises meant nothing.

Memories were suddenly, inappropriately, flooding back. One amazing night.

'We'll have children, practise medicine together, have an awesome life. Anna, will you marry me?'

And then that appalling dinner with her mother... handing back the ring and walking away.

Hell.

There were shouts from the jetty, torches beaming out over the water, guiding them in. Locals, who before Anna had arrived had never been permitted within the castle confines. She *was* making a difference.

He glanced down at the shrouded shape of what once had been Giulio. A life well lived, but a useless, stupid death.

That was how he felt right now. Useless. He'd vowed to make a difference to this island but people were still dying.

People would still die and they'd die tonight. He'd seen enough of those who'd already been shifted to the castle. It'd take a miracle, and what Anna was providing...

It was no miracle. She was doing her best but the long legacy of the Castlavarans remained intact.

History couldn't be changed.

She couldn't help.

He was twenty-three years old and he was dying under her hands.

She had the emergency room set up just as she'd envisaged it. She had staff working as a team. They'd cooled every burn, at least twenty minutes under running water. They'd administered pain relief. They'd coped with immediate shock and blood loss, treating lacerations and breaks from the impact itself. They'd made sure, as much as possible, that pain levels were under control.

Bruno and Freya were wrapping burned limbs with plastic film, which protected as well as helped with pain. Carla was coping with a fractured arm that, if not splinted, could well block circulation.

She had no idea what Leo was facing. What he was coping with on his own.

But she had little time to think of Leo. She was adjusting the oxygen on the fisherman she was starting to think she'd lose.

His name was Tomas. Bruno had recognised him when they'd admitted him, though how anyone could recognise the blacked figure was beyond her.

'He's my kid brother's best mate,' Bruno had told her, visibly distressed. 'Anna, I can't...'

None of them could. Bruno and Freya were nurse-practitioners whose experience of severe burns was almost nil. Carla had treated burns, but since her stroke she'd become increasingly unsure.

Family medicine hadn't prepared Anna for this. She was upping oxygen, trying desperately to think what to do next, but there was no option in her grab-bag of emergency training. She was watching Tomas fighting for each breath, listening to the rasping in his chest, watching him almost visibly losing the fight.

And then Leo walked into the room and she could have wept with relief.

She'd glanced up as she heard one of the nurses greet him but almost immediately her attention went back to Tomas.

'What's happening?' Miraculously he was beside her. Directed by the nurse? Everyone in this room knew how tenuous was Tomas's hold on life.

'Leo.' Even saying his name stilled her panic. 'Tomas and I could use your advice.'

Heaven only knew the effort it cost to keep her voice calm. What she wanted was to scream for help, tell him she was out of her depth and drowning, but Tomas was still conscious. The last thing an injured patient needed was their doctor confessing she didn't have a clue what to do next.

'Tomas, Dr Aretino's here,' she told him, unsure what Tomas could or couldn't see through his swollen eyelids. 'I'll give him a quick summary of what's happened to you. Leo, Tomas has oropharyngeal and neck burns. I've intubated but he's still struggling. We've cooled and wrapped the burns. We've administered pain relief and fluids. I'd have expected the intubation to assist.'

She paused then, and said nothing more. The next word, the most logical word in her description was 'but'. *But nothing's helping.*

She didn't say it. Tomas didn't need to hear it, and to Leo it would be obvious.

She stepped back a little so Leo could see.

The nurses had helped her soak, strip and cut away

Tomas's charred clothing. If she'd had to guess she'd say he'd borne the brunt of the explosion. His chest was a mess, with impact wounds as well as burns.

Intubation should have made a difference, but it hadn't brought the immediate relief she'd prayed for. There was reduced oxygen saturation, a delayed capillary refill. His chest was hardly moving—there was shallow respiratory effort and limited abdominal wall movement. It was as if he was so badly burned inside that nothing could work.

She watched Leo do a fast visual assessment and then she saw his hand close over Tomas's undamaged wrist.

'Tomas. You've got yourself in one hell of a mess,' he said. 'But, hey, you're the first patient to be treated in Dr Anna's Amazing Castle Hospital. How lucky are you? We have brand-new operating theatres, every state-of-the-art tool for any impressive piece of surgery we want to perform, and Anna and I are aching to try out our new toys. You're our guinea pig.'

It was a scary concept but Leo's voice was warm and strong and reassuring and Anna saw the tiny slump of relaxation, the lessening of the flight and fight reaction that told her Tomas trusted Leo.

Leo was known. He was an islander.

She'd never be that.

But this was hardly the time to think that. Leo was looking at her, signalling her with his eyes. To back him.

'Tomas, the plan is now to put you to sleep in one of Dr Anna's great new theatres,' he told him, but he was still watching Anna, sending a silent message to follow his lead. 'Something hot has banged hard into your chest. In the long run you'll have a really impressive scar to show your grandkids, but right now it's created a band of tissue that's injured and swelling. It's acting like a corset, restricting your chest and making breathing harder.

'You've seen those old movies where the lady faints because her corset's too tight? That's what's happening to you. What we need is to give you another neat scar while we loosen the restriction. It'll be like cutting the corset's laces. It's a quick procedure under anaesthesia so you won't feel a thing and it'll make your breathing a whole lot easier. Is that okay with you?'

Tomas hardly moved but his body seemed to slump. Letting go? Placing his fate into Leo's hands.

Which was pretty much how Anna was feeling. She was ceding to Leo.

She'd never seen anyone with this extent of burn and injury. What Leo was intending to do… The procedure was called escharotomy. She'd learned of it in her training— the slicing of injured flesh to relieve pressure—but she'd never performed it. And here was Leo, acting as if it was common-or-garden normal.

'Let's go, people,' Leo said quietly, as if there was no rush at all, but minutes later they were in Theatre. The Castle Hospital Theatre. Never used until now.

What good fairy had made her work herself almost to exhaustion to get this ready? Anna wondered. She'd checked and double-checked to have everything in readiness, even though she hadn't expected patients for weeks or even months. She'd paid for a surgical colleague to come from England and check it with her. The theatre was big, airy, superbly lit and right now it was fully staffed. Bruno had brought the drugs they needed, plus back-up equipment from the old hospital. Maria was acting as head theatre nurse and a younger nurse was working as her assistant.

Anna's role was to give the anaesthetic. That took all her skill and more, because giving anaesthetic to such a severely burned patient was way beyond her area of expertise.

Leo was operating as if this was entirely within his skill set.

He was also keeping a respectful eye on her.

'Is there anyone else who's more competent?' she'd whispered as they'd scrubbed, but he'd shaken his head.

'Carla's still unsteady. She knows her limits and she wants you to do it. You can do it, Anna.'

'Leo, with this amount of respiratory distress…'

'Just haul up everything you know and then some,' he told her. 'And if you want back-up, ask.'

'Ask you?'

'We've never had a qualified anaesthetist,' he told her. 'Carla and I have struggled through. We've read, teaching ourselves until we can spout oxygen saturation levels, respiratory flows in our sleep. But even before this last illness Carla's been slowing down, becoming unsure. Her arthritis has made her fingers stiff and it's knocked her confidence. I've been starting to share, backing her decisions at every turn. So if you have any questions, ask. I won't be judging.'

She wasn't considering his opinion of her. She wasn't beginning to think he was judging her. She knew he was simply grateful that he had a pair of hands with medical skill.

He'd do whatever it took to protect his islanders.

Hadn't she learned that the hard way?

There it was again, history, surfacing when she had no time to give it space and no inclination either. It had been with her for the full six months of her stay, in consultation meetings, when they were focussed on the complexities of getting this place up and running, when they were talking staffing, when he was striding through the building site, snapping questions... And now, when he was all doctor, with every fibre of his being focussed on keeping Tomas alive...

That was what she was, too, a doctor operating outside her skill range, dredging up every last thing she'd been taught in medical lectures so long ago.

And all the while she was conscious that this was Leo. Not just a colleague. *Leo.*

It was almost as if her body had an inbuilt warning sign and it was flashing red. Do not think about how much he cares for his people. Do not admire the skill of those amazing fingers, or admit that Leo is simply...

Someone she loved?

She shoved the thought away as she focussed on the dials that told her Tomas's heart continued to beat, his oxygen saturation was rising, he might just possibly make it.

Thanks to Leo. And Leo's decision to return here.

Which was why personal history had no place here.

Blessedly the technicalities of what she was trying to do took over. Leo was cutting through the constricting, charred outer layer of flesh. He worked with an assurance Anna could only wonder at, cutting skilfully along the mid-axillary line of the chest. There were so many constraints he had to be wary of. The last thing Tomas needed was more damage, but not for a moment did Leo act as if he was unsure.

And almost the moment the cut was made, Tomas's chest started falling and rising with less restriction, moving naturally as it needed to if Tomas was going to breathe on his own.

Finally Leo started cauterisation, sealing the wound to stop the bleeding. He was working swiftly, not with the painstaking care that he'd use if the scar he'd made would be the scar Tomas would carry for life. There'd be more scars on this chest, months if not years of treatment to get Tomas back to anywhere near normal. Skin graft after skin graft. An instant's carelessness in the harbour would be followed by years of regret.

Maybe everyone in the theatre was thinking that. The silence in the theatre was suddenly loaded.

'We need to leave him in an induced coma,' Leo said into the stillness. 'The brain needs to focus on healing rather than shock and pain. He'll be on the first transfer out.'

She nodded. She knew by now how much the islanders hated leaving the island for treatment but with burns this severe there was little choice. They'd done all they could for Tomas. 'I'll stay with him,' she told Leo. 'You head back to the fray.' And then she hesitated. She'd heard reports of what had been happening out on the water. 'Giulio?'

'He died,' he said roughly, and she heard grief and exhaustion in his words. One of the nurses fought back a sob and Leo's face reflected it.

These were his people. His home.

'Any man's death diminishes me.' She used to think of the quote from John Donne when someone in her small English village died, someone she'd cared for, but she hadn't been born there, raised there. She hadn't gone to school with the locals, shared their backgrounds. She wasn't entitled to share their grief.

She watched as Leo's shoulders slumped as he told them of Giulio's death, and then she watched as he braced and headed back to treat whoever was left.

She felt for him.

And stupidly she felt bereft—for herself.

Tomas couldn't be left. He needed intense nursing and none of the nurses had the skills to care for him. She stayed in the now almost empty theatre and she watched as Tomas's chest rose and fell, rose and fell.

He'd live because of Leo.

There'd be no regrets this night, she decided, or none from her. The bigger picture was that Leo had come back to do what was right for his country. The bigger picture was that she could keep this medical centre growing, help Tovahna free itself from the shackles of poverty.

They were huge things, and they shouldn't leave one inch spare for the moments of emptiness that wouldn't go away.

CHAPTER NINE

THE LAST HELICOPTER left at dawn. There'd been three, all manned with medics trained in trauma medicine. Tomas had been evacuated first. The others had followed. Every one of them had suffered burns. Every one of them would need treatment by overseas specialists.

The choppers had used the castle roof to land. That had been another thing Anna had done over the months she'd been there, clearing debris, removing any impediment to a large chopper landing.

She should feel good that it had worked, she thought, as she watched the last chopper lift and head into the rising sun. Instead she felt empty. She was watching Leo. He'd done the handover to the chopper's medical staff. Now he stood back. His shoulders were slumped. He looked…gutted.

'They'll all make it.' She said it quietly, because his body language spoke of solitude and she wasn't sure she had the right to intrude. 'Even Tomas. His arms and legs are okay. His throat was swollen but his face doesn't seem too bad.' He must have fallen to his knees as the explosion hit, she thought, as the flames had formed a band of burned flesh around his chest. The rest of his wounds seemed relatively minor.

'But at what cost?' Leo was still staring at the disappearing chopper. 'Have you any idea…?' He broke off. 'Sorry. There's nothing you can do.'

'There might be,' she said diffidently.

'There isn't. You've done enough. That you had the castle ready…that was a miracle in itself. We can't hope for more.'

'Maybe,' she said, and let the word settle for a while. Let her thoughts settle.

There'd been time for thinking in the hours she'd sat by Tomas, listening to the noises from outside her new theatre, the sounds of a medical team working hard, the distant cries of distressed relatives. She'd have to prepare a reception area out of earshot of the emergency centre, she'd decided. She'd thought of that during the long hours and she'd thought of a lot more.

'I might need to talk to Victoir,' she said diffidently, and waited. She wasn't sure Leo was in the mood to listen to plans.

She wasn't sure of anything.

'Why would you talk to Victoir?' His voice was flat, disinterested. Defeated?

'Because he's dishonest.'

'Sorry?' He turned to face her then, looking confused. Good, she thought. Anything to shake him from his distress.

'You know Martin went through the books while he was here?' she said, still diffidently. 'Victoir's been lining his own pockets for years, in all sorts of constructive ways.'

'So what's that got to do with now?'

'Because it seems that two weeks from now I'm holding a celebration,' she told him. 'A party to end all parties, a day to mark the opening of the castle to the island.'

'What… A celebration?'

'You haven't heard about it yet? How odd.' She ventured a smile. 'Okay, the place isn't near finished but I'm impatient and I want a party now. So it seems I've been planning one for weeks. I may need to do a bit of sleight of hand in my diary. The trustees do need the letter of the law to be followed but they're not about to inspect too closely.'

'I don't get it.'

'But I do,' she told him, willing the grief and shock to fade from his face. 'We're having an Open Castle Party to show everyone what we're doing. Any islander wanting to come will be welcome. It'll be awesome, and of course we need food. Lots of food.'

'Anna, I hardly think—'

'That talking parties now is appropriate? It is,' she told him. 'It must be. Hear me out. Leo, you may not know it but my cousin and my uncle seem to have been paranoid about supply. There's room here to store enough food to feed an army. There's a massive stockroom under the castle. Right now it holds tins of baked beans that are fifty years out of date. So many tins. We have a bank of freezers with enough space to store food for the castle for a year or more, and they're currently unused.'

'Yes, but—'

'So tonight I've been trying to figure a way I can help the injured fishermen. Their treatment, their rehab will cost a fortune. The terms of the Trust won't let me help, but if they were working for me...'

'They were fishing.'

'Exactly,' she said, and smiled again, pleased with the neat plan she'd devised. The night had been totally miserable until she'd found this sliver of an idea. 'So here's my plan, aided by the not-so-honest Victoir. There'll be a document discovered tomorrow, dated...a couple of days ago? I'll leave it to Victoir to figure the niceties. It seems two days ago I requested two Tovahnan boats to put to sea to catch sufficient fish to stock my freezers. There'll also be backdated requests for hiring chefs, and there'll be menus discovered that might just contain the fish destroyed in last night's accident.

'I agree, it's complex. It'll take a few people crossing their fingers behind their backs, and co-operation by the locals, but the bottom line will be that all those injured were employed by the castle. By me. For my personal pleasure. Therefore the Trust is responsible for all their ongoing medical care.'

There was a long silence. A stunned silence.

'Do you know how much we're talking?' Leo asked at last. 'Treatment by the best burns units. Specialist care. Rehab. And then there's Giulio. He died, Anna. There's his funeral, plus he and his wife lived on the boat. If he was on your payroll…'

'Leo, can I get it into your head that I don't consider this place mine? The money doesn't seem mine either, and compared to what's in the bank this'll be peanuts. I can't see myself doing much more than dinting the capital, no matter how I try. But I have to try. My relatives bled this island dry to fill the castle coffers and it's not my money. It belongs to the islanders. So… Dr. Aretino, is it a good idea or is it not?'

He stared at her, stunned. 'It's a brilliant idea,' he admitted at last. 'If you really mean it.'

'Of course I mean it. Do you think the islanders will come to my party?'

'When it's explained what it's for…you won't keep them away.'

'Excellent.' She sighed and rolled her shoulders and thought of her bed. She was bone weary, but to go to bed now… She wouldn't sleep. And neither would Leo, she thought. She watched his face and saw her exhaustion reflected there. But she also saw more.

Her help was appreciated, but underlying everything was the fact that he'd lost an islander tonight. One of his own.

She glanced downward at the waves gently lapping the shore under the castle walls. The morning sun was just starting to create its early-morning sparkle.

She felt tired and dirty and dispirited, and Leo must be feeling the same, only so much more. Left to his own devices he'd head back to the other hospital.

There was nothing major there. The nurses could cope. He had his phone—they could ring if anything came up.

If he put the ringer on loud they could hear it over the water.

So why not?

'Leo, I'm going for a swim,' she threw at him. 'Want to come?'

'What, now?'

'You were heading for a shower, right? There's a fresh-water shower down below. You can swim and shower and then you're on your way. Coming?'

He was torn. She could see it, but she wasn't about to push further.

'I'm heading down,' she told him. 'I even know my own way now. Three sets of stairs from here, turn left, halfway along there's a wooden door with huge brass bars. Lift the bar and you're at the castle swimming pool—you know it's sea bath hewn from rock with a channel at the end to swim out to the sea if you want? I do want. I might not think of this castle as belonging to me, Leo Aretino, but right now I'm thinking of that pool as mine, all mine. So join me if you want, the choice is yours.' And she headed for the stairs and disappeared.

He should go home.

He should check on his mother and then head back to the hospital.

His aunt was with his mother—bless her. And the hospital...

He made two fast phone calls. He wasn't needed.

Still, he should go home. There were so many reasons he should try for a couple of hours' sleep before the next crisis.

He glanced at the steps. From down below he heard a splash.

He glanced over the parapet, half expecting Anna to be waving up at him. Instead he saw her head down, stroking purposefully toward the end of the pool.

Almost naked. She was wearing knickers, nothing else, and her lovely, lithe body was streaking through the water like an otter's, as if swimming was second nature. Where had she learned to swim like that? It was almost as if she was an islander.

She wasn't an islander, he reminded himself harshly.

He should go.

But the sight of her swimming through the clear, sapphire water...the shock of the night...exhaustion... His head wasn't working as it should.

He wanted a swim. More, he wanted a swim with Anna.

He swore softly to himself, torn between sense and desire.

He was too tired for sense to prevail. He was too shocked, too exhausted, too needful.

His body only wanted one thing and his head had no power to resist.

He wanted to be with Anna.

The water was a blessing. It had always been.

Her mother had swum as if she'd been born to the water, and from the time she could remember swimming had been part of their lives. There'd been all sorts of complications in Katrina's life but when things had got truly bad somehow she'd end up at a beach or a lake or a swimming pool.

'You can forget when you swim,' she'd told her little daughter. 'Don't let yourself think how cold it is, or what you have waiting for you after. Let yourself be a sleek, shiny fish, and the water's all yours. It's your home, baby. It's your safe place.'

As she'd grown older, as she'd realised how few safe places Katrina had, Anna had learned to almost fear her mother's passion for swimming. She'd arrive at Anna's apartment totally out of control, after some disastrous love affair, or a drug bust, or some other catastrophe. 'Get me to a swimming pool, darling. Or, better, get me to the beach.'

There'd been midwinter swims at stony beaches. There'd been break-ins to local pools at midnight, and Anna had mostly gone along because she'd known that in the water her mother was at peace.

And now at the castle she knew why. Her mother's childhood had, by all accounts, been solitary and miserable, but in the water under the castle Anna had found a similar peace.

It wasn't cold here. There were no fences to break. The water practically welcomed you in. For the six months she'd been here she'd swum every day and, like her mother, the time in the water was her time out.

She'd left Leo on the parapet. She had no idea whether he'd join her but it almost didn't matter. She put her head down and swam.

And he did join her.

She was in the 'swimming pool', which was simply a hollow hewn out of rocks at the base of the castle. As long as an Olympic pool, its waters were constantly refreshed by the waters lapping over the edge at high tide. The base at the shallow end was sand. At the far end, sea grasses attached themselves to the rocky floor, and tiny fishes, safe in here from larger predators, darted among the fronds. Their bright colours glinted in the morning light.

Anna saw them as she passed, but her mind had gone into the almost meditative state that swimming induced in her.

But then Leo was swimming beside her and meditation went right out the window.

He was as strong a swimmer as she was. Maybe even stronger. She'd been swimming hard and fast, as she always did at first, until the troubles of the outside world subsided. There weren't many who could keep up with her but Leo did it easily. They swam stroke for stroke. Side by side.

There was no need for them to swim side by side. The pool was almost as wide as it was long, but she didn't move apart and neither did he.

He was wearing only boxers. His body was so close if she edged a couple of inches to her left she'd brush his chest.

Skin against skin.

She was wearing panties. Nothing else. Bras were useless when you swam, they didn't stretch enough, making her feel constricted. She could have headed back to her apartment and donned a swimsuit when she'd left Leo but the pool was hidden from view from the windows above, and all she'd wanted was to be in the water.

And now...their swimming was in such synchronisation it was as if they were almost one.

She knew every inch of this man. His body...oh, she remembered his body, but now he was ten years older. His frame was stronger, the delineation of muscles more striking. He was a gorgeous Apollo of a man.

She wanted his body against hers. She wanted to say, *Mine*.

She wanted *him*.

She couldn't have what she wanted. Hadn't she learned that the hard way? Ten years of making do.

She hadn't been miserable for those ten years. After the first few appalling months she'd set to and made the most of what she had. She'd built herself a great career. She'd had some very nice boyfriends.

She'd always felt that part of her had been ripped away.

He was still beside her and the tension was suddenly unbearable. Enough. She swerved and headed for the cut leading to the open sea.

The bay wasn't quite as private but it was close. This bay was protected by two headlands, both within the castle keep. Last night's permission for islanders to use the castle jetty had been a one-off. It was glorious, it was safe and it was hers.

That was a jarring thought. She wouldn't think it and she desperately hoped that Leo wasn't thinking it.

Maybe he was still in the pool. She wasn't looking. This whole night had her so disconcerted that her mind couldn't get anything straight. There was only the water, deep and clear and beautiful.

Rocks jutted up to the left, tiny islands, their surfaces worn smooth by the wash of high tides—or by generations of Castlavarians using them to sunbathe. Had ancestors sunbaked?

Sunbathing was free, therefore her ancestors probably had, she decided, and the thought of the miserliness of generations of Castlavarans had her kicking with extra strength.

She was filled with strange sensations, formed from the dramas and pressures of the night, the skills she'd had to dredge up, the sadness, and now the fatigue, the drop in adrenalin. But overriding all was the thought that Leo was somewhere behind her.

In the same ocean.

In the same world.

Will you marry me? The words were suddenly resonating.

He'd asked that of her ten years ago and she'd said yes. They said wedding vows were inviolate. Maybe, for her, engagement was the same. Maybe she'd felt part of this man for ever.

Which was nonsense. She kicked out again, heading across the bay, fast and hard, letting the water cool something heating inside. Something she couldn't put a name to.

There were fish swimming under her, seeming almost to use her surge of power to carry them along. That was what she started to focus on. She wasn't alone, she had fish.

And her dogs back at the castle.

She didn't need Leo.

She reached the final rock before the open ocean and surfaced—and Leo was just behind her.

He was very large and very male and very wet. His body was glistening in the morning sunlight. He reached her rock and held on.

Their bodies brushed, skin against skin.

She wanted her bra back on. It'd been dumb to swim without it.

Actually, she wanted more. What was she doing, swimming almost naked? It was as if she'd issued an invitation. She should head to shore, grab her clothes and run.

She couldn't. She was winded, or at least that was what she told herself.

She tugged herself up onto the rock and dripped and stayed completely still. And waited.

He pulled himself up and sat beside her.

'Impressive,' he said. 'Your swimming.'

'It's one of the few legacies of any value my mother left me.'

'Swimming—and a castle.'

'Is that of value?' she said, because suddenly it had to be said. 'When it's messed with my life?'

'How does it mess with your life?'

'Because it stopped the man I love from wanting me.'

And there it was, out in the open. Said.

'Anna…'

'Just shut up,' she said, because she couldn't bear it one moment longer. He was too wet, too gorgeous, too close.

He was too Leo.

'Can we not talk?' she asked. 'Just…for now? I don't know about you but this time, this moment…I'm done. Right now I have only one need in the world and that need is you. Kiss me, Leo, before I go out of my mind.'

* * *

Of course he kissed her. How could he not?

She was simply the most beautiful woman he'd ever met, inside and out. She was naked apart from a sliver of lace panties. Her gorgeous, burnt-red curls were wisping wetly around her face. Her nose still had just the right number of freckles. Her body was brushing his, every curve just right.

Her lovely green eyes were gazing at him with what was surely a challenge.

Kiss me, Leo, before I go out of my mind.

Ditto, he thought. How can I not kiss her?

And he did.

She belonged to him, as simple as that. She'd made a vow ten years ago and that vow was as strong now as it had been then. Every nerve in her body confirmed it for her. She'd given her heart to this man and it still belonged to him.

He was hers.

It wasn't even a vow, she thought. It was simply a fact, a knowledge so deep and so strong that nothing could change it.

She shouldn't be out here. She shouldn't be almost naked, kissing a man she'd had nothing to do with for ten long years.

But her body said it was right. Her hands held the wetness of his body against hers, she felt her breasts mould against his chest and she felt like…she'd come home.

This man. This body.

Hers.

His hands were holding her, claiming her, pulling her closer. His mouth was possessing hers, her passion answered by his and more. The warmth of him, the heat, the strength... This was right. This was where she wanted to be.

Her man.

He couldn't do this.

He was doing it. He was loving the woman he wanted with all his heart. But deep within, the ingrained learning was still there, and almost the moment he felt her body mould to his, the age-old lessons resurfaced. Like a ghost, taunting him from the past, refusing to be exorcised.

She was a Castlavaran.

Even as he took her into his arms, even as he succumbed to pure desire, the events of the night were still with him. The distrust of the men on the water. His demand that they trust.

They didn't trust Anna. Why should they?

They trusted him.

He was hers—and then he wasn't. She felt the moment he realised, the moment passion turned into something akin to despair. He pulled away and held her at arm's length, and it was all she could do not to sob.

'Anna, I can't,' he said, and his voice was ragged with emotion. She could almost see the war raging within. 'Not... I can't.'

'Why not?' Somehow she made her voice even. Somehow she stopped herself reaching out again.

But the world was moving in. She thought suddenly, stupidly, that the workers would be arriving at the castle soon. The new hospital wing was on the sea side, and windows were being installed. There'd be workers at those windows, and she and Leo were far enough away from the sheltering castle wall for them to be seen.

She raised her arms to her chest almost as a gesture of defence. Leo saw and grimaced.

'We need to get back. Are you right to swim?'

'Of course I'm right to swim.' It was almost a snap. 'But, Leo, about us…'

'There's no us.'

'Are you kidding? After this? You want me as much as I want you.' What was happening? She was so confused.

But the time for silence was over, she thought. They'd lost ten years. What did she have to lose by breaking the barrier of emptiness?

'Leo, ten years ago you walked away from me.' She was inordinately proud of how steady her voice sounded. 'I told myself that it was a teenage romance, nothing more. I moved on. Sort of. But now…the way I feel… The way you feel… Leo, this thing between us, it's real and it's strong. Can we continue to ignore it?'

'I think we must.'

'So tell me the reason,' she said, struggling to keep her voice even. 'You walked away from me. It seemed then that you betrayed me, you broke a promise, you broke my trust. But ten years later I still want you. More, I still need you.'

How much pride did she have to lose by saying that? she wondered, but she'd been six months in this place. Six months of knowing there was no other woman in Leo's life. Six months of knowing how much he loved his country, how strong his reasons had been for walking away.

'Leo, I believe I can trust again,' she said, and there was a wobble in her voice now that she couldn't disguise. She was laying so much on the line here. 'But can you?'

'I never stop trusting.'

'That's not true and you know it. You classified me as a Castlavaran and trust flew out the window.'

'It's not you,' he said, heavily now. 'But, yes, it's the Castlavaran thing. How can I go there?'

'You hardly have to go there,' she said with irony. 'In case you haven't noticed, you're sitting on a rock in the middle of the sea with an almost naked woman right by your side. This is not a large rock. Go there? I believe you're already there.'

'I shouldn't be.'

'So tell me why not? You don't love me?'

'Love's got nothing to do with it.'

'Really?' Anger was rising now. She was baring everything, her body and now her thoughts, laying everything on the line. But the look on his face… *He was about to say no?*

And here it came.

'Anna, do you know what you're asking of me?'

'What? It seems to me that I'm giving.'

'You are,' he said heavily. 'But that's part of the problem. Anna, we're poles apart and you need to accept that, because it's reality. I'm the son of an impoverished widow, and my father died because of the power imbalance, the money imbalance on this island. I've seen what power can do, and so have each and every one of these islanders.'

'It can change. It has changed and you know it.' The knot of anger, of resentment was growing stronger. She'd exposed herself so much, and here he was still classifying her. Just another Castlavaran. Just another power wielder.

'You need to think this through,' he said, urgently now. 'Let me paint the whole picture.'

'You need to.' She was shivering, despite the growing warmth of the sun. Rejection was all around her.

But Leo's face was resolute. Implacable. She thought

suddenly of the expression she'd seen on his face all those years ago and she thought, Nothing's changed.

'Anna, what would the islanders think if we married?' He closed his eyes for a moment as if reinforcing his own thoughts, and when he opened them again she saw resolution in spades. 'They're cautiously optimistic about what you're doing now. Of course they are, but what you expect of them is trust and you can't buy that with six months of building. It takes generations to build it. And, Anna, they trust me.'

'Why wouldn't they?'

'There's any number of reasons they wouldn't. Anna, they allow me to vaccinate their children, and if you knew how long it took me to get them to agree... There's little internet access on the island—there's no infrastructure and no one can afford satellites. Poverty breeds superstition and fear. Carla hasn't been able to persuade them in all her years of practising medicine. You know why? Because the sister of her great-aunt by marriage was your grandfather's wife. That's how she got the money to pay for her medical training. She came back here and the islanders were grateful for her skills but they still didn't trust her. She could treat the worst of cases but she couldn't change things.'

It was her time to close her eyes then. She felt so bleak she was almost ill.

'So I'm a Castlavaran and I'm tainted.'

'By association, yes. No matter what I want... Anna, I can't risk it. I can't risk what I've built.'

'So after ten years nothing has changed.'

'It can't.' There was despair in his voice but she couldn't listen to his despair. It was nothing, she thought, compared to how she was feeling. Exposed. Betrayed.

Helpless. All from a finger of fate she'd had nothing to do with.

'So that's that, then,' she said bleakly. 'We all live ever after, but happily doesn't come into it.'

'Anna, maybe you could—'

'Don't you dare,' she hissed, cutting over whatever he'd been about to say. There was nothing that could make this better. 'Don't even think about making suggestions as to what I could do or not do with my life. It has nothing to do with you. I'll get on with making this castle the best hospital I possibly can. I'll put every ounce of energy into making this island more liveable, making up as much as I can for the greed and selfishness of people I don't even consider my ancestors.

'But it seems I'm not allowed to love you. So I can't listen to what you think I should do personally. You butted out of my life ten years ago and obviously that decision sticks. Okay, I accept it. I've humiliated myself enough. From now on, you're my professional colleague and nothing more. So if you'll excuse me I need to get back to shore and get some clothes on. You set your barriers in place ten years ago and it's time I set mine up, just as rigidly.'

There was nothing left to say. She could feel tears slipping helplessly down her face.

He raised a hand as if to wipe them away, and she slapped it away.

'Don't touch me,' she managed. 'Not now and not ever.'

And she turned and dived into the water. She swam back to shore, hard and fast.

Sobbing underwater was hard, but she managed it.

She had the rest of her life to manage everything else.

* * *

Ten years ago Leo Aretino had walked away from the woman he loved because of loyalty to his country. He'd thought then that nothing could hurt more.

He'd been wrong. He sat and watched her swim away and the pain he felt was bone deep.

Ten years ago he'd argued that his cause was noble. He'd thought separation would cause Anna pain but she'd get over it. She'd been young, beautiful, talented. Her life was in England. Walking away from her had felt like he was cutting away a part of himself, but he'd been young, he'd been optimistic and he'd been sure that Anna's pain on rejection would be fleeting.

Now, watching her swim away, having her words replay over and over in his head, that surety was gone.

He'd hurt her as badly as he'd hurt himself and that pain was ongoing.

So swim after her. Gather her into his arms. Be damned to the consequences, you love her.

But marriage to a Castlavaran…

The impossibility was still there.

Things were changing, he thought. Anna was building a medical service that could finally equal that of its neighbouring countries. She was building not only a hospital but also apartments luxurious enough to attract medical staff. The castle would be transformed into a hospital that the islanders trusted and used.

But he had no doubt that tonight the boats had brought the injured to the castle because of him. Trust in him had allowed burned men to be brought into a medical centre that seemed almost foreign. More. Foreign didn't begin to describe the islanders' distrust of all things Castlavaran.

If he was seen to align himself with Anna… If he was to become part of the Castlavaran family…

Maybe it could work. Given time.

But if it didn't… If the islanders didn't accept assurances…

He thought of the fledgling vaccination programme that he'd worked so hard to get off the ground. He thought of the home rehab programmes he'd set up for so many people. He thought of diet charts, diabetic schedules, exercise regimes. He thought of child and adolescent health programmes he'd instigated. They all sounded simple, sensible, but for an island cut off by poverty for so long, they were huge.

They existed because he was seen as one of them. He was an islander the people themselves had sent away to train. He knew he was trusted.

He wasn't a Castlavaran.

Anna had reached the beach now. He saw her grab her clothes, slip a T-shirt over her head and start to make her way up the ancient steps, to disappear into the castle. To her fantastical apartments.

To where she belonged. To where fate had decreed she stay.

Whereas he belonged elsewhere. Not in her castle. Not even on this rock, or on this beach, which had been controlled for so long by a family who ruled by greed.

The weariness and grief he felt was making him feel ill, but part of that—a huge part—was grief for Anna. This morning he'd seen just how much he'd hurt her, but there was no escaping that hurt.

He was an Aretino, an islander. Anna was a Castlavaran. The middle ground was this magnificent new medical centre. Maybe it would work, because of Anna's generosity and because of the trust the islanders had in him and his staff, but that middle ground had to stay purely medical. The risks of muddying it were far, far too great.

Anna was gone. The castle loomed grey and forbidding and Anna was inside.

He had work to do. He needed to check on his mother. He had house-calls to make. He had a clinic to run.

Life went on. It had to.

And the love between two people? Like Romeo and Juliet, he thought suddenly, and found himself choking on a bitter laugh. Yeah, those two had sorted it well.

He'd always thought the story was ridiculous. Dying for a teenaged love? How stupid. They'd been kids. Given parental approval, given permission to see each other whenever they wanted, would they have been doing anything in their old age besides remembering with vague fondness—or even a bit of embarrassment—their first delicious romance?

Now he wasn't so sure—but he was sure that Romeo and Juliet had only thought of themselves and their grief. If Romeo had had the same level of duty and care as he did, could the Shakespearean ending have been the same?

That was crazy thinking, but at its heart he knew there was a germ of truth.

Given thought, care, the faith and dependence of his people, surely Romeo would have walked away.

Like Leo, he'd have had no choice.

CHAPTER TEN

THE CELEBRATION TWO weeks later, ostensibly to open the Castle Castlavaran Medical Centre, was definitely premature. The castle wasn't nearly ready but if Anna was to provide for the injured fishermen then the celebration had to be now.

'It's the opening of my special project,' she'd told the trustees in what was beginning to be a ritual contact rather than serious negotiation. 'You've let me build my hospital because I can't be happy practising my medicine without facilities to match. Now that the first section is open for emergency use, I need a party to celebrate.'

So the Deed of Trust, written so long ago, was invoked yet again. 'Funds shall be used for the pleasure of the present incumbent.'

Now, on the Saturday of what was to be a weekend of celebration, what she should be feeling was pleasure. She wasn't. Her morning's swim with Leo had pretty much destroyed her hard-won equilibrium, and she was back to being that dumb nineteen-year-old, in love all over again.

Which was dumb. What had changed? She still had her gorgeous apartments. She had her doofus dogs. She had her glorious beach. She had a project that took every waking hour, and she had an island home that'd make most millionaires swoon with envy.

She'd also had so little sleep she was running on empty and she was...desolate. That one kiss had thrown her straight back to feeling as if wedding vows had been broken.

But she couldn't think of that today. As the islanders streamed into the castle on this bright May Saturday, Anna walked slowly through the grounds, trying to see it through fresh eyes.

For the last couple of weeks she'd thrown everything into setting this place up so the islanders could see it as it would be. The plan was the Open Castle today followed by speeches and a feast, then a blessing by the local priest on Sunday morning. The whole weekend was designed to draw the locals in, make them see what she was doing—engender trust?

So now she did her own wandering through, trying to see it as the islanders were seeing it.

Outside areas first. The castle courtyard was to be separated into two. Right now it was filled with marquees, stalls providing food and drink, with hoopla stalls and fortune tellers—'Because an island party's not a party without them,' she'd told the trustees. But eventually— soon—it would be transformed, with an ambulance bay and reception area on one side, and a walled garden for ambulant patients on the other.

There were eventual plans to incorporate a visitors' precinct, art centre, tourist hub, formal tours of the underground labyrinth, history tours. For the hospital itself... She wanted a swimming pool, a rehabilitation centre to make major city hospitals weep in envy. Huge posters showed visitors her vision.

And now... The islanders certainly seemed happy— maybe they were—but everywhere she went, the moment she was seen, the noise level dropped to wary. She was greeted with politeness, with gratitude for what she was doing—but with distance.

She made her way up to the battlements, to the area that was to be converted to a massive patient lounge. This would be able to be cleared fast, at need, to be used as a helipad for patient evacuation, but there'd be covered areas with lounges, everything necessary for recovering patients to enjoy the sun and a view that up until now only Castlavarans had had the right to see.

There were more islanders here, showing huge interest as they inspected more posters showing plans. But there was still caution as Anna approached. She could still see distrust. What she gave, couldn't she take away?

She left the battlements and made her way down through what was still a rabbit warren of unused rooms, but with more posters showing them as individually designed wards, scrubbed, painted, hung with colourful curtains, with patchwork coverlets on the beds. Every detail had been meticulously thought out. There'd be work here for every islander who could sew. Yes, plain would be easier and even more hygienic, but this way there'd be wages coming into families who'd never seen such largesse.

'Pretty makes me happy,' she'd told the trustees, and, bemused, they'd simply signed off.

It did make her happy. Sort of. People were thanking her—awkwardly—but then turning back to their friends. To people they knew and trusted.

She walked into the last ward, the kids' ward. This had been a fun project and she'd started it early, so it didn't need posters to show what she intended. What had been the castle ballroom was now set up with cubicles, where removal of screens meant each child could become part of a communal recovery area.

She'd brought in occupational therapists to advise. The play area was designed for subtle rehabilitation, but it was fun and fantastical. It made her happy to see it.

But now she walked into the room and the customary silence fell. A group of locals admiring posters showing proposed play equipment parted to let her through.

Leo was at its centre.

Of course he was at its centre. He was part of this cautious, distrustful crowd. Part of the island.

During every step this last six months he'd talked to the islanders, told them what was happening, helped them to accept that there was no hidden agenda, no trap.

The islanders trusted him. If this was a democracy he'd be their elected president, she thought.

And Anna? She'd be the Crown. A figurehead, to be accorded respect but not friendship. There was far too much history for a Castlavaran to be a friend.

There was too much history between herself and Leo.

'Dr Raymond.' He greeted her with a smile, though the smile didn't reach his eyes. 'This is wonderful.'

'I know,' she said, and gave him the same forced smile back. 'We should all be proud of what we've achieved.'

'*You've* achieved,' he said, raising his voice so all the islanders could hear. 'You're giving us generosity without price. And what you're doing for our injured fishermen… Believe me, we're grateful.'

There was a murmur of agreement. The islanders were indeed grateful, but she glanced around and she still saw wariness. The history of her ancestors was still there, an almost tangible thing, a history of abuse for financial gain. But in what way could she possibly gain by this, she thought, except the satisfaction of seeing an island cared for?

'Believe it or not, I don't want gratitude,' she managed—but suddenly she was caught.

Leo.

She looked at him, really looked at him. She'd thought he'd been laughing as she'd entered. Maybe he had, but there was no laughter here. He looked exhausted. It wasn't unusual to see Leo look tired, but this was different. His fatigue seemed bone deep.

'Leo, what's wrong?' She said it before she could help herself, but he shook his head, as if to tell her not to go there.

Well, why should she? They had no choice but to be nothing to each other. She shouldn't care that he looked as if he was driving himself into the ground.

The islanders were being polite. Smiling warily at her. They were assuring her how much they appreciated what she was doing. The thanks were effusive and she thought, They still think I can snatch it away.

But Leo… What was with him? Why the bleak look?

She couldn't care. He didn't want her to care.

It was almost time for the formalities. She'd organised for the head of trustees to formally open the emergency department—that seemed as close a gesture as she could make to declaring it was being handed over to the people. Then she'd asked Leo to speak and he'd reluctantly agreed.

'It's not my place,' he'd said, and she'd almost lost it.

'It's your island,' she'd told him. 'This is for your people. Just do it.'

So he'd agreed.

There'd be feasting and fireworks on the battlements. There'd be a blessing in the island church in the morning and then life would move on.

For twenty years.

* * *

But Leo didn't play his part.

The head of trustees gave a wonderful, generous introduction but Leo wasn't there to take over. It was Carla who finally rose to take his place.

'He must have been called away,' she told the crowd. 'But Dr Raymond is already trying to organise additional medical staff for us, so our Dr Leo might be able to have a well-deserved rest.'

She spoke warmly and well, but the gap left by Leo was almost palpable.

Still, it was a party. The fireworks were spectacular. The music was brilliant.

Anna still felt empty.

The silence as she approached, the forced way people responded to her, the wariness... When would it end?

In twenty years?

And then Carla found her. She was flushed, big-eyed, obviously worried. 'Anna, can you help?'

'Of course.' She'd been wondering how soon she could escape. She wouldn't mind a bit of medical need to give her an excuse.

'I think Leo's mother's dying,' Carla said, and Anna's heart sank. This wasn't the kind of medical need she'd had in mind.

'She's slipped badly over the last week and we're not sure how close the end is,' Carla told her. 'I'm guessing... close. Her sister—Leo's aunt—is starting to be frightened, so Leo's been sitting up with her these last few nights. But now he's tired to the point of collapse. We've had medical dramas this week, plus more than our share of births, and I know he's exhausted. He won't hear of me helping and all his relatives are here. He wants them to stay, to be part of the celebrations, but he's there alone.

Anna, he's past exhaustion. If you're not needed here any more…would you go?'

'I'd go if I could be any use,' she said, puzzled. 'Carla, I'm not sure he'd want me.'

That was a heavy statement, but she knew it was true.

But now Carla was almost waspish, weariness and anger showing through her request for Anna to help. 'Of course he wants you,' she snapped. 'I know there are things between you—I'd be blind not to see it—but tonight he needs help, medical as well as personal. You need to get over yourselves, the pair of you, but meanwhile I need you…Donna needs you…to get over there. Here's the address. Can I depend on you?'

And there was nothing to say to that except, 'Of course.'

His mother was deeply asleep. There was time—even a need—to think of the events of the day.

The opening of this first step of the medical centre had been amazing. The plan was the culmination of everything he'd dreamed of for the island. It'd take a while to build a medical team with the skills to take advantage of the facilities Anna was providing, but already international interest within medical circles had been piqued. Doctors' quarters in a magnificent renovated castle would be a distinct lure, as was building a medical service almost from the ground up.

Island infrastructure was still a problem but Anna was already onto that. He'd heard her tell the head of the trustees…

'How can I be happy living here if I can't phone my friends on the other side of the island?'

There were so many issues facing the island, lack of

good schools, good roads, a decent port, but Anna was onto those, too. He knew she'd find a way.

She was astounding.

She was the woman of his dreams and he couldn't claim her.

Maybe in three or four years when the medical team had settled, when the islanders had finally started to trust…

Or maybe not. How deep did mistrust of the Castlavarans go? For him to ally himself with a family that had essentially killed his father…

It couldn't happen.

He closed his mind, as he'd learned to do so often in the past when things hurt to the point where his chest felt as if it'd burst. As his chest felt like it was bursting now. His mother was slipping quietly from this life. She might rally, as she'd rallied before, but he knew the end was growing closer.

As a doctor he knew that this was a time for acceptance, but this was his mother. For so many years there'd been just the two of them. His distress was for memories of what had been. It was also fatigue—and for a build-up of emotion he could no longer hold back.

In the distance he could still hear the celebrations from the castle. He wasn't a part of them. They belonged…to the woman he loved?

He'd never felt so alone in his life.

Talk about the worst house in the best street! Realtors often said these were the best buys, but there was nothing 'best' about the house Carla had directed her to. The stone terraces here were crumbling, the façades sagging with time. The ground here must have shifted, maybe with some long-ago earth tremor, Anna thought, as the walls on each seemed out of alignment, plugged with timber, all slightly askew.

Leo's house was at the end of the row and its skew was the worst. Its woodwork was brightly painted. Its tiny front garden was a tangle of gorgeous vines and flowers—someone here had loved gardening—but nothing could disguise the meanness of its narrow façade, and the way it sagged toward the cobbled waterway at the end of the street.

Had Leo been paid nothing for the work he'd put into this island? For the local doctor to live in such a place…

But she wasn't here to judge. She knocked tentatively on the door. There was no answer. She pushed and the door swung open onto a small sitting room.

'Leo?'

'Anna!' She heard his shock. She pushed open the next door and Leo was inside.

As a doctor it was a scene she was familiar with. Acceptance came with experience of situations like this.

One look at Donna told her that the end, indeed, was close. She was a tiny woman and disease had shrunk her even more. The mass of white curls around her face was practically the sum of her. She lay completely still, and Anna wondered if this was sleep or coma.

'Carla said you might need me,' she said softly.

The shock was still with him. His hand was holding his mother's and he didn't rise. 'Carla had no right.'

'Carla loves you—as all the islanders love you.'

There was silence at that. He turned back to look down into his mother's face and his distress was almost palpable.

'Unconscious?'

'She stirred a little while back. She asked for water.'

'She's asleep, then,' she said softly. 'Leo, when did *you* last sleep?'

'I can't remember.'

She nodded and walked across to lift Donna's emaciated wrist away from Leo. The pulse was steady. There was time yet, but who knew how long?

She put the old lady's hand back into his.

'You'll collapse if you don't sleep.'

'My aunt…she's the only one my mother trusts and she won't stay any more. She's scared.'

That happened. Death could be terrifying—or it could be a gentle slipping away, the culmination of a life well lived.

'Would you sleep for a couple of hours if I stayed with her?' she ventured. 'She doesn't know me but…'

'Of course she knows you. You're the Castlavaran.' It was said with something akin to desperation.

Now wasn't the time to argue. Anna simply nodded.

'If she knows that, then she'll also know I'm a doctor. She shouldn't be frightened if she stirs. But if she does stir and worries, Leo, I'll wake you straight away. I promise. Will you trust me that much?'

'You know I'd trust you…with everything I have.'

It was a big statement but she had to move past it.

'Then trust me with your mother,' she said. 'Let me take the chair. You go and find your bed and sleep.'

'Anna…after all I've done to you…'

'Don't go there,' she said softly. 'For now there's only your mother to think of, and your need for sleep.' He rose, and before she could help herself she laid her palm on his cheek. It was a caress of comfort, nothing more, and it seemed to ground them both.

'Sleep, Leo,' she said softly. 'I will wake you the moment you're needed. Know that you can trust me.'

'I do trust you,' he said, and his voice was ragged with fatigue. 'Of course I trust you. But the whole island—'

'Forget about it,' she told him. 'Just go.'

And with one last long look at his mother—and then her—he went.

In the end it was a time of peace, sitting in the dark, listening to the thready breathing of the sleeping Donna. Maybe she should be distressed. Maybe the events of the day should have left her disoriented. But there was something about this time, this night, that said her world was somehow settling.

She was a stranger to this woman but she didn't feel like a stranger. This felt like her place.

She sat and let the stillness of the night envelop her and the rest of the world seemed to fade to nothing.

She should be tired but she didn't feel it. As the night wore on there was nothing but the sound of breathing. The sounds of peace.

And then, just before the dawn, Donna woke. Her dark eyes flickered open, focussing. The nightlight illuminated both their faces, but not so much. Enough.

'You…' It was the faintest of whispers. 'It *is* you. The Castlavaran.'

'I'm Anna,' she said softly. 'Leo's sleeping in the next room. Yes, I'm the Castlavaran.' What was the use of denying it now?

'You're the woman my son loves.'

There was no answer to that. She took Donna's hand to tuck it under the cover but it was grasped and held.

'I'll get Leo for you,' she told her. 'I'm sorry that you had to find me here, but you know I'm a doctor? Leo needed to sleep.'

'Don't be sorry. I'm sorry. You're Anna.' She sighed, a huge, regret-filled sigh of sorrow. 'Anna, he loves you.'

'And he can't marry me.' Why not say it like it was? 'Donna, it's okay. Your son won't do anything to put his family, or the islanders, at risk.'

'I know that,' Donna said distressfully, obviously making an Herculean effort to speak. 'But he fell in love. He has a photograph of you on his bedside table. He sent it to me all those years ago— "This is the woman I'm going to marry." And then nothing. Finally he explained and I agreed. Impossible. But I thought…I thought he must get over it. Move on.'

'That was…sensible.'

'It was selfish,' Donna told her, fighting for each word. 'Did he tell you? How could you ever know…?'

'Donna…'

'Let me say it.' The grip on her hand tightened. 'You know the Castlavarans killed his father? The night my husband came down with appendicitis… Carla was here then, our first ever doctor. She said the appendix had burst, that he needed emergency surgery and she couldn't do it here. I sent Leo to the castle to plead. He was twelve years old and we thought—it was the only way—a child pleading might just break down the Castlavaran indifference. We needed money to hire a helicopter. He wouldn't survive a boat trip to where he could get help. But your grandfather asked what was in it for him and then he slammed the door in Leo's face.'

'Oh, Donna…'

'And the stories go on,' Donna whispered, obviously fighting for breath to speak each word. 'Every islander has a story. So now… Anna, if there was any way he could do the work he needs to do with you by his side… If there was any way I thought he wouldn't lose the islanders' trust… What you're doing at the castle… I'm so proud of you. If I could see a way…'

'It's not for you to see our way for us,' Anna told her, wiping a tear slipping down the old lady's cheek. 'Leo and I will sort it out. We must.'

'He can't. He's like his father. He's too honourable…'

'I know that.'

'You'll have to do something,' Donna murmured. 'Please.'

'I'll do what I can.' She leaned over and kissed her lightly on her wrinkled cheek. 'Meanwhile, I promised I'd wake Leo the moment you woke and I'm honourable, too. Believe it or not.'

'I do,' Donna muttered fretfully. 'But can the islanders?'

He was soundly asleep, and it almost broke her to wake him. For a moment she stood, watching the steady fall and rise of his chest. He was still fully dressed, sleeping on top of the bed rather than in it. A big man in a small room.

She needed to call his name. He'd be awake in an instant, she thought. She'd promised to call.

But she took a moment, a moment only, to look around her.

The room was sparsely furnished. It was the room of a man who spent hardly any time here. There were faded marks on the walls, she guessed from childhood, from posters finally fallen down from where they'd been stuck on ancient plaster. The rugs were threadbare and the iron bedstead minimalist.

A decent sound system sat on the bedside table with good-quality headphones and she thought, At least he hasn't deprived himself of everything.

And then she saw the photograph.

It was small, black and white, enclosed in a simple silver frame.

She remembered when it had been taken. They'd just passed their exams and had gone to a fun fair. There'd been a photo booth and, laughing, sticky with fairy floss, they'd entered.

The picture was of two faces laughing from behind their mass of cotton candy. They were squashed so tightly together they almost seemed an extension of each other. It had been blown up from passport-sized and had been grainy, low-resolution in the first place, but their love and laughter showed through.

She had the matching print tucked in a bottom drawer. After all these years it hurt too much to see it, but that neither of them had destroyed it… Maybe such a thing couldn't be destroyed.

'If I could see a way…' Donna's words were still reverberating.

What way?

But she'd told Donna that now wasn't the time and she was right. She'd made a promise.

She leaned over and touched Leo on the shoulder. He was awake in an instant.

'She's okay, Leo. She's awake and talking.' It was all she could say. It wasn't for her to say what he knew for himself, that things were shutting down. 'She's just woken up.'

'I'll go to her.'

He rose and raked his hair.

And suddenly she was seeing him the night his father had died. Maybe he'd been woken from this bed, in this room. She thought of a twelve-year-old, woken from sleep, walking across the darkened drawbridge to the great castle gates. What a thing to ask of a child. How alone must he have felt?

He was alone now, facing the death of his mother. Plus he was facing the ongoing needs this island had heaped on his shoulders.

She could help. She could share.

But for an Aretino to become a Castlavaran…

'If I could see a way…'

This island was so rigid but it had become this way through need—she'd accepted that. The castle and its owners were simply 'the Other'. You were an islander or a Castlavaran, not both.

If things could change…

They could change. With transfer of titles, with release of castle funds…

In twenty years.

It has to be possible, Anna thought. Her pride, her anger for the way she'd been treated had ebbed away. There was only aching need for this solitary man who'd done all in his power to make things good for his people.

He should be the Castlavaran, she thought. The ruler. He'd earned the right of respect, trust, the things a ruler needed. It shouldn't be her making these decisions. A tweak of fate had left the island in her hands but this man had earned it.

He stood, looking helplessly at her. His hand reached out for her—and then fell away uselessly.

'Anna, thank you. I'm sorry. I need to… You need…'

'We both need,' she told him, and something seemed to settle. Something solid. Something sure. He'd do what he had to do, this man. He was honourable. Dependable.

He was loved.

'Go to your mother,' she said softly. 'It's her need

that has to take precedence now—but know that I go with you.'

And before she realised what she intended herself, she reached up and kissed him lightly on the lips. It was a feather touch, no more, a kiss given before he could react or reject, and then she was stepping away. 'Do what you need to do, Leo,' she said, and amazingly her voice even sounded sure. 'But go with my love. And know that I'm here for you and I will be here for you. For however long it takes.'

CHAPTER ELEVEN

THE FINAL PART of the opening of the medical centre took
place the next morning. Anna had told the trustees that
she needed a party, and Carla had set her straight on what
else was needed.

'You're opening a medical centre and you want island
acceptance? A blessing is non-negotiable.'

So at ten o'clock Anna was sitting at the back of the
island's main church. She'd suggested she not come—
this should be the islanders' dream rather than hers—but
Carla had been adamant on that score as well.

'You can't give it away for twenty years and they know
it. They need to accept you.'

'Will they ever?'

There was no answer, so all she could do was stay as
inconspicuous as possible. As she waited for the service
to begin Carla sought her out and tried to drag her down
the front but she was having none of it.

'Leo's mother?' she asked Carla.

'She's a little better,' Carla told her, her face light-
ing up. 'I dropped by an hour ago. You must have done
her good last night. When I left she was even saying she
wanted to come here! Today! I have no idea if that's possible, but Leo's coming. He says he couldn't speak yes-

terday so he wants to speak today. Anna, my son's down at the front. Come and sit with us.'

'Please, no.'

So she was left. She'd found a seat in a nook behind a pillar where she had to peer sideways to see. The people around her cast her curious glances but left her alone.

That was how life was for her. The islanders were outwardly courteous, but always wary.

With no one to talk to she focussed instead on her surroundings. The church was ancient, and impressive.

'It was built for ceremonial occasions by the Castlavarans,' Carla had told her, 'but it's been neglected for generations as the Castlavarans lost their faith and the islanders had no funds to keep it up.'

It looked beautiful today, decorated with sheaves and sheaves of the island's wild roses, but the flowers barely disguised the need for repair.

How could she present restoration to the trustees, she thought. 'I need a church for my present happiness?'

And then the service started. It was a simple service, a blessing on what was being done, prayers of thankfulness for what had happened two weeks ago, hopes for what the medical service might mean to the islanders in the years ahead.

Might, she thought. *Might?* Still distrust.

And then Leo stood to speak.

The congregation had been a little restless, clearly there because they felt obligated to be but not ready to be too invested in what still might not come to pass. But the moment Leo stood, the stillness was absolute.

He had their absolute attention. Their absolute trust.

He should be the castle patriarch, she thought yet again.

And then he spoke, quietly, strongly, well. He spoke of a long-ago dream. He spoke of the near miracle of what he saw happening. He spoke of his hopes for what Anna was doing, of his pride in what had already happened, and his trust in what she was doing into the future.

He almost had her forgetting the distrust. He spoke simply, his emotion struggling to be contained. There was thankfulness in his voice, but also deep weariness. She could see it on his face, a man whose responsibilities had stretched him thin. This was a man who was there for every islander. A man who never turned from what had to be done.

Including the gut-wrenching decision not to take comfort in her body, not to let himself love her.

She knew it. As she sat there and watched, as she listened to what was indeed a personal thanks to her, she accepted their combined story for what it was—one of sacrifice. She'd been deeply hurt, but for Leo that pain must have been just as deep. There were so many things he'd given away.

She'd pressed Carla about Leo's love life once, and Carla had given a mirthless chuckle.

'Our Leo? When would he have time to do some courting? There are plenty of island girls who'd take him with joy, but his head's been taken up with the medical needs of this island.'

But it can't have been entirely, she thought. Not for all these years. She of all people knew how Leo responded to a woman, how much joy he'd found in her body. There must have been opportunities to marry one of his own.

One of his own. The phrase resonated as Leo finished outlining plans for the future, as he sought her face in the crowd and managed a smile, a smile of weariness and gratitude and acceptance, and as the congregation stood to sing.

One of his own. She wasn't one of 'his'. She was a Castlavaran.

But she wasn't.

Anger was suddenly her overriding emotion. A child's bad-tempered shout suddenly came to her, heard in some long-ago surgery when she was asking to see a spotty chest. *'No! Can't make me!'*

No one should be able to make her something she wasn't.

So what was she, then? A Raymond? Her mother had married briefly, but the name was all she had of the man who'd fathered her. Her tentative approaches to meet him had been met with rebuffs.

So if she wasn't a Raymond and she wasn't a Castlavaran, then what?

Things were clearing. The resentment she'd held for so many years was gone and in its place…determination.

Donna's words hung over her. *'If I could see a way…'*

Would there ever be a better time?

Would she ever feel this brave again?

And before she could change her mind she started moving out toward the aisle. She had to edge her way past a sea of curious islanders to reach it.

Leo was still standing beside the priest. The priest looked curiously down the aisle as he felt the stir of movement. He saw Anna.

And Leo… He, too, stood still.

Waiting.

Dear heaven, could she do it?

She had this one chance, she thought. If not now, then never.

'Help me, Donna,' she whispered to herself. 'Help me say it.'

For Leo this felt almost like an out-of-body experience.

He'd sat last night with his mother, half expecting her to slip away in the night. Then Anna had come and

Donna had stirred and demanded answers to questions he'd rather not think about. And then she'd demanded he dress her and carry her to the church.

And astonishingly she was here now, wrapped in blankets, surrounded by his aunts and cousins. They'd appropriated a nook to one side so Donna could watch and listen from her wheelchair. When he'd come forward to speak he'd been aware that his mother's eyes were bright and inquisitive, seemingly more alive than he'd seen them for months.

She couldn't last much longer. Her body weight… her fluid intake…impossible. But that she was here this morning was a miracle.

And now here was Anna.

She should have been seated in the front pew. He'd thought that as he'd entered and seen her, far up the back, trying to be invisible.

She'd be feeling that she had no place here.

He'd helped her feel that way, and he hated it. But as he looked around the sea of faces in the congregation, out to where his mother sat, once again came the knowledge that his way had been right. It was still right.

In time, given the medical services they deserved, the islanders could come to depend on him less, shifting loyalty to a myriad of other places. But for now he was still the Doctor. The man who'd persuaded them to have their children vaccinated, to eat less salt in their diets, to stop putting honey on their babies' pacifiers. He was the man they'd helped educate, who they'd supported to be here for them in times of trouble. The man they still needed to trust.

The man who'd had to turn away from his need of Anna.

But now Anna was out in the aisle, making her way steadily toward the front.

Toward him.

The entire church seemed to take a collective breath.

Anna had dressed conservatively in a soft grey suit and white blouse. Her curls were caught back into a demure knot. Her outfit was entirely appropriate for this community where women of a certain age still covered their heads.

It'd be a crime for Anna to cover her head, he thought inconsequentially. It was even a shame that her hair was confined to a knot. Those blazing curls deserved to be free.

Free. The word seemed to stick in his head and stay.

She wasn't free. Because of her commitment to the island she was trapped in the castle as surely as he was trapped in his lifestyle. If she walked away she could still command living expenses, she'd still be fabulously wealthy, but she couldn't justify all the things she was doing 'for her pleasure'. The things she was doing to make his island safe.

She'd reached him now. He'd taken the two steps down from the altar and for a moment he thought she intended to walk past him. Her eyes looked steely, determined. He wasn't sure what she was doing but by her position on this island no one would gainsay her right to do it.

But instead of stepping past, she paused and placed a hand on his arm. It was almost a caress. No, it *was* a caress, and why it grounded him…why it made his world seem to settle…

'Stand by me,' she said simply. 'Leo, I need you.'

And she took the final steps upward to the dais, leaving him to follow or not. As he willed.

The congregation was all islanders. That was where he belonged. But he looked back at her and saw determination and resolution. But also something more. A deep vulnerability, a hurt that had never been assuaged.

He stepped back to her.

She met his gaze without smiling and nodded, and then they both stood and faced outward. He stood so their shoulders were touching, not sure where this was going but suddenly sure that this was where he needed to be.

He watched her bite her bottom lip, a gesture he knew well. The gesture of a woman about to launch herself into the unknown.

And then she spoke.

'I ask your indulgence,' she said softly. 'The indulgence of all of you. Father, do I have your permission to speak?'

The elderly priest spread his hands, looking bemused, but he nodded. No one said no to the Castlavaran.

Anna bowed her head briefly in thanks, and then continued while Leo stood, stunned. He had no idea what was happening.

But now she was speaking to the congregation.

'I had no plans to speak today,' she said. Her voice was quiet but steady, and the acoustics of this ancient place meant it rang out over the sea of listeners. 'I felt I had no right. This medical centre should belong to you, the islanders, not to me. I see myself simply as its guardian for the next few years.'

There was a murmur at that, and it wasn't a great murmur. It was the sound of muted resentment that such a guardian was needed.

But Anna wasn't done. Indeed, those first few words seemed to have steadied her. She waited until the murmurs faded and then continued.

'But what I have to say now concerns that guardianship,' she said simply. 'It concerns all of us, so I ask your indulgence.' She took a deep breath and forged on.

'Last night I sat with Donna Aretino,' she told them. She glanced outward then at the sea of faces—and Leo saw her shock as she realised that Donna was here. But somehow she managed to smile at Donna and then she kept right on speaking.

'Most of you realise how ill Donna's been,' she told them. 'And last night, sitting with Donna, I saw things clearly, things that affect me, that affect you, that affect the island life that Donna represents. So at this time, at this blessing of all we intend to do, I need to ask a question. A question of all of you. First, though, a story.'

She had them all. The murmurs had gone. Every gaze was fixed firmly on the woman by Leo's side.

'You know that Katrina, my mother, was born a Castlavaran.' She was keeping it simple, keeping it slow. 'She left this island because she hated what her father and her brother were doing, but her grief at leaving Tovahna was profound. She married my father, an Englishman. I was born as Anna Raymond and my mother never spoke of Tovahna again. In my childhood, though, she taught me what she called her secret language. Your language. She sang me your songs. Her love of this island came through. And then at medical school I met a man who spoke your language as well. This man was your Dr Aretino. And I fell in love.'

Somewhere up the back of the church a baby gurgled but the gurgle was cut short. The hush that followed was absolute. Leo wondered what the mother had done to so skilfully quieten her child. Every ear was straining to hear, his own included.

What was she doing?

'And your Dr Leo loved me.' She said it strongly,

surely, and he knew by the steadiness of her voice that
ten years of bitterness and resentment had disappeared.
'We had six glorious months together before he asked
me to marry him and I said yes. But then my mother returned from overseas and Leo realised who she was. A
Castlavaran. From that moment I became a Castlavaran
in Leo's eyes. I know now the damage the Castlavarans
have done to this island. I know, too, the damage they've
done to Donna, to this gentle lady who, miraculously it
seems, is here today. I also know the hurt they've caused
to Leo himself. I understand why he had to walk away
from our vow to wed.'

There was another stir then. This was news to the islanders. A long-ago love affair… Leo looked out over the
congregation and saw the faint withdrawal. They didn't
like this. The connection of a man they'd trusted…

Trusted…past tense?

Anna must have sensed it, too, he thought, but she was
forging on. He was still standing beside her, his shoulder still touching hers. As the stirrings of distrust began
he thought maybe he should step away but he couldn't.
What she was saying was truth, and on this day, in this
place, there seemed no space for anything else.

'So Leo finished his training without me, and then
came back here, to his people,' she continued. 'As you
all know. He's given his heart to this island, to you, his
community, and of course to you, Donna. To his family. Though after all this time maybe every islander is
his family. The Aretinos have been islanders since time
immemorial. They've been fishermen, farmers, parents,
grandparents, friends, part of the fabric of Tovahna.
There's been care and respect and love for generations.
All the while, the Castlavarans have cared for no one but

themselves—and here I am, seemingly a Castlavaran, with no place among you.'

That created another murmur, but this time there was a tinge of confusion. Agreement, too, though. Anna *was* an outsider.

He felt her flinch. The flinch was tiny, momentary, but it was enough and he couldn't bear it. He took her hand and he held it.

That was a statement, too. The murmur this time was louder, more disapproving. He wanted to say something but it felt like a band across his chest was tightening. This was an impossible situation. It had been impossible for years. Nothing could change it.

Except he was holding Anna's hand. He should let go but he couldn't. There were moments in time when the impossible became inevitable. There'd be consequences, he thought, but quite suddenly he knew that letting this woman go was the new unthinkable.

And Anna was still speaking. Her fingers curved around his and held on, as if finding strength there for what she wanted to say, but there was nothing weak about the voice she used, or the words she was uttering.

'But families change,' she said. 'Names die out. The name of Castlavara died with my uncle. There's no one of the name Castlavara on the island any more.'

'But you're the Castlavaran.' It was a brutish fisherman, a man in his seventies whose boat had been impounded decades before for drifting too close to the part of the beach that had been declared for Castlavaran use for centuries.

'I'm not.' Anna's voice rang back, strong but not angry. Simply sure. 'You know I was born a Raymond. My hair, my skin, are my father's, and my name is my father's. I do have, however, Castlavaran powers and for the next nineteen years there's nothing I can do about that.'

'You're doing all you can.' That was Carla, calling out from the front pew. 'You're giving us so much.'

'I'm not giving,' Anna said. 'I'm returning. And I want to return so much more. But you'll all know there's much I can't do. The Trust prevents it. In nineteen and a half years, though, the Trust will end and the island will pass into the control of the islanders. Your land will be your own. That's a promise I can make, I do make, but with Leo's help I can do so much more.'

'Like what?' It was the belligerent fisherman again.

'Like become one of you.' She spoke softly now, tentatively. Every islander had to strain to hear, but the acoustics of the church were such that each word still hung there. 'And that's what I need to be, an islander with islander concerns. The Trust says castle funds can be used for my comfort and enjoyment. That's how we got the castle medical centre. It's supposedly for my personal enjoyment because I'm a doctor, and how can I enjoy myself without a top-quality medical centre?

'But we need a home medical service as well, and how do I justify that to the Trust? We need good schools, a new harbour, sealed roads. We need transport for our olive crops. We need light industry, places where our fish, our olives can be processed so we can reap the profits. We need tourist infrastructure. We need jobs to stop our children leaving the island. We need so much.'

She turned then toward Donna, and for a moment she spoke only to that lady.

'Donna, you've worked hard and long for this island,' she told her. 'I've heard the stories. But overriding everything else, every decision you've taken was for your love of your family. For this island. And Leo's the same.

His love for his father…the pain his death caused and the ripples of that spreading through his life… They've all helped to make him the man I know he is. He's devoted to you and to each and every person here. So that's why I'm standing here now. That's what I want for myself. Indeed, that's what I want for the whole island, and the thought of continuing without it is unbearable.'

She had them now. The blustering fisherman was looking at her through narrowed eyes. He was still suspicious, as surely every islander was suspicious—generations of mistrust couldn't be undone in a moment—but there was a collective waiting. *Wait and see…*

She glanced at Leo then, in her eyes a question, but her glance was fleeting, almost as if she was afraid of the answer she'd be given. And then she forged on.

'So here's my suggestion,' she said, and suddenly there was a tremor in her voice. The first sign of doubt? 'The Aretinos are a huge family. Leo is an only child but he has aunts, uncles, cousins, a family with members that must reach into almost every family on Tovahna. And because I love Leo, his concerns are my concerns. Donna, your concerns have become my concerns. Tovahna is becoming my family.'

But once again there was a moment when suspicion reigned. Leo was no longer sure where this was going but he saw the stillness, the closing of faces, the generations of mistreatment spreading its fog throughout.

But Anna saw it and faced it square on.

'That's why I'm here, now,' she said. 'If my family was a family such as the Aretinos, I'd love all my family and the Trust couldn't argue that my family's welfare wasn't a cause of my comfort and enjoyment. If my large and extended family can't access good schools, if my cousins can't fish safely, if the children of my family can't access good jobs…how can I be happy?'

They were starting to see it. There was the faintest lightening of expression on the sharpest of the islanders' faces.

Leo was before them. His grip on Anna's hand tightened still further and he tried to tug her to face him but she wouldn't have it. Her feet were planted squarely and her face spoke of determination to see this through to the end.

'Once upon a time Dr Leo Aretino asked me to marry him.' She was deliberately not looking at him, speaking only to the islanders. 'He turned away because of his love for this island. I've been here now for six months and I've learned to love it as well. Not only that, I've learned that my love for Leo hasn't faded.'

'So marry him.' It was Carla, of course it was Carla. 'Marry him, Anna. You have our blessing.'

'I have your blessing, Carla,' Anna said gently. 'But I need more. So this is what I'm saying. My mother was born a Castlavaran and she rejected the name. I was born a Raymond but that name means nothing to me. Now… what I want, what I believe Leo wants, and I hope… Donna, I hope you want it, too… What I believe the islanders *need* is for the name of Castlavara to be finally finished. Ended. And for the islanders to take over the island as they should. Legally we can't do that for nineteen years but do we need to wait that long? All it takes is a name change. All it takes is for one man to take one woman as his wife.'

'Anna…' It was too much. Leo broke his silence and tugged her around so she was facing him. 'What are you saying?'

'I'm asking,' she said simply. 'But not you, Leo, be-

cause you're too honourable, too worried about your islanders, your family. Your mother said to me last night…
"If I could see a way…" Those were her words, and I hope
she'll back me up now. With her help, I'm seeing a way.
So now I'm asking the islanders.'

She met his gaze full on. Something passed between
them. Something good. Something sure. Something that
could last…for ever?

She smiled, the faintest of smiles, and turned back to
the congregation.

'Ten years ago Leo asked me to become an Aretino,'
she told them. 'So I ask now, in Donna's presence, with
the man I love beside me, in the presence of every islander who could be here today, would you accept me
into Leo's family? Would you have Leo—and Donna,
too, for the time she has left to us—come and live in
our vast island castle? Live there we must for another
nineteen years if we're not to break the Trust, but will
you let us work from there for the good of the islanders?
Would you have me marry this man and be an islander
and—with our marriage—let the name Castlavara disappear for ever?'

Silence. Total silence.

The stillness seemed almost deafening. It went on and
on, as each islander thought of what they'd just heard.

Then there were mutterings. Whispers. Nudging.

And then suddenly Carla was on her feet. 'Come on,
you cowards, just do it,' she called.

And Donna, astonishingly strong, was calling from
the side, 'My loves, you have my blessing.'

And then someone started to clap—and amazingly it
was the belligerent fisherman. And then a child clapped,
because maybe children clapped when they weren't sure
if they should follow or not.

And what followed… Every single islander was on his or her feet and the applause was almost deafening. The priest was surging forward to bless them, smiling on this the most solemn of occasions.

And Leo was looking at this woman he loved with wonder. With disbelief.

With joy.

He kissed her. Of course he kissed her—and the thing was done. She'd come home. And then somehow he put her back, at arm's length and the look on her face said it all.

Yet still he asked.

'Anna, I deserted you ten years ago… Will you come back to me?'

'Truly, I don't think I've ever left.'

'So you'll still marry me?'

'It would be my honour.'

'Now?'

And the sounds around them seemed to still again, fading to nothing. There was just this man, this woman and all the love in the world between them.

'Oh, Leo…' She was half laughing, half crying. 'Of course I'll marry you. Yesterday if you want.'

And then she was back in his arms and he was turning to the priest, who looked bewildered at this spectacular turn of events.

'Father…'

And the elderly priest suddenly realised what was being asked. His bewilderment turned to a beam a mile wide.

'Yes, my son?'

'I know it's common for banns to be called,' Leo said. 'And for all sorts of formalities to take place before a wedding. But ten years ago I asked Anna Raymond to be my wife and she said yes. Would a ten-year engagement count as replacement for formalities? Would you marry us now?'

He turned back to Anna. 'If that's what you want, my love? Could you bear to marry without the full bridal? Could you marry me right now?'

And she was laughing, hauling the tie from her hair so her curls sprang free. Tugging off her grey jacket and tossing it to the side.

'How can you doubt it?' she asked, and she smiled and smiled. Her face was bright with love and laughter. 'A wedding. Now? Why not? I have everything I need. I think.' But then she wrinkled her nose. 'Flowers, though? Every bride I've ever seen has flowers.' But her eyes were laughing and he knew that flowers or not, their wedding was a done deal.

But flowers happened. The priest headed purposely toward once of the wall sconces, lifted out one of the sheaths of wild roses and proceeded to wrap the stems in an embroidered cloth covering a side table. The cloth was possibly as ancient as the church itself, but the priest obviously had different priorities.

'Here, my daughter,' he said, and then he fixed Leo with a stern look. 'What else? Rings? Do we have rings?'

Only about a hundred were offered on the instant.

But Leo shook his head as offers came from everywhere. He smiled at Anna and that smile, oh, it was just for her.

'I have two rings,' he told her. 'An engagement ring that was handed back to me ten years ago, and a wedding ring we bought at the same time. They've been in my wallet every moment since.'

They needed no more. They could do the legal formalities later.

'You have everything you need, then,' the priest said. 'If you're both sure…'

'We're sure,' they said in unison.

'Then let's do it,' the priest said, and smiled and smiled, and he turned back to the congregation. 'Dearly beloved…we are gathered here today…'

And thus they were married.

The vows were made. Leo took his bride out into the morning sunshine. Every rose in the church was stripped to produce petals to throw.

Anna hardly noticed, for Leo's hand held hers, and every islander knew that her hand would be in his for ever.

CHAPTER TWELVE

Nineteen and a half years later

THE PLANE WAS about to leave and Dr Anna Aretino was a sodden mess. She'd been sobbing since she'd woken this morning and her husband wasn't much better. Leo was just holding it together.

The two girls reached the top of the plane steps and turned to wave. These were the Aretino twins, non-identical, one a dark-haired beauty, the other redheaded, vivacious, gorgeous. The only thing identical about them was their smiles, both a mile wide.

'I can't believe they're going.' Anna was tucked under Leo's arm, hugging and being hugged, sniffing into his oversized handkerchief.

'Mama, leave it off.'

At fifteen, Georg was showing every sign of being just as good looking as his father—once he lost the braces from his teeth. He was currently waving to his sisters, but he was also laughing at his parents.

'Look at you both. Your daughters have scholarships to the same medical school you went to. They're off to see the world. They're so happy they're practically sickening, and you know they'll be back at first term break—and the next term break—and the one after. And they're already planning careers here. You don't get rid of kids from this island. You know we'll always want to come back.'

Anna had a final sniff and returned the handkerchief to her husband's pocket. Her son was right, they would be back.

This island was home.

'And now it's time we did what we promised to do all those years ago,' Leo said softly. 'It's a shame the girls' term started so early they couldn't stay to see this through, but the rest of us… Come on, Georg. Ready, my love?'

She was ready. Georg was right, her daughters were launching themselves into the world and she should feel nothing but joy for them. On this day of all days, she should feel joy for all the island.

And in the end what followed was almost an anticlimax. The lawyers' documents were ready to sign. Names, dates, signatures, witnesses and the thing was done.

Tovahna belonged to the people.

'Terrific,' Georg said in the tone of a long-suffering teenager who'd been dragged along to something that didn't interest him. 'Now can I go to football?'

So he was left at the football grounds and Drs Leo and Anna Aretino made their way back to the castle.

The castle was, after all, their home. Their massive apartment would stay in their name. A smallholding of beach-side farmland on the far side of the island—once worked by Leo's great-grandfather—was also retained. The rest was either transferred to the islanders whose home it was, or held as public property to be administered by the island council.

The battlements of the castle were thus no longer Anna's property but they hadn't been used as such for years. They were now, and into perpetuity, available to the patients, residents, staff of Tovahna's world-class medical centre.

For this day, though, it had been decreed that for one last time the battlements would revert to being Leo and Anna's own space. They'd asked for privacy and they had it.

So without children, without any encumbrances— apart from two doofus dogs because dogs had always been and would always be a part of their lives—they made their way to where they'd stood so long ago, looking out over the sea beyond their island home.

As they reached the parapets Leo took his wife into his arms and kissed her. It was a long, steadying kiss. It was a kiss that grounded them in the knowledge that what they had was wonderful. What they had was family, home and joy in spades.

'We've done it,' Anna murmured, when there was time and space to speak. 'Our family's launched onto a new and exciting path, and Tovahna finally belongs to our people.'

'*You've* done it,' Leo told her, kissing her ear. 'My lady of the castle. The last of the Castlavarans.'

'That's not who I am,' she said contentedly. 'I'm the wife of Dr Leo Aretino. I'm the mother of three gorgeous children. I'm the shared head of a dynasty of dumb dogs and I'm a family doctor to any islander who wants to use me. Castlavara? As of today it's a name that's forgotten. Leo, we have done right, haven't we?'

'I can't think of anything we could have done better,' he told her, and he kissed her again. 'Tomorrow the islanders will receive their land titles, but it hardly matters any more. You gave the island back to the people twenty years ago.'

'*We* gave it back. If I hadn't met you…if I hadn't fallen in love with you…'

'It doesn't bear thinking of,' he said. 'But now…we've asked for privacy for this one last time. Complete privacy. Are you thinking what I'm thinking?'

'Yes, but the windows…'

'I decreed that, too,' he said smugly. 'The battlements are to be ours for this final day, and the deal is that every window facing east shall have its blinds firmly drawn.'

'People will cheat,' Anna told him. 'If I was told to pull my blinds and not look then I'd cheat.'

'Then the islanders are about to be shocked.' Leo was already tugging her away from the parapets, down the stairs toward the beach below. 'Twenty years ago I swam almost naked with you, my love, and I almost made love to you. For twenty years I've been regretting that "almost". After today the islanders have the right to be here any time they want, but today it's ours, my lady. So what do you say? A swim and whatever comes after?'

'What's happened until now has been wonderful enough,' she told him, smiling and smiling, and she was already unbuttoning her blouse as they headed downstairs.

'It was simply a forerunner,' Leo told her. He turned in the stairwell and tugged her back into his arms, to kiss her, hard and strong. 'A family, an island, a nation… Why do I believe the best is yet to come?'

And then they reached the beach. Their clothes were gone. They dived into the sapphire water and started the long swim out to 'their' rock.

And if the islanders were shocked, then that was their problem, because Leo's belief was proven most definitely right.

* * * * *

TAKING A CHANCE ON THE SINGLE DAD

SUE MacKAY

MILLS & BOON

This one's for Lynne Mark.
Thank you for your wonderful support of my stories.

TAKING A CHANCE
ON THE SINGLE DAD

SUE MACKAY

MILLS & BOON

PROLOGUE

LEADEN SILENCE CRACKLED down the line, turning the arm-chair Brenna had inherited from her grandmother from snug and comfortable to something resembling a hard plinth beneath the suddenly tense muscles of her bottom.

'Hunter? I said I'm missing you.'

'Missing you too, Bren.'

The tension didn't back off. It ramped up. That was not the voice her fiancé used with her. At least that was what he would be if they actually openly acknowledged they were getting married next summer, and if they finally got around to choosing a ring to validate their en-during love for each other.

But Hunter seemed to have a lot on his mind at the moment that had nothing to do with them.

'Tell me what's happening in Kamloops. How're your parents?' she asked.

Again, that awkward silence. They didn't do silences—usually had too much to say to each other.

'Hunter? You're scaring me.'

'Hold on, will you?'

In the background she heard a door open, then shut, followed by footsteps on a wooden floor. Was he on the deck? Winter in the Okanagan wasn't even close to tropical. What he had to tell her must be something he didn't want his family to overhear.

Was his father in a worse state than his mother had indicated yesterday? All he'd said was that she had been in hysterics when she'd rung, saying the family orchard was in crisis and he had to get over there urgently for his father's sake. He'd left Vancouver within three hours, an overnight bag and his laptop over his shoulder, despair in his eyes and a one-way air ticket in his hand. He hadn't driven as snow had been forecast near the Rockies.

'Bren, I was going to ring you later tonight. Everything's in turmoil here.' The harshness of his voice frightened her.

What was going on?

Talk to me.

But if she demanded information from him, he'd shut down. Shut down? It seemed he was already under lock and key. She looked around the familiar, cosy sitting room of the house she'd grown up in, her gaze not alighting on any one object for more than a few seconds, her heart pounding faster by the minute.

Finally she had to say something or go spare. 'Do you want me to come across for the weekend?'

'Bren, I don't know where to start. Dad's—'

She heard him swallow, and a gnawing feeling there was bad to come began deep in her stomach.

'The business is on the verge of bankruptcy. I don't know if it can be saved. The insurance company's fighting paying out for the flood damage done last year. The same thing's happening with many of the orchards in this area. I haven't gone into the paperwork yet, but people are muttering about the company that owns the power station being at fault.'

'Can't the insurance company pay out and then go to

the power provider for the money?' Of course she knew that wasn't how these things worked, but anything to delay whatever was about to slam-dunk her.

'Insurance companies are not charities. If there's an out they're going to take it, and to hell with what Dad's been paying them over the years.'

The bitterness in Hunter's voice shocked her. But he was loyal to his parents so their troubles would be his, regardless of his own aspirations. Just like her and her family, especially her dad. She'd always been encouraged to follow her dreams.

'I guess I'm aware of that. I was hoping for more, that's all.' A fairer outcome for Hunter's family and a happy improvement in the way he was talking right now wouldn't go amiss.

'There's a lot to do here.'

Here it comes. Brenna waited, tensing as though Hunter had a gun aimed directly at her chest. More specifically, her heart.

'Dad's worried he's failed again. It's like he doesn't know what to focus on to get things sorted.'

Brenna swallowed hard. There was more to this—but what? 'Darling, I'm so sorry. What can I do? For you?'

The sound of a long indrawn breath had her fingers gripping the phone, her thighs tight.

She hurried to add, 'I'll come at the end of my shift tomorrow night to be with you. I'll pack more of your clothes too. Let me know what else you need. I can fill the car till there's no room left but for me. Fingers crossed the storm will have passed through by then.'

'No, Brenna. You can't come. There's nothing you can do here.'

'I can support you—be *with* you. I love you. You know that.'

'Yes, I do.'

Was that resentment in his quietly spoken words?

'Hunter?' Now her toes were tucking under and her knees were pushing together. There was ice in the air, yet the heat pump was blasting out a toasty twenty-two degrees.

He was dragging in a lungful of air. Then, 'The only thing I want you to do for me is pack up all my gear and send it across. I am not returning to Vancouver.'

'But what about your job? Your study?' *Me?* 'Vancouver's your happy place. You've said so a hundred times. We're a couple—we stick together through everything. I'll do whatever it takes to help you through this.'

'I have to move back to the orchard. It's the only chance there is to make the place viable again. Mum and Dad need my support to get through this.'

Did he mutter *again*?

'It's not the first time I've had to step up for them.'

'What do you mean?'

'It's how our family works. Ever since that quad-bike accident they've made me think I owe them for the trouble it's caused and that I can never repay them, but I keep trying.'

Hunter had just stolen any words she might have been about to utter. Their relationship wasn't being taken into consideration. Not at all.

'Hunter, we're a couple—for better and for worse,' she gasped through frozen lips.

It was happening again. Someone else she loved was deserting her.

'Would you pack up and move out here to join me?' he whispered.

Anger flared. How dared he ask her that? 'You know

I would—after I've finished my exams and when my dad's…'

The thumping in her chest slowed, creating a pain under her ribs and a knot in her belly. *Dad*. Her mainstay as she'd grown up trying to understand how her mother could leave and never contact her again. Not once.

'Oh.'

'Exactly. We've both got too many commitments. I don't want you putting aside your medical degree for me either. You're an amazing doctor, Bren, and you have to finish what you've started.'

Did he have to be so nice when he was breaking her heart?

'As for leaving your father now that he's been diagnosed with dementia—that's not happening. Not on my account. Nor can I see you doing it. Not easily, any rate.'

He had her there. Damn him. Tears spilled down her cheeks and she ignored them. Her dad needed her, along with her stepmum and half-sisters. She couldn't walk away from being there for them through this black time. All the love he'd spoiled her with since her mother had run away had got her through the bad times; she intended doing the same for him.

But she loved Hunter. He was her mainstay. They were supposed to be getting married when she qualified. Hunter loved her. He'd said so often. Yes, he did love her. There'd never been anything false about his declarations. They could make this work. They *had* to.

'Brenna, there's no easy way to say this so I'll be blunt. We are finished. We have to be. We can't hang in limbo for the next however many years, until my family is back on track or things have changed for you. I am truly sorry, but there is no alternative.'

When Hunter called her Brenna there was no arguing

with him. She'd tried and failed too often to risk it now. Though what more did she have to lose? Seemed she'd just lost the love of her life.

There was nothing else essential other than breathing. Dragging in air to make sure her lungs were still working, she closed her eyes and strove for something to make this all go away.

Not happening.

She could go crazy: cry and yell, plead and beg. Or she could dig deep for dignity, and not make Hunter glad he'd called it quits.

'Bad timing, huh?' she sniffed.

'The absolute worst, sweetheart.'

The endearment curdled Hunter's stomach. Brenna was the love of his life, the sunshine and the warmth, the reason he worked so hard to put aside money, so he'd be able to buy a home for her—for them—in the near future.

You don't have a future with Bren any more.

The urge to hurl the phone across the yard had his arm lifting. He needed to hear it smash into a thousand pieces just as his heart was doing. But he held on so tight his fingernails were digging deep into his palms, the harsh edge of the instrument pressing into his ear.

It was the most awful timing possible to have this happen to his parents, to Brenna, to him. Bren didn't know about his father's mental instability in times of crisis. Neither did she know how controlling and selfish his parents had been with him as he'd been growing up, and that that had been his reason for moving to Vancouver. He'd thought he'd escaped, that they'd finally accepted he had his own life to live. He'd been wrong, had been drawn in once more to straighten out their messed-up lives regardless of his aspirations.

It was an insurmountable problem he couldn't find a way around. He'd never forgive himself if he remained in Vancouver and his father carried out his threat to take his own life. And Brenna could not leave her father when he had dementia. Even with her stepmum and sisters there supporting him, Brenna was so close to her father she wouldn't dream of moving away. Neither could he ask her to put her medical degree on hold with less than a year to go. He'd never forgive himself when she came to resent him for requesting that. It was bad enough his own paramedic training was going on the back burner.

'Hunter? Stay in touch. Please.'

That would hurt worse than anything. To see Bren, talk to her, and not be able to share the future they'd started planning together would be hell on wheels. 'No. I can't do that. It has to be a clean break. Over and done as of now. So sorry, Bren, I really am.'

Do it. Now. Before you lose the courage.

'Goodbye.' His finger stabbed the off button, remained stuck to it, as though preventing him ever hearing from Bren again.

No woman had made him so happy and carefree and yet so determined to succeed. No woman, no person, had believed in him as much as Bren had. Her only expectations had been that he be himself, believe in himself and follow his own dreams—something his parents had never allowed.

He loved her beyond all reason, and yet he'd just put her aside for his family's problems. Old habits did not disappear in a cloud of happiness after all. If only he could be that man Bren believed in. If only he could make his parents understand he'd been trying to help the day when he'd overheard his father bemoaning how he couldn't shift the cattle himself because of his headaches.

Hunter had taken the quad bike out to round up the cattle and shift them to a field on the side of the hill. It had gone well until a bull had charged the bike. Only eleven, he hadn't been able to control the heavy machine and it had rolled, leaving him with a smashed leg and angry parents who'd said he'd made things worse for them by not being available to help around the orchard while his bones healed. From then on, they'd continued to make him pay for his misdemeanour with more and more demands.

None of this made tonight's decision about his relationship with Brenna easy. This time his father had threatened to swallow a bottle of paracetamol, and as he'd done it once before they couldn't take any chances. Not that he was telling Bren about his father's mental state. She might start watching him to see if he was unstable too. Not that she'd be seeing him again. He had to remain strong about that. He loved Bren with every fibre of his body.

His only hope was that by doing the right thing for his parents it would keep him focused in the months ahead when the going got tough. Because it was going to. Not a doubt in the universe. His own plans and needs and love would be shelved. Didn't mean he had the right to ask Brenna to put hers alongside his.

The phone lit up. Bren's number came up on the screen. Then the ringing began. He pressed Off. She tried again. And again.

Then Hunter did hurl the phone with all the frustrated strength he had. It soared over the back yard, across the fence to land with a splash in the trough.

'Goodbye, Bren. Love you.'

The back of his hand slashed at his face as he hunched over, letting the rain soak his clothes, chill his skin further. Not caring what happened to him. But he had to. He was needed here. There was no choice.

CHAPTER ONE

Six years later...

HUNTER FORD LEANED his shoulder against the doorframe and watched his son's tiny chest lift and fall under the light bedcover as he slept, and sighed with relief. 'You're happier already, aren't you, my boy?' he whispered through a thick throat.

Dylan's grandparents had already started grooming him to be compliant by having him running around after them for the hell of it—something he hadn't been able to prevent on the days he worked and Dylan didn't have preschool.

'You could learn something from him,' Jess murmured beside him. 'Stop worrying so much.'

'You haven't met Brenna.'

'Surely she's not going to kick your butt—verbally or physically?' Dave's wife never felt the need to hold back.

'I'd handle that.' Might even welcome it. But getting the cold shoulder from Bren would punch him hard. Neither did he relish the idea of being treated like a special friend who needed taking in hand to learn the ropes at the helicopter rescue base. Brenna Williamson. He knew nothing about what she'd been doing since that heartbreaking phone call. Had deliberately shut down on anyone telling him about her. He'd had to or go insane with grief.

Jess swiped his arm. 'It's been a long time. You've moved on, so will she have. Anyway, you can cope with anything. Look at Dylan. After everything he's been through, he's happy because of you.'

Hunter's gaze was still fixed on that small body in the large bed, despite the picture of Bren in the forefront of his brain. 'He trusts me to get it right for him.'

'Get it right for yourself and the rest will follow.'

'Is that your way of saying that if I'm happy Dylan will be happy?' That was Jess all over. But, then, she was a psychologist.

'At last something's got into that dense brain matter. Now get a move on. You're due at the base in twenty-five minutes, and even at five-thirty in the morning traffic around Kitsilano is more than what you're used to.'

'On my way.' So much for having breakfast before he hit the road. He'd spent ten minutes watching and absorbing the sight of his son sleeping; Dylan was his world, and one of the reasons he'd returned to the city where he'd been happiest. The first time he'd moved here had been within weeks of leaving high school; his best friend, Dave, right beside him. They were going to conquer the world and put Kamloops into the only-for-visiting-the-olds file.

He'd truly believed he'd escaped his parents. More fool him. His dreams had begun falling into place, then his father had had yet another mental breakdown and he'd been expected to pick up the pieces. Now here he was back again, the dreams altered but still there. Everything he did, worked for, would be about Dylan, not his parents, other than to make sure they were safe and comfortable. His son was not growing up under the weight of his parents' selfishness.

At last he'd learned to stop feeling guilty every time his father got ill. It wasn't his fault, and he shouldn't be expected to give up his life to fix their problems when they weren't prepared to try and sort things out themselves.

Oh, just call Hunter, get him to do it.

Hunter swallowed hard. Coming here had been the right thing to do. For his boy, and for him. Time to start over with a clean slate. There'd be memories of Bren around every corner, which he'd have to ignore once he got today done and dusted. He was under no illusion. Seeing her for the first time would be difficult. Yet it had to be done, then he'd get on with settling into Vancouver, the place where he'd been so very happy so long ago.

Not that he was the young guy any more who laughed at everything, thought the world owed him, and believed there might be a chance that if he worked hard enough, he might achieve the life he wanted. No, but something from that time lingered and had drawn him back, away from Kamloops and the darkness and frustration that lurked around every corner.

Straightening up, he took one last look at his boy and strode away, his eyes moist. At the front door he paused, said, without looking back, 'Jess? Go easy on him if he gets upset today, will you?' It wasn't Jess who needed reminding Dylan stressed at new settings with new people. It was him who needed reassuring that everyone had Dylan's back while he went to work. Deep down he understood Dave and his family were there for his son. It was just that he needed reassurance that he had done the right thing, coming to Vancouver.

'Get out of here, will you? I'm going back to bed to

snuggle up to my man for half an hour. *When* you get out of my hair.'

Hunter was pushed out the door, and the lock clicked behind him.

'I'm going, all right?' Not that Jess would hear, but habit had him getting the last word in. Zipping his puffer jacket up to his chin, Hunter slid behind the wheel of his four-wheel drive and backed down the drive.

'Here I go.' He headed to SW Marine Drive, trying to ignore the confusion in his head, and failing. Shortly he was going to see Brenna, hear her voice, her laugh, and he had no idea how he'd react. He wanted to be cool, calm and friendly. That's how he should be after all this time. Once they hadn't been able to get enough of each other, had believed the future was theirs for the taking. Hunter shook his head abruptly in an attempt to banish those memories, which were probably rose-tinted anyway. He was meant to be looking forward, to settling down in a city he loved, to a life he chose and not one dictated by guilt and strained loyalties.

When he'd decided to make the move west, he'd thought through all the consequences and while accepting he'd once loved Brenna more than life itself, he believed she wasn't going to be a problem—if he ever saw her. At the time he hadn't known he'd end up working alongside her for four weeks.

He should've turned down the request to work on the emergency helicopters the moment he'd heard her name. Hard to do when the base director had all but gone down on bended knees begging him to give whatever time he could manage, they were that short-staffed. Anyway, he loved emergency medicine. The adrenalin shot when racing out to an accident always made him feel needed and happy to be helping people.

The position he was taking up next month at Vancouver General would have plenty of those moments, but there was something about getting into an ambulance and racing to help someone. Since arriving in town he'd been walking on hot coals every day with nothing more to do than wait for his hospital job to start and to move into his house on the settlement date. With Dylan happy at his new preschool he was redundant for hours.

Jess had told him about the rescue service's need for a temporary paramedic and had offered to look after his son before and after school if he took it up. She was probably sick of him hanging around the house during the day.

The airport loomed ahead far too quickly, and Hunter was pulling into the rescue centre long before he'd prepared himself. Bren wasn't just a part of his past. She was still real, and, for a few weeks at least, a piece of his life again. Hopefully she was still always late to everything, and he'd get a few more minutes to pull himself together.

His palms were damp on the steering wheel. His ears filled with a thumping sound coming from behind his ribs. Was she as beautiful as he recalled? Would that regret over what they'd lost, which he'd felt the day he'd married Dylan's mother, return?

Would Brenna shoot him on sight just for turning up?

Hunter put the gear stick in Reverse. He was out of there. Doing a runner. He'd head for the hills until it was time to pick Dylan up.

His foot remained on the brake pedal. He had to stay and go into the hangar, sign on and do his job. Twelve hours and he'd be able to quit—until tomorrow, when it would be a little bit easier. The ice would be broken. With a sigh he turned the ignition off. Since when had he become so gutless?

Stepping inside the cavernous hangar, he headed in

the direction of the voices coming through an open door. Kevin, the base commander, and— He stopped. It was Bren's voice he was hearing. His skin tightened. Brenna. Not Bren. Those days were gone, over, finished, because he might stumble in his determination to make this move work if he allowed any feelings from the past to beat him around the head. As were the days over when he dropped everything and everybody to be there for his parents. He did love them, but they weren't playing the guilt card any more.

Brenna was saying, 'Sorry I'm late. A burst water main on my avenue had traffic diverted all over the show.' A metal locker door banged shut.

'You're fine. Nothing's happening so far,' Kevin said.

She thought arriving right on time was late? Change number one.

'Good. I want to go online and book the car onto the ferry before it's too late. When I got home late from Whistler last night I was exhausted and figured I'd find time today. Mum was supposed to do it but she ran out of time too. She's busier than ever now she's retired.' Brenna laughed.

That laugh, warm and endearing, and much too familiar, crunched Hunter's gut. His feet dragged towards the doorway, her voice winding around him, reminding him of sultry nights between the sheets. Spinning around to run for the car park was tempting. Instead he clenched his hands and tightened his leg muscles. Running wouldn't solve a thing. Beneath his ribs a heavy thudding felt as though he was being beaten with a stick.

This was far more difficult than he'd believed. The past would be harder to ascend than Mount Baker, and it seemed Brenna still had the power to make him *aware* of her. Right down to his toes. He'd once loved her with all his being. Now he didn't. Didn't? Or shouldn't? His mouth dried. He still loved Bren? Had he been in denial all along? No. He couldn't have. Then why these wild emotions brought out by the sound of her voice?

'Find anyone to cover for Patch while that broken femur heals?' she was querying.

'Yes. I heard about the man who's taking over as head nurse at the hospital's emergency department next month. He's had experience as an ambulance paramedic. Figured I had nothing to lose by approaching to see if he'd help us out. He was more than happy, which takes the pressure off for now.'

I'd still be a full-time paramedic if I'd been able to make the hours work around Dylan.

Hunter stopped in the doorway. Exhaled hard. His gaze was rooted to the woman before him. Beautiful, still as curvy. Those caramel eyes still sparkled with fun, her crazy curly auburn hair was still long and tied back in a ponytail, her mouth still soft and enticing and undeniable. Bren, as he remembered her, as he'd loved her. *Brenna.*

Tying up her bootlaces, she laughed. 'The man never stood a chance once you got your teeth into him. Who is he? Anyone we know?'

That beating against Hunter's ribs became a whipping. On a deep breath he stepped right into the room.

Kevin said, 'Probably not. He's shifted across from Kamloops. Name of Hunter—'

'Ford,' Brenna finished as she stared at the sexy apparition strolling towards her with all the panache of someone totally at ease with his world. Her head spun. This wasn't a vision brought on by a restless night. Only one man she knew swung his left leg slightly outward as he walked, thanks to a quad-bike accident as a kid. 'Hunter, what are you doing here?' she squeaked, thoughtlessly launching herself at her past.

'Hey, Brenna. Great to see you too. *Oof.*' He put his hands on her shoulders, keeping her from plastering her body all over him.

'I can't believe it's you.' Damn it, she was pushing close, wanting to lay her face against his chest like she'd always done back when they'd been together. Then reality got in the way. She jerked backwards. Hunter had dumped her. He hadn't wanted her any more.

Hunter gazed down at her, not a hint of enthusiasm in his eyes. 'You're looking good.'

Brenna took his reaction on board and reacted accordingly. 'Why wouldn't I?' He wasn't about to find out how hard it had been to get over him. 'You've scrubbed up okay yourself.'

The boyish good looks of six years ago had hardened into a strong, handsome face. Looking closer, she noted the weariness blinking out from those steel-grey eyes where there used to be laughter shining. Then his apathy registered. They were not lovers, not even friends, nothing but colleagues for the next few weeks. Brain slap for being such an idiot. Throwing herself at Hunter like she'd been waiting for this moment, like she had to have him, was ridiculous.

Stepping away, she flattened her mouth, swallowed her annoyance at having been so stupid. This was the man who'd *phoned* to say that after three years together they were over. Finished. Told her to go get a life and forget him.

What did people say when they first met each other after a long time apart? With their history? She said tartly, 'So you've returned to Vancouver.' Hope fluttered awake. She squashed it. *Don't go there.*

Hunter's hands fell to his sides as he too took a backward step. 'Yes.' This man used to talk non-stop, not coming up for air for hours.

His reticence spurred her on. 'How long have you been in town?'

Why haven't you got in touch? This is me, us. I'm not going to blast your head off for walking away from what we had going. Or am I?

Six years ago, she'd wanted to, but not now. What was the point? It couldn't be undone. Except there was a flame of attraction scorching her inside and out.

He left you. Don't forget that.

Like she could.

'We arrived ten days ago.'

We? Brenna stepped further away; widening the gap physically, if not mentally.

I threw myself at him as though we were still an item.

He had a significant other half in his life, and she'd done that. Her stomach shrivelled and all the moisture evaporated from her mouth. Her chest lifted, stayed there as a breath stuck in her throat.

I didn't stop to think. Instead, the moment I saw Hunter I reacted like I used to. How bad is that?

Now he'd get the wrong idea. 'How are your parents?' Banal but safe. Unless… The air finally whooshed out of her lungs. 'Sorry.'

'They're fine, living in a retirement village. Mum's having a wonderful time. Even Dad's happy. The orchard sold last year.' Hunter didn't look overly thrilled, but then he hadn't looked too happy about anything so far. Including her. He hadn't been surprised to see her. So, he'd known she worked here and had still taken the job.

Her teeth gnashed. He'd signed on despite the fact this was her space. About to spew her sudden anger at him, she bit down, kept herself under tight control. Having a spat wouldn't change a thing, only make the coming weeks even more awkward than they were going to be. 'That's great.' It was far from great, but it was better than saying what was really on her mind.

Kevin interrupted, looking pleased with himself. 'So, you two know each other.' Rostering staff problem solved?

Oh, no. She usually paired with Patch. She wasn't working with Hunter. 'It was a long time ago.' Hunter was back in town. For how long this time? How *permanent* was his permanent job at the emergency department? Why did she even care? He wasn't alone any more. Even if he had been, it still wouldn't matter. She was not revisiting their relationship. He'd broken her heart once; she wasn't handing it over to be devastated a second time.

'Then you'll have plenty to catch up on. Good thing I've rostered you together this week.'

Brenna tightened her mouth against protesting, and instead managed to say in a semi-steady voice, 'There'll be opportunities to talk over the coming weeks.' Though hearing what Hunter had been up to since they'd split might help soften the blow seeing him had inflicted, she did not need to learn how in love he was with another woman.

She stared at this man she'd once believed would share her life right through to the rocking-chair days. The good looks that had women falling at his feet were still there, somewhat jaded now, but somehow that made her soften towards him. Silly woman. Note that wariness in his gaze. It was foreign to her. Seemed the years away hadn't been kind to him. Through a sigh she asked, 'Want a coffee before our first callout?'

That tiredness dipped further, tightened his face before he rallied. 'Sure do. Might try to have my breakfast since I ran out of time at home.' He shrugged off the small pack slung over his shoulder.

Heading for the kitchen, she asked, trying to sound, oh, so uninterested, 'Is this a long-term move?' Again, the question arose—how permanent was permanent in his book? At her side her fingers crossed. She wanted him to stay? Or to be heading away again? It wasn't as though they would kick-start their relationship. That was finished. Besides, even if Hunter was available, she wasn't prepared to get involved only to find herself coming second to someone or something else again. She'd learned that lesson the first time.

Hunter answered in a manner suggesting he was wondering how much to say. 'The plan's to settle here long term. I've bought a house in Kitsilano and take it over in a fortnight.'

She gasped. Of all the places to move to. Not only was Hunter back in town, but he was right on her doorstep, apparently settling in for the foreseeable future. *Not fair.* Once more she struggled for calm. 'I can't believe you're here.' True. 'What've you been up to?' Truly? She wanted to know? No. Well, maybe. Depended on what he had to say.

'Nothing out of the ordinary,' was Hunter's acerbic reply. Followed by, 'I didn't expect to find you working on the choppers.'

'Why not?' she snapped, before engaging her brain. *Don't let Hunter see how rattled you are.*

Sure. Like that would work. This was the guy who could read her without a glance. Hopefully he'd lost that ability when he'd pulled the plug on their relationship.

'More than anything you wanted to be head of an emergency department before you were thirty-three.'

He remembered. Why wouldn't he? She *had* been driven about getting that position. Until they'd broken up and restless energy had overtaken her. Then she'd needed something more to her life than working in an emergency department. Not that that wasn't drama personified, but she'd wanted something for herself and, adding in her passion for adventure photography, flipping around the sky in helicopters and whipping down hillsides on skis or a mountain bike had given what she'd hankered after. It made her feel exciting and not a woman intent on studying and being the best doctor with nothing else to her name. 'I changed my mind.'

Tilting his head slightly to one side, he said, 'I hope you haven't regretted that. You were so determined I thought nothing else would do.' Was there a hint of annoyance in that? Surely, he wasn't thinking she could've moved to Kamloops to be with him instead?

'Not once. Because it was easier on Mum being where she could reach me at all times, I continued working in the emergency room until Dad died three years ago.' After her dad had gone her restlessness had become impossible to live with and that's when she'd gone in search of adventure.

'I heard about your dad. I'm sorry.'

'He lasted longer than expected.' Dementia was so tough. 'It wasn't nice towards the end.' A familiar sadness rubbed at her. She hated that it had been a relief when her father had left them, but he'd have detested what his life had been reduced to if he'd been aware.

'Dave told me. I would've come to the funeral but thought it might be inappropriate.' Hunter watched her too closely.

She nodded once. It would've been. 'How is Dave?'

'Married with two kids, living in Kitsilano. Happy as a pig in mud.'

Was everyone from her past moving to Kitsilano? 'Lucky guy.' She'd always got on well with Dave but after Hunter had left town, she'd deliberately stayed clear of his best friend. Seemed easier than being reminded about him all the time. 'Two anklebiters, eh? Who'd have thought?' Dave being the focused, suit type at one of the country's leading banks didn't seem the man to change dirty diapers or calm a crying toddler to sleep. Guess some people shifted focus when needed.

One day she'd like to have children. If she ever again went out with a man long enough to establish a loving relationship. Which wasn't exactly her life plan at the moment. Possibly never would be. Two failed relationships had kind of opened her eyes and brought caution to the fore.

'His wife would agree with you. She pinches herself every morning.'

Did Hunter want a family? He used to say he did. But then he used to look happy. Her skin tightened. He'd said *we*, remember? He might already have a brood. It was none of her business. She had to remember this was Hunter, a man she'd *once* loved, and now didn't. Though there was no denying how often she'd wondered if he still lived in the Okanagan, and if he'd continued training as a paramedic or had returned to his original career as a nurse. She'd be patient and who knew what she'd learn over the coming days?

As long as she remembered the past had to remain where it belonged, she'd be safe from the little vibe of heat trickling through her right now. Dropping the talk of family, Brenna answered his earlier query. 'I like the challenges of rescue work. Landing in a field one day, dropping into the bush on a wire cable on another, bringing in a mum and her baby from an outlying sound in a storm.'

'Seems like you've become an adrenalin junkie.'

'It's a way of using up excess energy.' The one thing she was never short of.

'Brenna, we're on,' Andy called from beyond the door. 'There's been a car versus bull out near Richmond.'

Relieved, Brenna placed the coffee jar back on the shelf and brushed past Hunter, aiming for the door, trying not to suck up a noseful of his scent. But he still used that spicy aftershave, the one she'd introduced him to as a birthday present during their first year together. Thank goodness *she* no longer sprayed the fragrance she'd worn back then over her skin every morning. That would be too much.

'Let's go,' she snapped. Her head was pounding, and she needed to be busy.

Hunter followed, grabbing the pack she indicated with a tip of her head. She was running hot and cold with him. This was unknown territory. How did a person act towards the man she'd loved with everything she had after he'd walked away so long ago?

'You want me in the back?' Hunter asked as they approached the chopper.

'Take your pick.' She leapt aboard and stowed her bag before sinking onto a seat, clipping safety belts in place and donning a helmet. 'Hey, Andy, how was your weekend?'

'You missed a great party, Brenna. Like seriously great.'

'Them's the breaks. Anyway, we had quite the shindig at Whistler after the last race. Lots of ice cream and hot chocolate.'

Hunter joined her, pulled on his helmet, looking confident and relaxed, apparently not afraid to face the monkey in the small space. 'You're into ski racing now?'

'Not quite. Photographing the participants is my thing. Which often means going as fast as the racers. I'm the doctor for a local school team and end up with more photos than broken bones at competitions.' When Hunter's eyes widened Brenna shrugged helplessly. This situation was spooking her. Made that morning's traffic woes a doddle. Hunter was sitting beside her. Unreal. A deep breath and she spoke into the headset mouthpiece. 'Andy, have you met Hunter? He's covering for Patch.'

'Welcome aboard, Hunter.' The rotors were spinning, and the engine noise was increasing rapidly. 'We'll talk later.'

Brenna creased her brows together, clasped her hands in a tight fist on her lap and spilled the question that was itching like a hornet sting, 'Why Vancouver?' Why Kitsilano when there were lots of suburbs to choose from? 'You get run out of Kamloops?'

He grimaced. 'Not quite.' Then his gaze met hers. 'I've got through the last years by keeping the idea of returning here at the front of my mind.'

That bad, huh? Her heart melted a little for him. Then it froze up again. Had he not once thought how this might upset her? Obviously not. Then again, ask her an hour ago how she'd have felt about Hunter returning to her city and she'd have shrugged and asked, 'What's the problem?'

They'd first met in Vancouver General's ED while working with a badly haemorrhaging patient. She'd been in her last year as an intern, gearing up to specialise in emergency medicine, and he had been tossing up where to go next. Hitting it off instantly, with sparks flying and the temperature rising, Hunter had asked her out for a drink at the bar next door where hospital staff flocked every day, and they had become inseparable overnight. Literally.

It had been wonderful. Until the day he'd received the call from his mother and had had to get home fast. End of relationship. End of story. Except now he was back on her turf, looking amazing. So strong, yet wary, sexy yet—*Sexy*. Her teeth ground together. 'Sounds like you have unfinished business here,' she muttered around the sudden yearning clogging her throat. That wouldn't be her.

'It's more about being somewhere I'm comfortable. Some place I can make things work for both of us.'

Brenna's face tightened at the reminder he wasn't alone. The yearning slowly abated, and she began to focus on what she was here for. Pressing the button on her mic, she asked in a monotone, 'What are the details, Andy? I didn't get the brief.' Too busy trying to ignore the fact she had to work with Hunter.

'Three male teens in the car, going to the skating rink for hockey training. Rounded a corner and smacked into a bull that'd escaped from the field. The beast took out the right front of the car. An ambulance is there, along with the fire crew, who are cutting the vehicle apart so you can retrieve the lads.'

'Messy,' Hunter commented, sitting a little straighter, immediately focused on what lay ahead. 'There'll likely be blunt force trauma injuries for the two in the front seats. Are we the only air base responders?'

Andy answered, 'The second crew's warming up. They won't be far behind us.'

'You'd better be landing on the road,' Brenna muttered. 'There might be more bulls wandering around in the field.' She wasn't a big fan of cattle, or any livestock. A city girl through and through, she preferred sheep on a plate as chops, and her beef definitely as steak, medium rare.

'I'll see what I can find.' Andy laughed.

Looking at Hunter, she grimaced. 'You'll be in your element.' Having grown up in the country, he'd have no fear of animals with hard heads.

'I learned to be cautious around cattle after my quad-bike accident.'

'Here we go,' Andy told them. 'Looks like the beast's been put out of its misery.'

Glancing down, Brenna noted the large animal on its side at the edge of the road, none of the emergency personnel taking any notice of it. Relief sneaked under her skin. Total focus was what mattered, and not on a bull. Nor on the temporary paramedic.

At the car wreck Brenna appraised the situation and listened to the ambulance officer's observations. The teens looked too young to be driving but according to a fireman two of the boys were seventeen.

'We'll see to the front passenger,' Brenna told Hunter. He'd taken the brunt of the impact. 'Carl and Nick will see to the driver when they arrive. The ambulance crew will continue with him until they get here, then take care of the boy in the back. His injuries aren't so serious and a road transfer's possible.'

Hunter squatted down beside the lad she'd indicated as their patient. 'Hello, there. I'm Hunter and this is Brenna.' Hunter's and her names in one sentence. She shivered. 'We're here to look after you. What's your name?'

'Johnny.'

'How old are you, Johnny?' Brenna asked. How alert was the lad?

'Um, fourteen? Seventeen. Yes, seventeen.' His mind was wandering, a sure sign of a possible neurological injury.

'You were going to the skating rink?' Hunter was digging into his pack for a neck brace.

Brenna began assessing Johnny's injuries. This was like old times: different setting, same questions and empathy for their patient. Different feelings for her medical partner. Kneeling opposite Hunter, memories flooded in of them working together. It was a struggle to ignore the flare of awareness that came with those.

Patient first, Brenna. Patient second, and last.

They needed to put that neck brace on Johnny in case of vertebrae injuries before anything else. Together they got it on, then she put her finger on the boy's pulse: rapid and erratic. Was he bleeding somewhere? With her other hand she felt under the boy's body, touched a sticky spot.

Johnny cried out.

'Easy. We'll give you something for the pain shortly.' In an aside she told Hunter, 'Torn tissue on the left side of his thigh.'

He nodded.

'H-how are my mates?' His breathing was rapid and shallow.

Without checking, Hunter told him, 'They're doing okay.'

Good move. Johnny didn't need anything else to worry about. 'Breathe long and slow, try not to panic. We're here to look after you.'

Hunter repeated a question to the teen, 'Where were you guys going so early in the morning?' By doing that, they'd know if he began losing awareness and if the neurological dysfunction had worsened.

'Soccer. No, hockey practice,' Johnny cried. 'This isn't fair. I'll miss the championships and I've worked so hard for them all winter.' He struggled to push up on his elbows and screamed as pain twisted his face.

Brenna gently pressed him back against the car seat, her fingers then doing a quick, light assessment of his left arm. 'Don't move, Johnny. I'll get you something for that pain.' They needed to administer morphine before he was lifted out of the wreck. In a quiet aside to Hunter she added, 'Fractured left humerus.' Glancing lower, she inhaled deeply. 'Also the tib and fib on the same side.'

'Add in some ribs where the airbag slammed him, I think.' Hunter nodded grimly, then added in a quiet aside to her, 'He's got a tough road ahead before he's back on the ice.'

'Of all the bad luck.' After Hunter checked the vial with her, Brenna began drawing up morphine. 'Right.' She leaned close to their patient. 'Johnny, I'm giving you something to stop the pain. Just a little prick in your upper arm, okay?'

Johnny didn't even murmur as the needle slid under his skin.

'Ready to lift him out when you are.' A fireman leaned down.

'We need splints on the left leg and arm, then we'll be good to go.' Hunter took a cardboard splint someone handed him and nodded to Brenna.

Working in sync, the splints were quickly in place and Johnny was being lifted from what remained of his seat and laid on a stretcher, leaving behind a pool of congealing blood where he'd sat.

Hunter immediately hunkered down to begin taking more obs, asking the lad questions to keep him focused.

Impressed, yet not surprised, with his total concentration on the job, Brenna cut away Johnny's track pants to ascertain the injuries to his thigh and buttock. Her fingers found the source of the haemorrhage, and instantly Hunter passed across thick cotton pads to apply pressure before taping them in place. It was like they were meant to be together. Each knowing what the other needed. Hell, they'd been like that in bed too. In most aspects of their lives. Except when he'd left her. Another shiver down her spine jerked her back to Johnny. She was the one who needed to concentrate.

'How's your lad?' Brenna asked Carl over her shoulder.

'Breathing difficulties, a piercing from the windscreen wiper in his chest.' Then Carl added, 'Air's building up in his lungs. We need him on the way ASAP, before his lungs can't take in any more oxygen.'

If the boy's breathing had been compromised, then the lungs would eventually malfunction. She made an abrupt decision. 'We'll send him first. Just say when you need to lift him out of there.'

'Now.' Within minutes the second teen was out of the wreck and lying on a stretcher, being carried to a chopper.

'What about the third boy?' Brenna asked.

The fireman answered. 'Loaded in the ambulance and about to go. He suffered whiplash and a bang to the head that might've caused concussion. He's the luckiest of them.'

'Johnny, open your eyes,' Hunter said. 'Johnny.'

Reaching for Johnny's wrist, Brenna felt for his pulse. 'Slow. Erratic. How's that bleeding?'

'I'm applying another pressure bandage over the top.'

'We'll load him as soon as you've done that.' Listening to Johnny's chest through her stethoscope, Brenna breathed a sigh of relief. 'I don't think there's any damage to the lungs, but I still want him on the way ASAP.'

Firemen lifted the stretcher on board their aircraft. All the time Johnny was groaning as tears flowed down his cheeks. 'I want to skate. Put my boots on.'

It wasn't happening any time soon, but no one was about to tell him. It would be bad enough when the traffic cops talked to him later about his friend's driving as the car had been seen by the farmer racing along the road moments prior to the impact.

In their helicopter Hunter continued talking to him, keeping him calm. Then he glanced up and nodded to her. 'You okay with this?'

'Of course,' she told him, sitting back into her seat and buckling in for the flight. She kept watching from under lowered eyelids, as though her eyes were drawn to him without any input from her brain. The red overalls didn't detract from the body filling them out. Like the exhaustion falling off him didn't tone down the raw handsomeness of his face. A face that used to turn her on with a smile, make her blood boil with anger when he was being stubborn, show compassion when she was struggling to cope with study and her dad's illness.

No wonder her next relationship hadn't lasted. There wasn't a man out there who came close to Hunter. So much for believing she'd got over him. There was still a way to go. Starting now.

CHAPTER TWO

BRENNA BLEW ON her mug of mushroom soup and watched the ferry ticket for her car download. So much for doing this at work. All coherent thought had flown out of her head the moment Hunter had appeared in the locker room.

The soup burned her lips, so she put it aside to cool a bit. Outside the wind slammed against the house and rattled the windows. It had been building since about four and she'd driven home in a deluge of rain. But it had been Hunter slowing her trip. Twice she'd been tooted at for not moving when the lights had turned green. But at least she had the night to get on with things and not have to hear his voice or see that magnificent body shaping his overalls in ways that brought hot memories to the forefront of her mind. Forbidden memories. Their relationship was history. No one got a second go at dumping her. No one.

If only it could be as easy to ignore him. She could try another tactic. Picking up her phone, she pressed speed dial. 'Hi, Mum. We're all set to go to Victoria, leaving at five.'

'Thanks, darling. So sorry I didn't get around to booking the ticket.'

In her family they didn't say they'd forgotten something any more. It came with too many memories of Dad as the dementia had begun taking hold of what had once been a very sharp mind. But this coming weekend would bring up a lot of things they only ever talked about once a year, and on past experience Mum would already be starting to get upset. 'Want me to confirm the time with the others?' Her half-sisters shared an apartment in Gastown.

'Em's here so I'll tell her, and she can let Fay know.'

Brenna could relax. Emily had bought the passenger tickets last week. They were good to go. 'I talked to Mrs Crawford and she's already been in to give the beach house a polish.' As only their neighbour at Whale Beach would. No house was ever too clean for Mrs Crawford. She'd have given the place a thorough going-over after everyone had left at the end of Thanksgiving weekend and would still go in to wipe down all the surfaces before they turned up on Friday.

Mum gave a tired chuckle. 'I'd be surprised if she hadn't.'

'You all right?" Brenna asked. It wasn't like Mum to sound so flat, though they were going to the island for the third anniversary of her father's death, so it was to be expected. 'Apart from the obvious,' she added.

'Think I'm coming down with a cold. Nothing major. How was the weekend? Get lots of amazing photos?'

'I'm hoping they're good. I haven't downloaded them yet. It was so late when I got back last night I just crashed into bed. The weather was perfect, and the snow excellent. Plus, the kids were amazing in their determination to do well.' Not mentioning how she'd nearly slammed into a boulder while concentrating on getting the best picture of the race leader on a downhill section. Her mum would have fifty fits.

The most caring woman, she'd always been there for Brenna from the day she and Dad had got together, not once making her feel any different from the two girls who'd come along later. She'd been very lucky, if she didn't think about her birth mother.

'Guess who I saw today?' Oh, bugger. Now she'd gone and set herself up for a lecture. But she had to tell someone, to get it off her chest, out of her head, and who better than Mum?

'Hunter Ford.'

'What? You knew he was in town and didn't tell me?' Her jaw tensed, and her fingers were claws.

'No, but I've only ever known you to speak like someone's got a rope drawn tight around your throat when you're thinking about Hunter. Oh, honey, I'm sorry it was Hunter. You don't need all that hurt rearing its head again.'

I talk differently when thinking about Hunter? Since when? Probably for the last six years.

'You're right. I don't. But it gets worse. He's working at the rescue base for a month.'

'You really have annoyed someone out there.' Mum sighed. 'How are you? It must be hard after all these years. Has he changed much?'

I'm coping. If I ignore the images floating before my eyes.

Brenna sipped her now lukewarm soup. 'Older, more worn, otherwise still Hunter as far as I can tell.' Until she knew more, she wasn't mentioning the mystery of who the 'we' was.

'Maybe you can get rid of that grandfather clock now he's here.'

Brenna gasped. What? Just turn up on his doorstep with a gift she bought more than six years ago? Hardly. 'Better go. I've got hundreds of photos to sort through and send to the school.' She regretted saying anything about Hunter. Though it had to come out sometime. As did the clock. Why had Mum kept it for so long for her, knowing Hunter was never coming back? She wondered how Hunter would react if he ever got to see the damned clock.

Why did you come back, Hunter?

Life had suddenly become a roller-coaster ride of emotions, none of which made a lot of sense. Why couldn't she just accept he'd once devastated her, and she wanted nothing more to do with him?

Because I'm still attracted to him.

And wasn't that the dumbest thought she'd had in years? Attractive or not, he'd hurt her big time and could do it again. Get a grip, be tough. Act the part if necessary. 'I'll see you Friday, Mum.'

'Okay, honey. Take care.' The phone clicked off with no parting shot about how to handle Hunter. Showed how tired her mother was.

But take care. Of what? It wasn't as though Hunter was going to feature in her life again. Other than working on the choppers with her for a few weeks. Too many weeks. One would've been more than enough. Hopefully Kevin would roster him with Carl later on. Why would he do that?

Because I need him to.

But if she wasn't going to get all hot and wound up over Hunter then it didn't matter if they worked together.

Plugging the lead from her camera into the computer, Brenna clicked on the icon to begin the download of the weekend's photos. And while she waited she clicked on 'Pictures' and scrolled back beyond six years.

Her and Hunter in Stanley Park with his dog.

Hunter lying on her couch sound asleep after a hectic night in the ED.

Her in a bikini on the beach just down the road, her windsurfing board at her side.

Hunter smiling at her as though she was the best thing that had ever happened to him. He'd always said she was. Yeah, and then he'd left her.

Click. The screen filled with images of snow and mountains and teenaged skiers wearing bright red and white outfits.

Her head remained full of images of Hunter. Smiling, laughing, sad, tired. These pictures were stored in her memory; pictures she'd forgotten, or deliberately pushed away. Why had she transferred those real photos onto her new computer? She hadn't kept more than a few of Shane when they'd separated last year, yet there were hundreds of Hunter. Pictures that she'd not looked at once since a month after he'd left town and she'd known the only way forward was to stop torturing herself over them.

'Poppy,' she called as she shoved up from her office chair. 'Walkies.' Selecting which photos to send to the coach could wait. She needed fresh air.

Poppy lifted her head from her paws and flicked her tail up and down on the carpet, before leaping to her feet and doing her customary circles around Brenna's legs. It was never too late for her to go walking.

Outside the wind whipped around the house.

Brenna shrugged into her puffer jacket and pulled on gloves. Poppy nudged her thigh and waited patiently for her lead to be clicked into place. 'It's not going to be much fun, Pops, but you need the exercise and I need to clear my head.'

It worked. By the time Brenna returned home Poppy was soaked, requiring a good towelling. Then, after a large bowl of food, the Lab snuggled into her big soft cushion for the night, and Brenna reheated her soup before sitting down to concentrate on the skiing photos, selecting the best, editing, chopping and making up a portfolio to send to the school's sports coach. By the time she climbed into bed she was exhausted, and soon unconscious.

When her favourite song romped into her brain at four forty-five she took Poppy for another walk. 'At least you'll be dry this time.' Rubbing her pet between her ears, they headed out onto the road to do eight blocks before returning to get ready for the day.

Another day squashed into the helicopter with Hunter sharing the same space, the same air. Twelve hours of being polite and not too nosy, while wanting to know every last thing that had happened to him in the intervening years.

Hunter, Hunter, Hunter. Why did you come back to my turf? Canada's a huge country, yet you've landed splat in the middle of Kitsilano. I don't get it.

Apart from the fact he'd said it was the area he knew and had been happy in, and where his closest friend now lived. Four weeks, minus one day. Somehow, they'd manage to survive. They had to. Hunter wasn't going to make her regret going into her favourite job every day.

Tossing her bag onto the passenger seat of her car, she got in and turned the ignition. *Grrr.* The engine coughed and died. What the heck? She tried again, same result. Dead. She flicked the light switch and swore. She hadn't turned them off last night. How hadn't she noticed they were on when she'd got out of the car? Too busy thinking about Hunter, that's how. Go on, blame the man. If he hadn't come to town, she'd be on her way to work right now.

Grabbing her phone, she pressed the button for Kevin. 'Sorry, I'm going to be late. Flat battery. I'll call a cab. Hopefully they won't be too long getting here at this hour.'

'Give Hunter a buzz. He's staying not far from you.'

'I don't have his number.' She didn't want it. Might be too tempting to ring him in the quiet times. 'A cab's just fine.'

'I'll ring Hunter for you. Does he know where you live?'

Arguing wasn't going to get her anywhere, and she did need to get to work on time in case there was a call out. 'Tell him my dad's old place. He'll know it.' Unless his memory was shot to pieces, which was highly unlikely. He'd know she didn't mean the house Mum and Dad had owned together. 'He might've left already,' she added hopefully. Hunter was always on time for everything, even to the dentist. But she was talking to herself.

Kevin obviously had better things to do than shoot the breeze with a grumpy woman at this hour. Who wouldn't? By most people's standards it was early for anything more than coffee, toast and driving to work with rock music in the background. Slamming the car door shut, she stomped down to the kerb to wait, trying to ignore the unease churning in her stomach. If only this wasn't happening.

Almost immediately headlights lit up the street. A four-wheel drive cruised to a halt beside her and Hunter stuck his head out the window. 'I hear you need a lift.'

'Thanks.' There were definitely butterflies batting around in her belly. Unbelievable. His second day on the job and he was picking her up, and she was falling apart. She'd had no intention of ever inviting him onto her street, let alone near her house. That was too close, too laden with memories. Yet here he was, a knight in a shining black four-wheel drive. Too close and laden with those memories. Like the one where she'd ogled his biceps and flat abs because he'd worn only jeans cut off at the knees as he'd mowed the lawns for her dad.

'You going to stand there all morning?'

Good idea. Ducking around the vehicle, she got in, saying, 'I should phone Roadside Assist.' She'd been too busy thinking about Hunter to do it before.

'You left a key with someone for them?'

'No, I could hardy go knocking on a neighbour's door at this hour. And before you ask, there isn't a spare under the door mat.'

'I've got a battery charger in the back. I'll deal to your car after work.'

That was the last thing she wanted. But what were her options? 'I'll see.' Inside the warm vehicle she buckled in and tried not to breathe aftershave spice.

He didn't blink at her terse reply. 'You forget to turn the lights off last night?'

'Yep.' She shook her head at her stupidity.

'Lucky I'm staying close by.' Was that a smile lifting the corner of his mouth? But, then, Hunter did like helping people out of a fix. Like the time she'd locked herself out of the house when she'd had the book group coming. They'd only known each other a week, though they'd begun *knowing* each other very well, and yet Hunter had left the pub where he'd been having a drink with his mates and raced around to lever the door open.

'Yes.' She should stop being grumpy. It wasn't his fault Kevin had asked him to swing by and pick her up. It *was* his fault her head was heavy and full of memories she no longer had use for. 'You can't have been far away when Kevin called.'

'I was running late, so now I've got an excuse.'

'You? Late? Um, hello. You are Hunter Ford, right?

The guy I used to know was always at the airport watching the flight before his leave for the same destination?' A chuckle rolled up her throat. She swallowed it.

'Says she who liked to swan in at the very last second.' Hunter flicked her a smile.

'These days I prefer early and prepared.' She was not falling into that smile.

'I was saying goodbye to my son. I hate leaving him. Especially while everything's new and strange. Though Jess says it's me with the hang-ups, and that Dylan's settling in like he's meant to be here.'

Jess *and* Dylan. The whole family package. Nice. Her shoulders dropped and her arms tightened against her sides. 'How old is your boy?' Might as well get it out of the way.

'Four last month. He's started preschool in Kitsilano with one of Dave's kids.'

He didn't seem to mind her questions, so she kept going. 'You said the idea of coming back here kept you going over the years, but why?'

Hunter slowed for a red light, accelerated away when it changed to green. His fingers were gripping the steering wheel, his face no longer as relaxed. 'Seemed like a plan to have at the ready, something to look forward to.'

A mind-your-own-business answer. 'We all need those,' she muttered. Not that she had any at the moment, her life being in cruise mode with lots going on to keep her busy and out of trouble. So, Jess. What was she like? How long had they been together? Were they married? Yes, they would be. Hunter used to say he wanted to marry the woman he loved, not live in a relationship without all the legal trimmings. That woman used to be her. Why bring her to Kitsilano when that had been where *they'd* been so happy? 'You and Jess been married long?'

Dylan was four. She and Hunter had broken up six years ago. She'd been replaced quick smart.

'Are we what?' Abrupt laughter filled the four-wheel drive.

'Concentrate on the road, will you?' she snapped, not sure what his response meant.

Hunter drove straight and true in the outside lane. 'Jess is Dave's wife. Not mine,' he added through gritted teeth.

'Oh.' So where was Dylan's mother? She was not asking. Not now when Hunter looked like he wanted to strangle her. Over an obvious question? *He'd* brought Jess's name up in the first place. Or was it the wife word that turned his mood from friendly to sour? Not asking that either. Brenna reached into her jacket pocket to retrieve her phone. No new messages. Great. Now what? Talk about the weather. Always a safe subject. Or she could go with shutting up.

'Dylan's mother and I were married for a couple of years, but it was a fail. Always going to be, I guess, since the only thing we had in common was Dylan, and I love him to bits, but he couldn't keep us happy with each other.' This was more like the Hunter she remembered. Not reticent with his words. 'Not that it was his role to.'

Now her heart ached for him. Reaching across, she touched his arm, felt him tense under her palm and quickly withdrew. 'I'm so sorry. That must be hard to deal with. So did Dylan's mum move to Vancouver too?' As in separately. If she'd moved first, he'd have come so he could spend time with his son, wouldn't he?

'No.'

Brenna waited for more. Got nothing. Back to being the taciturn Hunter she didn't know. 'So, you're a full-time dad.'

'Evie died in a car crash after we'd split up. She'd

dropped Dylan off so he could spend the night with me, and on the way back to town she crossed the road into the path of an oncoming truck and trailer unit. She didn't stand a chance. The police believe she was texting at the time.'

I think I prefer it when he doesn't talk so much. This was awful.

'Hell, Hunter, how did you cope? That's…' She paused. 'I don't know what to say really.'

'Don't even try. It's all been said, often, and none of it helps.' He pulled into the car park at the rescue base, hauled the brake on, turned the ignition off and slowly turned to face her. 'We were never in love. Evie fell pregnant soon after we met, and we decided to give it a go for the baby's sake. Bad idea. We got on better when we lived separately, and Dylan was happier.'

There was a whole load of self-blame resonating in his words, even when he hadn't been in the car and apparently not texting with Evie. No surprise there. It was who he was. A man who believed he had to stand up and help people, not destroy them in any way.

He destroyed me by standing by his parents.

Yes, and she'd survived, made a comeback, been with a man for nearly two years, got engaged, then unengaged. At least she wasn't so naïve any more. Nudging open her door, she said, 'I hope the move works out for you and your boy, Hunter.' Surprisingly she did. Once he left this job and took up his permanent one, she'd be absolutely fine with it.

Why had he gone and spilled his guts? Hunter shivered in the chilly air. While it was good to have the facts about Evie and Dylan out of the way, he hadn't needed to say half as much as he had. Or had he? Had he been trying to show Brenna that he hadn't fallen in love with another woman after he'd left her? But he'd noticed the sudden tightening of her hands on her thighs when he'd said how old Dylan was. She'd done the sums.

What he hadn't told her was that he'd hooked up with Evie because he'd been desperate for some warmth and kindness in his life, something to temporarily fill the gaping hole that only Brenna could fix. And would never get the chance to. He'd deliberately set out to put Brenna out of his life.

Yet here he was, encroaching in her work zone, and in her neighbourhood. Yesterday, spending time working together, being crammed into the back of the chopper or sitting in the tearoom, had rammed it home to him that he hadn't got over her as much as he'd thought. If at all.

The attraction that had seen them falling into bed the first time they'd gone on a date seemed to have been lying in waiting for the match that had fired his libido into a frenzy yesterday. A frenzy that could not get a look in. He and Brenna were long over. She'd have a man in her life, and when Bren did anything, she did it with everything she had, including loving.

Sadness, or jealousy, or longing, or some blasted emotion grabbed him, squeezed so tight he stepped towards his vehicle, needing to race away some place that didn't palpate with Brenna vibes. So much for returning to the one location he'd ever been completely and utterly happy. But Kamloops was no longer an option.

His boy was not getting tied up in the fiasco that was his parents' marriage and their inability to stand on their own two feet and help each other—when he wasn't available—for everything from snow on the lawn to the mailman being late. Plus, Mum had already begun telling Dylan about his grandfather's strange thinking and how there were voices in his head, and how Dylan had to be strong for them. Enough was enough.

'You standing out here all day?' Brenna called from where she held the outside door open.

Good idea. 'What's for breakfast?' He'd snaffled some buns from Jess's pantry when she'd been filling the kettle.

'Toast and jam.'

'You still eat that?' Some of the tension that had built up on the way here loosened, and he managed a smile.

'Hello? You think I stopped all the things I enjoyed when you left?' Her ponytail swished sharply across her back. Her eyes drilled into him. Then the door slammed shut between them.

What had he done? Why hadn't he tried harder to find a way around what had seemed like insurmountable difficulties and kept Brenna at his side? Because it wouldn't have worked. Over time they'd have come to resent the changes they hadn't anticipated and taken it out on each other. But what he would give now to have at least tried. There had been so many moments he'd missed out on and no way to get them back. And it hadn't worked out any better by walking away either.

His heart was heavy, sad. He'd lost so much that day, and to start thinking now that he might not have got over Brenna had him worried. Would he never be free of this tightness around his heart whenever he thought of her now that they'd caught up again?

On the other side of the security fence a helicopter began warming up, the rotors gathering speed as Andy did his checks.

Time to get to work, concentrate on what had to be done, not what might've been. Hunter headed inside to the tearoom, where his eyes were instantly drawn to Brenna's rounded bottom and short, slim legs. As toned as ever. Keeping fit had been an obsession with her, and had driven him crazy at times when he'd wanted to lie snuggled up to her warm body for the last minutes before starting a new day and she wouldn't have it. No lying around for Bren. *Brenna*.

'Here's hoping we have time for a coffee at least.' Again, he hadn't had breakfast before leaving the house because he'd been watching Dylan. Yesterday he'd been stepping into a big unknown with Brenna. Today his gut hadn't been churning when he'd picked her up, but he was very aware of her. Aware in ways he shouldn't be. Ways that his memory fed non-stop, tormenting him with images of them together. Despite his gut being quiet today, other parts of his body were waking up, as though from a long sleep. Which wasn't exactly true. He had been out and about occasionally, though none of the few women he'd befriended had had the power to knock him to his knees like this one.

Even now.

'You got kids?' he asked, in an attempt to cool his ardour. Because if she said yes then he'd know for sure there was a man in the picture.

'A gorgeous four-legged girl named Poppy,' Brenna answered in a neutral voice.

'She'd be a dog, then.'

'You remember.'

That she disliked cats? 'Yes.' Seemed six years wasn't long enough to delete all the irrelevant info from his brain. 'Lab or spaniel?'

The cupboard shut with a clang. 'Black Lab, a big softy. Tea or coffee?'

Trying to tell him she remembered nothing? 'Either.'

'Make that neither,' Andy said from the doorway.

'We're on. Heart attack on a cruise ship out in the passage. Fifty-nine-year-old man, no known history.'

Hunter shrugged. 'Do you ever get breakfast before the first callout?'

Brenna answered. 'Half the time.' Her eyes glinted at him as though she had lots to say but was holding back.

'If it's any help I didn't know you worked here when Kevin twisted my arm.' He watched for her face to soften. It didn't.

'He's good at that.' Slinging the pack over her shoulder, she told him firmly, 'Anyway, it's fine.'

'We can't change what happened.' He followed her out of the hangar, sure she wasn't going to speak to him again unless it was to do with a patient.

But, 'You're right,' she admitted. 'I'm acting like a four-year-old. Except Dylan's probably far more mature than me. I'm sorry.'

'I haven't seen you squishing banana through your hair yet, so I think you're ahead of my boy.'

'Yuk.' She shuddered deliberately. 'He doesn't.'

'Oh, yes, he does. He can throw some right tantrums when he's in a mood.'

He took the bag from her as she leapt aboard. 'Takes after his grandfather on his mother's side.'

'Not you?' Finally, Brenna was smiling in a natural, friendly, not-looking-for-an-argument way.

The knot in his gut unravelled as warmth flowed over him. Which was worse, because hope came with it. If only he knew what he was hoping for. They weren't getting back together. Too much had gone down in the intervening years for them to be able to pick up where they'd left off, strange feelings or not.

'I don't like bananas.' He gave her one of his best

smiles, felt cheated when she didn't blink, or shiver, or sigh, like she used to.

Pulling on the helmet, she pressed the speaker button. 'Andy, was the ship heading north or returning to Vancouver?'

Hunter had his helmet on in a flash, heard Andy say, 'It's due to dock in Vancouver in an hour but the doctor on board is worried the man is getting worse. They'll have him ready to lift when we get there.'

'So, it's a snatch and go,' Hunter commented just as his phone vibrated in his pocket.

Brenna nodded. 'It means one of us is redundant, but we never know what might go wrong.'

Hunter read his mother's number on the screen of his phone. She was early, even for her. His gut tightened. What had Dad done now? Sat outside all night? Refused to take his meds? The other day he'd got upset with other residents in the village and had been sulking ever since. His depression was under control, his selfishness wasn't. If Dad could cause trouble, he would. Breathe deep. He had to remember these calls were unavoidable. He'd deal with them one at a time. His finger tapped the phone as he debated trying to call back, but it was so noisy in here neither of them would hear each other. Anyway, that was giving in too quickly.

His finger worked the keys. Can't talk. In the heli. I'll call later. A heavy weight sat on his chest as he pushed Send. What if something serious was wrong? Something he had to deal with? Breathe deep, remember? His mother was not going to stop calling, pestering him, demanding his undivided attention just because he'd left them in a safe environment with all the medical help available to man. He was the one who had to make changes, to accept he was here for good, and he was not going to be diverted. For Dylan's sake. *And mine*, he admitted grudgingly. Shoving the phone deep into the pocket of his overalls, he leaned back in the hard, narrow seat and looked at Brenna.

She had her phone out too, reading a text. 'One of my neighbours on the other side of the service lane says their house was broken into last night.'

'Glad you've got a dog.'

'I wonder what time it happened? Poppy got restless around eight, kept pacing between the front and back doors. When I let her out, she ran to the gate and barked then came back inside.' Her slim fingers worked the phone. 'I'm letting Claire know in case it's any help to the police.'

Worry stormed through Hunter. 'You didn't go outside, did you? Who knows how many thugs were out there?' She might have a kick-ass attitude, but she was so small it would only take one half-formed male to overcome her. 'I'll check your house out when I drop you off tonight.'

'That won't be necessary. Whoever it was will be long gone.'

He was on a hiding to nothing, but offering help was his thing. Besides, this was Brenna. How could he not make sure everything was as it was supposed to be at her place? 'Let's see how Poppy reacts when you get home.'

Brenna glared at him. Then her eyes softened, and a small smile appeared. 'Okay.'

That was it? Okay? He'd won a point yet felt deflated. *Hey, so Bren stirs you like she always did.*

His stomach crunched. It was true. And not meant to be. There hadn't been a woman who came close to Brenna for waking him up, physically and even in the brain department. Not before or after those amazing years together. He had tried to accept they'd had a once-in-a-lifetime relationship and it couldn't be repeated so that he could move on, forge a future with another woman. Tried. Bombed. But that didn't mean there was a hope in Hades now. It wasn't why he'd come to Vancouver. Moving here, buying a house, getting a great job—all part of the making-Dylan-happy package that would make him happy on the way. Nothing to do with getting back with Brenna.

Nothing.

'Did you have your own house back in Kamloops?' Brenna asked.

She seemed hell-bent on learning all that he'd been up to since they'd split. Why? Same issues as him? But she didn't look at all tempted to get close. With nothing to lose by filling her in on the mundane, he said, 'I moved into the cottage behind the packing shed soon after I left here. I needed my own space, and I think Mum was afraid I'd leave if I didn't have some breathing room, so she convinced Dad to agree.' His father was hard to live with, his depression dragging everybody down. He probably would've gone crazy himself, living with his parents and the constant bickering and mood swings.

'Handy.'

'It was. You live alone?' There hadn't been any sign of anyone else in the house when he'd picked her up. No lights on, no other vehicle in the lane.

'I do at the moment, and, to be honest, living on my own doesn't bother me. I'm hardly ever there so I don't have time to get lonely.' Brenna was smiling to herself.

Hunter's heart slowed. There mightn't be a man living with her but that didn't mean there wasn't someone special in her life, and that smile suggested she was thinking about whoever was her up-close, extraordinary partner.

Whoever he was, Hunter wanted to meet him at dawn, guns loaded. 'What about your mother?'

'Lives in an apartment closer to the beach.'

'Ten minutes out.' Andy came through the headset.

Ten minutes and he could get active, do something constructive, like transferring their patient onto the stretcher and hauling him on board using the hydraulic pulley, not planning the murder of someone he'd never met. Brenna could stop cruising through his head like she had every right to annoy him, wind him up, reminding him of what might've been if he hadn't been caught between doing his best for his family and having the future he and Brenna had planned on.

It had been such a tough choice. Whichever way he'd gone would have been fraught with consequences that would remain with him for ever. In the darkest hours of his father's depression he'd think about Bren and what might've been if he'd taken the other road. But he'd never have been able to live with himself if Dad had carried through his threats to end everything. Not that it had been easy living without Bren at his side, supporting him, loving him. There'd been no one to talk to in the easy, say-anything manner they'd had. Evie hadn't come close.

Hunter glanced across as Brenna read more messages on her phone, a little smile teasing the corners of her mouth. Longing stabbed him. Hard. The lines at the edges of her eyes were an added attraction, making her appear wiser and more experienced than he'd known her, and she'd been no slug. Now an adrenalin junkie who'd taken up photography professionally in a part-time capacity. Who'd have believed it? This was a new Brenna to him. Of course, studying more hours than were available on the way to becoming a doctor hadn't left her room for other interests.

But haring down a mountainside while using a camera to catch other people's moves? Did she understand how quickly things could go wrong? And the damage she could do to herself? He'd learned that the hard and painful way, he did not want the same for Brenna. He'd been struck dumb when she'd mentioned what she'd been doing in Whistler. And dumber still when, after his shocked expression had registered, she'd shrugged and asked, 'What's for me to lose?'

That kind of said it all and had made him feel shorter than his phone. Talk about rubbing it in. He'd taken away what she'd hoped for and she'd been telling him she'd never allow herself to be vulnerable to another person again. She could relax. He had no intention of attempting to rekindle their defunct relationship. Hurting her again was not an option. Neither was having his own heart broken again—despite that longing that had snagged him a moment ago. But it didn't mean he wouldn't worry if he knew she was doing something hair-raising. It terrified him, knowing from his quad-bike accident how quickly things could go belly up.

Life in Kamloops had been busy, physically hard at times, but dangerous? Not really. Not even his heart had been in danger with Evie. He was glad he'd hauled the orchard out of debt and got a good price for it so his parents could move to town, but he didn't miss the memories of the trees he'd climbed to hide when his father had been in a particularly foul mood. There were some good ones, like gorging on peaches, nectarines and apples after school, but all in all he was glad that time of his life was finished.

When he'd realised he had to take Dylan away from the Okanagan, Vancouver had been the first—only—place that had come to mind. Dave was here. This was the one place he'd been truly happy, and he'd wanted, needed, another chance at happiness. The only snag was that Brenna lived here, but she wasn't why he'd returned. Or was she? Underneath all the talk, was Brenna part of his reason for coming back?

CHAPTER THREE

'I'M COMING TO your front door,' Hunter told Brenna in his don't-argue-with-me voice that she recognised from once upon a time. He'd attached the battery charger to her dead car, and now all she had to do was wait for her battery to suck in some energy. 'Just in case that thief's been back to the neighbourhood.'

'Your telling-Dylan-off voice?' she grumped unfairly. He hadn't done anything wrong, had insisted on bringing her home and hooking up her car when it would make him late to see Dylan. She couldn't blame lack of sleep, more like she'd been out of sorts since he'd turned up on Monday.

'Not even close. He'd ignore me if I spoke like that.'

'Again, I'm outsmarted by a four-year-old. I have to meet this kid.' Shouldn't have said that. Hunter would think she was looking to get friendly with him. 'Come on. I know you want to get cracking.'

Hunter was beside her in an instant. 'Does Poppy stay inside while you're at work?'

'No, she's around beside the garage in a kennel with a large run.'

The sensor light came on as they headed around the corner, sending their shadows across the lawn, tangling them together as they walked in sync. Warmth stole through her. The tension she'd worn all day softened.

When was the last time she'd come home with a man? Not since Shane. Not that Hunter was coming inside to settle in for the evening. Or to make love in her big, soft bed. He might be causing these random feelings of longing and possibility, but he could not return to her life in any way other than as a colleague.

Though that was a temporary position, whereas if he became her life partner again there'd be nothing temporary about it. And she was afraid to try for that. Her mother hadn't stayed around to see her grow up. Hunter had left her once. It was all too scary.

'Hey, Pops, how was your day?' She'd shower her beloved pet with all the love she'd stored up and have it returned without question.

Poppy stood on her hind legs to place her paws on Brenna's shoulders for her customary pats. Her tail wagged non-stop and her tongue lolled as Bren's fingers worked through her fur.

Brenna kissed the top of her head. 'Missed you too.' The best part of coming home was the welcome she always got. It warmed her and made her feel loved.

'She makes you look smaller than ever,' Hunter muttered, his gaze fixed so firmly on Poppy he had to be avoiding looking at her.

Was he having similar errant thoughts about her as she'd had about him over the last two days? 'We make a good team, don't we, Pops?' Small? He used to like it that she was slim and short, used to rub it in about how she should carry a ladder with her everywhere she went. But tonight's comment didn't seem like he was teasing. He also used to say short on stature, big on attitude. He hadn't mentioned that tonight either. But, then, how would she feel if he did dredge up things like that from the past?

'Dylan wants a puppy, but he has to wait until we're settled into the house. I doubt we'll get such a large breed, though.' Finally, a glint of humour entered his dark gaze. 'Though if Poppy can contain herself and not drag you all over the show then Dylan can definitely con a Lab into watching out for him.'

Brenna unclipped the chain that attached her pet to the wire running the length of the back yard. 'Poppy, this is Hunter. Play nice with him.'

The dog dropped her front feet to the ground and strolled nearer to Hunter, watching him, her tail moving slowly from side to side, her I'm-sussing-you-out move.

'Pat her so she knows you're friendly.'

Hunter crouched to do as he was told. The wagging intensified. 'Hello, Poppy. I'm glad you're here to protect Brenna. I don't like her coming outside on her own. Especially at night,' he growled.

Brenna stared down at him, gripping her hips, her fingertips pushing deep, her chin forward. 'You do realise you're giving me the willies when it's entirely unnecessary, don't you?'

He looked chastened. 'It worries me, thinking of you out in the dark if some brute's hanging around.' His expression softened. 'Then again, if I'm making you more vigilant it's not a bad thing.'

This was true Hunter. Caring, concerned, willing to put himself out there for someone. For her. She would've melted at the intensity in his voice, except she had to be strong and keep him at arm's length. Damn. It wasn't easy. And it should be.

'I've been doing it every night since I brought Poppy home. She'd be the first to warn me if anyone undesirable was hanging around.' She headed for the door. 'I'm going inside. You want to come in?' Brain slap. She should not be letting him into her space or there'd be further images to deal with. Too late. She couldn't retract her invitation without looking lame. 'I've made a few changes.'

Don't leave too much scent in the air. I have to live here after you've gone.

'Does your stepmum still own the house?'

'No. When Dad went into full-time care I bought it off them. Mum sold their other house at the same time to buy the apartment, so she didn't have to worry about lawns and maintenance. It also meant there was money for Dad's expenses.' Topped up by her and her sisters so that Mum never needed to count the cents.

Hunter had no compunction about following her indoors but hesitated in the kitchen to look around. He seemed disappointed.

'Hunter?'

He swallowed. 'Nothing.'

Oh, yes, there was. She stared at him, trying to fathom what was causing that tight look in his face. 'What were you expecting?'

He shrugged. 'You're quite the interior decorator, aren't you?' Did he have to make it sound like a fault?

'It's paint and fabrics mostly, with tiles replacing the hideous old carpet.' Bi-folds instead of sliding glass doors, stone benches to replace the old, chipped laminate ones. 'You don't like it?'

'I haven't seen enough to know.'

Got it. He'd been expecting everything to be the same as it had been when they'd lived here, renting it off her parents. Before he'd left and she'd bought it. Because— Because he was stepping back in time to when they'd been in love and had had plans of one day buying this place together.

Reality shocked him, brought it home that she had moved on, was living life, not waiting for it to tick past, not sitting in a holding pattern in case the day came when he returned to her. Was this why he'd insisted in coming to her doorstep—not to check she'd be safe? No, there had been genuine concern reflected in his eyes, but obviously there'd been more going on behind that. Might as well get the elephant out of the way.

She tried for a shrug, got it half-right. 'Take a look around.' Really see my home as it is, not was.

Woof, woof. There was no getting away with not feeding Poppy right away. 'Come on, girl. Bring your bowl.' She walked away, leaving Hunter to his musings. Whatever they were. Did he actually think there was a chance of them getting together again? Truly? Would she have to be blunt and spell it out for him even before he said anything to indicate he might? Like…'I am not getting back with you. I'm not sure if I ever want to try another relationship. The pain when they go wrong is horrendous.'

Anyway, Dylan meant she had no place in Hunter's life. Sure, Dylan had to come first, always. She got that, would be upset if he didn't. But Hunter had shown he was incapable of blending all aspects of his life so that everyone had a place with him and weren't put aside for someone else. Hunter made choices between everything, everyone.

While Poppy guzzled down chicken-and-rice-flavoured dry food, Brenna put the kettle on to make tea. Wine would be better but then she'd have to offer Hunter one and she really needed him gone. She mightn't *want* him to leave—damn, she really didn't know what she wanted—but for sanity's sake it would be best if he headed away because there were already vibes making her body pulse and had her watching him out of the corner of her eye as he stood in the middle of her sitting room, staring around. Vibes that could do with a cold shower.

To hell with it. The fridge door swung back against the wall. Snatching the open bottle of wine, she slammed the door shut again and reached for two glasses in the cupboard above. Wine sloshed as she tipped it into them. 'Here, welcome back to Vancouver.' She shoved one glass at Hunter.

Damn the man to hell and back for returning, for walking into her life like nothing had gone wrong between them, like they could start over, like she wanted to see him and remember all those steamy sessions—some of which had happened in this house—like she needed to be aware of him and learn what his goals were and how he'd been married and now had a child, and that there was no future for them because she was afraid of being rejected again. She gulped a large mouthful and gasped as it went down the wrong way.

'Careful.' Hunter's splayed hand was between her shoulder blades, banging only hard enough to affect a cough.

Fine, if she wasn't remembering those palms and the mischief they could cause to her libido. Stepping away, she sipped the wine, stared at her feet and wondered what the hell to say next.

Go away. You're screwing with my head.

Hunter wasn't getting the vibes or the message. Instead he stared at the collection of framed photos on the far wall. 'You were always good with a camera, but these are outstanding.'

Her fickle heart swelled with pride. Was nothing on

her side? Putting aside her glass, she replied, 'Thank you. I won an international photographer's award with the one of the tandem skydiver.' It was her favourite photo of the thousands she'd taken since giving in to the need for adrenalin rushes that shut down thoughts of a sedate family life—with Hunter.

'You skydive now?' He was still staring at the photos, holding his breath as his gaze flicked from one photo to the next.

Watching his face, she replied, 'I've done a couple of jumps.'

Hunter looked down at her, amazement warring with anger all over his face. 'Why, Brenna?'

Because I couldn't have the life I wanted so I found another one.

She had to push him. How else could she deal with this man standing in her house looking gorgeous, and sexy, and so—so Hunter-ish? Her shoulders were tense as she rolled them. 'Why not? People do it all the time.'

'You enjoy living dangerously? You want to hurt those who love you when it goes horribly wrong?'

Said the man who'd hurt her badly. 'There are always plenty of safety measures in place.'

'They've been known to fail.' He stepped closer, taking her shoulders in his hands. 'Did I do this to you, Bren?' There was pain in his eyes, darkening the silver shade to brooding clouds. 'Did I?'

She sagged into his grip. 'It has little to do with you, Hunter. Believe me. It's about me and my life.' He'd added to her need to prove herself worthy of attention when he'd left her, but he hadn't started it. 'There was a day after my mother left us—I was eight—when I climbed the Douglas fir in the neighbour's yard. All the way to the top.'

'Let me guess. You refused to come down until she came home.'

'You've got it.' She could smile about it now. 'Dad cajoled, and begged, and growled. Nothing worked. He started climbing up to me, and the higher he got the more the top of the tree swayed. I held on like grim death until he reached me.' She could still remember his warm hand wrapping around her ankle in such a tender manner that had told her how naughty she'd been, and how loved she was, that she was lucky one parent cared enough to climb the tree for her.

'There was no colour in his cheeks and I had to talk him down. He suffered from vertigo.' He was the best dad anyone could ask for.

'Promise me you'll never tell Dylan that story. I don't get vertigo, but I hate climbing trees and getting jabbed by branches all the way.'

'That could cost you.' She smiled sadly. 'About a month after you'd gone, I woke up one morning and decided I could either find another tree and hope you'd find me or I could get out there and enjoy life, even take some risks. Calculated ones, I assure you.'

'Things can still go wrong, no matter how many safety precautions you put in place,' he murmured.

'I think we've both learned that lesson.' She could admit she hadn't fought to keep Hunter in her life, hadn't decided to move east with him, but then she'd be admitting she'd been afraid to risk losing the love of her father when he'd been there for her when her mother had deserted them, and for everything afterwards. Her chest rose on a breath, and she shifted the conversation sideways.

'I tandem dive but haven't been solo. I tried but sitting on the edge of the plane, staring down at the ground way below, knowing it was entirely up to me to land softly and not someone attached to my back making the right moves, seriously scared me.'

'Thank goodness for something.' His sigh whispered against her cheek. 'I was starting to think I don't know you at all.' Relief flickered in the depth of his gaze. 'That would be too much, would make a mockery of my memories.'

Her heart rocked. Hunter had memories too? Good ones? Like hers? Low in her belly heat unfurled. For a moment she didn't feel quite so alone. As though she might be able to find someone to warm her heart, to keep her safe and happy. Because, as much as she denied it, that was what she truly wanted. A partner to share everything with. Could she begin to let go some of the knots that had held her together over the years?

'Where have you gone?' His finger brushed over her hair.

'I'm not sure,' she answered truthfully. The pounding in her chest got louder as she looked into the dark gaze she'd never forgotten, had been looking for over the years. 'I'm really not sure.'

Hunter was leaning towards her, his hands ever so gently drawing her closer to him.

Brenna tried to straighten up, away, but couldn't. It felt right being there, close to that strong chest and the warmth emanating from his whole, long, wide body. Flipping her head back, she gazed up at Hunter. He was— He was Hunter. The man she'd sworn to love for ever, to have babies with, to grow old beside. Her heart skipped a beat. All those wonderful things that she still wanted. Something deep inside began melting as her body re-acted to the need that she'd been fighting for days took over. It pushed aside her fear of making a mistake, letting hope take over. Her mouth dried as the gap between them lessened.

His scent swirled around her, his warmth heated her, the light stubble on his chin reminding her of how it felt on her skin, blocking out all thought. As if by their own accord, her feet lifted onto her toes and she was reaching for him, her arms sliding around his neck, her mouth seeking his.

Hot. Hungry. Demanding. Giving and taking. Brenna pushed hard against him, her mouth devouring his, her hands pressing into him. Hunter returned her kiss, hot, hungry, his tongue teasing her mouth, his body plastered to hers, one hand clasping her bottom.

Yes. Haze and longing and heat swamped her. Burned her.

Thud, against her thigh.

What?

Thud.

Wrenching her mouth away from the maelstrom threatening to drown her, Brenna jerked out of Hunter's hold. 'Poppy.'

Thanks for the wake-up call.

She'd just made the most horrendous blunder. Thankfully they hadn't gone too far. Her fingers slid across her bottom lip, already swollen from that kiss. 'Hunter, I…' Words failed her. They'd kissed as though six years didn't lie between this and their last one.

'Don't, Bren. Let's not dissect what happened. We got carried away when we shouldn't have.' Regret scored his words and darkened his eyes as he turned for the door. 'I'll see you tomorrow when I come to make sure your car fires up.'

'I can do that.'

'I'm sure you can, but I'll be here at five-thirty.' He

disappeared out of the room, his heavy tread the only sound in her house until the front door clicked shut behind him, leaving an eerie silence in the hallway.

So, he wasn't going to avoid her after that kiss. Then again, he couldn't when they had to work together. She needed to take immediate vacation leave. Starting now, and not finishing until Hunter began his hospital job. Brenna sank onto the nearest chair before her shaking legs dropped her in a heap on the floor.

'What the hell just happened?' Her teeth dug into her bottom lip, making her wince when she bit too hard. The absolute last thing she'd wanted to do was to be anything more than friends, not even close ones, and she'd gone and kissed him.

Poppy dropped her head onto her knees, her big brown eyes staring at her.

'Thank you, girl. You saved me making a total moron of myself.' Who knew how far they'd have gone if she hadn't got a head butt from her dog?

Thump, thump went Poppy's tail.

'What? Oh, walkies?'

Thump, thump, thump.

'Let's go,' Brenna sighed. She could think about Hunter and his soul-destroying kisses just as easily walking the streets as she could here. If her legs actually managed to gain enough strength to hold her upright. Who'd have believed that after all this time Hunter would still have the power to knock her off her feet?

She needed to toughen up. Fast. Before tomorrow morning. Because, awkward or not, she would be going into work and doing what she loved most in the world, flying around saving people.

What she loved most, not *who*.

Hunter had no part of the who bit. He was the past,

had to remain there, could not be given the opportunity to come back into her world only to leave when it suited him. So, if anyone was leaving the rescue service during the next three and a half weeks it would be him, not her.

She was being harsh, but harsh had got her over him, and into a life that had brought adventure, fun and even another man for a couple of years. Shane had proposed on a skiing holiday in Banff and she'd believed she loved him, had been pleased for a second chance at happiness. But somehow her hours at work had increased and setting the wedding date had never happened.

When Shane had said he couldn't continue the way they were going she should've fought harder to keep him by cutting back hours to be with him more often and settled on a wedding date so she could move into domestic bliss, where she'd be immune to Hunter. Seemed she'd reacted instinctively, protecting herself again, only it hadn't hurt with Shane the way it had with Hunter.

Fabulous man that Shane was, he wasn't right for her. Or she wasn't right for him. One or the other, it was the same result. They'd split up amicably and could have a coffee together without the world exploding into a star storm of lust. Or anger and arguments. *They* were better friends than a couple. Hell, she even got on fine with his new squeeze.

Stars twinkled through the bare branches of the elms, no exploding going on up there. Brenna shivered in the chilly air and lengthened her stride to outpace the ghosts of her previous life. 'It's you and me, eh, Pops?'

At the sound of her name, Poppy wagged her tail and a reluctant smile lifted Brenna's tender lips. 'Perhaps I should find you a big bruiser of a mate and breed puppies. We could have a complete family of four-legged brats to keep us happy.'

Poppy stopped abruptly, her nose checking out a pile of leaves.

'You don't like that idea? Me either.' What she really needed was to call up her single girlfriends and go out. Not happening this weekend, though. Unfortunately, a weekend with her mum and sisters in the beach cabin wasn't going to produce a sexy man to play with.

Any man whose name wasn't Hunter Ford.

Not one to fall into bed with a guy within hours of meeting him, getting some fun and light relief wasn't happening any time soon.

No, Hunter Ford was not an option.

'Daddy,' Dylan shrieked, charging at Hunter. 'I coloured in a picture of a horse today. Want to see it?'

Hunter swung his little man above his head and held him there, smiling up at the excitement in his eyes. 'Of course, I do, but you've got to get down first.'

Dylan tried to swing his legs downward and laughed when his dad held him tighter. 'Let me go.'

'Tell me what else you did at preschool first.'

'I did three wees and had chocolate cake because it was Amber's birthday. We sang "Happy Birthday" and clapped. Put me down.'

'Okay, kiddo.' Reluctantly Hunter set Dylan back on his feet. If he had it his way, he'd never let him go, but he wasn't going to stifle him, even when he wanted to protect him from absolutely everything, including tripping over his feet in his rush to get the coloured-in horse.

Dylan yelled, 'Ow!' and straightened up just before he crashed into the wall.

'Slow down,' Hunter called after him.

'Here, get this on board. You look like you've had the day from hell.' Dave was handing him a beer.

Nothing wrong with his day. It was the early evening that had tipped him sideways and had him questioning every damned thought about returning to Vancouver to settle down properly. He would not think about helping Brenna or going inside her house. Definitely not thinking about that kiss. Not for a moment. Or how her body had turned his brain to mush whenever he'd touched her, which he'd done way too often, once being more than necessary.

'He's late. Wonder what kept him from getting home on time?'

'We don't always finish bang on the dot of six, Jess,' he growled, before swallowing a large gulp of beer. He hadn't got to tasting his wine back at his last stop, the distraction in the room being too huge to focus on anything else. He didn't even remember putting the glass down, but he must've since it hadn't come home with him. Why had he kissed Bren? *Brenna*. As if he'd had any choice when she'd been so close, smelt delicious, looked like the woman of his dreams. That's because she *was* the woman of his dreams. He swore and downed half the bottle of beer.

'Tsk, no swearing in front of children,' Jess growled, before saying, 'Let's try *who* got you in such a sweat. Wouldn't be Doc Williamson, by any chance?'

'Want another beer, bud?'

Thank goodness for sensible pals. 'Please, Dave. That one hardly touched sides.'

'I'm taking that as a yes.' Jess smirked and sipped her wine. 'I have to meet this woman who gets you in a twist.'

'Take it any way you like,' Hunter gave back, focusing his annoyance on her and away from the images of a kiss that had knocked his knees out from under him and set his blood racing through his veins, bringing memories and longing and putting a hex on his careful plans for the future.

'Here's my horse, Daddy.'

'Thanks, kiddo.' Hunter took the paper Dylan held out to him and focused entirely on the yellow and green animal standing in a red and grey stall. 'That's clever. You've done a great job. We'll put it on the wall in your new bedroom when we move into our house.'

Our house. Dylan's bedroom. Their life.

'I'll do more colouring in tomorrow. Can we play I Spy?'

'Sure.' It was nearly Dylan's bedtime, but Hunter wasn't giving up play time. 'Then I'll read you a story in bed.'

'Dinner in thirty,' Jess said.

'Great.' If his stomach could handle food at the moment. 'Come on, Dylan. We'll play in the other rooms, give the adults some quiet time.' He ignored Dave's smart-ass comment to that and headed out to the conservatory to start their derivative of I Spy, which involved colours and not letters as Dylan wasn't up to speed on those yet. His friends' two boys joined in and soon the house was full of shouts and laughter. So much for quiet. Hunter grinned to himself. Served Jess right. Nosy creature. But she'd be the first to have his back if anyone hurt him. That was how she operated, unless she disliked you.

So, Brenna, what did we do? Was it wrong? Right? Whichever, they definitely needed to put the past back in its box and padlock the lid.

He didn't need Jess harassing him with questions, he managed fine all by himself throughout the night. They hadn't quietened down by the time he turned into Brenna's service lane early next morning. She'd started the car, removed the charger and was about to head to work. 'Want to share a ride?' he asked. Not because it made sense to share the trip but because he wanted to know how she felt about him this morning.

'Sorry but I go to aqua jogging straight after work on Wednesdays.' She slid inside her car and closed the door.

So, he wasn't top of the pops. Hopefully there'd be no complications arising while they worked together. Like their previous relationship, last night's kiss was history. Knowing that was one thing, remembering it another. So far, he hadn't been doing a good job of remaining neutral around her.

'See you at the base,' he managed, without the disappointment that was clamping around his throat creeping into his voice. Dropping the charger into the back of his four-wheel drive, he climbed into the driver's seat and reversed out onto the road. Thirty minutes to give himself a talking-to about wanting Bren and not having her, and when he pulled into the rescue centre park he added a wish for a frantically busy day for good measure.

It was the only wish that came true all day.

'Aircraft accident at Boundary Bay airport, two injured, one serious.' Andy drained his mug of coffee and headed out to the helicopter at a fast clip.

'The pilot's not really with it, says he's got pain then goes quiet on us,' they were told when they arrived at the upside-down Cessna. 'He'd started to take off when the plane suddenly shot sideways and flipped.'

'Name?' Hunter crawled between the strops to the open door.

'Alan.'

'Hello, Alan, I'm Hunter, a paramedic. Can you hear me?'

'Yeah.'

'Can you tell me what happened?'

'Sharp pain in my chest. Blacked out, I think.' Nothing wrong with his speech or awareness.

'Any history of heart problems?' Hunter was tearing open the man's shirt and taking the ECG pads Brenna passed through to stick to Alan's chest.

'No,' Alan shot back, too fast. Was he telling the truth? Or had he hidden some of his medical history in order to keep his licence?

'Any other pain, before or after impact?'

'My left arm hurts.' Then he quickly added, 'That started after we crashed. Not before.'

Left arm pain could be an indicator of cardiac dysfunction. Or Alan might've broken it when he'd been thrown against the framework as the plane had rolled.

'Ventilation required,' Hunter told Brenna, and nodded when he saw she had the equipment in her hands. Naturally she hadn't missed a trick. He turned away from Alan and spoke in a low voice. 'I'm wondering about the cause of the accident.'

Brenna nodded. 'According to the other guy on board, the take-off was going according to plan then suddenly the pilot groaned and grabbed his chest, letting the controls go. It all ties in with CA. But you're wondering about past history, aren't you?'

See? She had a finger on everything. He nodded but refrained from answering in case Alan overheard. No point upsetting him further. 'In case there are fractures I'll check him over before we extract him with some help from the onlookers.' At this hour there weren't many, but he only needed a couple of strong men to get Alan's small frame out of the tiny cabin.

On the flight back to the hospital emergency department Hunter filled in the report form, making sure all the details were correct, including the pain Alan had suffered before the accident, but not the suspicious way he'd replied to questions. His medical history would be looked into by ED staff. Whether the man should've been behind the controls was for the medical insurance company to determine.

'I'm not happy thinking that accident might've been preventable,' he told Brenna as they returned to the helicopter from the ED. 'His arm wasn't broken, or even badly bruised. What if his passenger had been seriously injured? Or worse?'

'One of the bystanders said he'd renewed his licence two months ago and they have to pass a medical first so it's probably a new medical event.'

'Or he's been denying pains and pretending nothing's wrong.'

'Are you always this suspicious?' Brenna glanced his way, amusement lightening those intense caramel eyes for the first time all morning.

'Just being observant,' he growled, because he had to avoid falling into the warmth surrounding that amusement. 'I hope we've got time for coffee.'

'In need of a fix?'

'Something to keep me alert. Dylan woke twice last night and had to be talked back to bed, no easy feat.'

'Does that happen often?'

'Less than it used to.' He wasn't mentioning how their kiss had kept his body fractious when he hadn't been awake, being the responsible dad.

The coffee grains hadn't had time to dissolve in boiling water when Kevin poked his head around the tearoom door. 'Gas explosion in an apartment downtown.'

'Not in Gastown?' Brenna asked, her voice thick with apprehension.

Kevin quickly shook his head. 'No. Nowhere near Emily and Lily.'

'Thanks.' Brenna pressed her lips together, seemingly

fighting the relief her sisters were safe while other people obviously weren't.

Kevin continued, 'There's a fire on the third floor of the building and so far firefighters have found two bodies, along with one badly burned, unconscious woman.'

'Internal and external burns very likely,' Brenna said as they ran to the chopper.

'The worst injuries possible in my book.' Hunter grimaced. 'Especially those to the lungs.' Hopefully, and very likely, the patient would be unconscious, otherwise she'd be in agony.

The woman was out of it, and her breathing was shallow, while her heart rate was rapid as it tried to compensate for the lack of oxygen. Black mucus at the edge of her mouth indicated internal burns. Brenna immediately began giving oxygen via a manual ventilation bag while Hunter cut away the woman's clothing so he could cover the burns to her skin with cling wrap to prevent infection or dust contaminating the wounds.

'I need large-bore IV access here for saline,' Hunter told Brenna. Fluids were essential for the woman to have any chance of surviving.

'There's a trauma to the head.' Using her free hand, Brenna was carefully feeling around the woman's skull. 'She must've been thrown against something solid in the explosion.'

'The left wrist is at an odd angle too,' Hunter noted as he applied tape to keep the large-bore in place before letting the saline solution run into the vein. 'We need to get her to hospital ASAP.'

'Do we have identification details?' Brenna was looking at the cop standing nearby, not at their patient.

'I've got her name and where she works. That's all I've been able to find out,' the young woman replied. 'A police unit has gone to her work for more info. They'll pass it on to the emergency room.'

'I hope neither of the deceased are related to her. She's got enough to fight at the moment without having to deal with that loss,' Hunter said with a heavy heart. Some people got some lousy breaks. 'Let's go.'

On the way back to base Andy called up Kevin. 'Put the kettle on, will you? We could all do with very strong coffee and breakfast.'

They got to smell the coffee before the next call came in. 'A woman in labour and the baby's head's out but nothing else is moving. It's been in that position for thirty minutes. The midwife called it in.'

The moment they entered the bedroom at the house they'd run to from the helicopter, Brenna was introducing herself. 'Hello, Amy. I'm Brenna, a doctor. I hear you're having trouble bringing your little one into the world.'

Hunter nodded to the man looking distraught on the other side of the large bed. 'I'm Hunter. Your wife?'

He nodded abruptly, pain in his dark eyes. 'Do something. It's not meant to be like this.'

'We're onto it.'

As the midwife filled them in on the details, Brenna talked softly to Amy and explained what she was doing. Pressing above the pubic bone slowly and firmly towards Amy's lower back. 'I'm trying to reposition baby's shoulder. Sometimes they get stuck.'

'I tried that,' the midwife said. 'No change, which was when I called your lot.'

Hunter smiled as he unpacked the portable trolley they'd brought with them. 'You did the right thing. Brenna's just trying once more. We'll be on our way very soon.' Unless baby's shoulder shifted, and then it would arrive in a rush.

It didn't. 'Let's go.' Brenna straightened up and between them they helped Amy onto the trolley.

Immediately Hunter began wheeling her outside and
across to the helicopter sitting in the middle of the road,
where neighbours were keeping back traffic and other
people coming to see what was going on. 'Let's go,' he
told Andy as soon as Amy was strapped in and the door
shut.

'I've called the details in,' Brenna told him. 'They've
got an obstetrician on standby.' Surgery looked like
Amy's best option now.

'Baby was delivered safe and well by C-section, and is
in PICU to keep an eye on things. Mum's been given
heavy painkillers so not very aware just now. The husband sends his thanks,' Kevin told Hunter and Brenna
when they sat down to eat lunch at four that afternoon
after numerous callouts.

'That's the best news of the day.' Brenna fiddled with
her sandwich. 'What about the burns lady?'

'No change.'

As she made to drop her sandwich back on the paper
bag Hunter said, 'Eat it. I know it's hard to swallow but
we're no good to anyone if we don't have food.'

'And I've got to deal with sixteen energetic and rowdy
teenagers later.' Her perfect white teeth bit into the bread
and chicken. Her eyes closed as she worked at chewing
and swallowing. She looked so vulnerable Hunter had
to tighten his hand around his mug of soup to stop himself from leaping up and going to cuddle her until she
smiled again.

Instead he said, 'Thought you were aqua-jogging.'

'We are. It's part of the keep-fit regime their skiing
coach insists on.' Her eyes popped open and he was

blasted with a caramel-coloured look. 'It's wind-down time. Last weekend's competition was the final one for the year, yet the kids aren't ready to hang up their skis. Or stop their fitness training. They're a good lot who like doing things together, and I go along to keep them orderly. At least, I try.'

Her phone vibrated on the table and she picked it up. 'That's not good. A friend of mine has to fly to Toronto tonight as her mother's been admitted to hospital.' She tapped a reply, then put the phone aside. 'Now what am I going to do?'

'Problem?' Hunter asked, even when it was obvious there was. Worry was darkening that toffee colour to coffee grinds.

'Gina dog-sits Poppy for me when I go away. She likes getting out of the apartment she shares with two other women and coming to my house for peace and quiet. She also adores Poppy.'

'Where are you off to this weekend?' More downhill races? Leaping out of perfectly good flying machines?

Brenna's face tightened. 'This weekend is the third anniversary of Dad's passing and the family's going to the cabin over on Vancouver Island.'

'I'm sorry. The date didn't register.' If he'd been around it would've been indelibly marked in his head.

'Hunter,' Brenna sighed. 'Don't apologise. I did not expect you to know the significance of this weekend.'

She was right. This stuff was hard. With nothing to add he went with a change of subject. 'Why not take Poppy with you?' He'd spent some amazing weekends with Brenna and her family at the holiday house. The dog would love running on the beach and in the forest behind.

'She gets bad motion sickness, especially on the ferry,

which I found out the hard way the first time I took her over there.'

He laughed. 'Not nice.' So Poppy would be home alone unless Brenna came up with someone else at short notice. 'Dylan and I could stay over. It'd give Dave and Jess a break from us.'

Shock registered in her face. 'Thanks for the offer, but I'll come up with something.'

He had spoken without thinking it through and saw how she might feel about him being in her personal space. 'The offer's there if you get stuck. Dylan and I could do with time away from Dave's lot too.' He and Brenna wouldn't see each other except maybe at the beginning and end of the weekend, and he wouldn't go delving into her rooms and cupboards. But he wouldn't beg. It wasn't that important, yet the longer he thought about it the more he'd like to have two days when he didn't have to fit in with another family.

In his pocket his phone vibrated. 'Hello, Mum, how's things?'

Brenna stilled.

'Mum, you know perfectly well Dad's capable of doing that by himself.' Hunter stood up to wander outside.

Brenna had begun fidgeting with her coffee mug. As for the look on her face—he didn't want to think about that. She didn't know about Dad's bouts of depression, therefore wouldn't understand what he was saying to his mother.

'If you hadn't moved away, I wouldn't have to worry.' His mother was using her best petulant voice.

It wasn't working. 'We discussed this. You and Dad have all the help you need at your fingertips. You don't need me there to fix every little thing that crops up.' Through the doorway he could see Brenna rinsing her mug at the sink, a grim expression tightening her mouth. So, she thought he'd drop everything and run back to Kamloops over a phone call.

Isn't that what you did last time?

Dad had been thinking about suicide then. Today he was refusing to take Mum with him to the supermarket. What if it was something far worse? Was Brenna right in believing he'd pack up and leave for good?

'No, Mum, I live here now. I am not returning to Kamloops except for visits.' And the first one of those wasn't happening for a while yet. They had to learn to get on without him there twenty-four seven. 'Let Dad do what he wants. He's not hurting anyone.'

Get that, Brenna? My life is now here in Vancouver.

Kevin waved at him. 'You're on again. Car versus bus on Highway 99.'

'Got to go.' He hung up. Hard but necessary for all of them. As long as he was there for every mishap or disagreement, his parents were not going to start sorting out their own lives. Thankfully the staff at the village they lived in were on his side.

As he strapped himself into the seat beside Brenna, he told her, 'Families, huh? They sure keep us busy.'

'Worth it, though.'

She could've said she hoped his had been worth what he'd given up. She hadn't. He relaxed. 'That's what I tell myself when Dylan wets his bed at two in the morning.'

'He still does that?'

'Occasionally, when he's upset about something.' Usually something one or other of his grandparents had told him. 'It hasn't happened since we moved.' Long may that last.

'So he's happy here?'

'Very.' It was true. Dylan seemed to grow every day,

expanding his horizons, not looking for trouble in cupboards. 'Which is why we're here. And not leaving,' he added for good measure.

At ten past six Hunter slung his day bag over his shoulder and headed out to his four-wheel drive. He was exhausted. Every muscle ached, his head throbbed and he couldn't wait to get home to his boy.

'Hunter?' Brenna stood by her car, her elbows on the roof. It was hard to read her expression in the overhead light's sharp glare.

'Yes?'

'Can I take you up on your offer to look after Poppy after all?'

'Not found anyone else?' he asked, not liking to be second best.

She straightened and came across. 'I haven't asked. Turning you down was a knee-jerk reaction because it felt weird that you might be staying in my house after all this time.'

Don't pull any punches, will you?

He gave one back. 'We have moved on, Bren.' Idiot. He'd just shown how far his journey had gone. Nowhere. 'I meant Brenna. When do you head away?'

'Friday afternoon. I'll be back about six on Sunday night.' A little smile flicked on. 'Poppy is fine with children, in case you're wondering.'

'It didn't cross my mind. You wouldn't have accepted if you thought there'd be a problem.' See? They did know each other well. Too well, if the memories his body had dredged up during the night were anything to go by. 'If anyone's in danger of being over-petted, it's Poppy. She'll be begging you to come home early. Dylan adores dogs.'

'Good.' She turned to open her car door.

'Brenna,' Hunter called. 'I hope the weekend goes

okay for you. I know how much you must miss Chris.'
Her father had been her rock after her mother had deserted them when Brenna had been a child, apparently not once letting her down. He still remembered her grief the day Chris had been diagnosed with dementia. Even though she'd been expecting it, hearing it for real had hit her hard.

'It doesn't get any easier, but somehow going to the cabin where we all had so much fun as a family helps. I don't go very often any more.'

That was sad. 'I guess I understand, but it seems a waste.'

'Shane and I used to go a couple of times a year, but not any more.'

'Shane?'

Her face closed down. 'Another story.' Flapping a hand at him, she slipped into her car and gunned the motor.

In a hurry to get away from him? His gut squeezed tight when it shouldn't. There was no reason for Brenna to stay around talking about things he knew nothing about, like this Shane. Who the hell was he anyway? What was he to Brenna? He didn't live with her. Wasn't housesitting this weekend.

'See you tomorrow when I collect the key to your house,' he called to the taillights as she roared around the corner.

Hunter slammed his door shut and snapped on the ignition. Whoever Shane was, Hunter was sure he wouldn't like him.

CHAPTER FOUR

HUNTER DRANK COFFEE and stared at the photos covering the wall before him. The hairs on the back of his neck lifted and he glanced around the room, but Brenna wasn't there. She was still over on Vancouver Island.

But, hell. The images in front of him were her. Sure, the skiers were younger, taller, shorter, male, female, blond, dark—but all he felt, saw was Brenna. Like a painter, when she created a photo it came from within her, using her talent to bring the excitement, fear, joy out in the participant's face, body, angles.

He could see them breathing, moving, and hear the skis on the snow. Draining his mug, he placed it on the mantel, and spoke aloud in an attempt to remove this sense of Brenna being here. 'As for that parachutist, I'm up there with him, floating to the ground, absorbing the shrinking vista.'

No wonder she'd won an award. Her work was exceptional. Typical Bren, she mostly shared it with a team of teenagers who obviously played up the moment she focused her camera on them. Even the funny, cute photos of kids racing down the slope spoke to him of Brenna and how she enjoyed being a part of other people's fun.

But it was the shots taken when someone was focused on winning and doing all in their power to make it happen that made his skin tighten. It was like she got into other people's heads and knew what they were thinking, feeling.

'Something to remember,' Hunter muttered as he flicked off the lights and headed for the bedroom he was sharing with Dylan. No photos in there, thank goodness. He might get some sleep, unlike last night when he'd lain awake for hours, going through the good times they'd had, memories brought on by being in her space— a space he'd once shared.

So much for believing he was over her. He might've been, but now he doubted that. Lingering love in his heart? Or buried love now making itself known again? He could no longer deny how much a part of him Bren had been, and still was. Apparently, it wasn't possible to cut her out of him.

Now what? That was the question. A hard one, at that. Did he really want to get back with Brenna? Six years in between when they'd both dealt with crises and moved on in different directions told him to be cautious. They weren't the same people as the two who'd had everything ahead of them and had believed their love could survive anything. It hadn't. If he did still feel something for Brenna it would be tainted by the past. His neglect of her when his parents had demanded his presence, her acceptance without a fight for him. His child was another biggie.

Bending over the bed, he gently kissed his boy's forehead. 'Love you, Dylan.' He was the best thing that had ever happened to him. It might've been a disaster with Evie, but they'd made the most amazing kid between them. A child who'd forced him to look outside the circle that was his screwed-up family and go for what was important. Did that include starting over with Brenna?

He had no idea. Did he think he might want to? The answer to that would have to wait until they'd spent more time together.

Shedding his clothes and slipping into the other bed, Hunter lay on his back, his hands behind his head, and stared upwards in the darkened room. A part of him felt as though he'd finally come home, but the other side of him was filled with wariness. Had he been working towards this? No, he could honestly say he hadn't.

Yet the memories of the good times were rampant now he was in this house. He and Brenna had been so good together, like nothing else he'd ever experienced. She'd brought him alive in ways no one and nothing else had. The years back in Kamloops had toughened him, taught him that if anyone was to help him face up to what his parents were doing to him that had to be him, but he hoped the accident that had taken Evie's life had made him more compassionate towards others. Dylan had certainly brought out a fierce protective streak in him, including keeping him safe from his grandparents. Yeah, there had been some good to come from the decision he'd made six years ago.

His eyes closed, and his breathing slowed. 'Hey, Bren, I've missed you.' His short marriage to Evie had brought home what a stupid move it had been to leave Brenna. They could've made it work if they'd sat down and talked it through. But he'd been so determined to do right by everyone that he'd screwed up big time. He should've focused on the big picture, not only sorting his parents out.

Now what? He could hardly make it up to her—it was too late for that. Wasn't it? Had she missed him? After she'd got over the initial shock of being dumped? But he was only just beginning to understand how much he'd missed her—all the time. It had taken seeing her again to start the truth unfolding, and now he had to decide if he liked that.

'Dad, look, Poppy's doing wees again.'

What was with this fascination with pee? Hunter shook his head at his son. 'That's what happens when you drink water.'

'I don't want any more, ever.' Dylan loped along behind the dog to her kennel, where she lay down with the bone from last night's dinner.

'Yes, you do. It's good for you. Give Poppy a break and come help me find the lawnmower.'

The whole street had gone crazy that morning, the strident sound of small engines blaring from yard to yard. The sun was out in full strength, hinting that spring was finally waking up. The less obvious signs were the green buds beginning to appear on the trees lining the street and the grass getting long.

'Can I push the mower, Daddy?'

'We'll push it together.' It would be a quick job since Brenna kept the grounds in top-notch shape. The key he'd found on the hook inside the boot room fitted the shed lock.

Dylan pushed past him. 'It's dark in here. There might be ghosts.'

'If there are, they'll be friendly.'

Hunter flicked on a light and stared at the array of gear in front of him. Bloody hell. She really had become an adrenalin junkie. A windsurfing board and its sail leaned against the wall nearest to him. There was a paddle board and pole with an assortment of life jackets. Nothing too dangerous there. The two mountain bikes next to the board were as clean as the day she'd bought them, their wide tyres in perfect condition, but the scratches in the paintwork indicated a collision with the ground at some time. His heart squeezed tight. Brenna really did like living in the fast lane.

'Nothing to lose, Brenna? Just your ability to move around as you like if you make a bad landing.'

Dylan was tugging the lawnmower towards the door. 'Come on, Daddy.'

'Let me do that, chum.' He took the handle from Dylan's small hand, looking back at that stack of gear.

Who are you, Brenna? Where's the woman I loved?

Was this what their break-up had done to her? Or had she always had a hankering for adventure? There hadn't been any indicators when he'd known her. A few hours riding a windsurfer on a calm sea down the road had been her idea of sporting fun. Now look at her collection of gear.

Hell, he'd gone back to Kamloops to run the orchard in an attempt to save it while also working in the local hospital's surgical ward. All safe and serious. Necessary if he was going to help his parents, but he should've had more fun along the way. More than an odd beer with his friends, but he hadn't had the energy left at the end of the day for more than looking after Dylan.

But I did have fun; with my boy.

Lots of great times squeezed in between all the hard work and stress that had gone on at the orchard. He'd organised Dylan's third birthday party in the packing shed with robots and clowns for entertainment. Yep, there'd been good times in the last few years, most of them centred around his boy. If that made him boring, then he'd put his hand up. He was a father, first and foremost, and not too proud to tell anyone asking.

But he needed to start doing things for himself, like

getting back into softball this summer, maybe coaching a junior team. He could try dating Brenna.

Like that was going to happen.

Crunch. Splat. The mower's engine raced.

'Dad, look where you're going. That was Poppy's ball.'

Once again Brenna had messed with his head.

'Sorry, the ferry was late leaving Victoria,' Brenna called out as she barged into her house on Sunday night and headed to the kitchen, where she dumped her bags. 'I didn't expect you to stay until I got back. I do have another key.' But it was lovely seeing him here. Especially when she felt restless and sad.

Hunter was standing behind the bench, looking right at home and devilishly handsome in his navy-blue jersey and blue and white checked shirt. 'Dylan didn't want to leave Poppy on her own.' He grinned.

'They got along, then?'

'Inseparable. Though Poppy's take might have something to do with the food titbits she received whenever I wasn't looking.' His grin widened. 'I know it's not healthy for a dog to eat toast and honey, but routine takes over again as of now.'

'As long as chocolate wasn't involved, I can live with that.' Brenna opened the fridge to retrieve the bottle of wine she'd put in there on Friday for a pick-me-up when she got home, knowing how drained she'd feel after the emotional weekend.

'I told Dylan chocolate makes dogs very sick. He wants to know when we can come and stay again.'

'You'd have to fight Gina for it. She's always looking for a chance to get away from her flatmates and their boyfriends.' Damned top wouldn't crack open. 'Anyway, it's unlikely I'll be away again before you shift into your house.'

'Here, let me.' He took the bottle from her hand, got a glass from the cupboard and poured her drink, before picking up his beer and raising it to his lips. Lips she'd had the hardest time forgetting since Wednesday. 'Dylan will be disappointed, but then he doesn't know I'm going to get a dog when we're in our own place.'

'Where is he?' She'd met the cute little guy, a replica of his dad without the lines on his face and worry in his eyes, on Friday when they'd arrived early with their overnight bags and groceries so that she could introduce Poppy to the boy.

'Fell asleep in his dinner. I put him to bed until I'm ready to leave. He's been running around outside non-stop all day. And before you ask, Poppy's sprawled on the mat beside the bed.'

'That explains my non-welcome home.' Parking her butt on one of the stools at the counter, she sipped the wine, and finally allowed full rein to the exhaustion bugging her. 'It's good to be home.'

'A big weekend?' he asked gently.

His concern was like old times. 'Very. I don't know why this one was more intense than usual when it's now three years since Dad went. Mum cried a lot, and Em and Lily weren't much better.' Nor was she.

'There's no finite date for moving past something as hard as losing someone you love. Some people swear you only need a year; one anniversary for all the important dates you shared. Others say it happens when you're ready.'

'I thought I was.' That was before Hunter had reappeared in her life and stirred up a load of memories. Not all those memories were about them in bed together, or laughing, sharing food, dates. Some were from the times they'd spent with her family at the cabin, and during the weekend she'd been very aware of those occasions. 'The maple tree we planted three years ago has turned up its roots. I'm going back with a new one when spring's settled in.'

Hunter laughed. 'Chris and his maple trees. Not to mention the syrup he poured over his breakfast every day. That man had the sweetest tooth I've ever known.'

It was nice hearing Hunter laugh over something she, Mum and the sisters had cried about more than once since Friday. Dad had had the sweetest tooth ever and originally planting the tree had been about acknowledging that. 'Nothing was safe from his bottle of maple syrup.' Brenna smiled. 'Hard to believe how much he got through and still had normal glucose levels. Even on his worst days with dementia a dollop of syrup made him smile.' She brushed her eyes before lifting her glass to her mouth.

'You're the same about chocolate. I had to put a lock on the pantry to keep Dylan out.' Another laugh filled the air between them. 'You need another pantry for normal food. There's no room in that one.'

'I try not to eat too much, but it is my go-to treat.'

'No wonder you're into aqua jogging. It's got nothing to do with those teenagers at all. You're your father's daughter.'

'Yeah,' she sighed. 'I am.' Nothing like her birth mother, except for the over-the-top curly hair and mud-coloured eyes. 'I found my other mother two years ago.' Sort of.

Hunter leaned his elbows on the counter, his legs splayed behind him, and locked his eyes on her as he sipped from his bottle of beer. 'How did that go?'

He knew how much she'd wanted to meet up with the woman who'd given her life, even if only to tell her how cruel she'd been to desert her and her dad. 'Dad left me an envelope not to be opened while he was alive.' The wine sweetened her mouth when it might've turned sour. Because she was with Hunter? Breathing deep, she smelt something hot and savoury and tasty. 'What's cooking?'

'My pine nut and chicken casserole. I figured you might not have had dinner and thought we could share a meal. If you want to be left alone I won't take it with me. Not all of it.' His smile was devastating because it was kind and gentle and all about doing something for her. It undid some of the knots that had formed the first day he'd walked into the rescue base.

'Dinner sounds delicious, and I'm more than happy to share. After I've finished this glass and poured another.' This was her private time—Hunter notwithstanding— to have a drink and think of her father in the context of the anniversary without looking out for Mum, Emily and Lily. It had been a difficult weekend, everyone sad, but at least they had been there for each other and able to let their hair down, say anything they liked, and no one took offence. They'd all unreservedly adored Dad.

Although there was one thing she would've liked to have had out with him. 'Dad didn't want me to know about my birth mother while he was alive.' It wasn't as if she'd missed out on getting to know the woman because of his reticence, but he still should've told her. 'Unbeknown to anyone except Mum, he'd been trying to find her for years. All he'd had to go on was that she came from Australia.' Apparently, her birth mother hadn't been big on sharing facts about herself.

'Big country, that.'

'Which makes it all the more remarkable that he

eventually found her family. Two sisters living in Perth. My aunts. They didn't have much to say except that my mother had returned to Australia after leaving us, and she'd died from cancer not long after.' She'd never mentioned Brenna or her father to the sisters. 'They got a shock when Dad got in touch, and I gather it took photos to prove he wasn't lying. Once they accepted the truth, they got all concerned he was after the family fortune.'

'That's not like Chris at all.' Hunter locked eyes with her. 'Or you.'

'I don't think the aunts believe me when I say I don't want a cent of it, but they'll get used to the idea eventually, I guess.' Hunter knew her well. Right now, feeling decimated from the emotional two days, it was hard not to fall into the depth of his steady, reassuring gaze, to fall and hold on until the sadness drained away. Hard, but not impossible, if she straightened her spine one vertebra at a time. 'I flew out to meet them, and learned I have cousins as well.' Four, all determined not to make her a part of the family. No doubt because of that fortune.

Hunter took her glass from her clenched fingers and topped it up. 'They hurt you.' He understood without being told.

Another notch of emotion dropped away. 'They want nothing to do with me.' All she'd wanted had been familial recognition, to be able to phone them occasionally for a yarn about what she'd been up to and in return hear what they'd been doing. Instead, she'd received the same lack of interest and concern as her birth mother had given her. None, except for the determination to keep her from the family coffers.

'I have accepted I can't change their minds and let it go.' There was no point staying churned up over what she couldn't alter. 'But I still get bitter at times. What's so wrong in talking to me? And how could my mother not even tell her family about me?' That had really hurt, deep and hard, a hurt that wasn't going away so easily. Was she so unlovable her own mother hadn't wanted her? But her stepmum had accepted her straight away, buck teeth and temper tantrums and all. People did leave her. Some people. She raised her eyes to the man before her. He'd left her.

Yeah, and how hard did I fight to keep him?

She gasped. *What?*

'They're the losers.'

'Pardon?' Who were losers? Her and Hunter?

'Your Aussie relations.'

Phew. 'I reckon.' Brenna also reckoned this wasn't the time to be thinking about where she and Hunter had gone wrong. She was emotionally exhausted and anything she came up with could be utter nonsense. It was something to think about later. Not now. Taking a big sip of wine, she studied the man who'd broken her heart and yet had managed to walk back into the perimeter of her life without too much resistance from her. Meaning what? She had no idea and right now all she wanted was to unwind, enjoy her wine, eat dinner and maybe even enjoy the company. 'Can we eat? I'm suddenly starving.'

His gaze was steady, but there was a question in his eyes. Had he picked up on her thoughts? Of course he had. He knew her, remember? But all he said was 'Sure. Everything's ready. The rice has been steaming for hours.'

Brenna watched as he began plating up, relieved he'd kept whatever was causing that shadow in his eyes to himself. Yet his movements were relaxed, his focus on what he was doing calm, as though dinner was the most important thing on his agenda at the moment. Glad to follow his example, she asked, 'So Poppy sealed the deal about getting a dog?'

'Not just any dog. A Poppy dog.' Hunter grinned. 'Can you put me in touch with her breeder?'

'No problem. Step one in settling into that house you've bought.'

His grin diminished, became a tight smile. 'Yes.'

'You're not changing your mind about moving here?' He couldn't. As he'd told her, this was as much for Dylan as himself.

'Not at all.' The tightness backed down a little. Placing their meals on the counter, he reached into the drawer for cutlery. 'It's just that I feel bad about the location I chose. It's your home turf, and I don't want you thinking I'm deliberately trying to upset you.'

She picked up a fork and toyed with the rice and gravy. 'At first I was annoyed. It's a big city, why chose Kitsilano?' Where we'd been so happy once. Because he was over them. As she was or should be. 'But then I came to see that it's the area you're most familiar with. More importantly, your friends are here, which will make the move easier over the coming months.' Raising her laden fork, she tasted the food. The flavour explosion from the gravy was delicious. 'Oh, yum. That's good.'

'But you'd rather I'd not landed on your patch.'

'No, I'm a big girl. I'm over my funk.'

'Not so big.' Back to grinning at her.

'Let it go. Short, slim and big on attitude. That's me.'

His laughter filled the room, and her heart unfortunately. 'I've been missing that.'

And I've been missing you since you turned up. You're here and yet you're unavailable because I can't have you. I'm too afraid. I'm over being left behind by those I love. Except Dad never deserted me. Mum's still a huge part of my life. My sisters give me grief, but they've got my back as much as I've got theirs.

If they got back together, would Hunter leave her again when he was needed elsewhere? When his parents called? If something happened to Dylan? Of course, he had to do whatever was necessary to keep his son safe and well. But he could let other people help, share the load, not walk out of their lives without looking back. Gulp. The emotions were building again, this time not about dad. Not good.

She swallowed the heaviness in her throat and filled her mouth with chicken. Savouring the delicious flavours bursting across her tongue, she dug deep and moved on to something light and easy. 'Eat your dinner or I'll have it after I've finished mine.' It was that tasty. She was that hungry. 'When did you learn to cook like this?'

'Evie was an exceptional home cook and taught me the basics, and then I didn't want to go back to boiled vegetables and steak every night of the week, so I used what she'd shown me, along with the internet, and found a passion for putting cheese with broccoli and meatballs and making something flavoursome.'

Brenna settled into enjoying her meal, almost effortless now that Hunter had helped her relax by listening without criticism, by understanding her without having to go into details. He'd known her family well. Dad had been thrilled when they'd first talked about a wedding. Then the dementia had begun raising its ugly head and they'd thought about getting married while he could give her away knowing what he was doing, but with her studying, Hunter working long hours, and the family trying to cope with her father's illness, they'd never got around to organising it.

If they had, the last six years would've been very different for one of them. Probably her, as she'd have moved east to be with Hunter while he sorted out his family's problems. But then he wouldn't be a dad. Or would he? Would they have had the children they'd talked about sooner than first thought? Children. Her a mum. Yes, that had been one of her dreams.

Hunter was shaking her arm. 'Go sit in a comfortable chair while I clean up.'

Blinking up at him, she asked, 'Did I just nod off?'

'More like you were miles away, thinking about who knows what. You were about to fall off the stool.' Mischief twinkled in his eyes. 'I've already picked up one person from the table tonight. Must be something about the food I cook.'

'Leave the kitchen. I'll fix it.' In the morning. 'You need to get Dylan home to his own bed.'

'Shortly.' His hand was still on her arm, sending pulses of heat over her skin.

She shouldn't, couldn't, give in to those light beats ripping through her. But, hell, she wanted to. More than anything. It had been a long, hard weekend, and this was the balm she needed. Hunter. His touch, his scent, his heat. Some things in life were impossible and turning away from Hunter right now was one of them. Placing her hand on top of his, she squeezed gently before lacing her fingers with his.

He moved closer. Lifted their hands to his lips. Ran the lightest kiss over her knuckles so that she tightened her hold on him. Next he'd… Lick between her fingers on that super-sensitive spot. A shiver ran down her back as desire rose from deep inside. Then Hunter's eyes locked onto hers, and their silver grey darkened with heat and desire.

Tugging their hands her way, she slid her mouth over

his thumb and ran her teeth over the pad, felt the shiver rippling through Hunter.

Then he took her head in those large, familiar hands and, holding her at just the right angle, leaned in and began kissing her blind.

All the emotions swamping her twisted into a new shape—hot, craving, desire for this man. The only man who'd ever made her feel so wanted, so sexy and desirable. It had been a long time, but the moves hadn't changed. His kiss was like a switch. Every sense in her taut body was on full alert, her mouth on his, their tongues dancing together. She leaned closer, needing his strength to stay upright as everything but the feel of Hunter's mouth on hers disappeared.

And then his hands were holding her upper arms and that beautiful mouth was slowly sliding away.

As air came between them Brenna jerked her head back. 'What?' They couldn't stop. Not now when her whole body was vibrating with need.

'I can't, Bren. I've got to take Dylan home.'

'You haven't got time to finish that kiss?'

Poke me in the eye, why don't you? You can't just stop kissing me like that—unless it meant nothing.

Concentrating hard, she lifted her shoulders and her chin, stepped backwards. He was right. They shouldn't be kissing again. The first time had been a mistake, this time foolish. They hadn't talked about the past, and that wasn't going to disappear in a cloud of desire. If they'd ended up making love it would still be there to haunt them afterwards. Hunter had been right to stop. She should be grateful his brain was obviously in better working order than hers.

'Goodnight, Hunter.' She wasn't thinking about the

other option—that the kiss meant less than nothing to him. That would keep her awake all night.

At three a.m. Brenna admitted defeat and climbed out of the large, now chilly bed, because she'd forgotten to turn the heating up, and went to put the kettle on for a cup of tea.

Hunter hadn't hung around after her terse 'Goodnight', had simply bundled Dylan into his arms and headed for his four-wheel drive.

While the water came to the boil she opened her laptop. If she wasn't getting any sleep then she might as well prepare the photos the ski team had ordered to be printed. The job might even make her nod off.

Fat chance with Hunter rampaging through her head non-stop. She didn't need her photo bank to recall past occasions with him. Wandering through Stanley Park, sitting at the front of the ferry being soaked with incoming waves, partying with their friends, barbecuing in the back yard with her family. The only pictures not on her computer, but just as vivid in her mind, were those like the ones she'd happily have made tonight if reality hadn't stepped in.

Brenna groaned and jammed her fingers through her knotted curls, pulling at her scalp. So much for keeping him at a distance. Why, why, why had she been so eager to kiss the man? She didn't even know what she wanted with him any more. Her excuse was that coming home emotionally worn out and talking to him had relaxed her, had made her feel half-human again to the point she'd forgotten to be on guard with Hunter.

Stirring the teabag vigorously, she shook her head. 'Poppy, your mum's gone and blown her well-planned life out of the water.'

Not that anything would change. Except her head space, and it seemed that was already messed up.

The dog didn't move, except to open one eye briefly.

'You're agreeing, huh?' Then, 'Oh, great.' The teabag had burst. 'Maybe I should go back to bed, lie quietly and turn my mind off.'

Like that had worked for the last five hours. She got another teabag and started over.

'So, Pops, what do I do next? Tell Hunter to leave town before lunch?' Now, there was a thought. 'We can't have one of those pathetic conversations where we say we have to get over what happened and move on pretending everything is the same as it was a week ago.'

A week? That's all it had been since Hunter had turned up on base and complicated her life. One week.

This didn't have to be problematic. All she had to do was remind herself she loved her work, enjoyed going on trips with the skiers and riding down mountainsides with the bike group from the hospital, and taking scary photos in situations that fed her adrenalin need. There was no time for a relationship even if she'd wanted one. Forget that she'd decided to get in touch with her girlfriends for a night out. When she wasn't rostered on the helicopter her weekends were fully booked with one thing or another. Except the next one. A trip to the hairstylist on Saturday and lunch with Em and Lily on Sunday wrapped it up. Very staid for her and it would leave too much opportunity to ponder about Hunter and this need she had going on for him.

The tea and photos were a success. The ringing phone woke her. Scrambling out of the comfy armchair, she dashed across to grab it before whoever it was hung up. The screen showed six-fifteen and Kevin's name. Uttering an oath, she banged the phone against her ear. 'Kevin, sorry, I'm still at home, I overslept. I'll be there as quick as I can.' A thirty-second shower and no walk for Poppy.

'Slow down. I was checking you were all right. We're off to a quiet start, but if a call comes in, I'll take your place.'

She was never late. Blame Hunter. Why not? He messed with her head all the time. 'I am really sorry.'

'Relax. How was the weekend?' He knew where she'd been, and probably thought the emotions had made her tired. Which was true, but they hadn't caused her sleep pattern to change so drastically.

'It went well, lots of laughter and tears. We decided it was the last time we'll do it. Everyone's ready to look forward despite the emotional upheaval.'

'That's good. Okay, see you soon but, Brenna, don't rush. We've got this covered. Hunter's here and raring to go. You have some breakfast and take Poppy for her walk before coming in.'

As the phone went silent Brenna burst into tears. Everyone was so damned nice. They were there for her even when she didn't ask them to be. Except Hunter was now back in the picture. Not as a lover or partner. No, she had to put a stop to that. No more kisses. The number of times his mother phoned him nagged at her, reminding her he could just as easily pack up and disappear when the woman needed him too much. Which meant he still had the power to hurt her, if she gave too much of herself.

But she wouldn't deny he was here and that she'd like to see him occasionally. Last night, talking about Dad and her birth mother had shown what she'd missed about him almost as much as the loving. Or was it all part of the loving? He knew her, understood her, which was very, very special. Not even her close girlfriends got it as right as Hunter.

Everyone needed someone to offload on, knowing they wouldn't be laughed at or embarrassed. Hunter was that someone for her. Always used to be, and she hadn't managed to replace him in that aspect. Not in any way. Except for the adventure and photography, which gave her a sense of fulfilment on a certain level.

Now all she had to do was find a way to make friendship with him work without giving too much of herself away. Without kissing him again.

Loud laughter came from the staffroom when Brenna finally walked into the rescue headquarters. Her toes curled, and her blood zinged. Always a sucker for Hunter's laugh, her stomach squeezed tight. Just as well she hadn't managed to swallow any breakfast, or it might be revisiting. Right, time to straighten up, pull on the poker face and go join the crew for a coffee. She strolled in as though this was any normal morning. 'Morning, everyone.'

'Sleepyhead's arrived.' Hunter didn't look at all repentant for causing her lack of sleep. Did he know the effect he'd had on her? Worse, he didn't look as though he'd missed a moment's shut-eye all night.

'The morning's been quiet. The other crew are out attending a motorcycle accident beyond Richmond. A fractured leg and an angry patient apparently.' Kevin shrugged. 'Guess now you're here I get to sit behind my desk for the rest of the day.'

'I can swap if you want some work experience,' Brenna said. That way she didn't have to sit squashed into the tight space in the back of the helicopter, breathing in spice overlaid with rock-solid male testosterone. Taking the front seat in the chopper would show she was avoiding Hunter and he'd pick up on it straight away. He'd probably already worked out that's what her offer to Kevin was all about. Her brain wasn't in first gear this morning. 'I have some medical notices to get through.'

'You hate those things.' Kevin placed a coffee in front of her.

'Doesn't mean I can ignore them.' Okay. Partial truth time. 'I'm very tired so it might be best if you cover for me this morning.'

Kevin nodded. 'You're looking peaky.'

The corners of Hunter's mouth were lifting into a smug smile. 'Very peaky.'

Instead of yelling at him for being a smart-ass, she gulped a mouthful of coffee and stared at the table between them.

I will not let him see how much he's got to me.

'I think Poppy's missing Dylan. This morning she kept going to the bedroom he used to sniff around.'

'Told you they hit it off.'

'You'd better get a puppy sooner rather than later.'

He didn't miss a beat. 'Got the breeder's details in your phone? Because I don't think I'm going to get away with a miniature poodle.'

'Diamonds on the collar?' Trying not to imagine Hunter and a poodle because she'd laugh herself sick, she tugged the phone from her pocket and tapped on contacts and found the number. 'Here, I'll send it to you. What's your number?'

One dark eyebrow rose.

Did he really think she was trying to get his details for her own use? When she hadn't had them while he'd been in her house for the weekend? She slid her phone across the table to him. 'Put it in yourself.'

After tapping in the number, Hunter handed her phone back. 'Thanks. I'll get in touch this week. Though I can't take a pup while we're still at Dave and Jess's. It wouldn't be fair on anyone.'

'Have they got a large house, or are you all crammed in on top of each other?' On top of each other brought connotations she'd rather not think about when stuck in a small room with the man.

His eyes widened. Obviously, he'd had the same idea. 'Five bedrooms, two sitting rooms and an enormous yard. They got lucky when Dave's work colleague had to downsize urgently. They snatched the house up and I can see them staying there until their grandchildren are old enough to have babies.'

'What's your new place like?' As long as they stayed on innocuous subjects, she'd handle this.

'Three beds, one sitting and an average yard.' Hunter leaned back in his chair and stretched his legs to the far side of the table. 'It's a humdinger. There's lots of renovating to do, including updating the basic kitchen and bathroom. But it was the large, spacious rooms and the windows that let in lots of sunlight in winter that hooked me. Of course, it might be like an oven in summer, but we'll deal with that when it happens.' He really wasn't fazed one little bit by last night.

Where did that leave her? 'I'll go settle into the office, Kevin.'

Andy poked his head around the door. 'We're on, guys.'

Brenna sank onto the chair behind Kevin's desk and opened the first set of notes from the medical board. *Proposals for dealing with the increase in diabetes.* Scintillating stuff, and nothing to do with her day job, but she read everything that arrived in her file from the board. Who knew when she might quit the rescue service?

* * *

The week crawled past. Brenna had a mild cold and a pounding headache so she stayed on Kevin's desk, giving him more time doing what he liked best. It had nothing to do with avoiding working with Hunter, of course. He dropped in to chat about mundane things a couple of times a day, and she joined everyone in the tearoom whenever they were there. Slowly, she began to feel comfortable with him again, and by Thursday afternoon she was more than ready to get back into the flying seat beside him. Not that she'd resolved where they stood, or what she wanted from him, but she was happier. 'The desk is yours next week,' she told Kevin over coffee as they waited for the minutes to click down to eighteen hundred and home time. Three days off, then she'd be on nights.

No more calls came in and the night shift arrived. Everyone leapt up, eager to get away. With her bag over her shoulder, Brenna headed out to her car.

'Brenna,' Hunter called as he followed.

When she turned around, he was looking at her thoughtfully, which had her foot tapping impatiently.

'Are you doing anything on Saturday?'

'Not a lot for once,' she answered warily.

'I'm going to a wedding.'

'That's nice.' Where was this going?

He came closer and she could see the awkwardness in his face. 'This is very short notice, but I need a partner. Would you come with me? Please?'

What the hell? 'Sorry?' Had Hunter asked her to go on a date?

'Sorry you can't? Or sorry you won't?'

'Sorry I don't know if I heard you right. You want to take me to a wedding? Whose?' Not that she needed to know. She wasn't going. That would be too personal and remind her of what they'd both once wanted.

'Dave's brother, Toby, is marrying his childhood sweetheart. They got back together last year after working at opposite ends of the country for four years.'

'Nice.'

'Well?'

'You don't need me there. You know Dave's family as well as your own. It's not like you'll be stuck at the table furthest to the back with all the second and third aunts.'

'You're right. I'll be stuck with the groom's family. Right beside Dave's sister, because Dave thinks we'd hit it off together.'

Brenna's stomach dropped. Dave wanted Hunter and his sister to get together? She remembered Molly with braces on her teeth and long mud-brown hair in ponytails. Guess she'd grown up some. 'You're not interested?' She held her breath.

'No.' He was watching her way too closely. 'Molly is cute and lovely but not my type, even if I was looking for someone.'

He wasn't in the market for a partner. That was good news. She could forget that kiss entirely. Her lungs began working again, although unevenly. 'So tell Dave.'

'I have, without being too blunt. It's tricky since we're so close and Molly's his kid sister.'

'In other words, you are trying to find another way to deliver the blow by taking someone else to the wedding. But why me? Dave will see through that in a flash.'

'Maybe. But it's worth a try. So, yes or no?' Hunter shrugged too nonchalantly.

Brenna hesitated. It would be fun catching up with Dave and meeting his wife and kids, but could she spend hours with Hunter and not start wondering how they might get back together? 'No.' Even as she uttered the word disappointment filled her.

'I'll have to pull the wild card. I helped you out last weekend.'

'Low blow, Ford.'

'Needs must.'

She couldn't stop the smile that spread across her mouth. 'You're that desperate?'

'Could be.'

'I like it. What time?' Damn, giving in came too easily. Hopefully attending a wedding wouldn't be as close and personal as a candlelit dinner date for two. Not that she'd been asked on one of those.

'Kick-off is at five so I'll pick you up a little after four.' Hunter returned her smile.

'You always were full of yourself when you won.' She couldn't be mad at him when there was a bubble of excitement building inside her. Against all the warnings she'd given herself since their last kiss, she wanted to go out with Hunter, to have time together that didn't involve BPs, airways or heart rates. Though heart rates might come into it if it was a hot date. 'I can still retract my agreement.'

'Don't even think about it,' he tossed in her direction as he headed for his vehicle. 'Did I mention I'm moving into my house on Sunday?' He knew he hadn't.

That soon? She wasn't reacting. Not even moving her lips. His plans for settling into his new home had nothing to do with her. Anyway, she was having lunch with her sisters. She pinged her locks and ignored that well-honed body leaning against the four-wheel drive.

What would she wear? A mental appraisal of what was in her wardrobe and she grinned. Tomorrow she'd go shopping for a dress and shoes. Slapping the steering wheel, she laughed. This might be fun after all. It had been ages since she'd had an occasion to get all glammed up. It had been even longer since she'd gone out with a hot man.

Though she was not supposed to get excited about that. No more kisses, remember? But she could have fun.

CHAPTER FIVE

HUNTER SWALLOWED HARD as he stared at the woman standing before him. Brenna looked more stunning than any of his memories recalled. Her svelte figure filled the sleek red dress to perfection. His eyes travelled down her shapely legs to the colour-matched high heels that brought her head a little closer to his shoulder and he felt a tightening in his groin.

There was a time when they'd—

Don't go there.

Dragging his gaze upwards, he stared at the wild curls that were her signature. They'd been coaxed into a soft style framing her face and highlighting her eyes.

'Bren, you get more beautiful by the day,' he whispered.

Was this why he'd asked her to accompany him? Because he'd wanted something good back from the past? Something to help him through the mire of their current situation? Needing a woman to deflect Molly had been an excuse. He knew it, Dave knew it, which meant Jess did. Hopefully Brenna didn't. It might create a stumbling block when they were trying to move past the bog that was their history.

She blinked, squirmed in those unreal shoes and finally laughed softly. 'You scrub up all right yourself.'

He took her arm to lead her out to his four-wheel drive, paused while she locked up. 'Where's Poppy?'

'In her run. Where's Dylan?'

'In the back of my vehicle. Along with Dave's two. It's a bit of a squeeze. I had to put one child on the jump seat, in the appropriate car seat, of course.'

Her eyes widened, whether in disappointment or relief that they weren't going to be alone he couldn't decide. Then she said, 'Hang on, I'll get Poppy and clip her in the back too.'

Laughter pushed past the tightness in his throat. 'A carsick dog would not be a good look at the wedding ceremony.'

Her sigh was OTT. 'I hate it when you're right.'

'Come on. Let's move.' They weren't late but he couldn't stand here bantering with Brenna all afternoon. Well, he could, but then they might never make it on time. Also, the kids would start getting stroppy over being belted in for too long and going nowhere.

'Hi, guys,' Brenna called as she slipped into her seat and reached for her belt. 'I'm Brenna. I know Dylan. What are your names?'

'Joshua.'

'I'm George.'

Hunter shut his door and turned to the back. 'Everyone ready?'

Shrieks of 'Yes!' and 'Hurry up!' answered him.

'Shouldn't have asked,' he muttered to Brenna. 'Hope you brought your earplugs.'

'They're in my purse.' She grinned.

That grin was dangerous. It tightened parts of his anatomy that he needed to stay quiet for the rest of the day. And night. Concentrating on driving was the only way to go for his passengers and his libido. 'Thanks for agreeing to be my partner.'

'I'm not sure why you needed me when you've got three escorts right here.'

He glanced sideways, got whacked with another, bigger grin. 'They're not coming with us. I'm dropping them off at a friend of Jess's who's bravely volunteered to look after them until the morning, when Jess will take over again.' Tomorrow he'd be busy moving into his house.

'It seems Dylan's making lots of friends fast.' There was a worried glint in her eyes that he was sure had nothing to do with how his son was fitting into life in Vancouver. Wondering how their night might pan out?

'The last legal requirements for the house purchase went through yesterday.' A surge of pride had him saying, 'We'll be living close to the preschool he's attending, and the primary school is only another street away, so I'm hoping the friendships he makes will roll over from one school to the next. Friends are so important.'

'Good ones, yes.' Her gaze was fixed beyond the four-wheel drive.

Was she having a crack at him about being friends, not lovers? 'Brenna, I am really grateful you're coming to this wedding with me. It means a lot. I know it's not easy for you.'

Her sigh resonated between them. Then her hand was on his arm, squeezing hard. 'You want me to sit at another table?'

He laughed, as he was sure he was meant to. 'We'll see.' How had he ever managed to leave her? They were so attuned to each other, surely they should've been able to make it work. There'd been long dark days at the time. Days when he'd had to restrain himself from driving back here and snatching her away from her study and work and

family. Days when he'd come close to tossing the towel
in with his parents and leaving them to sort out their own
problems. 'Family first' had been his mother's mantra all
his life, especially when his father was in his dark space
threatening to end it all. Now Dylan was his number one
priority, but he'd managed to accommodate his parents
as well since his son's birth. Could he add Brenna to the
mix? Safely? For both of their sakes. He wanted more,
the whole picture. A wife, more kids maybe.

'Brenna, can we play I Spy?' Dylan piped from behind.

'Good idea.' Another squeeze and her hand left him.
'I'm going first. I spy something green.'

'How'd you know not to use letters?'

'Grass.'

'Tree.'

'Dog.'

'I do have some contact with kids.' Her eye roll was
a five out of five. 'Who said dog?'

'Me,' shouted Joshua.

'You need your eyes tested, buster.' Brenna laughed.
'I don't see any green dogs out there.'

'Yes, there is. On that letter box.'

'Now who needs their eyesight checked?' Hunter
pulled away from the traffic lights and turned into the
street where the kids were going to spend the night. Unless he kept them with him as chaperones. Every time
he glanced across to Bren his heart stuttered. She was
so beautiful.

But more than that, she came with so much good from
the past that he was beginning to believe he could make
the move to Vancouver work in more ways than he'd anticipated. In ways he hadn't dared hope for. Heading back
over the Rockies the next time his parents really needed

him wasn't happening, yet he still had to prove to himself more than anybody how determined he was to stay here.

Brenna sat at the white cloth–covered table with a glass vase of daffodils in the centre and tried to relax. Hard when Hunter sat right beside her, looking good enough to eat. Just as well they'd already consumed the banquet. She glanced around the room at the other tall, good-looking men. None were a patch on her date.

'Here.' Hunter passed her another glass of champagne. 'Get that into you.'

'Looking dehydrated, am I?'

He gave her the once over before those intense steely eyes locked on the curves of her breasts peeking above the top of her dress. 'There's nothing dry or shrivelled about you.'

Corny, but cute. Deep inside the tension was weaving tighter. Time for a change of subject to something less intoxicating. She tapped the rim of her glass against Hunter's. 'I like Jess.'

'She likes you too.'

Brenna choked on her mouthful of champagne. 'You've been discussing me?'

'No one *discusses* with Jess. She says what she thinks and we mere mortals learn to deal with it.'

Just then the band struck up and Hunter leaned close to say, 'I should never have introduced the two of you. My life is going to be hell from now on.' He breathed deeply, savouring the heady scent of summer that was her perfume.

'You'd better believe it.'

As they watched the newlyweds take their first married dance Brenna relaxed further. Despite all her misgivings about coming here, she was having fun. Hunter was good company, when he wasn't being sexy just by breathing. He didn't leave her to her own devices while going off to talk to the people he knew. The only time he'd wandered away was when she and Jess had been talking. If he'd known they'd get into a push, prod, what do you know about Hunter, what do I know you don't, kind of conversation he'd have stuck to her like glue. Or taken her out to his car and clipped her into one of the children's seats for the rest of the night.

'Shall we dance?' Hunter asked, a hesitancy in his voice she hadn't heard all evening.

Looking directly at him, she said, 'Yes, I'd love to.' There hadn't been a lot of dancing going on in her life lately. A few outings to bars and nightclubs had been it since she and Shane had parted ways. There hadn't been a lot going on with Shane either. He reckoned he had two left feet when it came to moving to music. She might as well make the most of what was on offer and deal with any consequences later.

'As long as the band doesn't play music where I have to hold you and direct you around the floor without mashing your toes,' Hunter quipped as he led her onto the floor amongst everyone else flocking to dance too.

Mashed toes might be easier to deal with than his hand on her waist where heat shot in all directions. 'You're not into doing a two-step, then?' She certainly wasn't.

'Lucky if I can move one without getting out of rhythm.' He still held her hand, his fingers threaded through hers.

Standing before Hunter, looking up into that handsome face, seeing his mouth twitch with laughter and his eyes rest on her without demanding anything from her, Brenna felt as though she'd finally come home. Of all the places, surrounded by strangers, holding Hunter's hand, doubting they were going anywhere with this, everything still felt right, and she wanted more.

Suddenly, she wanted it all. Tugging her hand free, she began moving her hips, her feet, tipping her head back so her hair brushed across her shoulders in time to her movements. She wasn't getting it, even if it happened to be on offer. But, hell, she was going have a great time. Tomorrow could bring what it liked. She was tough, she'd survive.

Hunter pulled into the kerb outside Brenna's house and switched the ignition off. 'Thanks for coming with me. I had the best time in ages.' He meant it. They'd been easy together, the most relaxed since he'd arrived in town.

'Me too.' Brenna tipped her head back against the headrest and smiled a beguiling, private little smile that pushed under his ribs and rattled his usually quiet heart.

Picking up her hand, Hunter engulfed it in his to rub his thumb back and forth across her wrist; he sat quietly, staring out at the street, thinking about Brenna's body pressed against his as they'd attempted the two-step that the band had inevitably played for the grandparents. They'd both been hopeless but having her that close had meant he'd been loath to stop pretending he had everything under control. Everything except his libido, and that had raised its head far too often to be comfortable. 'I should be going. After I walk you to your door, that is,' he added in a hurry.

'Yeah, right,' she sighed through those lips that he'd been eying up all night.

Lips that could tease, tantalise, torment. He wanted to be teased, tantalised, tormented. Right now. Withdrawing his hand, he reached for the door handle. 'Come on.' Finishing the night in her bed was foremost in his brain but having Bren rebuke him for suggesting it would be hard to stomach.

Who the hell am I trying to fool?

He'd take what he could get, as long as she wanted the same. 'Come on,' he growled again.

Brenna was silent as they walked up the path, balancing on those ridiculous, sexy heels like it was normal to walk on stalks thinner than his mother's knitting needles. At the door she slid her key into the lock.

The sound of it opening was heavy, loud, and reminded him this was as far as he went. Hands on hips so he didn't reach for her, Hunter stared down into the face of his dreams. 'Goodnight, Brenna. Thanks again for helping me out.' If his feet hadn't been made of concrete that's when he'd have left.

She was staring right back, the overhead light making her face harsh yet highlighting the longing in her eyes. 'Hunter.'

His heart missed a beat. Then another. The breath he'd just inhaled hurt in his chest. His tongue glued itself to the roof of his mouth. Leave. Now. Please.

Her shoulders lifted, fell softly, and then her hand was on his chest. 'I know what we said about nothing happening between us again, but—' Her hand clenched into a small fist, knocked on his sternum. 'Can we have this one night?'

His arms reached for her, lifted her up against his chest and he leaned down to kiss her softly on those delightful lips. 'Open the door, Bren,' he gasped through the need roaring through his body from his hard-on to his chest to his mouth. 'Now.'

Down the hallway into her bedroom, right up to that enormous bed she apparently slept in all by herself. What a waste. But not tonight. Tonight they'd make love, pile up more memories, and worry about where this wasn't going tomorrow. He set her on those amazing heels, turned her round slowly, savouring the view in the light thrown by a bedside lamp she must've left on earlier. He palmed her shoulders, spread his fingers across her satin skin, closing in on the zip that held that figure-defining dress in place. His mouth found her neck, where he laved the sweet skin behind her earlobe.

'Hunter,' she whispered. 'Let me touch you.'

'No way, sweetheart. This is for you. One touch from you and it'll be all over for me.' His desire was explosive. It wasn't happening until he'd made Brenna fall apart in his hands. Right on cue her lithe body shook. Her head tipped back so that her wild hair spilled down her back as he tugged the zip down to the top of her bottom. Then she stepped forward, to shimmy out of the dress. He gasped as her perfectly curved bottom in the red lace G-string moved from side to side. Then she turned to face him, swinging her hips in the same way she'd done on the dance floor earlier. Her full breasts in their lace cups swayed in time with her hips. Her widespread hands slid over them, pausing to rub her nipples before moving lower, over her belly to the lacy V that was the front of her panties.

Hunter groaned. 'Don't do this to me.' Yet he was incapable of moving, his eyes tracing every movement of those fingers, his body thrumming with desire, his head whirling.

Her lips lifted into a sensual smile, teasing and taunting him. 'Or what?'

'Or I'll throw you on the bed and take you. Now. Urgently.'

'Perfect.' She reached for him, using his tie to tug him close. Held on as she sank to the bed, and began dealing with his belt and trousers, his boxers. And, at last, his body. With her mouth.

'No, Bren,' he gasped. 'No. Not yet.' He had to touch her, feel her need. Now. Pulling back, he reached for her head, lifted it away from him, before sweeping her up and spinning around to sink onto the bed with her straddling him. 'Ladies first.'

And his hands and mouth proceeded to show her exactly what he meant by that. When she cried out with such need and relief and depth in her voice, he finally sank into her heat and knew he'd come home. If only temporarily.

There was nothing temporary about the rest of the night. Neither was there much sleep, just snatched minutes before he'd reach for Brenna again, or roll into her arms as she gripped him and began touching, tasting, giving herself.

When the sun lightened the edges around the curtains, they both looked at each other and smiled.

'I'm exhausted,' Brenna said. 'I'm not getting up till I have to get ready to go to lunch with my sisters.'

'I'm starving and exhausted,' he gave back. 'What's for breakfast?'

'Ow!' She winced. 'I didn't do the shopping yesterday.'

Hunter sat up and swung his legs over the side of the bed. 'I'm going out to get bagels and smoked salmon, and proper coffee. Then I have to go. I've got the movers coming at nine.'

Brenna shot upright, her eyes wide. 'I totally forgot it's moving day for you. Why a Sunday and not Saturday, like normal people?'

'Because I had a wedding to go to, and Dave wouldn't have been available.' He ducked through the door into the en suite bathroom. A quick shower was needed before anything else.

'What can I do to help? Unpack boxes, set up your kitchen?' Brenna followed him into the bathroom. 'I've got a few hours free.'

'Get back to bed and play catch-up on that sleep you want until I bring back the breakfast. As for unpacking, there's not a lot to do and anyway Jess has taken charge of the kitchen. Mostly dumping her old stuff on me. Not that there's anything wrong with her last dinner set or the salad bowls and casserole dishes she put away when a whole new lot was delivered last week.'

Brenna laughed. 'You're getting the cast-offs, eh? Didn't you bring your own things from Kamloops?'

The water was hot and worked at his muscles as he soaped away the scents from the night. 'There wasn't much I liked, most of it being from the cottage at the orchard. In other words, rubbish. A mix of Mum's old sets.' Nothing like the one decent collection of Wedgwood blue dishes, plates and bowls stacked in Brenna's cupboards.

'So, you don't want me to help?' There was something wistful going on in her eyes.

Which made him feel a heel when he said, 'Thanks, but there're going to be too many people hanging around already. Jess will be bringing the kids with her as well. Bedlam.' Having Brenna in his house, opening boxes of books or mugs, as he moved in and got established in the new life he'd been dreaming of raised the stakes about where they were headed. He wasn't ready for that. Despite the incredible night they'd just shared, he had to think about how far he was prepared to go with her.

The brakes had to go on until he was a hundred per cent sure what he wanted for the future. He wasn't about to set Bren up only to hurt her again.

So why stay last night?

Like he'd been able to say no to her.

The bathroom door closed with a loud click, but not before he saw the withdrawal darkening her eyes.

His heart was heavy as he lathed his skin with soap. The words that slid across his lips unprintable. Again, he'd stuffed up with Bren. What was the harm in having her help unpack his gear? He didn't want her just as a woman to make love to and then get up and disappear out the door, but having her in his house, leaving her scent, her presence in the rooms for him never to be able to avoid her if it became apparent he had to, wasn't on. Snapping the water off, he snatched up a towel from a pile stacked on a stool. It smelt of jasmine and Bren. His lungs expanded as he breathed her in. Brenna. His Bren.

Was he falling in love with her all over again? Or had he never fallen out of love? Was that why he and Evie hadn't made it? Had he been too distracted by the woman who'd held his heart? The same questions he'd found himself asking over and over since first seeing Brenna again, and still no straight answers. He'd worked so damned hard to get over her, to shove her out of his life so he wouldn't go begging for a second chance, and he'd thought he'd succeeded.

He might've spent the intervening years having moments of longing for that smile, those curves, the attitude that told him where to go when she didn't agree with him, but he had stopped loving her. Or so he'd thought.

Hunter's skin lifted in cold bumps. If he still loved her, where did it lead? Brenna had been quick to kiss him, even quicker to get him into her bed last night, but he doubted she'd have him back other than as a friend with benefits. He'd hurt her when he'd called their relationship off. While she hadn't tried to stop him going—he wasn't admitting to her calls that he'd refused to answer—and she hadn't made a move to go to Kamloops to be with him, in her eyes he'd deserted her as her birth mother had in the past. Almost as though she expected people to dump her, which was hardly fair on her father, who'd stayed around all her life.

Back in her bedroom he found his shirt on the floor where it'd been dropped in their frenzy to get naked with each other. Pulling it over his head, he looked around the neat room with its feminine furnishings and smiled. No photos of hair-raising skiers or parachutists in here. The only photos were of her father and stepmother, and her sisters. No one else. This was Brenna's room, her haven from the world, the place she tended to her soft side. His smile dipped. The room felt lonely.

He found her in the conservatory off the kitchen, a mug of hot water clasped in her hands, a thick navy robe wrapped around her slim body, and Poppy sitting at her feet. That sense of loneliness grew inside him. This was a side to Brenna he hadn't known before. Because it hadn't been there then? Another thing he was responsible for?

'Hey,' he called softly. 'I'll be back shortly with the bagels.' It was the least he could do.

Those curls had become riotous overnight and now they hung over her cheeks like curtains, hiding most of that still expression. Most of it, not all. 'Don't get me one. I'll find something in the freezer when I'm ready for breakfast.' She sounded as though food was the last thing she needed.

Brenna wanted him gone, not coming back with a smile and a bag with something to eat in it. 'Fine.'

What else could he say? *Come round for a celebratory drink later when I've unpacked the glasses?* Not that he didn't want to show her his home. He wanted to very much, and yet he didn't.

His phone vibrated. Digging it out of his pocket, he

grimaced. 'Mum.' Letting the call go to voice mail he noticed there were two other missed calls.

'She's up early.' There was censure in Brenna's voice. Did she think he'd be racing back to Kamloops today? Any day?

Not that he could fault her for that. He'd done it before. He hadn't talked to her about his folks since returning to Vancouver, hadn't told her much at all about anything important. 'She's still learning I'm not there to jump every time she wants something.'

She was staring out of the conservatory, her knuckles white around that mug. 'It's a hard one, that.'

So, she definitely still had issues about his family. 'I've moved here for good, Brenna. No matter what happens, I am not going back to Kamloops.'

Silence. Tense and heavy.

He rushed on, needing to explain himself. 'I've made sure there are support systems in place, and the medical people at the retirement village are up to speed with Dad's depression bouts.'

'They're serious?'

He nodded. 'Very. You won't find a headache pill anywhere in the house because of them.'

'He's tried to commit suicide?' Understanding was dawning in her face, as was disappointment—in him. 'You never once told me about this. I thought we had a strong relationship.'

He squirmed. 'I'm sorry, but it's hard to tell people your dad's suicidal and selfish and all the rest of what goes on with his depression. I told a close friend once and he never looked at me the same again. As a teen I used to worry I might turn out the same. It wasn't until I moved to Vancouver, away from it all, and could spread my wings, that I knew for certain I am nothing like my father.'

'I still should have known.'

'I tried more than once to say something, but the words kept banking up in my throat. I had this irrational fear that if I told you it might turn out I mightn't be the happy, hardworking guy you knew.' He drew a deep breath. 'Now it's all about looking out for Dylan.'

'You could do that in Kamloops.'

'To a certain extent, but it isn't the life I have worked for. I feel most at home here, in a vibrant city where I've got friends who believe in me, where I can do the work I trained for on a larger scale, where Dylan can grow up unshackled by his grandparents' need to force their woes onto him.'

Now he had her attention. Her eyes widened as they locked on him. She straightened her back and really looked at him. 'They what?' she demanded.

He shoved his hands in his pockets to hide the shaking that had started up. Against his fingers the phone started vibrating again. Blindly pressing buttons till it stopped, he took a breath and spilled.

'They're already grooming Dylan to do as they want. Mum tells him how Dad hears voices in his head and that Dylan has to be careful or Granddad will tell the monsters to get him.' He might be being disloyal, but he was fighting for his integrity here. He needed Brenna to believe in him again. Didn't matter if they had a future or not, she had to believe in him like she once had. 'Dad demands my lad be his general runabout, getting things, doing jobs that are beyond a four-year-old.'

'That's wrong.'

'Yes, it is.' He knew too well where it would have led if he hadn't taken Dylan out of the picture. He'd had the same grooming all his life. Except for when he'd been living in Vancouver. His parents had given him space then, for a few years, and he'd begun to believe he was free to get on with his own goals. But the cord had been there all along, and when they'd begun winding it in, playing on his guilt for the quad-bike accident when he was a kid believing he was helping them, he'd gone along with it.

'It's not happening any more.' To Dylan or to him. He *had* paid his dues.

'Good.' There wasn't a lot of conviction in that one word.

'Brenna, I know what I have to do and I'm getting on with it.' Pulling his hands free, he crossed to her and leaned down to place a kiss on her cheek. 'Believe me.'

Please.

CHAPTER SIX

'How did the move go?' Brenna asked Hunter as they sat
with the rest of the crew members in the rescue centre's
kitchen, eating dinner. She wasn't avoiding the subject
and how he hadn't wanted her helping. That would be
giving it too much importance. It stung, though, because
it showed how he felt about anything more than a friendship, and even that had boundaries. Kisses and sex fine,
domesticity not.

'Not bad. I could do with more furniture. I'd thought
the house was quite small but there're a lot of empty
spaces.' Hunter leaned back in his chair, plate in one
hand, fork in the other, scooping up noodles and green
curry from his Thai takeout.

'What do you need?' Andy asked. 'We've got a second
house lot stored in our garage from Mel's mother's place.
You're welcome to help yourself to anything you fancy.'

'Thanks for the offer,' Hunter answered. 'But I'm
looking forward to going shopping and having a crack
at matching up furniture with the rooms and eventually
the colours.'

'Study colour charts first.' Brenna smiled. They were
on nights this week and so far the shift had been slow,
only one callout for her crew to pick up an elderly gentle-
man from another cruise ship who'd fallen and broken

his hip while trying to prove to a woman he could do a backward flip into the swimming pool. Those cruises weren't always as safe as people expected.

'I'll talk to an interior decorator,' Hunter agreed, a light smile going on over those lips that had turned her on something shocking on Saturday night.

Pushing away from the table, Brenna took her plate to scrape away the remains of her meal. Her appetite had been subdued since Hunter's revelations about his father's depression and how Dylan had been treated. She now understood his determination to make the move here work, but his parents could be extremely persuasive when it came to getting their way. Water dripping on stone came to mind. Hunter had already had at least one call from his mother since starting work three and a half hours ago.

'Does Dylan like his new home?' It would be a major problem if he didn't.

'He didn't want to go to Jess and Dave's tonight. I think he's worried we won't go back home in the morning when I finish here. He's as happy as a piglet in muck there and has used sticks from the neighbour's trees to mark out where the dog kennel's going. Shame it's where I intend putting in a vegetable garden.' Hunter smiled, a wistful gleam in his eyes as he watched her.

'Dog or fresh veg. Quite the dilemma,' she agreed, while thinking how he should've talked about his home life other than glossing over the basics when they had been a couple. Relationships like theirs were meant to be open and honest, otherwise what was the point? Now she knew, she had to go back to keeping some distance between them. Hunter had made it as plain as white flour that there was not a lot of room for her in his life, the occasional occurrences they'd already shared being the exceptions. She'd been warned—don't get close.

If it isn't already too late.

The plate slid from her lifeless fingers and hit the tiles, shattering into jagged pieces. 'Damn.' It couldn't be. She wasn't in the habit of giving her heart away easily, if at all. Or had she never really gained it back from Hunter the first time?

'Saves washing it,' Hunter quipped.

Smart-ass. Did nothing rattle him? Bending down, she began picking up the shards and dumping them in the bin. She knew Hunter got wound up quicker than a rope on a pulley when someone he cared about was being hurt. Except he didn't seem to notice how he hurt her.

'Think I'll try for some shut-eye while it's quiet.' There were single bedrooms upstairs for the night shift crews. Not that Brenna expected to drop off—it wasn't yet ten o'clock, but she had to get away from Hunter. She might be feeling relaxed but every time he said or did anything she felt herself winding tight again. Saturday night had been wild, and she wanted more—without the rest. Without knowing how he intended staying here and leaving his parents to cope, without knowing how focused he was on getting it right for Dylan, without knowing he really meant this to be for ever.

Because now she understood how important this all was for Hunter she couldn't go for half-measures. It was all or nothing, especially with Dylan to consider. And she worried Hunter would never compromise enough to make a life work that included all of them. And if he couldn't then it had to be nothing. If only Saturday night in bed hadn't cranked up the hope for more than sex. That wasn't happening again. Nothing was the word to live by now.

Andy looked up from the dispatch phone he'd been talking into. 'Afraid not, sunshine. We're wanted north of Horseshoe Bay.'

Yay. Something constructive to distract her. 'What have we got?' she asked as they raced for their flying machine.

'Drunk driver went over the edge of the road into the river.'

'Hypothermia, fractures, trauma injuries, all or any of the above, here we come,' Hunter muttered as he went to give her a hand up into the chopper.

She dodged him. Feeling that hand on her tight skin would be like hot chocolate sauce on ice cream, leaving her a molten blob incapable of pulling herself together. 'You forgot the belligerence, if our patient's conscious.' She was still aware of where the bruises had been from her last intoxicated patient three weeks ago.

A shadow crossed his eyes as she kept a gap between them. 'Didn't forget, merely hoping the driver will play nice for once,' he growled.

Sinking onto the hard seat and buckling on the helmet, she put everything aside and went for normal. 'I talked to Poppy's breeder this morning. She's got a litter due next month and is happy to put your name down if you still want a Lab.'

'You what?' Now Hunter looked confused.

Who could blame him? She was all over the show, first friendly then decidedly cool. But she had a problem here. To admit how wonderful it was to have Hunter back in her life, even if only partially, or to deny, deny, deny. Doing both was not working out so being pals was it from now on. 'I thought it was something I could do for you both without getting in the way. If I've overstepped the mark, I'm sorry. The final decision's yours, of course.'

'You can say that when you've met Dylan?' Finally, the smile was back, on his mouth and in his gaze.

Grinning, she snuggled down further into the seat and

clipped the safety harness in place. 'He's really got your number, hasn't he?'

'He was born with it tattooed on the inside of his forehead.' That tenderness that she'd observed when she'd seen Hunter with Dylan filled his eyes. This man adored his son, and nothing, no one, was going to get in the way of that.

Maybe, just maybe, his parents were going to have to learn to stand on their own feet from now on. Crossing her fingers at her side, she said, 'I like that. It should keep him out of trouble for years to come.' Even if it meant her chances at reconciliation of the full and totally involved kind had truly flown the coop. Her heart sank at the verification of what she already knew.

So, what was her problem? Nothing had changed from last month when she had been happy living solo, doing all the adventurous escapades her photography took her on, eating what and when she wanted, not having a rumpled bed that looked like a whole football team had been having a practice session in there, no hot male scents filling the corners of her room.

Nothing different, except hope had raised its head and wasn't ready to be put to rest again. A work in progress, that. She'd keep at it and go mad in the interim.

Hunter closed them in, put his gear on and stretched those legs that went for ever towards the back of the chopper. 'He's a tough little nut, for sure. Just like his mum.'

'Oh, yeah, and his father's an absolute wimp. Softer than whipped cream, and about as useful in the hot sun.'

He grinned. 'Hold back, why don't you?'

'Nah, it's way too much fun baiting you.' It was true. They'd always been like this together, and while she should be avoiding anything that reminded her of their previous relationship, it wasn't possible—because that's who they were. 'Tell me about Evie.'

He blinked and tipped his head forward in her direction. 'Pardon?'

She'd surprised herself as much as him. 'You say she was tough too. Yes, too. You are a strong man, Hunter. Is that why you decided to make a go of marriage? Because you both believed in doing the right thing for someone you love and that if you tried hard enough, you'd succeed?' Ouch. That was a loaded question, and she hadn't seen it coming.

He'd suddenly found something intriguing with his boots, his gaze firmly fixed on them. 'I never really thought about it. I think you're partially right. There was no walking away from our responsibilities on either side. Evie cared a lot about people, would never deliberately hurt anyone, least of all her child.'

'I'm surprised you split up, then.'

'I think I mentioned Dylan was happier after we separated. The tension between us got to him and it wasn't fair. Eventually it would've held him back.'

Another reason for her to stay away from Hunter. They fluctuated from hot and happy to cool and reserved. The little guy would pick up on that as quickly as he'd fallen in love with Poppy. 'He's had a lot to deal with for a little fellow.'

'Sure has.'

'Hope you guys have got your armour plating on.' Andy's voice came through the headset. 'Seems our patient had passengers who weren't happy at being dunked in the river and then told to stay away from their friend while the paramedics see to him.'

'The cops haven't arrested anyone yet?'

'Doesn't sound like it. But being annoying isn't a felony, as far as I know.' The helicopter lurched. 'Hold on. Bit of bad weather ahead. I'll try to go around most of it.'

Brenna's stomach settled back into place. She loved flying, even the rough bits, but her stomach was full of curry and noodles, and she didn't want to regurgitate it. 'If it was daylight, I'd take pictures of the cloud formations. The colours in a storm can be amazing.'

Hunter shook his head at her. 'You really do like pushing the boundaries, don't you? I saw all your gear in the shed.'

'Thanks for mowing the lawn, by the way. I didn't notice until I took Poppy on her walk this morning. You didn't have to do it.'

'I had time on my hands.' He shrugged.

'Dylan deserted you for Poppy?'

'You could say that.'

The engine pitch changed.

Brenna glanced out the tiny window. 'We're on.'

Flashing lights greeted them and made Andy's job difficult until someone wised up and had the tow-truck driver switch them off until the helicopter was safely on the ground.

'Calvin Banks, thirty-one, was semi-conscious but now alert, though that could change. Way over the limit, according to the cop who breathalysed him, and no seat belt, which, ironically, probably saved him as his pals were able to haul him out through the smashed front window.'

The ambulance officer who met them gave as much info as he had as they stood under umbrellas. 'Wide gash to the forehead, some water inhalation, broken tib or fib on right leg, and generally foul-mouthed. We haven't administered painkillers but have cut his sodden clothes off and wrapped him in a survival blanket.'

'Nice,' Brenna muttered as she approached the man

lying on a stretcher in the back of the ambulance. The rain was heavy and getting heavier. 'Hey, Calvin, I hear you've been in the river.'

'So what?'

'Nice,' she repeated to Hunter, who stepped inside after her. 'Want to tell me what happened?'

'I got sick of the road, thought I'd try another way home. What do you think, woman?'

'Okay, that's enough,' Hunter snapped. 'We are here to help you, not get into an argument. Understand?'

The guy's eyes shifted. 'Who are you?'

'Hunter. I'm the paramedic who's going to get you on board the chopper for a ride to hospital. There are two ways of doing this. Entirely up to you which one I choose.'

Brenna knew Hunter would never hurt a patient, no matter how rude and difficult they were, but hopefully Calvin was beyond working that out and would go for the easy option.

'You wouldn't hurt me. It's against the rules.'

'Rules are made to be broken, pal.' Hunter was drawing up an injection. 'I'm going to give you something for that pain.'

'Thanks, mate.' Calvin relaxed a tad. 'The other idiots wouldn't do it, said they weren't allowed to. I reckon they were being mean.'

Who could blame them if this was how Calvin had treated them? But if either of the ambulance crew were registered to give injections they would've done so. 'You're some way out of town, and the folk who man the ambulances are mostly volunteers. Not all of them are qualified to give injections,' Brenna told their patient as she began reassessing his injuries.

'That's stupid.'

She dodged a flailing arm. 'It's safe, Calvin. Now, take it easy. We are on your side here.'

'The pigs aren't.'

The 'pigs' were decent men, doing a hard job of trying to save people like this man from killing someone with their vehicle while drunk. Brenna watched Hunter as he put the syringe away. 'Ready to go?'

He nodded. 'The sooner the better. That weather's turning nasty.'

The sooner they were shot of Calvin the sooner peace and quiet would return, but then the poor staff at the ED would get their share of abuse and obnoxious behaviour. Sometimes she wondered why any of them wanted to work in emergency jobs.

No one wanted to hang around in the rain, so everyone quickly moved the stretcher towards the back of the chopper and Calvin was transferred inside, where Brenna changed the survival blanket for a dry one and topped it with a wool blanket for added warmth.

Andy had them up and away in no time, apparently as eager as the rest of them to make their delivery, but the weather hadn't finished with them. 'I'm going out over the strait,' Andy informed them. 'The storm's increasing in intensity.'

As the helicopter lifted off the ground Brenna shivered as water from her ponytail dripped down between her shoulder blades. 'It's guaranteed we'll be full-on busy for the rest of the night now.'

'Here.' Hunter handed her a small towel. 'Wipe the water off your head and face.'

'What about me?' Calvin demanded. 'I'm the patient, not her.'

'Dr Williamson has already wiped you down and replaced the blankets with dry ones. There's nothing more we can do except monitor your heart and blood pressure and keep an eye on you until we reach hospital.' Hunter clicked his harness into place. 'We won't be moving around much. There'll be some turbulence on the way.'

Calvin's eyes widened. 'We'll be all right, won't we?'

Right then the helicopter lurched sideways.

Only a small lurch but enough to put fear into their patient's eyes. 'Let me out,' he yelled. 'I don't like it in here.'

'Calvin.' Brenna leaned forward in her seat. 'Listen to me. You're going to be fine. Andy's our pilot and he's one of the best in the business. He's going to fly around the storm, not through it, but we will feel some bumps on the way. They're normal and the helicopter is made for these condtions.'

'I don't like flying.' Apparently, the man could do quiet and worried.

She did feel a little sorry for him. He was incapacitated in a situation that held a lot of fear for him. 'Not everyone does. I promise you're going to get to hospital just fine. It'll take a little bit longer, though, since we're avoiding the weather as much as possible.'

'Can't I go by road?'

'It would take a lot longer and you need to be treated sooner rather than later.'

Andy spoke in her ear. 'There're trees reported down across the road between the accident site and Horseshoe Bay. And thanks, Brenna, I owe you a drink next time we're hitting the town.'

'A big one,' she agreed, before telling Calvin, 'The road's closed. This is your only way out.'

'Oh.' He remained quiet for the rest of the flight, squeezing his eyes tight every time they hit a bump in the sky.

Finally back at base, Brenna shook her head to get rid

of the water in her hair. 'I'm having a hot shower and getting into dry clothes.' Then she looked around. 'Unless we're heading out again?'

'No, you're good to go on the shower,' Margaret, from the other crew, told her. 'But don't muck around. I suspect the calls will start coming in shortly. The roads are slippery and vision is limited, according to the state police when they rang to update us thirty minutes ago.'

So dry clothes weren't going to stay that way. Shucking off her overalls in the bathroom, Brenna stood under the shower with the water as hot as she could take it until the feeling came back into her hands and feet. Once dried off and dressed in a second pair of overalls, she headed downstairs to toss the wet clothes into a drier. 'I bet I'll need them again before the night's out.' Next trip she'd make sure her wet-weather gear went on board the helicopter with her and wasn't left languishing in the hangar.

'Tea's made, and ham-and-cheese sandwiches are in the toasty maker,' Margaret told her.

'You're a treasure,' Brenna said as she sipped hot tea.

'Just what the doctor needed.' Hunter strolled into the kitchen looking sexy with his damp hair sticking up in all directions and the dry overalls a tad tight on his frame so that muscles everywhere were accentuated.

Her next sip of tea went down the wrong way.

'Hey, careful.' His hand slapped her lightly between her shoulder blades. 'Told you before about rushing your tea.'

Looking up into those alert grey eyes, she melted. He was so sexy, and cheeky, and—well, just Hunter. 'I seem to have forgotten that message,' she croaked around the tea and her despair that she'd never be able to watch him walk away at the end of his short tenure at the rescue service unscathed.

'I'll forward it later.' The cheeky element in his gaze changed, replaced by worry. His hand fell away, damn it. 'Those toasties look like the best thing out,' he said to Margaret. 'Thank you.'

'You're welcome. I suggest you don't delay eating them in case the phone goes in the next five minutes.'

'I've got big pockets,' Hunter said, before taking a mouthful and glancing across at Brenna. He'd gone all thoughtful.

She knew better than to ask what was up. He wouldn't say, which would only frustrate her. Hell, the man frustrated her in more ways than one, especially the physical. She wanted him again. Staring at the phone on the wall she begged silently, *Please ring. Now. Before I turn into a melted puddle at his feet.*

The phone rang.

Brenna's mouth fell open. *Seriously?*

'Not pretty,' Hunter said in a low voice as Margaret reached to answer.

Snapping her teeth together, she turned away, heat flooding her cheeks as embarrassment whipped her. Snatching up a toasty, she headed out the door in preparation for flying off on their next mission, whatever it was. It could be a stubbed toe, for all she cared. She'd asked the universe to help her out and it had. Holy cow. Hopefully she wouldn't be asked to make a major sacrifice as payback.

'I've been feeling odd in the chest,' the forty-five-year-old woman lying in her bed told Brenna, almost before she got through the door the elderly neighbour had indicated. 'People say not to muck about if your chest feels strange in case it's a heart attack, so I called 911.'

'You were right to do so,' Brenna reassured Carla Brown. 'We'd rather find there's nothing wrong than learn tomorrow you'd had a heart attack and told no one. Now, tell me about these strange feelings you're getting.'

'Um…well, they're not as bad as they were.' Embarrassment started filling Carla's face. 'I think I panicked with the terrible weather making me think no one would be able to get here if it really was serious.'

'It's fine.' Brenna slipped the BP cuff on Carla's arm and pressed the start button. 'What does it feel like in your chest?' She wasn't asking leading questions so Carla wouldn't give details that might be misleading.

'Tight when I breathe in. My head was pounding at one time, and my arm tingled.'

'Which arm?'

'Left one.'

'Carla, I'm going to open the front of your pyjama top so we can attach pads to see what your heart is doing. Is that all right?'

'Yes,' she whispered, her eyes straying to Hunter, who had his back to them pretending to be busy preparing the heart monitor.

So he'd cottoned on that this woman was not at ease with a man attending her. Go, Hunter.

Brenna took the pads he handed back to her and she stuck them on Carla. 'All ready, Hunter.'

Together they watched the readout of Carla's heart. 'Nothing wrong with your heart, Carla.' Brenna gave her a smile. 'How's that make you feel?'

'Lots better.' She smiled too. 'But why did I feel so strange?'

'Are you stressed about anything?'

Her face dropped. 'I might be losing my job because the store I work at isn't doing so well, and I need it because I'm on my own. I don't have any qualifications for something half-decent. Shop work is all I'm good for. It keeps me awake at night, worrying how I'll cope.'

Hunter turned around after a quick glance to see if the pyjama top was back in place. 'Have you been to put your name down at the shops in the mall?'

'No, because I don't know for sure if it will happen. What if I get another job and don't lose the one I've got?'

Brenna began packing up their equipment, watching Hunter weave his magic over Carla.

'Be proactive. Take control of what happens to you. Go to every shop in the mall and introduce yourself, leave your work résumé with them. Don't wait for someone else to tell you what's happening.' He gave one of his devastating smiles.

Which worked for Brenna, waking up the butterflies in her stomach.

Carla didn't look so sure. 'You make it sound easy.'

Hunter slung the bag over his shoulder and hoisted the monitor in his other hand. 'It's not, but it sure makes you feel good when it starts coming together.'

Like telling his parents they had to take charge of their own lives because he was now doing the same for Dylan and himself. Yes, he knew what he was talking about. But what happened when it came crashing down around his ankles? When his father twisted things to amp up the guilt so that he returned to Kamloops? Brenna swallowed the threatening sigh and followed him out of the room. She couldn't afford to find out. If Hunter left Vancouver again, he would not be taking her heart with him this time.

'Want to go get breakfast?' Hunter asked as they headed for their vehicles bang on six the next morning. 'I'm starving.'

'Don't you want to collect Dylan?' Brenna replied.

'He won't wake up for at least an hour. We'll be done by then.'

She seemed to be weighing up something, taking for ever to say yes or no.

'Problem?' he asked a little harshly. 'It's only breakfast, Brenna.'

'You're right. Where shall we go?'

He named a chain food outlet down by the beach at Kitsilano. 'See you there.' He wasn't waiting around for her to change her mind. But what had been going on in her head? They'd had a good night, talking and laughing between patients, for which there'd been way too many unnecessary calls due to the inclement weather and people worrying they mightn't be able to get help when needed.

Swinging out onto the waterlogged road, he drove carefully as skidding was not an option. Brenna was running hot and cold with him. Like he was doing any better. Protecting himself meant being on guard—until they got close and then all reticence and barriers were shot to pieces with one look.

He could put it to her that they have a full-on fling and get whatever this was out of their systems.

Except what if that didn't happen and they found they wanted to be together all the time, to pick up where they'd left off?

He glanced in the rear-view mirror to make sure Brenna hadn't changed her mind about breakfast, and smiled when he saw her car behind his. No, he wouldn't be wrecking the camaraderie between them this morning by suggesting they either have a fling or quit seeing each other. He'd carry on as they were and see how things panned out by the time he'd finished his weeks on the helicopters. Gutless? Possibly, though he preferred to see it as taking things slowly and not rushing into anything—a bit late for that—and making a colossal mistake. He'd shifted here for a reason and he would not be leaving so he had to be cautious—especially with his heart.

Pulling into the food outlet, he held his breath until Brenna's car rolled in beside his. He really wasn't confident about her and how they were getting along. Stepping out into the drizzle, he tugged his jacket collar tight around his neck. 'I'm over this,' he commented as he held her door open.

She swiped his arm. 'Toughen up. The weekend's predicted to be fine and warm.'

Ignoring the tingles where she'd touched him, he deliberately grumped, 'The weekend's days away. We could have snow and more rain before then.'

She ran for the building, pausing at the door to wait for him. 'I hope not. I'm going mountain biking on Saturday.'

More crazy action. He bit his tongue as he tried to keep his thoughts to himself. 'You go with a group?'

'Always. I'm not stupid, or reckless. Accidents do happen, even to the best of us, but I work hard at avoiding them.' She stared up at the menu on the wall.

Glad she realised that. 'I'm having the full breakfast.'

'Pancakes with bacon and syrup for me.' Her hand delved into her pocket, withdrew with her wallet.

'I'm getting this.' He stepped up to the counter and gave their orders, handing over his card before she had a chance to do anything about it.

'Thank you.' She gave him a killer smile that made him wish they could head back to her place and forget all about eating.

What about after he'd dropped Dylan at preschool? He sighed. Wasn't he supposed to be taking things slowly? 'You're as bad as Chris when it comes to maple syrup,' he said as they sat down.

'Got to keep the tradition going,' she agreed. 'It's almost as good as chocolate.'

'You don't eat chocolate for breakfast?'

'Only on the days when the night shift has been crazy and I've had no sleep. Or when there's a *pain au chocolat* within reach.' Her eyes were misty. 'I like how you mention Dad as though it's no big deal. Most people step around the subject, and I don't like it that he's supposed to be spoken about any different to when he was with us.'

'He was a part of my life when we were together, and I don't see any reason not to talk about him.' Snatching a serviette out of the metal box, he passed it over. 'Here, clean your face, it's splotchy.' Time to lighten the atmosphere before she had a full-on meltdown in public, something she was allergic to.

'Thanks for the compliment.'

'Someone's got to keep you in line.'

She laughed. 'You think that's your role now?'

'I'd rather emulate Chris in raising my boy. He was a great dad, and I want to be the same for Dylan.' So much for diverting the touchy subject.

Brenna's hand was soft and warm as it wrapped around his. 'From what I've seen, and the little you've told me, I reckon you've got fatherhood sussed. You're never going to load Dylan up with guilt or make him follow your decisions on how to live his life. You're better than that, Hunter.'

His chest expanded, and his eyes got some dust in them so he wiped them surreptitiously with his sleeve. Except, of course, he didn't get away with it and Brenna handed him more of those serviettes.

'Blow your nose and sit up.' She grinned.

'For someone who hasn't had a lot of sleep you say the nicest things.'

'Maybe that's why.' Her grin turned into a gentle smile. 'No, really, you've got the right instincts.'

'You understand that's why we're living in Vancouver and not Kamloops? I'm doing what's best for both of us.'

'Got that in spades, and if I can help, be a part of it, then here I am.'

Was now the time to suggest a fling? No, that'd be crass. Even when his body was crying out for it, his brain was trying to forget the idea. 'There is a paint scheme to deal with.'

She laughed and took the plate the waitress had arrived with. 'Yet you didn't want me there on Sunday.' Her mouth twisted sideways, and the laughter died in her eyes.

Hunter nodded. 'I had a panic attack, thinking how I needed my own space. We've got together really quickly.' Her eyes widened at that. He carried on putting his foot in the mess. 'Not together all the time together, just sometimes having fun and enjoying each other's company together. Then suddenly I took a step back. If I hurt you, I didn't mean to and I'm sorry.'

'I get it. It's okay.'

Forgiven as easily as that. This really was like old times. Frightening or exciting? He didn't know so went for testing her further. 'Feel free to drop by any time you like.'

'I'll wait until you've finished unpacking and then you can give me the grand tour.' Dribbling maple syrup over her bacon, she forked up a mouthful and rolled her eyes. 'Delicious.'

So are you, looking gorgeous beyond description.

'You could be waiting a while, then.' Unpacking all those cartons crowding the smallest bedroom wasn't a priority, mainly because the whole idea of deciding where to put everything didn't thrill him. He was far happier outside, planning the vegetable garden he intended planting as soon as winter finished dumping on them. Which should've been a couple of weeks ago, except the weather god wasn't playing nice.

'You going to look at furniture today?'

'What do you think?' He'd only shifted in yesterday.

'That's a no, then. Why not?'

Because he had a son he'd rather spend time with, finishing arranging his bedroom and toys, rather than wandering around a large store, tossing up between black or navy couches, between a double or a queen-sized bed with or without a steel-framed headboard. 'I'll get there.'

'You stalling?' she asked, then colour flooded her cheeks. 'Forget I said that.'

'How am I supposed to do that?' She had put it out there, and he knew it wouldn't go away in a hurry. Hell, they couldn't even get through breakfast without the on-off button coming into play. 'I am not going away, Brenna,' he repeated. 'Vancouver is home now, more specifically my house is where I intend living for a long time, at least until Dylan has grown up and left to follow his own aspirations.' Forking up hash brown and egg, he chewed and watched the play of emotions passing over her face.

Get it, Bren? I mean every word.

Finally, Brenna pushed her half-empty plate aside, picked up the paper mug of coffee, took a sip and put it aside as well. 'I do believe you. I hear it in your voice and see how much you want Dylan to be settled and happy here.'

But? He continued eating and waited.

Her chest rose on an indrawn breath, dropped as she exhaled. 'Give me time to get used to it. It's not long since you walked into work and I'm all over the place about how I feel about that. We've argued, been intimate, dated, got angry. There's a lot to come to terms with, and I'm still working my way through it all. Okay?' She was pleading with him.

He hated that. 'It's fine. I know exactly where you're coming from. You and I weren't part of the plan for coming back here.' She winced, and he rushed on before she could bite his head off. 'What I meant was that I was always going to get in touch with you. What I didn't know was where that would lead. I had no plans of getting back together with you. But I wanted, still do, to see how things are for you, and if we could at least be friends.'

Retrieving her plate, she replied, 'Like I said, give me time.' Her eyes were lightening so he knew she wasn't cross with him.

Best to leave it at that while they were at least smiling at each other. But there was a long way to go in sorting out just what they wanted from each other. 'What have you got planned for the day after you've caught up on sleep?'

'I'm taking Poppy to get her teeth cleaned. Should be a barrel of laughs.'

'Sounds like you'll need a coffee afterwards. Drop by if you've got time.'

'I'll see.'

He had to accept her reluctance. He wasn't the only one confused right now. At least he'd had the sense not to raise the fling idea, or about now he'd be out in the car park, trying to pull the knife out of his back.

CHAPTER SEVEN

BRENNA KNOCKED THE shower handle to make the temperature higher and stood with water pummelling the aching muscles in her shoulders. That spot between her shoulders always hurt most during and after a bike ride.

It had been a hard ride out at Fraser. The track had been muddy, the trees sodden from last night's downpour—so much for the fine weather forecast for the weekend. Like her, the four other cyclists she'd gone with had all returned to their vehicles covered in mud from helmet to toe grips. The owner of the local bar they'd stopped at had laid newspaper on the seats before they'd sat down but at least he'd let them in and given them prime position by the roaring fire he'd had going.

Sponging her face again in case she'd missed some mud, she bashed her elbow and gasped. Falling off at a sharp bend and landing on her arm and hip had given her bones a knock. Colourful bruises were making themselves known along her arm and down her leg, and by tomorrow she'd be stiff. All part of the thrill of speeding over root-strewn tracks. She hadn't been the only rider to come a cropper today—one of the others had managed to leave his seat and land hard, luckily with no injuries anywhere except to his pride.

Tell that to Hunter. If he knew she'd come off, he'd be

locking up her bike and throwing away the key. Yes, she'd seen his angst when she'd mentioned going mountain biking. He only saw it as another way for her to risk her life. He didn't understand that she had to prove she was capable of pushing the barriers and surviving, that she was worthy of people loving her. Sure, her family adored her, no doubt at all. But two people who should've loved her unreservedly hadn't, and Hunter was one of those.

There was always a certain amount of risk involved in high intensity sports. Ask any successful skier, snow-boarder or—yes, mountain biker. Anyway, it was a lot of fun. The option of staying at home sitting on the couch with a book didn't spark her interest nearly as much.

Snapping off the shower, she reached for a towel and pressed the warm softness against her face. Hunter, Hunter, everywhere she went, he was there, in her head, driving her crazy with longing and at other times with annoyance. Right now, it was a mix of both getting to her.

Drying off, she pulled on black jeans and a thick red jersey before attacking her curls with styling cream and the blow-dryer. Then she applied a light coating of make-up, though why when she was only keeping Poppy company for the rest of the day she had no idea.

While the kettle boiled she rang her mum. 'Hi, I'm home in one piece.' She always reported in. Hunter wasn't the only one to worry about her escapades. 'I had a great day out at Fraser.' Not mentioning coming off the bike.

'You must've been half-drowned from what they're reporting on the weather channel.' Her mother's second favourite TV program after the news.

'There was a bit of rain coming down.'

'How's Hunter?'

Where had that come from? She dragged out her answer. 'He's fine. Still unpacking.' He'd been at it all week, though she suspected it was only half-heartedly. Which begged the question. How permanent was permanent? Brenna sighed. She should probably move past what had happened in the past and accept Hunter was here to stay. It had been in his voice and face the other morning at breakfast when he'd talked about his move. He was strong; he'd do it. If it was what he wanted.

'What's the house like?'

'I haven't seen it.'

'Why ever not? Even if you're not getting back with him, that seems sad.' Her mother had made no secret of her hope that Hunter's return to Vancouver would encompass Brenna as well. 'You can at least be friends again.'

'We are.' Sort of.

'I'm sure it's not easy with his reasons for going back to Kamloops, and you not rushing after him.'

'He suggested I give him some tips on the interior decorating. I think he's winding me up. It's not really my area of expertise.'

'You've done all right so far with the house.'

The house, not *hers.* Some things never changed in her family. Laughing, Brenna said, 'I've done three rooms in as many years, Mum.'

A text popped into her phone and she sneaked a look. Hunter.

You home? Dylan wants to see Poppy.

'Mum, I'm going to take Poppy for a walk before it gets too late. I'll call you tomorrow, okay?' Not the whole truth, but close enough. She didn't need questions later about how they'd got on, or if she was seeing him again outside work.

It took ten minutes to finish that call, then she texted

Hunter back. Poppy and I are coming to visit. Will be a little while. She wasn't asking if that was all right. No more avoiding the truth. Hunter had moved into his own home, not far from her. It was time to see his house and give him his housewarming gift. Better late than never. It would be a firm step in the right direction.

Hunter stared at the grandfather clock standing beside Brenna's car. No wonder she'd backed right up to his porch. This wasn't a throw-over-the-shoulder piece of furniture. Not her small one, anyway.

He caressed the woodwork, the glass, the fine carvings. He opened his mouth, closed it again. Speech was beyond him. He walked around the clock, scanning every last detail, and still couldn't utter a sound.

'You still like it, then.' Brenna sounded relieved.

His head dipped. 'Like it?' he croaked. Like it? This had been his clock from the moment he'd seen it. He'd had to have it. He'd never felt like that about an inanimate object before. Except he hadn't been able to afford it at the time because every cent had been going into the 'buy a house' account, and later there had seemed no point. 'When—? How—?'

'I put it on layby the day after you took me to see it. It was going to be your housewarming present when we moved into our own place.' Now she was looking distinctly embarrassed. 'After we broke up, I sold it. Actually, Mum sold it for me. To herself.'

'I think you need to explain that.'

'I'm not sure I can.' Now there was full-on embarrassment colouring her cheeks. 'Mum knew how much it meant to you and thought there might come a day when—' Her chest rose. 'When I might want you to have it. I discovered it when I was storing some of Dad's gear in the lock-up.' Her voice broke, but she carried on. 'So here it is. Remembering how much it meant to you, I'm not churlish enough that you can't have it.'

'Oh, Bren.' He reached to wrap her in his arms and pull her close. 'It's as beautiful as I recall.' It was almost the same as the one his grandfather had had in his hallway when Hunter had been a kid, and he'd been allowed to wind it up and have the bells chiming on the hour every time he'd gone to stay in the old nineteenth-century house. When Granddad had died the clock had disappeared and he'd been as distraught over that as losing the man who'd loved him unconditionally.

She twisted around and regarded the clock. 'It's been stored in an insulated cupboard along with Mum's excess furniture, and she's had it checked over every couple of years by a clockmaker.'

What did it mean that she'd brought it to him? Hadn't taken an axe to it instead? 'I don't know what to say.'

'There's nothing to say. It always had your name on it. It's nice that you're still smitten. Let's get it inside out of the weather. Though the sun has finally agreed to make an appearance it's just as likely to change its mind when we're not looking.'

Taking an end each, they carefully carried the clock in through the front door. 'It's not light,' Hunter noted. 'How'd you get it into your car?' She'd dropped the back seats so it could fit through the trunk.

'The security guy at the lock-up gave me a hand. Poppy was under threat of death if she threw up. I drove so slowly it's a wonder I wasn't picked up for dangerous driving.'

'You've still got to get her back home.' Hunter shifted the clock to the left, away from the sunlight filtering through the bay window, his fingers trailing down the woodwork again to make sure this wasn't a dream.

'I'll work something out. She managed once, maybe I can push my luck and try again.' Brenna was looking around the spacious sitting room. 'Minimalist approach on the furniture, I see.'

'Still haven't made it to the shop.'

'It's early days.' She was rolling her shoulders awkwardly.

'You hurting?'

'I always get a snag in my muscles from riding. It's nothing to do with moving the clock.'

'Bren, I don't know how to thank you.' The words squeezed around the emotion blocking his throat. He reached for her again, careful not to hurt her shoulders.

Again she winced. But before he could say anything, she placed a hand on his chest to stop him getting closer. 'It's Mum you should be thanking. Not me.'

Leaning down, he kissed her lightly, as a friend would. A friend who didn't know if he meant more to her or not. 'Let's celebrate with a glass of wine. I haven't got any champagne, sorry.' Though exactly what he was celebrating was a mystery to him. The clock, definitely. But there was more, he just couldn't identify the emotion. It felt familiar yet different. More than friendship, more than gratitude, less than love. Less than love? Or full-blown, heart-totally-involved love?

'Dad, Poppy's done wees on the step.'

Thank goodness for little boys and their intrigue with pee. 'Fill the bucket by the tap outside the back door, will you?'

'I'll see to it.' Brenna headed outside, leaving him to stare after her, wondering what he was going to do next.

This had moved everything to a different level. One he

wasn't sure he wanted to stop on. Face it, he didn't have a clue what was going on, and judging by the wariness in her eyes he suspected Brenna wasn't faring any better.

'You mentioned wine,' she said a few minutes later.

'Did I?' He shook his head. 'Right.' In the kitchen, he carefully poured two glasses, aware how shaky his hand was. 'Follow me for the grand tour.' He led her through the house, forced himself to laugh when she joked about the floor-to-ceiling stacks of cartons waiting to be unpacked, tried not to groan out loud when she bent over to push a train along the track on Dylan's bedroom floor. It wasn't the train disturbing him. Rather it was her sweet bottom with its perfect curves.

He wanted her. Now. Here against the wall. He couldn't have her, even if she was willing. His son was out in the yard, playing with her dog. Not everything about fatherhood was perfect. She'd probably turn him down anyway. There was wariness in her eyes, and she didn't look at him very often.

'Come on, let's sit on the back porch so we can keep an eye on the kids.' Out of temptation's way.

'Good idea.' She seemed fixated on walls and carpets and furniture—or the lack of it. She might find something else to take her interest outside.

'Brenna, can Poppy stay for dinner?' Dylan stood in front of her, hands on his hips.

He was a right little copycat of his dad, Hunter acknowledged.

'Probably not tonight,' Brenna answered after a brief pause.

'We're having pizza. I can order extra if you'd like to stay.'

'Yes, say yes, Brenna. Then Poppy and I can play some

more.' Dylan jumped up and down, his arms in danger of connecting with Brenna.

Leaning back, she laughed. 'I can hardly say no to that, now, can I? Yes, I'd like to stay for pizza.'

'Whoopee,' Dylan shouted, and ran around in circles on the lawn.

'Where does he get his energy?'

'Asks the woman who never seems to get tired.' How come his son got her to laugh so easily?

'Believe me, I'm feeling it in my legs right now. Uphill cycling takes it out of me every time. I really should get into a training routine but I'm not disciplined enough.'

Was that why she was limping a little? 'Doesn't sound like you.' She'd been very strict about her spare time when studying medicine, as she'd needed to be in order to qualify.

'That's because it's not the end of the world if I bomb out on a ride occasionally. I do it for fun, not to be the best.' Her gaze wandered around his back yard. 'You've got a reasonable amount of space out here. What are you going to do with it?'

'Put in a dog run and kennel and dig a vegetable garden. That'll take care of most of it.' With spring supposedly on the way, though apparently delayed, the gardening would be a priority.

'Have you talked to the breeder again?'

'I put an order in for a male yesterday. It's happening. I haven't told a certain person yet, otherwise there'll be no shutting him up until the day it comes home with us, which is weeks away.'

She was watching Dylan dragging Poppy around on a short rope. 'He's not afraid of Pops at all. That's a good sign.'

'As long as he recognises the difference between gentle dogs and aggressive ones, I agree.' Hunter stood. 'I'll phone the pizza house.'

Brenna looked up. 'This is so relaxing.'

'Nothing like your normal Sunday afternoon, then?'

'I don't sit around very often. There's usually something needing my attention.' Finally, a smile radiated out at him, sucking him in and turning him to mush. It might've been better if she'd kept up the wariness.

'Any preference for your pizza?'

'Surprise me.'

A perfect end to a not-so-bad week.

Brenna rinsed the plates before putting them into the dishwasher, trying to ignore the dull throbbing in her arm and leg as she straightened up. 'Shall I make coffee?'

'Can Poppy stay the night?' Dylan stood in front of her. 'Please?'

'I don't think so. We've got to get up early in the morning so I can go to work.'

'Please let her. I'll wake her up very early.'

This kid was gorgeous, and so like his dad when he wanted something. That hands-on-hips thing was classic Ford. 'Not tonight, I'm sorry.'

'You can stay too.' He didn't give up easily.

Neither did she. 'It won't work, Dylan.'

'Would it make a difference if I agreed with Dylan? You could stay for some of the night.' That deep, raspy voice lifted the hairs on the back of her neck and sent her stomach into overdrive.

'I could?' Why not? It was what she'd been wanting for the last hour, after she'd finally abandoned the caution over getting too close and friendly for tonight. Then what he'd said impacted. '*Some* of the night?' He didn't want her here when he woke up to get ready for work?

Too intimate in that it was snug and cosy and spoke of more than just sex? She could work with that if it meant having off-the-scale sex with Hunter.

Trollop.

'Dylan, take Poppy outside for a few minutes in case she wants to do wees again.' As boy and dog disappeared, Hunter turned back to her. 'Dylan's still getting used to moving away from his grandparents and his friends at preschool, and making new friends and settling in. I don't think he's ready to deal with you being in my bed when he gets up in the morning. He'd want to know what's going on.'

'And since we don't know the answer to that, we'd only confuse him further.' Fair cop. She remembered her mixed feelings the first time she'd seen Mum coming out of Dad's bedroom and she'd been twelve. Her heart sank. This getting to know Hunter again wasn't straightforward, but she was up to it. When the doubts weren't biting. Which they weren't at the moment. 'Some time together is better than none.'

Hunter leaned in and kissed her. Not on the brow or her hot cheeks, but smack on her lips, a full, deep kiss that had her holding onto his shirt to stay upright.

When he finally pulled away, she ran her tongue over her lips and said, 'What time does Dylan go to bed?'

Hunter laughed. 'After a shower and a story and a drink of water, followed by another drink and the demand for food, which doesn't get a look in.'

Brenna hugged herself. This felt—great. Homey, but nice. Normal, if this was a family. It was. She was just sneaking in on the periphery for a few hours. 'I'll take Poppy for a walk round the block while you get started on the evening ritual. She can sleep on the floor beside Dylan's bed until I go home.'

'Hopefully Dylan gets that memo and doesn't make her jump up on the bed with him.'

'If he does that, I'll never get her to leave.'

Half an hour later she stepped back inside the house, her bruised leg aching from the exercise, but her head was clearer than it had been in hours. She was going to spend time with Hunter, and it wasn't a spur-of-the-moment thing. She'd been turned on when he'd asked her to stay, but even with time to think about it she still wanted to be with him, to make love, and to forget everything else for a while. Progress in getting to know him again? Or was this how she balanced it all, and worked out what she wanted?

Hunter sauntered into the kitchen, a grin on his face. 'Can we borrow Poppy every night? No demands for food or games, just, *Where's Poppy? I want to go to bed.*'

'I'll take her along to his room.' And say goodnight to the little guy she'd begun to feel a strong affection for.

'Brenna, can you read me a story?'

One look into those grey eyes that were a replica of his father's, especially when filled with entreaty, and she caved. 'Sure. Which one?' There was a stack of books on the bedside table. One was particularly thick. That had to be avoided or there'd be no sleeping or making love going on before sun-up, by which time it'd be too late. 'How about this one?'

'Yes, that's my favourite.'

Saved by a random choice. Perhaps she should try that more often with other things in her life. Settling onto the bed beside Dylan, she ignored Hunter's laugh from the doorway.

'You've been conned.'

'"The digger's stuck,"' she read.

'See?' Dylan pointed to the picture of a big yellow digger in mud.

'I do.' She lifted her head and grinned. 'See?' she asked his dad.

'Oh, yes. I'll go put the kettle on. We're going to be a while.'

'"We have to get help pulling the digger out."' She continued with the story and felt a lump growing in the back of her throat as Dylan snuggled in close. This was something else. She could get to like it. A lot.

Getting ahead of yourself.

When she finished the story, Dylan was sound asleep. Slowly easing off the bed, she carefully moved the boy down the bed and pulled the covers up to his chin before dropping a kiss on his forehead. 'Night-night, make sure the bedbugs don't bite.'

'Better not be any bugs in this house.' Hunter dropped an arm over her shoulders and led her to the kitchen, where he had a steaming mug of tea waiting for her.

'Or what? You'll pull it down and start again?' She laughed around the raw emotions filling her throat. 'I think Dylan would have something to say about that. He's gorgeous, by the way.' *How soon can we make love?* 'Does he always fall asleep instantly?'

Why make love? Why not have sex? Gulp. The tea went down the wrong way, making her cough. She had to move so that Hunter didn't bang her on the back and aggravate the bruises that were playing up more as the night wore on.

'Not always, but he was exhausted after playing with Poppy. Hopefully he's out for the night.'

'Not good at sleeping right through?' *Please stay asleep for a few hours.*

Hunter picked up his tea and sipped it. 'He's better

than he was back in Kamloops, where he woke at least twice, sometimes three times a night. Now it's usually only once, and Saturday was a first. He didn't stir at all.'

'Nothing's easy, is it?'

'I'm hoping it will be—for a while anyway. Can you hurry up and drink your tea?' He looked at her over the rim of his mug, his eyes lit up with need.

Glug, glug, glug. She put the mug in the dishwasher. 'How's that?'

'Not bad.' He took her hand and all but ran down the hall, only pausing to check on Dylan. 'Good boy.' He high-fived Brenna. 'Must've been your mesmerising story-telling that knocked him out so fast.'

Hunter locked his bedroom door. 'I don't like doing this, but it would be worse to have him barging in and leaping up on the bed at the wrong moment.'

And seeing her in bed with his father. She turned the bedside light on. The soft shadows it threw highlighted Hunter's height and those wide shoulders. How had she managed to get through the years since they'd broken up? Especially the last few when he'd stopped lurking in the back of her head.

Hunter grabbed her around the waist and pulled her against his chest, his flat stomach and the rest of his hard body.

Her mouth dried as it met his. Desire rose, expanded through her body, heating muscles and skin, softening her stomach, tightening her toes and thighs. 'Hunter,' she whispered against his mouth before driving her tongue inside. 'Let's make love.'

Yes, she was making love, not having sex. She was going for broke.

Then Hunter clasped her, his finger rubbing her hot spot, and she had no idea whether she was standing, lying or kneeling. Everything was exploding in her head, throughout her body, until she couldn't take any more.

Hunter gave more. She tried to reach for him, to hold that pulsating organ pressing into her stomach, but he held her hands. 'Let me give you my full attention.'

She let Hunter work his magic.

After her body returned to earth and she could move, she rolled over on top of him and began kissing every inch of skin. It took time. He wasn't small. Anywhere. All the while he groaned and demanded release, and she continued with her lips, her tongue until she was as feverish as Hunter and she finally gave in and straddled him, taking him deep, clamping around him, crying out as they climaxed together.

Yes, she'd made love to Hunter. She'd given him everything of herself. What did she do next? Wait and see how this budding relationship unfolded? She'd come to see that it wasn't the old one being cranked up. They'd both changed too much for that. But they might be building on the bones of the past. Did she want that? Was she prepared to risk being put aside again if Hunter couldn't handle having her full time in his life along with his son, and the problems that were his parents?

'Hey, where've you gone?' Hunter wrapped his arms around and hugged tight.

Pain in her arm snagged her. Funny how it hadn't been a problem when she'd been having an orgasm.

'You all right?' The concern in his voice warned her. 'What's wrong?' He sat up and put her away from him to look her over. 'You're covered in bruises. What have you done?' His mouth flattened. 'You came off your bike.'

This wasn't the way to finish up a lovemaking session. Maybe it had been sex. No. Not for her, it hadn't been. She did love Hunter. This one, or the man she'd once loved, she couldn't be sure. But it was love thumping through her chest, hurting as much as those damned bruises. Love that wasn't reciprocated or Hunter would be looking at ways to make it work too.

'You're black and blue. No wonder you aren't moving comfortably.'

Reaching for her panties, she slid them up her legs, refusing to acknowledge it hurt to lift her left leg. Then she picked up her jeans and pushed her feet into them. 'I was moving just fine a few minutes ago.'

Hardly noticed a thing except for what you were doing to me.

Now she could leave without feeling like she had been sent to purgatory because he didn't want her here when Dylan woke up. Not that this argument had anything to do with that.

'Did you see a doctor?' he growled.

'Two of the people I ride with are doctors.' An orthopaedic surgeon and a GP. Her injuries were covered.

'Gees, Brenna, why do you do this to yourself?' Not long ago he'd been calling her Bren. 'Don't you care that you might break a collarbone or, worse, your spine?' he roared. 'What about the people who care about you? It doesn't matter if you hurt them?'

'Enough. You'll wake Dylan if you don't keep your voice down.' And make her regret falling for him again. Still. Whichever, it felt the same, hurt the same.

'Daddy?'

Too late. The young voice from the other side of the door sounded on the verge of tears.

'Coming, son.' Hunter glared at her as he snatched up his trousers and stepped into them. 'This is why I have no intention of getting into a permanent relationship.'

'I didn't wake him by yelling the roof down,' Brenna

said as she hauled her jersey over her head. 'I don't want to upset Dylan either.'

'Then stay away from us.' He swung the door wide and scooped Dylan up in his arms. 'My boy's a sucker for love, needs someone to focus on him, and that can't be a woman who might not come home at the end of the day.' If Hunter had yelled that at her she might've been able to absorb it without wanting to break down and cry, to beg to be given another chance. But he spoke softly, without menace or emotion, without kindness or anything close to the love she felt for him, just putting his opinion out there for her to know. Because Dylan's mother hadn't come home from that accident.

She spun away, swiped a hand across her eyes and turned back. 'For the record, I am leading my own life, and don't need anyone stepping in to tell me to do otherwise. I don't push too far, but neither am I going wrap myself in cotton wool.'

'Guess we know where we stand, then.' Hunter stalked out of his bedroom, Dylan wrapped in his arms.

Better now than later; though, in reality, it was already too late for her. Now she'd have to start over, putting her heart back together, piece by piece.

As she walked—not ran because that would show Hunter how distressed she was—down the hall a phone rang.

'Hello, Mum. This is a bit late for you to be calling. What's up?' Hunter's tone sounded light but when Brenna glanced over her shoulder the tension was obvious in his tight shoulders and the hand gripping the phone to his ear. Because of her or his mother, who could say?

Did she stay to see if he needed comfort or help if something was wrong back in Kamloops? One look at his eyes told her 'not wanted'. She went into Dylan's room to wake a reluctant Poppy and, hand on collar, headed for the front door.

'How bad are his injuries?' Worry inflected Hunter's question.

Again, she faltered.

Then, 'His shoulder's broken. That's going to take some time to heal.' Hunter's voice faded as he entered the sitting room.

The front door shut behind her with an abrupt click, like even the house wanted shot of her. Loneliness rose, filled her, making her eyes water. Which was ridiculous. She had her mum and her sisters, girlfriends who were always at the end of a phone, workmates to share time out with, the cycling gang. She was not lonely, not by any standards. A head nudged at her thigh, thankfully not the bruised one, and she gave Poppy a pat. 'Yes, and then there's you, my girl.' My dog, not my child.

I don't have a soul mate.

Brenna turned to look back at the house. Hunter stood behind the window, still talking on the phone, Dylan still tucked against his chest, his gaze fixed doggedly somewhere to the right of the path she was on, staring unseeingly at something she had no idea about. She knew it wasn't her.

Forgotten already.

Yet again supplanted by his parents.

She was better off without Hunter back in her life. No expectations to get blitzed.

CHAPTER EIGHT

POPPY HAD TO be pushed into the car.

'I'll drive slowly, promise.'

When the engine failed to turn over first time, bile soaked her mouth. 'You might be in luck, Pops. We could be walking home yet.' Going back inside to ask Hunter for help would be embarrassing. He'd probably deny he had a starter pack.

No, he wouldn't. He was better than that. He cared about people, didn't like to see anyone in trouble. But he might tonight. With her anyway. They'd pushed each other's buttons too hard. This time they'd gone way past the point of no return. Any chance of reconciling had evaporated. She'd been kidding herself to think they might get back together.

Please, start. Please. I'll get you serviced this week. I promise.

It was long overdue. The ignition turned and the engine spluttered to life. Thank goodness for small wonders. She drove away, in a hurry to get home and hide out in her space. She'd go online and book the car into the service station for Friday. Might even take a look at the photos that were her life to remind herself why she participated in some of the adventures that filled her weekends.

Poppy whined.

Oh, hell. Lifting her foot from the accelerator, she let

the car slow to ten kilometres an hour and reached across to rub Poppy's head. 'Sorry, girl. Got a lot on my mind. I've gone and stuffed up with Hunter.'

Mum would add 'again' to that sentence if she were within hearing distance.

Apparently, I didn't try hard enough to keep Hunter in my life last time.

Was she trying now? Or driving away without having a deep and necessary conversation with him?

The thing was, even if Maxine Ford hadn't rung, tonight hadn't been the time to sit and talk it out. They had both been angry. She was hurting, and she didn't mean her bruised muscles. Who knew if Hunter ached for what they might've had or could have? Things would be calmer in the morning. Not that they'd be talking about the deep and personal, but they could work at smiling and making coffee for each other on base.

It didn't work out like that.

'Hunter's not coming in today, and probably not tomorrow,' Kevin told her the moment she walked into the hangar. 'You'll have to put up with me.'

'That's fine,' she told him as disbelief welled. He was avoiding her? Or worse. Something horribly wrong had happened? 'Did he say why?'

'Only that someone's sick. I didn't think I had the right to ask for a full explanation since he has stepped up to help us out when he's obviously got a lot going on.'

Not again. His mother phones and he disappears. Thank goodness they hadn't got too far down the track of re-establishing their relationship, then. *If* that had been on the cards, and after last night she really doubted it. 'I'll put the coffee on.'

'Problem?' Kevin asked in a quieter tone. She'd forgotten this man rarely missed a thing when it came to his crews and their emotions.

'Nothing I can't deal with.' She found him a smile to show she was all right. On the outside, anyway. But when she put her bag in her locker, she found herself waiting to hear the gravelly laugh that was Hunter. Leaning her head against the locker door, she drew in some deep breaths and waited for her stomach to settle. It was going to be a long week. First there were the days Hunter wasn't here and she'd be fighting this intense yearning to hear him, work with him, laugh and share breakfast at midday. Then he'd be back, and she'd actually have to work with him, while denying her feelings were out of control.

Brenna got lucky.

On Tuesday night, as she trudged through the hangar to head home after a gruelling callout where a six-year-old girl had suffered severe injuries from being repeatedly hit over the head with a hockey stick by a seven-year-old boy, Kevin called out from his office. 'Got a minute?'

How many did he want? She had plenty to spare. 'What's up?'

'Like a drink? I think we deserve it after that. Hell, how can a child do that to another?'

'I'd love one.' Brenna sank into the chair in the corner and crossed her legs. 'The police and the welfare services have got their hands full. What if Ebony doesn't survive? It's not as though a seven-year-old can be prosecuted for manslaughter. Or murder.' They'd been to the rougher neighbourhood of the city, but no one could've predicted what they'd seen. Ebony's mother had been beside herself with fear and tearing up the street after the boy's parents, ready to kill them if she got her hands on them.

'We did everything we could. Focus on that. There's

no understanding what some people will do, and I've learned not to try and figure it all out. Only gets me wound up and doesn't solve a thing.'

She took the glass he handed her and gave him a small smile. 'You're being very wise tonight.'

'Yeah, right.' He looked as tired as she felt. Problems in his camp too?

'You okay?'

He nodded slowly. 'I'm fine.' He didn't sound it, but Brenna recognised the stop sign.

Sipping her drink, she changed the subject. 'How's Patch? I haven't spoken to him for a few days.'

'Fed up with being stuck at home. I'm thinking he could come in and do some of the desk work while I cover the callouts. I'll give him a buzz before I head home.'

'So next week I'll be working with you?' Giving him an eye roll she added, 'Guess I can handle that.'

'Actually, I'll be with you for the rest of this week too. Hunter's not coming back.'

'Oh.' The drink sloshed in her stomach. Not coming back to the rescue base? Or not coming back to Vancouver? Not that she'd established he'd left the city to race across to the Okanagan, but why else had he not come into work?

'You two have quite a history, don't you?' When she didn't answer, Kevin added, 'It's been impossible not to hear you talking about your past.'

It wasn't as though they'd tried to hide it. 'We were together three years, and talking about getting married, then life got in the way and we went in separate directions.' Put like that, it sounded so uncomplicated, as though neither them had cared too much, hadn't felt devastated and broken.

'What were the chances Hunter would be the man I hired to cover for Patch, hmm?'

'Took me by surprise.' And some. 'But he would've eventually got in touch, so you were only fast-forwarding our reunion.' Now it seemed the finale had come about equally fast. Not that she knew for certain Hunter had headed back east, but a lot of words had been spoken on Sunday that wouldn't be easy to forget. She was working on it, but now she had to factor in that Hunter wasn't returning to work here, and that felt like the final straw. Downing the last of her drink, she stood up. 'I'd better get cracking. Poppy will be chewing at the wire of her cage if I don't take her for a walk soon.'

Kevin was studying her as she moved to the doorway. 'I don't know what went down to break you two up but be patient, Brenna. He's a good man, and you're not so bad yourself.'

'Thanks, I think.'

Her heart lifted a little. *Glad someone believes in me.*

Hunter's comments about her reckless antics had stung. She did push the limits but she also did everything possible to be careful. No racing downhill over rocky terrain with the guys. No skiing off cliff edges to hopefully land on soft snow several feet below. Semi-fast and sedate was her approach to things. Even Hunter, if these past days were anything to go by. But playing safe was all very well. She did not want to reach seventy without having had some adventures, and for her those were not turning out to be the happy family variety.

So she'd replaced those dreams with ones of seeing amazing locations and getting dirty in them. Not the same as waking up to a four-year-old's cute smile or reading a bedtime story, or snuggling up to a man she loved, but better than knitting scarves for the old people's home.

She'd get around to doing that in her twilight years. 'See you in the morning.'

She was aiming for seventy now? At least she was being positive about something.

Brenna fastened her helmet under her chin and looked around. 'This is going to be epic.'

'I reckon,' one of the cyclists with whom she'd driven across to Squamish agreed.

'For once there's no rain in sight,' she said.

'Tempting fate,' someone warned.

'True.' Brenna couldn't wait to get on the track and feel the air in her face. Her bruises had gone, and two weeks of all work and no play had made her stir-crazy. Being between summer and winter, none of the sports teams she worked with needed a photographer as they were either winding down and putting their skis and hockey sticks away or shaking off the winter blues and getting out the softballs and bats, or sailboards. She was temporarily redundant—and restless as hell. She'd even given the house a floor-to-ceiling spring clean and packed up junk from the cupboards and taken it to the recycling centre, where hopefully they'd make a few dollars for charity.

'Let's do this,' one of her friends said.

'Before I jinx it any more.' Brenna grinned as she swung a leg over her bike. The bruising from her small crash two weeks ago was gone and her body was ready for some strenuous exercise. Hopefully it would shut her mind down for a while. Nothing else had worked.

She focused on the rough track, glad that for once she wasn't pedalling through thick mud. It meant she could go faster with less risk of the front wheel not going in the direction she wanted.

It was smoother riding than she'd had in a while and soon her mind was wandering again. The other night, exhausted from sleepless night after sleepless night, she'd gone through her wardrobe and tossed out a huge pile of clothes that she'd hardly ever worn. Then she'd started on the shoes but had quickly stopped. Blouses and trousers were one thing, giving away her heels was quite another.

To stop pacing around the house looking for something to prevent herself phoning Hunter and begging for another chance, she'd gone online to look up what the house over the road was on the market for and got a shock. Prices must've skyrocketed since she'd bought the house from the family. What would she get for it? Comparing rating valuations with other houses in the street, and especially the one on the market, showed she'd done well in the last three years.

So what? She wasn't going to sell. Not the house she'd grown up in. There were too many memories she couldn't walk away from. Though it might be time to do that. How long should she hang onto the past? But her father had been her rock, and she still needed something to anchor to, and the best she could find was this house.

The bike bounced over rocks and roots, settled back into a comfortable rhythm. Brenna grinned. Ahead the rest of the group were racing downhill, shouting with glee. This was fun, letting rip, and putting aside the horrors and sadness of her everyday job.

Then the others were slowing. Braking, she slowly joined them. 'What's going on?'

'Looks like someone's come off.'

Brenna stretched her neck to look past her friends. A cyclist lay sprawled at an odd angle over the track and another knelt next to him, a phone in his hand. 'We might need to put our doctor's hats on. That doesn't look good.'

'Agreed.'

Bikes were set aside as Brenna and Ash removed their helmets before approaching. 'Hi. We're doctors. Can we help?' said Ash.

'Thank goodness.' The man stood up and stepped aside. 'There's no phone reception out here. I don't think Geoff's in good shape.'

Brenna knelt down. 'Hello, Geoff. I'm Brenna and this is Ash. We're doctors.' She didn't like what she was seeing. 'We'll take care of you, all right?'

The man opened his eyes and nodded, then he tried to push up. 'Thanks.'

'Don't move,' Brenna said hurriedly, her hand instantly on his shoulder to hold him down.

Ash nodded to her and began removing Geoff's shoes.

Looking around for the other two in their group, she said, 'Can you go on until you get phone reception? We need the helicopter here,' she said, before mouthing silently, *ASAP.*

'On our way.'

'Can you feel me touching your feet?' Ash, the orthopaedic surgeon, asked Geoff.

'No. Why would I when I've got shoes on?'

Brenna's heart plummeted. It was looking worse by the minute. Lifting his hand, she took his pulse, asking, 'You can feel me doing this?'

'Yes. What's wrong? Why won't you let me sit up?' Worry was building in the man's eyes.

'It's a precaution, that's all.' It was not her place to tell him he might've broken his back. Anyway, they didn't know for sure. There'd be an array of tests to be done first. Where was that chopper? That was if the others had got far enough down the hillside to have been able to phone for help yet. Geoff's raised pulse was brought on by shock. 'Any pain?'

'In my left shoulder blade.'

His friend told her, 'He landed on a rock, then kind of flew along the track into that tree.'

'Don't tell Miriam that, will you? I'll just tell her I fell off going too fast and got me some bruises, otherwise she won't let me go biking again.'

Brenna shivered. He hadn't worked it out yet, but it was possible he wouldn't be walking again, let alone biking. Whoever Miriam was, her life might be about to change in a way she'd never expected.

What about the people who care about you, Brenna?
Shut up, Hunter.

'We were going pretty fast,' the friend said.

Another shiver ripped up her spine. This could happen to anyone, including her. Life as she knew it over in a flash. But it wasn't. It was Geoff's life that needed attending to. He might be numb from pressure on some nerves, not a damaged vertebra. In the meantime, she and Ash would treat him as though it was the worst-case scenario and not exacerbate the damage, whatever that was.

An hour later she and Ash watched the chopper lift away.

'I don't like his chances of dancing at his wedding,' Ash said.

Geoff had got quite garrulous before shock had overtaken him and shut him down.

Rubbing her arms, Brenna stared at the retreating chopper with the cyclist and her colleagues on board and shivered. 'Let's hope there still is a wedding.' Picking up her cycle, she prepared to head down the hill. Slowly.

Ash had also found a new, much slower than usual speed.

When they reached the other two waiting at Ash's four-wheel, drive Brenna felt the tension leave her legs, arms and stomach. Pulling the phone from her bag, she called her mother. 'Hi, letting you know another ride over and all went well.'

'You're home early.'

She winced. 'We're still at Squamish.'

'What's up? You don't usually call until you're back in town. It's quite late.'

When would she learn she could never put one over Mum? 'We came across an accident and it took a long time before the rescue team got here. But we're on our way now. Any chance of dinner when I get back?' She didn't want to go back to her empty house. Not yet. Not while Hunter's accusations about her taking risks were flapping around her skull, making her feel small and selfish.

'It's pasta.'

Not even her least favourite food could stop her calling in. 'Sounds great.'

'Try again.' Her mother laughed as they cut the connection.

Over ravioli in homemade tomato mushroom sauce Brenna chatted about her shock at finding Geoff and what she and Ash suspected were his life-changing injuries. She tried to keep the conversation light, but Hunter's words kept interrupting and making her sweat. In the end she put her fork down and eyeballed her mother. 'I'm sorry if I've caused you worry. It's just that I wanted to prove something to myself.'

Mum placed her hand over hers. 'That you are invincible.'

Brenna gasped, then shook her head slowly. 'Never could fool you about anything.'

'Tell me something. Has this got anything to do with Hunter?'

Oh, hell. But this was why she was here. Not to avoid her empty house—well, that too—but to talk about what was bugging her with this wonderful woman who'd love her no matter what, while at the same time giving her sound advice that might or might not offend her.

'He told me I was thoughtless, didn't care about my family and friends if I was prepared to take risks like I do. I disagree to a point. I am careful, take all proper measures not to have an accident, but after working with that man today I can see I might push things a little too far.'

Mum fiddled with her fork, her eyes thoughtful. Then, 'You don't think you're pushing yourself physically because you were, and still are, afraid to push for Hunter? That skiing down a steep slope is safer than connecting with a man who hurt you badly and might do it again if you give him half a chance?'

Denial rushed to her support. 'But I've been skiing, cycling, doing all those hair-raising things for years. Hunter only turned up a few weeks ago.'

'Brenna, you can do better than that.'

She pushed her chair back and stood up. Sat down again, reached for her glass of water. Hunter had never really left her. Even in the years when she'd truly believed she'd got over him he had been there, waiting in the wings. Nothing she'd done had stopped her loving him. It mightn't have been obvious, but it'd been there all along.

Instead of going after him with everything she had, she'd put her energies into sports, photography and other people, throwing herself at everything to prove she could bounce back, and no one need be worried about leaving her because she was a survivor, no matter what.

'You're right, Mum, I can.'

But where to start?

'Don't rush this. You need to be one hundred per cent sure.' More words of wisdom from the woman who'd always been there for her. 'After six years a little longer won't matter.'

'You seem certain I want to get back with Hunter.'

'Don't you?'

If he stays. *If.* 'Yes.' But she wasn't going to rush this. Mum was right. She had to be absolutely certain first or she, and Hunter, would get hurt all over again.

Hunter picked up his phone and brought up Brenna's number. His finger hovered over it, his mouth drying and his heart heavy.

Just press the damn number.

Dropping the phone on the bench, he filled a glass with iced water from his new, state-of-the-art fridge and glugged it down like a man who'd been in the desert for a week. Digging a garden was hot work.

Three weeks into his new job at the hospital and Hunter felt as though he was finally getting into his stride. He had a routine going whereby he dropped Dylan off at Jess's before seven and picked him up from preschool after he knocked off around three. They'd go home for biscuits and cold drinks before heading to the beach to play in the sand, and twice Dylan had gone into the water to splash around. Life was unfolding as he'd planned.

Except for Bren.

There were still stacks of cartons to unpack and furniture to buy, but apparently Rome hadn't been built in a day either. He was happy in a quiet way and thrilled that every day Dylan got louder and happier. His boy was settling in, which was what the move had been about.

It had not been about Brenna and falling back in love with her. If he'd ever stopped loving her in the first place. Which he now knew he hadn't.

But was he going to do anything about it?

The fact he hadn't heard from Brenna at all hurt. At first, he'd been angry to think she couldn't find it in herself to enquire after Dylan's health. Kevin must've said why he was not going back to work with them. Then he'd remembered he'd told Kevin someone in the family was sick and knew immediately Brenna would be thinking he'd done a bunk, gone back to his parents to help them out of another crisis.

That really stank. Seemed she hadn't heard a thing he'd said over the previous weeks. No, she'd have been watching and waiting for him to repeat his mistakes, more like, and was now probably congratulating herself on being so clever.

'Dad.' Dylan raced into the kitchen. 'I want to see Poppy.' *I want to see Poppy's owner.*

'Sorry, Dylan, but I've told you we can't. Poppy and Brenna are busy.'

His face dropped. 'They're always busy.'

'Want to go see the boys?' Jess and Dave were having a family day at home and they were invited to drop in any time they liked. It might be good to shoot the breeze with his friends and forget everything Brenna.

When Dylan raised his little fist in the air, he knew he'd avoided an argument.

For how long, who knew, but he'd take whatever he could. Tapping him lightly with his own fist, he said, 'You put some warm clothes in a bag, and I'll grab some beers and chips.' Sounding like a real pro, Dad. Well, it was a work in progress. Still a lot of learning to do. Like that would ever stop.

His phone rang. His heart rate picked up. Bren? Air whooshed across his lips as he answered grumpily. 'Hi, Mum.'

This was good. He didn't want to talk to Brenna. He wasn't missing her. He didn't love her. The phone started sliding from his fingers. Pardon? 'Can you repeat that?'

'I said Dad's started playing bowls. Just as well he broke his left shoulder and not his right.'

No, not that. The bit about how he didn't love Brenna. 'Mum, sorry, can I get back to you? I've got to go. Everything's fine. Bye.'

Twice in as many minutes he'd admitted he loved Bren. He'd loved her from the moment she'd walked into the emergency department and up to the bed where he had been trying to stem a patient's critical blood loss. She'd looked directly at him and said in the sexiest voice he'd ever heard, 'Hello, I'm Brenna Williamson, a doctor. Want some help?' And he'd been a goner. Together they'd saved the man from bleeding out and had gone to the pub for a celebratory drink at the end of their shift. It had been the start of something amazing. Something he'd walked away from. But he hadn't stopped loving her.

Yet now you expect Bren to have the utmost confidence that you won't do that to her again?

'Come on, Dad, I'm ready.'

'Give me a few minutes, will you? I'm not as fast as you.' Should he promise Bren he was here for good? That nothing would entice him to leave again? Words weren't easy, but they were simpler and quicker than the wait and I'll show you strategy. Those were the only choices and he'd go for both—if he was absolutely certain he wanted to spend the rest of his life with Brenna. No, that wasn't the question. He already knew he did. But did she want him? The big unknown in all this. When they were making love or sharing a meal, he believed she did. But her lack of trust in him was a hurdle to overcome, if it even was surmountable.

'Hurry up. I want to go now.'

'Behave, or we won't be going anywhere.' Putting the six-pack of beer on the bench, Hunter stared out at the garden he'd been digging whenever he'd had a free moment over the last couple of weeks. It was going to be large, and hopefully productive. Pride swelled in his chest. This was working; he was making a go of getting a new life happening, everything he'd dreamed about for so long was beginning to take shape. He had to hang onto that, not let his relationship with Brenna wear him down. Damn but she frightened him with her devil-may-care attitude when it came to her physical safety. Why couldn't she see that?

If you want her to believe in you, you've got to give back.

If she believed he would head east again for any reason, of course she'd play safe where her heart was concerned. He would.

You already are. You're not calling Bren and laying everything out there for her to see how much you want it to work between you.

'Dad.' Dylan stamped his foot. 'Come on.'

Since he'd been so distracted, Hunter let Dylan get away with that one. Picking up the beer, he ruffled his boy's hair. 'We're outta here.'

'Why doesn't Poppy want to see me any more? I love her.'

'She loves you too, buddy, but sometimes everyone

gets very busy and there's no time to visit.' And some-times people just had to take the raging bull by its horns and risk everything. 'We'll stop in and say hello on the way back from Jess's.'

'Yippee.'

If only he could please everyone as easily.

CHAPTER NINE

BRENNA WHISKED THE softened butter to a cream, added vanilla and then icing sugar. She was probably about to make a fool of herself, but some things were worth the risk. She'd kept her word and spent days thinking about Hunter and their future, all the time knowing she had to talk to him and tell him everything about how she felt and apologise for the past.

Icing sugar flew through the air, and she slowed the beating she was giving the icing enough to save most of it for the cake and not the walls.

Poppy sat up on her haunches, watching every move, waiting expectantly.

'I'm not giving you the whisk to lick, Pops.' She'd have it herself. 'But the good news is we're going for a walk as soon as I've iced the cake.' Around to Hunter's house with her peace offering. Now the procrastinating was over, it was time to step up and lay her heart on the line. At least then she'd know for sure where her future lay.

Banana cake with buttercream icing had been his favourite. She hoped it still was. Not that she believed a cake would win him over, but it might soften his stance when he remembered the other times she'd made it for him, and allow her to apologise for leaping to conclusions. Conclusions that might turn out to be right, but she'd finally realised she had to ask him, not blindly accuse him.

She owed Geoff Carr. His cycling accident had brought her to her senses. That and her mother's quiet way of putting everything into words that registered through the pain and confusion that had taken over her mind these past weeks. She didn't need to throw herself down mountainsides to prove she could cope with anything. She'd survived her birth mother's betrayal and her father's death. She'd even made it past her and Hunter breaking up, maybe not in one piece but she was here, doing well as an emergency doctor and surrounded by family and friends.

It was time to be realistic. That could've been her breaking her back the other day, or any of the days she'd skied, snowboarded, cycled or leapt out of planes. While not about to turn into a couch potato, she'd begun backing down on the need to throw herself at everything. It would break her mum's heart if anything happened to her, and she couldn't do that when Mum had accepted her as her own from the day Dad had introduced them. Neither did she want to hurt her sisters, or anyone else, or be beholden to whoever got the short straw and had to look after her if the worst happened.

Hunter had been correct when he'd said she was selfish. But at the time it had been the only way she'd managed. With Dad gone from her mentally and her family trying to cope, there'd been no one to talk to about how much she loved Hunter despite him walking away.

'Walkies.' She rubbed Poppy's head as she licked the whisk, trying to ignore the longing in her pet's eyes. 'You wouldn't like buttercream icing.'

Poppy sank onto her belly and dropped her jaw onto her front legs with a sigh as if to say, 'Try me.'

'I know, it's your favourite treat.' Or would be if she got half a chance.

With the cake iced and put into a container that went into her backpack Brenna clipped Poppy's lead to her collar and headed out the front door, glad to be doing something positive instead of mooching around the house.

By the time they reached Hunter's front path sweat was dripping down her face and pouring between her breasts. When spring had decided to come out of hiding it had done so with a vengeance. 'I could do with some iced water, Poppy. Bet you want a drink too.'

The house was all locked up. 'So much for ice in my water.' She found a hose lying in the back yard and turned on the tap for Poppy to lap at the water, then did the same for herself. Looking around the yard, she whistled.

Poppy stood alert, watching her.

'Down, girl. Look how much work Hunter's done out here. The garden's enormous, like he plans on feeding the whole street with his vegetables.' He hadn't been wasting any time getting it prepared. A lightness she hadn't felt in a long time crept up on her. Hunter was serious about this move. Just as he'd told her. As she'd refused to accept. 'I've been an idiot.'

A cautious idiot looking after her own heart. Since that revealing conversation with her mum she'd spent days going over and over what Mum had advised, weighing up the consequences if it worked out—and if it didn't. Every night as she lay in the dark, waiting for sleep to submerge her, she'd admit she had to give her and Hunter a chance. If, after six years, she still loved him, then what was there to lose? There was only one way to find out if he felt the same.

Except he wasn't home.

Now what? She had a cake to deliver.

Just as well she'd put ice packs in with it because now she placed the container and packs on the back step in the shade. No need for a note; not that she had a pen or anything to write on.

Then she headed away, aiming for the beach where Poppy could chase her ball into the water and expend some of her energy.

'Poppy's not home,' Hunter told Dylan after calling out and ringing the doorbell three times. Damn it. Where were they? As if he had any right to demand an answer, but now he'd made up his mind to talk to her and lay his heart out for her he couldn't stand having to wait.

'Can I see Brenna?'

'She's not here either. They've gone out together.' He ignored the ache behind his ribs. When he'd finally found the courage to visit and beg for forgiveness she had to go out. Like a punishment, except there was no way she'd have known he'd call round.

'I want to go to the beach.'

'Might as well.' Better than returning home to mope around the house, wondering where Bren had gone.

Pulling into the last vacant parking space at Kitsilano beach, Hunter hauled on the handbrake and got out to unclip Dylan's seat belt.

Dylan slid out and stepped onto the sand. 'Poppy,' he shrieked, and began running.

'Dylan, come back here now.' Hunter chased after him. 'Stop. Now.'

'Poppy, Poppy, it's me.'

Hunter skidded to a stop, his eyes finally lifting off his son and following the direction in which Dylan was scampering. Poppy was barrelling towards them.

Followed by Brenna, walking slowly with a cautious smile on her face.

He owed Dylan for suggesting the beach. 'Hi,' he said as he closed the gap.

'Hello to you too.'

'We've just been to your house.'

'Poppy and I went by your place.'

They stared at each other.

He tried breathing but it wasn't easy with all the longing building up in his chest. Longing to love and be loved. To share their lives as they'd always meant to do. Hell, he loved this woman. Always had, always would. How could he have been so callous to call her out on her activities? She was right, they were her choice. Just as when he'd headed back to Kamloops to help his parents had been his. Whether they were right or wrong, it didn't matter, though the consequences of his actions had mattered big time. 'I'm sorry. For everything. Right back six years.'

Bren stared at him, her eyes watering and her mouth softening. 'So am I.'

'You didn't do anything wrong.'

'Yes, I did. I could've followed you out to the Okanagan, finished my training in the hospital there, come home to visit Dad every second weekend.' Brenna swiped her eyes with the back of a hand.

'Don't cry, Bren.' He took a step towards her, his heart floundering. He'd lay the world at her feet if she'd have him back. 'I wouldn't have let you do that to your career. Or to your dad. It wouldn't have been fair on anyone, and eventually it would've come between us.' Would've caused irreparable damage.

'None of it was *fair*.' She took another swipe, but the tears kept coming. 'I dug my heels in and stayed away, blaming you for everything.'

'You're forgetting you did try. I refused to answer your phone calls, remember? I deleted your emails unopened and burned the letters you wrote. I had to, or I wouldn't have survived.'

Her smile widened. 'We can both be stubborn when we want to be.'

'Now, there's something I agree with wholeheartedly.' He sighed. This wasn't going too badly. Yet. 'It's all very well looking back and saying we shouldn't have done this or that, but at the time that's how we dealt with what was happening.'

She reached a hand to him and he took it, wrapped his fingers around hers and held on for dear life. Maybe it was going just how he wanted it. They were finding their way back to each other, though there were still things to sift through, making sure they didn't crash and burn a second time.

'Dad, can I go for a swim?'

Hunter groaned and dragged his eyes from the woman holding his heart. 'All right. I'll get your towel from the car.' He looked back at Brenna and his heart stuttered. 'This is real, isn't it?'

Her fingers touched her lips, and she nodded. 'I hope so.' She was still smiling, and there was something he was afraid to identify in her gaze in case he got it wrong. Love. For him? For him.

'Bren?'

'Go get Dylan's towel, and maybe lock your vehicle.'

He spun around and muttered an oath. 'That's your fault for distracting me, Brenna Williamson.'

'I know.'

'Brenna, Poppy's swimming.' Dylan stood next to her, hands on hips, staring down the beach. 'I want to swim too.'

'In a minute, kiddo.' Dylan was giving him breathing space, yet he didn't want to stop telling Brenna all the things that had been building up inside from the moment he'd first walked into the rescue hangar, to let free all the words that were freefalling through his skull onto his tongue. He increased his strides, reaching the four-wheel drive and grabbing the bag with Dylan's gear. Picked up his wallet from the seat and shoved it deep into a pocket. Shut the door. Pinged the locks. Took a deep breath and gazed down the beach to the woman who held his heart in her hand.

Then he was back with Brenna and they were strolling down to the water, hand in hand. 'Okay, Dylan, now I'm here you can go in.'

He didn't need any more encouragement.

'I can't move away in case he gets into difficulties,' Hunter told Brenna.

'I'd beat you round the ears if you did.' She moved closer, and he wrapped an arm around her shoulders.

'Now, there's a surprise.' He stared at Dylan and the dog but wasn't really seeing them. It was the past rolling through his head. 'I loved you even when I told you it was over.'

She nodded. 'I know. I was only thinking of myself, wanting you to come back to me. After you kept refusing to answer my calls and texts, I began to get angry. You were another person leaving me, and I didn't look beyond that to the fact that you'd told me so often how much you loved me and wanted us to spend our lives together.'

'When I stopped coming into work at the rescue centre it was Dylan who was sick. He had some gastro bug that was doing the rounds at preschool.'

'Poor kid. That's not nice.' She locked her gaze on him. 'You must realise I wondered if you'd gone east after hearing you talking to your mother, and I tried not to think of that as a rerun. Then I wised up, accepted you meant you are staying and if you had to go visit your parents then that was what families do.'

Relief softened away the last drop of tension in his belly. 'Thank you.' There was one more thing he had to get out in the open before the past was done. 'I'm not sorry about Evie. Neither can I imagine life without Dylan.'

'You shouldn't.' Under his hand she stiffened, then relaxed. 'I nearly got married myself. I met Shane about three years ago and we hit it off straight away.'

A pang of jealousy he had no right to flared. 'Go on.'

'We were easy together, sort of drifted along, enjoying similar things, comfortable really.'

'Sounds dull.' Hope replaced the envy.

'Not dull, but there was no excitement. Yet when Shane proposed I accepted. You were out of the picture for good as far as I could see so I wanted to try for that happy family I'd envisioned when we were together.' She stopped. Her right foot drew lines in the sand, smudged them out. 'But it was wrong, for both of us, and in the end we called it off. We're still friends with no regrets. Shane's found someone else and this time he's definitely in love.' She sounded happy about that.

Hunter let it go. Shane was her Evie and, face it, if neither of them had had relationships in the previous six years they probably wouldn't be much good for anything now. 'Will you come back to my house when these two have finished swimming? There's a top-notch bottle of champagne in the fridge, and dinner waiting to be heated.'

Bren looked up at him and grinned. 'Is that all?'

'Hell, no.'

He couldn't wait to get home and put Dylan to bed, but it was only four in the afternoon. 'This is going to be the longest afternoon of my life.'

'Half the fun's in the build-up,' she retorted, before rising on her toes to kiss him thoroughly so that he'd have pulled her down onto the sand and had her there and then if not for his son only metres away. And half the population of Kitsilano on the beach.

Finally, dog and boy had had enough. Hunger had overtaken the need to stay wet and sandy. Hunter packed them into his vehicle, Poppy in the back looking concerned. 'It's all right. I'll go very slowly.'

'Unless you want a mess to clean up, that's wise.' Brenna rubbed Poppy's chest. 'You'll be fine, girl.'

And she had been. Frustrating as it was, Hunter had driven slower than a snail, making Bren laugh.

'Relax. It's not as though Dylan's going to sleep as soon as we get there.'

'No, but he'll have dinner straight away and be ready for bed.'

And we'll be in my bed not long after.

At last they rolled into his driveway and parked. 'Phew. Thought we'd never get here.'

'We've waited more than six years, Hunter. What's a few more hours?' Brenna teased.

'You mean this is like it used to be?' His heart waited for her reply.

The laughter diminished, was replaced with a soft, gut-wrenching smile. 'Yes. When we were openly in love. Not lately when neither of us knew what we wanted or were denying the feelings we had for each other.'

'Then we're in for an amazing night.' If Dylan didn't

wake up. Be just their luck if tonight was be one of his restless sleeps. 'Let's get dinner under way.'

'I'm not sure I can eat at the moment,' Bren confessed.

'Soon fix that.' He laughed. 'What's this?' There was a container by his door and when he opened it the smell of banana wafted out. Dipping a finger into the creamy icing, he poked a dollop into his mouth and grinned. 'You made this.'

Brenna nodded. 'Like I said, Poppy and I came round earlier. I wanted to sit down and talk about everything and figured making your favourite cake wouldn't hurt.'

It was silly. It was only a cake, right? But right then he knew what he had to do. He couldn't let Bren get away again. Handing the container to Dylan, he said, 'Take that inside for me, will you?' Then he reached for Bren's hands. 'You're shaking.'

She nodded. 'I'm scared. I don't want to lose you a second time.'

'It's not going to happen.' Hunter leaned in close and kissed her gently. 'Bren, I love you, never stopped. Will you marry me? Help me raise Dylan? Have more children with me? Live in my house and make it ours?'

She blinked once, twice, three times, and then her eyes were ablaze with love, like she'd finally let go all her worries. Because of him. For him. 'Yes, yes and yes. And yes. All of the above. I love you so much I want this more than anything. Us and those dreams we once shared, however much they've morphed into other ideas.'

Hunter tugged her close and covered her mouth with his. Their kiss seemed to go on for ever. Brenna had never tasted so sweet, so exciting. She was back. They were back. 'Love you,' he whispered.

'The things you'll say to get someone to plan your colour schemes for the house.' She grinned.

He slapped his forehead. 'You see through me too easily.'

'I might want to paint it lime green and orange.'

'You can do what you like as long as you keep making those cakes.'

'I've forgotten the recipe already.'

He led her through the front door. 'Welcome home, Bren.'

If he'd thought she'd been crying before, he hadn't had a clue. 'This is going to take a box of tissues to deal with.'

Both her hands wiped at her eyes, her cheeks, and then she gave him her best, melt-the-toes, tighten-the-groin, smother-the-heart smile. 'I must've had an inkling. I've been talking to a real estate salesperson about selling my house.'

'You've what? Why? That's your haven.'

'Exactly, and it's time I let it go. Especially now we're together again. For ever together.'

She truly loved him. 'It might be me needing those tissues,' he croaked.

'Shall we tell the kids?' She stepped inside his—*their*—house and closed the door on the street. Shut them in with their love and dreams and family.

* * * * *

* * * * *

COMING SOON!

We really hope you enjoyed reading this book. If you're looking for more romance, be sure to head to the shops when new books are available on

Thursday 3rd October

To see which titles are coming soon, please visit

millsandboon.co.uk/nextmonth

MILLS & BOON

Coming next month

FROM HEARTACHE TO FOREVER
Caroline Anderson

'I wasn't brave, Ry, not at all. I was just doing what had to be done, and then once it was done I just felt empty.'

'I shouldn't have left you.'

She took his hand and kissed it, then held it in her hands, warm and firm and kind, Beth all over.

'I sent you away, Ryan. I couldn't deal with your grief as well as mine, and that was wrong. We should have grieved together for our daughter, but we didn't know each other well enough. We still don't, but we're learning, day by day, and we'll get there.'

He nodded slowly. 'Yeah, I suppose so.' He glanced at his phone and sighed. 'Beth, I'm sorry, I need to go.'

She chuckled softly. 'You need to get to bed. You've had a hectic few days, you must be exhausted.'

'I am. I tell you what, that bed had better be comfortable,' he said wryly. 'Did you try it?'

'No, I didn't have time, but if it isn't there's always the sofa.' She cocked her head on one side, her eyes searching his. 'Are you all right, Ry?'

He laughed softly and nodded. 'Yes, Beth. I'm all right. You?'

Her smile was sad. 'I'm all right. I'm used to it now.

'Don't be silly.'

'I'm not. I mean it. You're the strongest person I know, Beth, and the kindest, and I don't deserve you. Thank you.'

She hugged him back, then let him go. 'You're welcome. I hope you sleep well.'

He laughed. 'I'm sure I will.'

She walked him to the door and he turned and kissed her, just the slightest brush of his lips on hers, and let himself out and drove home, then paused a moment on the drive, staring up at the stars twinkling in the clear, dark night.

He loved the stars. They never changed, untouched by all the madness around him, the one constant in a changing world.

He let himself in, checked his email and looked at the bed—his new bed, carefully put together by Beth to save him the trouble because that was the kind of person she was—and felt another wave of guilt for leaving her alone when she'd been so sad and lost and torn with grief.

She would never have left him. He knew that, but at the time she'd been adamant that she didn't need him. Only now it turned out she had, but she'd been unable to cope with his grief, too, because they didn't know each other well enough to grieve together.

Well enough to make a baby, but not well enough to lose one. Maybe, given time, they would find that closeness and with it some closure. He hoped so.

Continue reading
FROM HEARTACHE TO FOREVER
Caroline Anderson

Available next month
www.millsandboon.co.uk

LET'S TALK
Romance

For exclusive extracts, competitions
and special offers, find us online:

 facebook.com/millsandboon

 @MillsandBoon

 @MillsandBoonUK

Get in touch on 01413 063232

For all the latest titles coming soon, visit

millsandboon.co.uk/nextmonth